WILLOW WINTERS
MELANIE HARLOW & CORINNE MICHAELS
CARRIE ANN RYAN • K.A. LINDE • J.D. HOLLYFIELD
ALEATHA ROMIG • JENNIFER BENE
SKYE WARREN & AMELIA WILDE • DYLAN ALLEN
LIVIA GRANT • HARLOE RAE • TIA LOUISE
NANA MALONE • JENNA HARTLEY • NIKKI ASH
AMELIA WILDE • MARNI MANN

flirting with a good night

WILLOW WINTERS

In our small town, all of my friends have found their soulmates and here I am, moving from one crush to the next but never actually settling down. The reason why is standing only a few feet from me now. He's joking with my best friend's husband, as I sit on their sofa trying not to stare. With his sleeves rolled up, the tattoos he got while he was away in the marines are on display, curved around his toned muscle that flex with his rough chuckle.

Cade was years older and left right after high school. I never told him how I felt, we were so young and there was no way he'd ever go for a sophomore like me. Times have changed and now he's back… and I can't stop staring and pining over the man I've been longing for.

And when he looks my way, with that handsome smirk, rough stubble and gorgeous baby blue gaze…

chapter one

Sharon

"JUST SMELL IT."

Magnolia's command is murmured with aww, even if it does crack me up. Both of us take a deep inhale that has my back pushing against the cream sectional sofa. Her eyes are closed, her nose just a centimeter above the practically bald little one's head. He has just a small smatter of dark brown hair at the very top of his noggin and with the little jostle, he coos, putting a wide-eyed Autumn on edge.

"There's nothing like it in the whole world." Magnolia's statement is met with both another coo from Cameron, the two-week old little one fast asleep in her arms, and a long exhale of relief from his mother. Autumn's arms are still up as if she was getting ready to snatch her newborn and quickly rock him back to sleep if he woke from the two of us taking a nice long whiff of that baby smell.

I bite back my smile, unable to not see the humor in the room with Magnolia completely missing Autumn's stress.

"Seriously," Mags presses, "There's something about the way they smell…" I finally let out a laugh when Mags closes her eyes and lays back with the little boy.

"If you keep creeping me out, I'm taking my baby back," Autumn's response is given with a broad smile. You'd never know she just went through almost thirty hours of labor earlier this week.

There really is something about that sweet baby powder like scent, though. I have to agree with Mags, pulling my legs up on the sofa and then resting my pointer against Cameron's little cheek. "He is freaking adorable Autumn," I murmur and feel my heart swell with happiness for her and Trent and their other two boys.

"I want another baby." Mags cradles the baby closer and Autumn's eyes go wide.

"If you wake him, you keep him," she comments while dragging the basket of clothes across the kitchen island to be closer to her. She's all the way at the end of it, now perched on a stool, while the two of us, strike that, two and a little a bundle, are huddled at the end of her sofa where the living room meets the kitchen.

Our Wine-down Wednesdays have certainly changed recently. Mags with her … shall I say love life dilemma, and Autumn with her ever-growing family.

"I'm not going to wake him up," Mags admonishes Autumn then makes an 'oops' expression as Cameron wiggles in her arms.

The little man has only been on this earth for less than 2 weeks but he knows how to make the whole world stop as he nestles in tighter.

"I would steal him away from you," I start and then we all hear the front door open and the sound of several boot steps filter in through the house. "But I have to get going," I finish as the sight of two men interrupts the conversation.

With a charming smile, the first man pauses to cup the little one's head. Giving me the perfect comparison of father and son.

Cameron looks just like Trent, Autumn's husband. His little nose and those large brown eyes. They are all Trent.

With a pout from Mags, and her pulling the baby into her arms playfully, as if to say 'he's mine, off,' Trent chuckles and makes his way to Autumn, planting a kiss on her cheek before setting down a number of plastic bags on the counter next to his wife.

What is it with men and carrying every single bag from the grocery store in at once?

"Thanks for giving him a ride while his car is in the shop," Autumn's gratitude is met with a little nod from the second man.

The one who has my heart stuttering from my place on the sofa.

"No problem," his deep voice echoes and I take the chance to drink him in.

In our small town, all of my friends have found their soulmates and here I am, moving from one crush to the next but never actually settling down. The reason why is standing only a few feet from me now. He's joking with my best friend's husband, as I sit on their sofa trying not to stare. With his sleeves rolled up, the tattoos he got while he was away in the marines are on display, curved around his toned muscle that flex with his rough chuckle.

He was years older and left right after high school. I never told him how I felt, we were so young and there was no way he'd ever go for a sophomore like me. Times have changed and now he's back… and I can't stop staring and pining over the man I've been longing for.

And when he looks my way, with that handsome smirk, rough stubble and gorgeous baby blue gaze… Lord, have mercy.

"Cade Jameson," Magnolia calls out as she gently sets the infant down for the first time since she snatched him from me. The little bundle lays effortlessly into the rocker at our feet.

With a gentle touch, I rock the little one, still bundled in a 'choo choo', blue plaid, train swaddle and look anywhere but at the man who's become the center of conversation.

In my periphery, I gauge the friendly hug between them. It's nothing more than polite. Well maybe a touch comical considering how short she is and how he has to bend down to hug her in return. She's a bit petite and Cade is a wall of muscle, taller than most.

"It's good to have you back. You staying long?

"I am," he answers proudly and I only notice that I'm staring, waiting with baited breath for his answer, when his gaze lifts past Mags to where I am.

I'm quick to look away although I continue to eavesdrop about how he'll be home through the holidays and how he's stationed here now, hopefully permanently.

My little heart pitter patters at the thought of him being back home for good.

"You staying for dinner?" Autumn questions and it takes me far too long to look up and realize she's asking me.

"Oh, no. I have to head out and I already ate." I answer her but then realize once the words were spoken that she already knew that.

I told her the moment I got here and stole Cameron from her before Magnolia could.

"You're walking home?" she questions further, the room of eyes on both of us. I ignore the heat that comes with Cade's prying gaze.

"That's how I got here," I cock a sarcastic brow Autumn's way and wonder why she added concern to her tone. I always walk to her house, she knows that. It's one of the reasons I love this neighborhood so much. As I stand, I stretch out my back slightly, focusing on the cream throw I'm folding rather than the man whose gaze is falling down my body.

Years ago I thought the tension between us was imagined. Or at least one sided. But this is the third time I've seen him since he's been back and I swear it only gets more and more obvious that I can't keep my eyes off of him and I know he does the same. Stealing glances each time we've had a run in together.

"Why doesn't Cade take you home?" Autumn offers, folding a tee-shirt in her lap and then adding it to a pile on the counter.

Oh, the betrayal. She doesn't have the decency to look me in the eyes. Instead she focuses solely on Cade as my heart completely halts in my chest. "You can take her home on your way, can't you Cade?"

Alone with this man? In his truck? Late at night with my ovaries still doing flip flops at the sight of a newborn?

Oh, no, no, no.

"Of course I can," he answers easily, a touch of southern hitting his last word as he slips his hands, which I already know are rough from years of manual labor, into his jean pockets. His asymmetric smile greets me, "Ready when you are, Shar."

Shar. It takes great effort not to swoon just from the way he says my nickname.

chapter two

Cade

THERE'S NOTHING LIKE THE AUTUMN LEAVES, HUES OF GOLD AND RED, being carried down the gravel road of this old town. Or the smell of the apples and the laughter of kids playing at the edge of the orchard that lines this half of the neighborhood I grew up in.

Nothing like the soft sigh that comes from Shar's plump lips either or the way the wind blows her brunette locks as I help her into my truck.

It's all a part of home to me. A home I missed dearly for years.

Her hand is small in mine and the blush that rises up her chest and into her cheeks is certainly from my hand on the small of her back rather than the chill in the air. I've always had an effect on her, one that forces a hint of a chuckle from me and she peeks up through her lashes and then finds her place in the passenger side.

"Thank you," she whispers shyly, letting me shut her door after giving her a small nod and a "no problem."

Shar has no idea how much I thought about her while I was overseas. How the stories Trent would tell me, keeping me up to date on this town, always seemed to come back to her.

It didn't matter what news was filtering through the town gossip, I needed to know about her and what she was doing, if she was with anyone. I had no right, she doesn't even know how I feel about her, but there was a piece of me that needed to hear she was doing alright without me.

Coming home every so often and catching up with a beer and friends was never complete until Shar idled in. Her confidence hitching just like her breath did every time she saw me.

I felt it, whatever it is that crackles between us now, but I never acted on it because it would only be days until I was gone again.

That changes now though.

The truck rocks gently as I pull my door shut after helping her get in on her side.

"You know you don't have to," Sharon speaks first as I bring the truck to life with a rumble and turn down the music so I can hear her caressing voice that much better. "I could walk."

My window's already rolled down and I set my elbow there, resting my chin in my hand, my pointer running along the rough stubble of my jaw as I stare at her and wait for her to look back at me.

"I like the opportunity to be a gentleman when I can be."

"Mm," she murmurs. "You imagine you're some kind of gentle beast, huh?" she jokes, but there's a breathlessness to her taunting. Both of her hands find her lap and then fall between her knees, which makes her thighs part.

A gentle beast? I'm not so sure of that. Not with the thoughts running through my mind right now. Imagining how I'd part those thighs of hers, barely covered by her burgundy cotton dress.

"I might be all brute, I think," I comment back, half-jokingly. "But I at least try."

She laughs gently, her chest rising and falling easily. With her hair swept across her shoulder she leans back, closing her eyes and listening to the faint music.

"Well thank you, Cade."

My cock twitches just from her saying my name. It's too rough a word for her seductive lips. Readjusting, I put the car in drive.

"Blue house on the corner, right?" I ask her and she nods.

"Right across from the lake."

"Yeah I remember now. It's been a year since."

"Since you dropped me off when I was wasted?" she questions and shakes her head, her beautiful gaze on the auburn leaves that blow in the wind as we drive by. "Thank you for that by the way… It was not my best night."

"We were all wasted," I attempt to appease her. If I was being fully honest, I'd admit to her that I'm glad she was too far gone that night. My fingers itched to hold her and if she'd been more sober, I'd have leaned in for a kiss. I'd have wanted more. Only for me to be called away the very next day. It was meant to happen, to give us more time for when it'd be right.

A time like now.

I lay my forearm on the center console, daring to get a little closer to her, my hand only inches from her.

"Seriously, thanks for that night. It was ..."

"A good night," I stop her from finishing the word 'embarrassing.' "I love coming home and getting to hang out with you." I almost say 'you guys,' but I cut it off deliberately, choosing not to hide anymore. Not to hold back.

"Oh, is that right?" Shar swallows thickly, the sound of it bringing my attention to her slim throat and the dip just beneath it that begs me to lay an open kiss right there.

With the heat climbing in the cabin, no matter that our windows are both open, I pull up in her drive and park the truck. "You like hanging out with me?" she asks, a hint of reverence playing in the sweet cadence of her question.

I can only nod, my grip slipping slightly on the wheel as my palms turn sweaty.

"I like the way you look at me," I push her gently, calling her out and finally being a man when it comes to her and what's between us.

"I look at people, yeah," she tries to play it off.

"You blush the same way too? When you look at other people."

I'm only given a deeper hue of red as she sits in that seat, biting down on her lip. A lip I'd like to suck while my hand roams between her legs. I have to shift in my seat and I notice she squirms in hers too.

The crickets and nightlife are the only backdrop as I turn the keys in the ignition and let the silence take over.

"You don't make me blush, Cade," she lies and then stares out her window to correct herself. "Well... you make all the girls blush so it's not the same."

"I don't notice it with other women. I don't notice anything about them."

"Now you're just trying to prove a point and make me blush," she accuses.

"Tell me you didn't look at me different from the other guys?" Damn, it's odd how much thinking that's a possibility hurts. The pain vanishes the second Shar looks up at me with wide eyes.

"I feel like you always did," I admit.

Her breathing is shallow and her lips slightly parted.

"Do you want to come in?" is all she says, her fingers digging into the leather of the seat beneath her, as if she has to cling to it to keep her seated there.

"And why do you want me to come in Shar?" I don't know why I tease her, why I prolong the tension, other than that I need her to admit it too.

"Because I don't want to be alone tonight?"

"You answered that like you were asking another question."

Her gaze drops and insecurity flashes in her gorgeous eyes.

"Come on, Shar. Tell me the truth. Tell me all of this isn't in my head and something I just made up."

My heart rages against my chest and my pulse races, waiting for her to answer.

She shakes her head gently, swallowing first, and then admitting, "If you mean the fact that I've wanted you for years and that I've dreamt what could have happened that night a year ago… then no. It's not in your head."

"Then, yeah, I want to come in."

chapter three

Sharon

HIS LIPS WERE ON ME SO FAST, HIS HANDS ON MY WAIST, PINNING ME against his truck. The only reason my eyes aren't closed as he devours me is because I need to see it, to know I'm sane, and that this all isn't a dream.

Cade Jameson, the boy who stole my heart in high school and left with it for years is back a man, demanding the very thing I've wanted since I first laid eyes on him.

With his large hands at my hips, his lips drifting down my neck and the chill of the autumn night air leaving goosebumps along my exposed skin, I can barely breathe, let alone believe this is real.

It's the site of my neighbor, Miss Clare Jane peeking through her blinds that snaps me out of the haze.

All hot and bothered, I'd feel shame if I wasn't living out a fantasy I'd trade all my modesty for in a heartbeat.

"Cade, inside," I whisper at the same time he rakes his teeth up my neck and smiles at the shell of my ear.

He whispers, "You have no idea how long I've dreamed about doing just this." His grip on me loosens and with a gentle hand in mine, helping me find my balance, he leaves a kiss just beneath my ear and adds, "But I was more of a brute than a gentleman in those dreams, Shar."

Pulling back, he gives me a charming smirk, "I'll mind my manners until we get through that front door of yours."

Oh, my… not a single word can finish that sentence. None come to mind even.

All the heat that had gathered between my legs burns its way up my body as I somehow find the ability to walk at a seemingly normally pace to my front door.

I'm already on edge just from knowing he wants me. Just from that short moment he had me pinned.

His strong hand wraps around mine, his deft fingers slipping against mine and caressing in soothing circles as I open the door.

The chill behind me isn't from the night air, it's from his immediate absence as I walk in and turn in my foyer, the light from the porch shining a light on his hulking body as he stands in the doorway.

"I have to apologize," he starts and with a quick intake, my heart betrays me, squeezing tight at the thought that he isn't going to come in. But then he does. A single step and then another. Each one of his, is met by one by me, luring him deeper in the house, until my back is pressed against the wall and the front door closes with a resounding click.

"I swear next time I'll lay you down right," he whispers although his words scream in my head, the lust making the quite polite words sound dirty. It's his hungry gaze that seems to tear my clothes off even though he's not touching me. His careful steps as if I'm his prey when he's aware I'm willingly already his.

"But tonight, I have to do this," he finishes the thought that seems to take forever to complete all the while my body heats and the desire takes over.

He's on me in an instant, my back arching from the intensity of his kiss. His lips press against mine as his hands roam down my body, lifting up my skirt and pushing my underwear aside.

My lips mold to his and I moan in his mouth as his thick fingers brush against my swollen nub and then drift lower, through my slick folds and to my heated core. He groans, his head falling back for a moment before he rests his forehead against mine. His lids are still closed and I stare up at him, my heart racing, needing more. My entire being depends on the words that are sure to fall from his lips.

"You're so fucking wet for me," he comments with reverence and before I can respond, I'm in his arms, my legs wrapped around his hips. With my back against the wall, he balances me there, his left hand pulling at the strap to my dress which falls carelessly, seemingly also affected by the unfair spell he's always had over me.

If I could speak, I'd tell him that. I'd admit I've been ready for him for longer than he knows. I'd confess how much I want him, if only every nerve ending wasn't lit along my skin, making his harsh touch filled with desperation ignite a craving both of us need to satisfy this very instant.

"Cade," I cry out his name as he rakes his teeth down the curve of my neck and pulls my dress down lower, taking my bra strap with it until I'm exposed to him.

"I promise next time I'll give you more attention," his calm words, force the haze of want to subside for only a split second, just enough to hear the unzip of his jeans. Then I'm gone, gone far away and higher than I've ever been with my lips dropped into the perfect "o" as he fills me in a swift motion, his thick length stretching me.

With my heels dug into his ass, my body freezes, paralyzed by the sudden wave of pleasure that holds me hostage.

"I'll give you time," he groans against my neck, still buried deep inside of me. My thighs tremble around his hips, my core stretching to accommodate his size.

"This is how I pictured it," he murmurs and I half wonder if he's telling me, or confessing a sin. "This is exactly how I've wanted you," his rough timber vibrates against my heated skin.

If I could speak, I'd admit the same, but he rocks just then, his pubic hair pressing against my clit and sending a moan to take over the words I dared to utter.

His lips find mine again as he rocks in and out, a gentle beast for a moment, before his pace picks up. My fingers dig into his skin, raking down his back and I find myself clinging to him, surrounded by his masculine scent. He fucks me, hard and rough until I have to silence my screams by biting down on his shoulder. The sudden movement awards me with a deep rumble of a groan that spurs him on. Faster, harder, relentlessly until I'm crashing hard against the wave of my release and he's doing the same.

He's gentle when he sets me down, although my legs are weak.

My head's dizzy and my body's numb all too soon. The climax

still wracking through my body and leaving me so limp I nearly fall to the floor.

Nearly, but I don't. Disbelief still forcing me to have some semblance of grip on reality.

I just slept with Cade Jameson… No, no, Cade just fucked me against the wall of my foyer. They're two very different things and all I want from him now is *more.*

"Do you want to stay?" I dare to ask him, not even waiting to catch my breath. "You want to stay with me tonight?"

Cade lifts his gaze to mine as he pulls up his jeans, buttoning them and already appearing put together. It's not fair, because he's left me shattered and I know I look the part.

I'm a well fucked mess and his tussled hair shows the evidence of what I've done to him, but nothing else does.

Insecurity wraps its way around my heart until he speaks.

"I'm a pretty easy-going guy, Shar. This could be one good night. It could stay between us. It could be more."

Leaning against my foyer wall, still feeling him inside of me, it takes everything for me to believe this really happened. It's happening right now.

"I want it to be more, but that only matters if you want that too. So you tell me." Vulnerability shines in his light blue eyes when he asks, "You want me to stay?"

If you loved this sexy little short, you'll devour the first novel in this small town romance world.

Preorder *Tequila Rose* today, releasing February 23rd or dive into these other standalone romance novels tonight!

about the author

Thank you so much for reading my romances. I'm just a stay at home mom and avid reader turned author and I couldn't be happier.

I hope you love my books as much as I do!

More by Willow Winters
WWW.WILLOWWINTERSWRITES.COM/BOOKS

baby, it's cold outside

MELANIE HARLOW &
CORINNE MICHAELS

chapter one

Harlow

"UGH!" I SCREAM AS I TRY TO PULL THE DAMN TREE THROUGH the glass doorway of my new apartment building—unsuccessfully. I've been at it for ten minutes and even in the freezing cold December-in-Chicago weather, I have sweat beading on my forehead. What the hell was I thinking trying to move a six-foot-tall live tree by myself?

Oh, I know, I was listening to Willow talk about how a tree with lights would be magically jolly for my psyche, and necessary to get out of the foul mood and bad luck I'm enduring. Pfft. I should've known better. Willow may be the best boss and top matchmaker in Chicago, but she was wrong on this.

I don't feel jolly. I don't feel festive. I feel sweaty and frustrated, and I would like to shove this tree right up Santa's …

I give it another yank and my hand scrapes against the bark, ripping a hole in my glove.

That's it. I'm over it all.

"Stupid Christmas and all its stupid holiday crap. Santa … blah! Who needs him and his jolly elves when life sucks? Stupid tree, stupid holiday, and stupid joy!" I kick the stump, then wince because it hurt.

"Well, that's not very festive," a deep voice says from behind me. "I don't think the tree did anything to deserve your hatred."

Of course someone is standing here, watching me like a freaking idiot. What a sight I must be too. I'm holding the cut end of a tree, trying to drag it through the heavy door that keeps closing, ripping off branches as I pull harder. I'm not sure whether I should laugh or cry.

I huff, my hair falling into my face, obstructing my view of my current life crisis. "Sorry, I'll apologize to it later." I don't even turn to look at the stranger because *whatever* with it all anyway. "Once I get it in the stupid door."

I'm a damn mess, but what else is new?

Two weeks ago, I got dumped. Merry-fucking-Christmas to me. Instead of the gorgeous ring I was hoping for, I got the gift of finding out my boyfriend of six years wanted to ride someone else's sleigh. So I packed my shit and left. Thankfully, my boss had just moved in with her fiancé, so she gave me the keys to her fully furnished apartment and told me to add plants because plants cure everything.

I should've gotten a bunch of fake ones—that way I wouldn't kill them—but Willow insisted I get a real Christmas tree to push myself into the holiday spirit.

And even in the absolute craptastic state I'm in, I wanted to fake it till I made it. I'm vying for partner of My Heart's Desire and every little thing helps, right? I should've known better. Now I'm going to have a big half-alive, half-naked tree to look at, one more reminder of how I'm failing at life.

Well, if I can get it upstairs.

I pull on the tree again, tug-of-war style, needles flying everywhere. I debate just leaving it here. There's no tree in the lobby, so I can just call it a contribution, right? If it was my name on the lease, and not Willow's, I might do it. Or maybe if I didn't care about my job or had another place to live, but alas, I don't. So the tree must go to its final resting place where it will undoubtedly die before the big fat guy makes his way on the 25th.

"Are you planning to put that in your apartment?"

"Yup," I say as I yank again. It doesn't budge. "Well, maybe."

He lets out a chuckle. "Need help?"

"Nope," I say through gritted teeth. "I got it." I wipe my brow where the sweat is now dripping and groan aloud. "I'm fine. It's fine. I got this."

"You know I can't leave until you get this tree inside."

I can hear the smile in his voice. At least I'm amusing him.

"I'm happy to help since you're struggling."

This is the worst week of my life.

The voice behind me sighs loudly. Giving in, I turn to ask for the help I so clearly need, ready to deal with the embarrassment of my life.

"I'm not strugg—" I start, but when I turn, I want to die. Because in front of me is the most attractive man on the planet, standing there with a smile on his face.

He has dark brown hair that's pushed to the side, but not in that slick way—it's as though it just moved there because he commanded it to. His jaw is strong and covered with a dusting of stubble that I want to brush my fingers against. And then there are his eyes. Jesus Christ. His eyes are the most stunning shade of blue. They're not quite royal blue, although I could see specks of it. They're a deep, rich sapphire color with traces of green, or is it just a lighter blue? Either way, I can't stop looking at him.

My mouth hangs open just a bit as I try to get my brain to form words. What do you say to a god?

"I can see you're not, but … I'm a gentleman, it's Christmas, and you know … I have somewhere to go before New Years."

"What?" I ask, not remembering if there was a question or whether I am supposed to do something besides stare at him like the present I'd like under my tree.

"Are you ready for me to help?"

Yes, the answer is yes. Yes to anything he wants. Yes!

"Huh?" is what comes out past my lips.

"The tree. Are you going to let me help you?" He grins at me, knowing my only other choice is to leave it here, stuck in the doors.

"Help?"

"*Yeeeeah,*" the word comes out slowly, which is apparently the cylinder I'm firing on. He puts his coffee cup down and then extends his hand. "I'm Michael."

What a name. It's simple, classic, and so totally him. I think there was an angel named Michael, right? Maybe a god? If not, there is now. The god of Sexy Men. That is Michael.

I sigh, my eyes blinking slowly as I stare at him.

His head tilts just a little, lips pursed as he waits expectantly.

Shit. I should talk. "Harlow."

"Harlow?"

"Yes?"

He smirks. "Your name is Harlow?"

If the ground could just open me up and swallow me, that would be cool. "Sorry," I say as I take his hand like I should've to start with. "Yes, I'm Harlow, and this is my tree that is resisting its new home." I'm hoping I can recover from this horrific introduction with a modicum of self-respect intact.

"I hear that some trees are just difficult."

"This is apparently the story of my life."

Men. Trees. People. Parents. They're all difficult. What's that saying about the common denominator? I'm starting to wonder …

"Well, let's see if we can't get the tree upstairs and willing to behave."

"Doubtful, but I appreciate it."

Michael moves to the double doors and pushes one to the side and then slides in a locking mechanism I didn't know existed, and then repeats it on the other side.

Seriously, I hate my life. "That *would've* made it easier …."

He gives me a panty-melting smile and his brows rise. "And probably saved a lot of branches."

"That too."

"Why don't you grab the top?" he suggests.

I move to the front of the tree, resisting the urge to punch myself in the face.

"Ready?"

I nod.

With almost no effort, we move the tree through the doors and to the elevator. "Thank you, I can get it upstairs."

Michael gives me a look that says he's not so sure of it, which I've earned. "I'll help you get it to the apartment. You know, there are two more doors to get it through."

I laugh, because what the hell else can I do? "I'm never going to recover from this. This is the most embarrassing thing ever."

"I'm sure I have you beat."

"Really?"

He shrugs. "Have you ever been to Cancun for spring break?"

I've never gone anywhere outside of Chicago. "Can't say that I have."

"Then I promise, you're not even in my wheelhouse of embarrassing moments."

I appreciate his attempt to make me feel better, but this definitely blows. If he wasn't so attractive, maybe I wouldn't care, or if he wasn't a guy, it would be fine. However, he is both and I am mortified.

I push the button to go to the twentieth floor and will myself not to say anything stupid on the elevator ride up.

"So, are you new to the building?" Michael asks.

"Yeah, just moved in about a week ago. It was my boss's old apartment, but since she and her fiancé just bought a townhouse, she's subletting it to me. You?"

"I've been here about a year. I live with a buddy from college."

"I used to live with my boyfriend, but I don't now. Nope. Now I'm alone. *Totally* alone. And single." I'm also wondering if I can sew my mouth shut to stop myself from blurting out stupid stuff.

Michael gives me a smile and runs his fingers through his hair. "Well, that's …"

"A lot of info?"

He laughs.

"I swear, I have my shit together most days, but it's been a rough week."

"Well, the holidays are either great or total shit, right?"

"I'm definitely on the shit end."

His eyes roam over my body and his lips turn up as my blood heats under his stare. "Here's to hoping today shows you it's not all shit, then. Maybe we can turn your luck around."

He stands there, holding the trunk of the tree and then the elevator door opens, not allowing me to think any more on that statement.

chapter two

Michael

DO NOT STARE AT HER ASS. DO NOT STARE AT HER ASS.

I try to tear my gaze away, but … it's really fucking hard to do with those leggings she's got on.

It's been a long time since I've had a reaction to a woman like this. I could've stood in that hallway all damn night watching her. She's beautiful in an imperfect kind of way. Her long brown hair is falling out of her ponytail, and there are a good amount of pine needles stuck in there too, but it just makes her more adorable. Not to mention how the tip of her nose is just a little bit red from the cold. I can't remember the last time I found someone's flaws so cute.

We get the tree into the apartment without any issues. "Do you have the tree stand?" I ask.

"The what?"

"The stand … that the tree goes in."

"You mean, it doesn't just … stand on its own?"

I can't tell if she's kidding, and I fight back laughter because the look in her eyes says she's not and she's halfway to tears.

"Not a big deal," I say quickly. "It can sit in the corner while we go get a stand." I don't know what possessed me to say it. I don't know this girl and she doesn't know me, but I'll do anything to not have her cry.

"Right now?"

I look down at my watch and then back at her. Fuck the family party I'm supposed to be at. I didn't want to go anyway, and I'd much rather help someone who is clearly having a bad day. My sister will understand, and if not, she can kiss my ass.

I smile at Harlow. "Yeah, we'll go to the store, and then I'll help you set it all up."

Her eyes brim with unshed tears and now I wonder if I fucked up by offering to help. "You'd do that? You don't … I mean, you're all dressed up. Don't you have somewhere to go?"

I lift my shoulder, not really thinking much of it. "I think helping a neighbor is the Christmas spirit thing to do, don't you? Besides, if you don't get it in the stand with water, who the hell is going to help you get it out of here when it's dead?"

The sound of her laughter goes straight to my cock. It's soft but lacks all restraint, and I find that I want to hear it again.

"I probably would just toss it out the window," she tells me.

"And that is why we're getting a stand now."

"Can you give me a few?"

I nod. "I'll wait here."

Harlow rushes out of the room and I look around at the apartment. Knowing she just moved in a week ago, I'm shocked at how organized it is. There aren't any boxes, unlike in my place, where my buddy and I have lived in for two years and still haven't finished unpacking. Everything in here is neat and clean. There are a few photos on the table where she tossed her keys, and I wander over to them.

I pick up a framed picture of an older couple, assuming it's her parents. Harlow looks exactly like the woman in the photo, only younger. A guy I'm guessing is her brother is in a cap and gown next to her.

Ugh. Northwestern.

"Hey, where did you go to college?" I yell out.

It's best to get the important things out of the way.

"Me? Oh, I went to U of I!"

Okay, so it's just her brother that is the enemy.

Setting that frame down, I move to the next photo, where Harlow stands next to another woman in an office. The other woman's arms are wrapped around Harlow's middle and the smile is so wide, it could break the glass. Who the hell has photos in their house with their boss? They must really get along.

"Hey. Sorry," she says quickly as she comes up behind me. "Find anything interesting?"

I laugh because it's clear I was doing what any normal person would when left alone in a stranger's house. "Nope. Seems you're normal."

"Sorry to disappoint."

"Is that your boss?"

Harlow nods quickly. "That's Willow. She's my boss-slash-friend. She owns the company I work for, but I'm going to come on as a partner soon. Well, if I'm able to match this client who is totally a pain in my ass."

"Match?"

She bites her lower lip. "Yeah. So. I'm a matchmaker."

"Like …"

"Like exactly what you're probably thinking, yes. I hate the term and really wish we could come up with something a little less cheesy. Like, Destinymaker or Couple Counselor. I don't know, I'm still mulling it over, but the point is that I cut through the crap and find what people want in a partner."

"I think you found your new job title—crap cutter."

Harlow rolls her eyes with a grin. "I'll be sure to float it to management. It's super romantic."

"I'm a romantic guy."

She tilts her head. "Are you? Interesting."

I groan, seeing the wheels start to turn in her matchmaker brain. The last thing I need is another woman in my life trying to set me up. My mother and sister are bad enough. "Actually, no. I'm not romantic at all. I hate romance."

"You and me both, buddy."

"Wait a minute. You make your living as a matchmaker, and you hate romance? Isn't that sort of a detriment to your career?"

She sighs and blows the stray pieces of hair out of her face. I notice she's put on lipstick. Her cheeks look a little brighter too, and she's put cover-up or something on her nose, but it's still pink. "I suppose it is. I haven't always hated romance. It's more of a recent occurrence."

"I see. That boyfriend you mentioned …"

"Ex-boyfriend," she says sharply.

"Right. Ex-boyfriend. Is he responsible for your hatred of romance?"

"Probably." She crosses her arms over her chest, not easy to do since she's still wearing her puffy winter jacket, and her lower lip juts out. It's angry and adorable all at once. "I thought he was going to propose on Christmas Eve, but he dumped me right after Thanksgiving. After everything I did for him, he dumped me!"

"What did you do for him?" I ask, curious.

"Oh, God." She shakes her head. "I was so dumb. I loaned him money to get out of debt, because I thought he was going to buy a ring. Instead, he bought two tickets to Maui and took his little side dish on Christmas vacation! Mele fucking Kalikimaka!"

"Ouch. How long were you together?"

"Six years."

"Six years!" The thought of a six-year relationship—seventy-two months, over two thousand days and nights of unrealistic expectations—nearly makes my knees buckle. "Damn."

"I was an idiot. But I kept thinking he loved me and eventually he'd want to marry me."

"Why'd you want to marry him?"

She thinks for a second. "He was cute enough. And he had a steady job. However, he also had a gambling habit I didn't know about."

"Got it." I look around. "So if I open drawers in here, will I find a little voodoo doll with a Hawaiian shirt on?"

Her brown eyes light up. "That is a great idea."

I laughed. "Why don't we stick to the tree stand for now, huh? I'll run out to the store. Where do you want your tree to go?"

She drops her arms and turns in a slow circle. "Maybe over there by the window?"

"Good choice." I check my watch. If I hurry, I can go buy her a tree stand, set it up by the window, and make it to my sister's party by nine, ten at the latest. "Okay, I'll be right back."

"Wait! I'm coming with you."

"You don't have to. It's freezing out there. Why don't you stay in and get warm?"

"I am warm."

"Oh yeah?" Unable to resist, I reach out and touch her nose. It's still chilly. "Doesn't feel that way."

She sighs. "My nose always gets so red from the cold. I hate it."

"I think it's cute."

"Cute like Rudolph?" She eyes me warily. "That's what my ex used to call me."

"Let me just say right now that your ex was a real big asshole who didn't deserve you, okay? And I don't care what he looked like or how steady his job was. Even if he kicked the gambling habit, he was never going to deserve you."

"But you just met me," she says softly. "How do you know that?"

"I just do." And the urge to kiss her at that moment is so overwhelming that I have to take a step back. Like she said, I just met her. I don't want to be that guy. "Come on. Let's go."

We walk the three blocks to the drugstore with an icy Chicago wind blowing in our faces, the cascading flurries growing thicker. I'm not sure how much snow we're going to get this evening, but it could make for a long ride out to my sister's house in the suburbs.

"Can we slow down a little?" Harlow asks, her shorter legs scrambling to keep up with my long ones. "I'm dying here."

"Oh, sorry." I shorten my strides and move a little less briskly. "I was trying to hurry because the weather's getting worse. I have a long drive tonight."

"I knew it!" She whacks me on the arm. "I knew you had somewhere to be. You should have told me. I can handle this myself."

"Harlow, you were never going to get that tree up to your apartment if I hadn't intervened. And even if you did, what was your plan—decorate it lying down?"

"I told you, I hadn't really thought that far ahead. I don't know anything about Christmas trees! We had an artificial one growing up. It stood on its own. Why shouldn't a real one?"

"Oh my God. Come on in here." I put my arm around her to shepherd her through the revolving door to the store, and it feels so good I wish I had a reason to keep it there.

"They have tree stands here?" Harlow looks around. Her nose is bright red again, and I want to warm it up with my lips. What the hell is wrong with me? I don't even know this girl's last name. And other than putting makeup on, she hasn't really given me any indication she's interested in messing around tonight.

Tearing my eyes from her face, I look for the holiday aisles. "Over there," I tell her. "Aisles eight and nine."

chapter three

Harlow

WE MAKE OUR WAY TOWARD THE OTHER SIDE OF THE STORE, AND I grab an abandoned shopping cart along the way. "I might need some other things too."

"Like what?"

"Like decorations. Lights and ornaments."

He glances at me. "You don't even have lights or ornaments?"

"No, and stop making me feel bad. Getting the tree wasn't even my idea, it was my boss's."

"What did you do last Christmas?" he asks.

My spirits sink even lower as I remember. "I put up a tree with the asshole ex in our apartment, but it was fake, just like his love for me. And I don't want any of the stupid ornaments that we hung on our fake tree with our fake joy in our fake happiness. It was all a lie."

"Oh, Jesus." Michael sighs heavily.

"I'm going to grab some vodka too. Be right back." I veer off down aisle four and head for the booze section. They probably won't have my favorite brand here, but beggars can't be choosers, and I really need something to take the edge off this holiday angst.

Too bad Michael won't be able to stick around long enough to have a drink with me. It sounds like he has to drive somewhere, and the weather is getting worse by the minute. I'm lucky we ran into each other and he had mercy on me—I'd probably be stringing lights on a tree still stuck in the lobby door if he hadn't.

God, he's so damn cute. And charming. And sweet. There was a moment in my apartment, right after he touched my nose, that I thought he was going to kiss me, but he didn't. Did I imagine it?

Duh, of course you imagined it, you dummy! All you've done is make an ass of yourself and talk about your ex. He probably looks at you and thinks crazy ex-girlfriend. And look at the way he's dressed—that man is too hot to be alone on a Friday night. He's got a date.

I pull a bottle of vodka off the shelf and place it in my cart. Then I add a bag of Hershey Kisses, a box of candy canes, and a tube of ready-made sugar cookie dough. In aisle eight, I grab a few strands of lights and a box of colorful ornaments. Since we're on foot, I don't want to buy too much, but I can't resist picking out a star for the top.

I find Michael in aisle nine looking at a box in his hands. My stomach flip-flops a little as I approach. He's so tall. I wonder what he looks like underneath all those clothes, and for a moment I fantasize about unwrapping him layer by layer. The winter coat and scarf. The suit and tie. The buttoned-up shirt. I wonder if it has French cuffs or not.

I love French cuffs.

He catches me staring at his hands, which are strong but elegant-looking, with long fingers. "Do I need a manicure or something?"

Embarrassed, I feel my face get hot. "No! Sorry, I was just wondering something."

One of his eyebrows cocks up. "About my hands?"

Oh, dear God. "Uh, about your shirt actually. Whether or not it has French cuffs."

"Why were you wondering about my shirt?"

Because I was thinking about taking it off of you is not an appropriate answer, although I'm almost tempted to give it. I mean, why not—I've been spewing every thought in my head without a filter all night long, haven't I?

But in the end, I don't.

"I guess I just like a nice dress shirt with French cuffs."

He looks amused. "And why's that?"

I shrug, figuring I might as well be honest. "I think they're classy and convey there's something powerful about a man. But it's an understated kind of power. Like he might drive a Range Rover and drink expensive scotch, but he'll still pull your hair and say dirty things to you."

He doesn't say anything for a moment, but his eyes stay locked on mine. The tension between us ratchets up about a hundred notches. "Yes."

I'm so lost in the heat of his gaze that I forget the question. "Yes, what?"

"Yes, my shirt has French cuffs." He places the boxed tree stand he's holding in my cart. "Yes, I drive a Range Rover." Then moves closer to me, so close I can feel his breath on my lips. "Yes, I drink expensive scotch."

I can barely breathe. My throat is dry. "And the other stuff?"

He smiles the slightly sinister grin of a well-heeled villain. "Come on. I have to let *some* things come as a surprise."

While I'm standing there, equal parts turned-on and dumbfounded, he takes the cart from me and pushes it toward the front of the store.

Jolly Old St. Nicholas! Is this guy for real?

I feel like I might look for him again only to find he's been nothing but a figment of my imagination. Do guys like Michael exist outside of fantasies and romance novels? Is he secretly a serial killer? Am I going to wind up tied up in my closet tonight?

Actually, the idea has some possibilities …

It takes me a couple minutes to recover my senses, and by the time I find him near the registers, he's already paying for all my loot. "What are you doing?" I ask, frantically tugging on his sleeve. "You don't have to buy all this!"

"Harlow, it's not that big a deal." He pulls out a credit card from his wallet, but before he can swipe it through the reader, I grab it.

Michael West.

"Hey, that's funny," I say.

"What is? You stealing my Amex?"

"No. Your last name is West. Mine's North. North … West … we have the same kind of last name." I don't know why it makes me so happy, but it does. We're both directions! We're both witches from Oz! Together we're Kim Kardashian's baby! It has to be a sign, right?

"Nice to meet you, Harlow North." He quickly snatches the card out of my hand and swipes it. "Now quit being a pain. I've got this."

I huff and pout, but there's not much I can do since the transaction is complete within seconds. "Thank you. It was really nice of you to help me at all, let alone pay for my drunk tree-trimming party supplies."

He laughs and gathers up three of the four bags, including the bulky one holding the tree stand box. "Is that what all this is?"

I grab the last remaining bag, which contains my candy and cookie dough. Maybe I'd just eat it right from the tube. "Pretty much."

We exit the store and immediately, a frigid blast of air hits us. The snow is coming down hard and heavy now, and it's tough to see even five feet ahead. The ground is slippery too, and I slide a little as we make our way down the sidewalk.

"Careful." He switches all his bags to one hand so he can take my arm. His touch sets off a spark that warms my entire body. I swear every snowflake that lands on me sizzles.

"So where are you headed tonight?" I ask, hoping it sounds like an innocent question.

"To my sister's in Lake Bluff." He looks up and down the avenue. "But the drive is going to be so fucking slow."

"Do you have to go?" Inside, I'm shrieking for Christmas joy that he's not going on a date. Visions of sugarplums and his naked body dance in my head.

"I should. It's my family's Christmas party, and I skipped it last year."

I nod, focusing on the sidewalk again as my sexy visions go poof and vanish. Unless … "You know, your sister probably wouldn't want you on the road in this blizzard."

"Oh no?"

"Definitely not. In fact," I tell him as we reach our building, "I think you might want to call her and tell her not to expect you."

"Really." He sounds amused as we make our way to the elevator.

"Of course!" I punch the button. "I mean, no pressure or anything, but I know I wouldn't want my brother on the road tonight."

The elevator doors open. It's empty.

"Ah. Very sweet of you." He lets me enter first, then hits twenty.

"It's just too dangerous," I insist as the doors close. "You could get in trouble out there."

He leans back against the wall and looks over at me, his expression smoldering. "I could get in trouble right here."

chapter four

Michael

WHAT THE HELL AM I DOING FLIRTING WITH THIS GIRL (WHO IS clearly going through a breakup) instead of being with my family (who are going to kill me for this) and wondering if her tree isn't the only thing we're going to get erect tonight?

I never think like this. I'm a logical guy who makes logical choices. I don't walk girls to get tree stands in the middle of a blizzard, no matter how red their noses get.

"You know, they say that decorating a tree is not something you should do alone," Harlow says as we reach her door.

"Who says?"

"Everyone."

"Is that so?"

She nods. "It's the Christmas law. I heard about it on the internet and you know that everything you read there is true."

"I would hate the break the Christmas law."

Harlow's brown eyes sparkle as if I just gave her the best present in the world. "Really?"

"Under one condition …"

"Name it."

She agreed to that way too quickly. My mind wanders a bit before I remember what I wanted to say. "We don't mention your shitty ex one more time tonight."

She extends her hand, and I take it. "You got yourself a deal."

We enter the apartment, tree still standing in the corner, thank God, and get to work. Harlow puts some cheesy Hallmark movie on the television and then brings in a mug of hot chocolate. "Here, it's also law that we have to drink this."

"This is a law I don't mind." I have a feeling her laws are only going to get more numerous as the night wears on, but I have a few laws I hope to enact as well. I'm such a dick. I have to stop my mind from going down this road each time she looks at me.

But she's so damn cute. When we got back, she put on a pair of way-too-fucking-short shorts, a tank top (as if it's not ten degrees and snowing right now), and tortoise shell glasses. She's got that hot-for-teacher vibe going on right now and I'm dying.

I take a sip and it's hot, but it's not hot chocolate. "What the hell is in this?" I ask.

"Whipped Vodka, you don't need the whip cream when you have it in alcohol flavor."

"You know, drinking and tree trimming is probably a bad idea."

She smiles. "Are you worried that you'll get into trouble, Michael?"

"I'm worried *you're* what's going to be trouble."

"Well, I've been on the nice list for a long time and it's gotten me here … maybe trouble isn't so bad." Harlow bites her lower lip before bringing the mug up to her mouth. She takes a slow sip, watching me over the rim and my cock goes hard.

"Are you flirting with me?"

She sets the mug aside and sidles closer. "Maybe."

"I think you are and I think you want me to kiss you," I challenge her. I love when a woman is assertive and it's clear that Harlow is testing her boundaries. She's about to find out that there are some games I won't lose. Enjoying the surprised—and pleased—look on her face, I place my mug on the coffee table next to hers.

"And what if I do?" she teases.

I raise my gaze upward, and feel a sly grin form on my lips because right above her head is mistletoe. While I don't need the excuse, I'm happy to use it to my benefit. "Well, sweetheart, look up."

"Huh?" Harlow tilts her head back and I take that opportunity to grab her and pull her to my chest.

She lets out a squeak in surprise and her hands grip my arms. "What does the law say about mistletoe?" I ask.

Her tongue darts across her lips, and I don't wait for her reply, taking that as invitation enough, and I kiss her. She tastes of chocolate, vodka, and sweetness. I've never been so attracted to a woman this quickly, but Harlow is like a siren song, one I want to answer.

At first, the kiss is slow and tentative, but then she moans and all of that shatters. Her lips part and I delve into the heat of her mouth. She kisses me back just as rough. I love when a woman doesn't hold back. Her hands drift up to my neck, holding me to her.

I slide my palms beneath her tank and up her bare back. Her skin is soft and warm and—

CRASH!

Harlow squeals and we jump apart as the tree hits the floor.

"Damn that tree," she says breathlessly. "It's evil and it hates me."

I have to laugh at her indignant face. "It's just a tree. How could it be evil?"

She arches a brow. "Clearly you have never heard of a Whomping Willow."

"Can't say that I have."

"Don't tell me you haven't read Harry Potter."

"Why not?" I manage to right the tree and prop it in the corner again.

"Because then I won't know if we can become friends."

I give her a look over my shoulder. "Is that what we're doing tonight? Becoming friends?"

"Of course. What else would we be doing?" Harlow pushes her glasses up her nose and gives me her best innocent little lamb face, all the while standing there in those fucking tiny little shorts.

I'm not sure she's wearing a bra either. If she is, it isn't doing much to hide the fact that her nipples are hard. It's hell trying not to stare at her chest.

I slip out of my suit jacket, tossing it on the couch. "Well, my friend, why don't you help me get this tree in the stand? Maybe all it wants is a permanent home. Some nice decorations. A drink of water."

"I have to water the tree?"

"Yes, Harlow. You do." Shaking my head, I grab the box with the stand in it from the drugstore bag. "It's a good thing I'm here."

"I'll drink to that," she says, picking up her mug again and taking a sip. "Okay, tell me what to do to help."

We manage to get the tree into the stand, the bolts secured, and some water in the base. Harlow doesn't have a tree skirt, but she does have a red fleece blanket she drapes around the base of the tree, and once it's in place, she stands back and claps her hands. "I love it! Let's decorate!"

I glance out the window. The snow is falling even heavier now, and if I stay even one more minute, I will never make it to my sister's house. She'll make me pay too—my entire family will. Nobody can work a guilt trip like my mother, and my sister can hold onto a grudge like it's keeping her alive. They have the ability to make my life very unpleasant.

But when I look at Harlow again, she's standing on tiptoe to hang an ornament high up on the tree, her bare legs beckoning. My cock stirs again in my pants.

Yeah, fuck my family Christmas. There's something I want to unwrap right here.

"Hey, I need to make a phone call real quick," I tell her.

"No problem. You can use my room if you'd like privacy," she offers, pointing to a door off the living room.

"Thanks. I'll be right out." I head into her bedroom and shut the door behind me.

Curious, I take a moment to look around her room before I make the call. It's feminine and neat, no surprise there. Pink, black, and white bedding. A million decorative pillows perfectly placed. One nightstand stacked with books, the other holding only a lamp, which is on. I lower myself to a bench at the foot of her bed and call my sister.

"Hello?" She already sounds peeved.

"Hey, it's me."

"Let me guess—you're not coming."

"Laura, the weather's terrible! I can't drive in this."

"How convenient."

"Look, I wanted to come this year. I really did."

"It's like you *knew* I was planning to set you up tonight!"

"Set me up?" I frown. "With who?"

"I forget her name. She's a friend of Reid Fortino's fiancée."

"Who the fuck is Reid Fortino?"

"God, you don't remember anybody! He's a co-worker of mine, and you've met him at *least* five times."

"Oh. Well, thanks but no thanks. I don't need to be set up."

"Michael, you can't keep turning down every single girl I send your way!"

"Um, yes. I can, actually." In the living room, I can hear Harlow singing "Have Yourself a Merry Little Christmas," and it makes me smile because it's so off key.

"You're going to wind up old and alone."

"That's a chance I'm willing to take." I get up and open the door to peek at Harlow, stifling my laughter at the sight of her stringing Christmas lights around her body.

"Good Lord, what's that noise? Did you adopt a sickly cat?"

"No," I tell her, quickly shutting the door again. "It's a neighbor singing. I have to go."

Laura sighs dramatically. "What am I supposed to say to this girl if she shows up hoping to meet the man of her dreams?"

"Say Merry Christmas. Pass her the cheese plate."

"You're a big jerk," she huffs. "I'm giving your present to somebody else. And if that girl shows up and she's perfect, you'll be sorry you're not here."

"I'll take my chances," I tell her. "Bye, sis. Sorry to miss the party. Give my apologies to Mom and Dad, and I'll see you guys soon." I end the call and hurry out of the bedroom.

The perfect girl is already mine tonight.

chapter five

Harlow

MICHAEL SHUTS THE DOOR TO MY BEDROOM, LEAVING ME ALONE IN the living room. I can't help dancing around as I admire my tree and start hanging ornaments on its branches.

"I'm sorry I called you evil," I tell it softly. "You're the perfect tree, and I'm having the perfect night."

Opening up a box of lights, I wonder who Michael had to call. For a second, a wave of fear rushes through me as I imagine him calling his girlfriend—or wife!—making up some lame excuse why he's going to be home late. But before I panic completely, I remember that he said his sister is having a party tonight. He was probably calling her to say he can't make it because of the weather.

Scolding myself for assuming the worst, I sing along with the soundtrack to the holiday romance on the TV as I unwind the lights. Not everyone is a two-timing asshole like my ex, and I have to get over it and start trusting people again—like the hot, sexy man in a suit who rescued me this evening. The one in my *bedroom*.

"Have yourself a merry little Christmas," I croon loudly, even though I am a terrible singer and Willow says I really should not ever sing in public. "Let your heart be liiiiiiiight." I loop a strand of lights around my waist and toss one end over my shoulder, twirling in circles. "From now on our troubles will be out of sight."

"Wow." Michael shuts the bedroom door behind him, his expression amused. "That's quite the vocal talent you have there."

I laugh. "I happen to have many talents. Singing, alas, is not one of them."

"I gathered that conclusion from the next room."

"Everything okay?" I glance at the phone in his hand as he walks towards me.

"Everything is great." He tosses the phone onto the couch next to his coat. "I am not expected anywhere else tonight."

"Perfect." I can't keep the smile off my face as I twirl around, showing off the lights I'm wearing. "I was just about to test these and make sure they work."

He puts his hands on my hips and pulls me closer. "Want me to try to turn you on?"

"Yes, please." I lift my lips to his and he kisses me, and I would not have been surprised if every damn bulb on the string lit up just from the current between us.

His mouth moves down my throat, sending sparks to the farthest reaches of my body. His hands slip beneath my tank top and slide up my sides. His breathing grows heavier as his palms move down the back of my shorts and grip my ass. He pulls me against him, and I can feel how hard he is. My belly hollows, and my core muscles clench.

I reach down between us and run my hand over the warm, hard length of him, and my legs go weak. Is it wrong that I want this near-stranger to fuck me senseless tonight?

"How am I doing?" he whispers, his breath warm on my neck. "Are you turned on yet?"

"Um, yes—and then some." I want to move into my bedroom, but I worry it might be too forward. Luckily, he's not nearly so concerned.

"Think the tree will mind if we give it some alone time?"

"Not at all," I reply, a little breathless. "Want to—"

But before I can finish my invitation, he scoops me up and carries me toward my room, throwing open the door and then laying me down across the foot of my bed. My heart pounds wildly as he closes the door, returns to the bed, and removes my glasses, setting them aside on the nightstand. I'm happy the lamp is on, so I can see him, but I'm still freaking out a little.

"I've never done this before," I blurt. "Brought someone into my bedroom the first night I met him."

"I've never done this before either," he says, holding up one end of the stand of lights wound around my body. "Removed Christmas tree lights from someone in bed."

"I'm a different kind of girl," I tell him, giggling as he unwinds the string and drops it to the floor.

He loosens the knot in his tie and stretches out above me. "I like that. I like everything about you, Harlow North."

"Even though I'm clueless about Christmas trees?"

"If you weren't, I wouldn't be here." He grabs my tank and lifts it over my head, revealing a red lace bra that is more decorative than anything else. His bright sapphire eyes pop. "And I'm *really* fucking glad to be here right now."

I smile as I wrap my legs around him. "Good."

We make out just like that for a good long while, and I can't believe how hot it is—the material of his dress shirt against my chest, the way his cock rubs against me through layers of clothing, the way I'm nearly naked but he's still wearing a fucking tie.

He moves his body over mine in a way that lets me know exactly how good it would feel if we got rid of all the barriers between us. I'm not exactly sure how far we're going to take this, but it's not long before he's got me panting and writhing beneath the weight of his body, frustrated by the need to get closer to him.

How bad would it be to have sex with a stranger? I mean, is he still a stranger? I know his last name, right? And I know where—roughly—he lives. We're practically neighbors! And I know he's the kind of guy to rescue a damsel with a tree in distress on a snowy December night ...

Good enough for me.

Apparently he's feeling the same way, because just as I'm about to swallow my pride and reach for his belt, he picks up his head and says, "Hey, before this goes any farther, I just want you to know, you can tell me to stop at any time."

"Okay."

"So," he says, kissing his way down my chest, "do you want me to stop?"

"Not even one little bit."

He looks up at me, his mouth hooking into a smoldering crooked grin. "Good."

He takes his time.

I don't know whether he's worried he'll never see me again or really does just want to lavish every inch of my skin with attention, but he undresses me with an agonizing lack of haste—first my shorts, then the bra, then finally the matching panties, which make him groan when he sees them.

"Did you know what you were doing?" he demands, moving down so his head was between my legs. "Did you put these on knowing they'd drive me crazy?"

"Maybe," I tease.

"You are definitely on the naughty list," he tells me, and then his hands are pushing my thighs apart and his mouth is on me and I can feel his lips and tongue making me wet right through the lace. Eventually he drags them down my legs and tosses them aside, circling his tongue right over my clit until I'm so close to orgasm I could weep. He drives me to the brink of insanity, taking me right to the edge of a climax I'm desperate for, and then backs off again.

"Please," I whisper, clawing at my comforter.

"Please what? You have to ask for it."

"Please let me come."

"Do you think a naughty girl like you deserves it?" he asks, sliding two fingers inside me.

"Yes!" I cry out, both in pleasure and in answer to his question.

He laughs and gives me what I want with his mouth and his hand and tongue and I'm rocking my hips beneath him, shameless and needy and moaning so loud I'm positive the neighbors can hear me.

But I don't care—it's the best orgasm I've ever had.

When my body stops its rapturous pulsing, I push his head away and scoot back. "Stop, stop," I say, totally out of breath. "I can't take any more."

"Oh, but you will." Michael stands up and removes his cufflinks, and it's so fucking hot watching him, my toes curl. When he pulls out the knot in his tie, I bite my lip. He's just starting to unbutton his shirt when I hear a voice in the living room.

"Harlow? Where are you?"

Michael and I exchange a surprised look.

"Expecting company?" he asks, his hands paused.

"No!" I stage whisper. "It sounds like my boss, but I have no idea what she could be doing here!"

"How did she get in?"

"She must have kept a key. This used to be her place, remember?"

"Hey!" Willow knocks on my bedroom door. "You in there? Get dressed, we're going out!"

"Um, one second!" I scramble to find clothes as Michael laughs silently, shaking his head. "I'll be right out."

I manage to tug on underwear, my shorts and tank, and a robe that was hanging on the back of my door in about ten seconds. Putting a finger over my lips, I look at Michael, and he nods. Then I open the bedroom door just enough to slide out, pulling it shut right behind me.

Willow is standing in my living room, hands on her hips. "That's not what I had in mind for a festive holiday party outfit," she says. "Can you put something else on? And maybe brush your hair?"

I pat my bedhead hair and tighten the robe around me. "What festive holiday party?"

"It's a Christmas party hosted by Laura Thompson from Reid's office, and it's always super fun. Plus, there's someone there who wants to meet you."

"Who?"

"A guy." Willow's expression is sly. "Laura Thompson's little brother. She showed me his photo last year and he's hot as hell. I know he'd be perfect for you. I don't need to remind you that I'm a spectacular matchmaker, do I?"

"No, but—"

"Then hurry up, we're already late. Reid's waiting for us in the lobby."

The last thing I want to do is leave my apartment to go meet someone's little brother at a Christmas party. "Thanks, but no thanks. I'm not feeling well."

"You're feeling fine, you're just depressed. Although nicely done on the Christmas tree." Willow gestures toward the spruce in the corner. "That's a step in the right direction."

"I'm not depressed, I swear. And you have to go now." Taking her by the shoulders, I spin her around and walk her toward the door. "Bye. Say hi to Reid. Have fun at the party."

Willow sighs as she steps into the hallway. "Fine. But if that super hot guy is there and asks about you, you'll be sorry you spent the entire night holed up in this apartment."

"Maybe."

"You can't just retreat, Harlow. You have to go after love if you want to find it. You're not just going to look up and find it standing there."

It almost makes me burst out laughing. Maybe I hadn't found love tonight standing there in the lobby, but I had found a damn good time. "Night, Willow. I'll talk to you tomorrow. Drive carefully in this weather, okay?"

Before she can try to drag me out again, I shut the door in her face, put the chain on, and rush back into my bedroom.

I close the door, toss my robe aside and lean back against the wood. It feels extra cool because I'm still burning up from that orgasm. "Hi."

Michael smiles. "Hi. Everything okay?"

"Yeah, my boss was just ... it doesn't matter."

"Come here," Michael says crooking his finger at me.

six

Michael

While Harlow stepped out to deal with whomever it was that stopped by, I lay there trying to make sense of what the hell is happening.

How did this girl, whom I just met, manage to get me to break all of my rules? I never fuck on the first date. And I usually spend a good amount of time making sure I don't end up with a stage-five clinger.

Still, I can't seem to help myself.

"Kiss me," I demand.

And she does.

It takes me no time to get hard again. The second I saw those brown eyes after she closed the door, flushed and still glowing a little after she came on my tongue—it's all I need. She tastes like sugar and spice and everything fucking fantastic.

"You have too much on," Harlow says as she stands at the edge of the bed right between my legs.

"Yeah?"

"Definitely."

"Well, what are you going to do about it?"

She grins. "I'm thinking that *maybe* we should remove some of it."

"Just maybe?"

Her fingers move to the buttons of my dress shirt. She slowly pushes each one out of its hole, moving down lower and lower. I groan as she lets her nails scrape down my undershirt, loving the way her breath hitches when she feels the muscles beneath.

Harlow drops to her knees. "I need to be eye level," she murmurs, her voice thick with desire. I swear, I'm going to blow like a teen on prom night if she wraps that fuckable mouth around my cock.

I close my eyes for a second, thinking of anything unsexy to try to get a grip.

Spiders. Pizza. Elephants.

Then she makes a low moan and there's not a damn thing I can think of to reduce how fucking turned on I am.

"Promise me you're not crazy," I find myself saying, because this girl is pretty damn perfect. Not that I think crazy people realize they're nuts, but I'm praying she's not. My last girlfriend was a money-grubbing bitch. All she wanted was the family money and status.

It's why I've sworn off dating anyone who knows who the hell I am.

Michael West, heir to the West Investment millions.

She looks up through her sooty lashes. "I'm not. Promise me you're not an asshole who is going to treat me like a pariah tomorrow."

I take her chin in my hand, forcing her to look at me. "I promise."

"Good, then you're still overdressed and I'm very much wanting to get back where we were."

"Me too, baby."

Fuck, I'm calling her baby. And not in that condescending way that some dudes do. The way I say it is like all that happened tonight was what was meant to. Like some fucking Christmas miracle is happening and Santa brought me exactly what I asked for.

A beautiful girl with red bra and panties that I want to ride all night.

Harlow goes for the button of my pants and I stand. That right there is a sight. She's on her knees in front of me, the perfect height to take my cock right now.

And then she brings her face right there. She hooks her fingers in my pants, taking the boxer briefs down with her.

"Merry Christmas to me," she says with a look of awe.

Yeah, that's every man's fantasy right here. A girl who looks just as turned on to suck my dick as she was when I was eating her out.

"I think we were both on the nice list," I say as I run my fingers through her hair.

"Let's find out."

Harlow doesn't hesitate. Her perfect lips wrap around my dick and she takes me deep. "Fuck." I let out a groan, head falling back as she sucks.

I've always been more of a giver when it comes to sex. I get turned on by the woman getting off, and I love nothing more than pushing her past her limits. Right now, though, it's really nice to receive. Her hot mouth is exactly where I want to be. Harlow's fingernails scrape against my thigh, sending a myriad of sensations through my body.

She bobs her head up and down, and then I slip my fingers in her silky brown hair. "Let me fuck your mouth."

Harlow moans and I take that as permission to do as I please. God, this is best fucking night.

I start to move my hips, her hands now gripping my ass. "You look so hot on your knees with my cock in your mouth."

She takes me even deeper and the surprise of it almost makes me lose it.

I jerk my hips back, not wanting to come too early and then I pull her up. "I want you."

"I want you too."

"We can stop now." I give her another out.

Harlow's big brown eyes are filled with desire. "No, no stopping."

Yes, Virginia, there really is a Santa Claus. The quote from *It's a Beautiful Life* springs into my head instantly.

I don't say a word as I lift her up and gently lay her down on the bed. She's so damn beautiful. It's funny that in just one night this girl has me all mixed up. I blew off my family party, carried a tree, and took her shopping, all just to see her smile.

I can't remember the last time I cared about something so simple.

She isn't here because I'm some rich guy who can afford to buy her entire apartment, let alone a tree stand. Sure she might not be able to sing worth a damn, and she doesn't know how to open a door properly or have even a basic knowledge of plant life, but she's kind.

She cares about her friends and her job. And she has the most stunning smile I've ever seen.

Which she's giving me right now as I look down at her.

"Hi," she says.

"Hi."

"What are you thinking?"

"That your smile is beautiful," I answer honestly.

Her eyes soften and she touches her hand to my lips, moving her thumb. It does something to my heart.

"You have no idea how glad I am that you rescued me," she says softly.

That makes two of us. I'm hoping I can rescue her a lot more too. I want to wake up with her in my arms on Christmas morning and start a whole new tradition of holiday unwrapping. I want to bring her to my parents' house, introduce her to my annoying sister, and then ring in the New Year with a kiss at midnight.

Where the hell did this feeling come from? Jesus, I'm losing my damn mind.

I shift the conversation back to the sex. Sex is what she wants. Sex is what we both want. I don't need to think beyond it. "Because you're about to have some earth-shattering sex?"

"No, that's just a bonus."

"Condom?" I say, trying to keep myself distracted. Because I can't possibly be falling for her. No, it's the snow. The cold has somehow frozen my brain. That's all.

She reaches over to the nightstand. "I'm really hoping Willow left some condoms." Harlow digs around in the drawer and then screams with delight. "I found some! Oh, we have a whole strip."

I take it from her hand, ripping the wrapper open with my teeth and roll it on.

"Here, let me help," she says as her hand slides down my dick, unrolling the condom as she goes.

Not wanting to wait another second, I take her wrists in my one hand and pin them over her head. Then I surge inside her with raw force.

"Oh! Oh God!" she moans and I give her a second to grow accustomed to my size.

After another second and feeling the way her pussy grips me, I start to move. I hold her down, thrusting inside her over and over. Her eyes close and she moans again. I move my free hand down between us and rub her clit.

I'm so fucking close.

I want her to come again, this time around my dick.

"Harlow," I urge her. "Come, baby. Come again."

Her eyes close and she takes her lower lip between her teeth. "I'm going to come," she moans and I increase pressure on her clit.

I feel her tighten. "Yes, that's it, Harlow, let go."

And she does.

I thrust harder, chasing my own release, which comes in record time. The feel of her pussy milking me is too much. I surrender to it, taking the last moment of bliss, and work to catch my breath.

That was … whoa.

After a few seconds I lift my head to look at her. Her hair is spread out on her pillow, her lips are swollen, and a lazy smile plays on her face.

Her eyes open and she lets out a soft chuckle. "If that's being on the naughty list, I'm never coming off."

I laugh and rub my nose against hers. "Are you okay?"

"I'm glorious. I'm pretty sure I heard angels sing on that last one."

"Me too."

"Glory be to God and all that."

"Pretty sure God wasn't with us, but I'm open to you thinking I'm close to being one," I tease.

"You earned it."

I kiss her once and then reluctantly get off the bed. When I glance back at her, she's now clutching a pillow and curling herself up. Her ex is a goddamn fool, and I'm very happy he is.

chapter seven

Harlow

BEST. SEX. EVER.

Like, ever, ever.

People write songs about the sex we just had and they aren't sad ones. Jesus, who knew I could have multiples?

I want to scream into the pillow but manage to pull myself together. I told him I wasn't crazy, and that might give him some doubts. But this day has been a whirlwind and I'm not really sure how to process it all.

First, I had mind-blowing sex. That in itself is worth screaming about.

Second, I really freaking like him. Michael is fun and even though he's a little naughty, sometimes it's good to balance the goodness I tend to lean toward. I'm always the good girl, doing what people ask, finding them love, blah, blah. Maybe putting my tiara away and grabbing the broomstick will be a change that leads to more fun.

And by fun I mean multiples.

Third, I am not a one-night-stand girl, and this is a problem.

My sexual conquests always have meaning, and I at least know the guy a little, but I don't know Michael at all. But he's sweet, he can put a tree up, and he must have at least some feelings toward me, right?

Do I ask him to stay?

Do I see if he wants to go for another round?

I don't know the rules in this situation, and that's something I'm not used to.

All of these are first-world problems, but it's the world I live in.

I chew on my thumbnail as I mull it all over and try to think logically. If Michael wants to leave, he can—it's not like he has to drive. And if this is all we ever have, I can be a mature adult. Not to mention, this isn't my forever apartment, so if it gets super awkward, I'll just move.

It's not that serious. It's just a night.

One incredible, unforgettable night.

"You okay?" he asks, and I jump a little.

The pillow is covering my bare breasts, and again, I'm faced with not knowing where to go with this. "Uhh, yeah, I just need to … use the bathroom."

He smiles, his naked body on full display and it takes every ounce of my restraint not to stare at his cock. I really like it. It did magical things, and I'd like to see if it was just a fluke or not.

I mentally slap myself. I promised not to be crazy and I will uphold my end of the bargain.

I do my business and walk back out. When I enter the bedroom, Michael is on the bed, covers up to his waist, but his chest is bare. God, he is a work of art.

"Come here," he says with his arms open.

And I go without pause.

"I know you said you never do that …"

I look up. "I don't. I'm a serial monogamist. Not really by choice, but I typically only sleep with guys I really like, and never on day one."

"It's not really my normal, either. I usually at least know more than just some basic information."

That makes me feel marginally better. "What do you want to know?"

"Family?"

"My parents are still happily married, for over forty years now. I have one brother who isn't married, and I swear never will be. Even though I've tried to match him at least three times."

"So your matchmaking skills are a questionable thing."

I sit up with narrowed eyes. "I'm the best in this city."

He grins. "Good to know."

I sense challenge in his voice so I don't let it go. "Seriously! I have more marriages than Willow, who owns the company, and her sister, combined. I'm like a *super* matchmaker."

"One who doesn't believe in romance?"

I sigh and pull the blanket up to cover my chest. "Okay, if we're talking about *me*, that's different. In my experience, romance is fleeting. It comes and goes and people claim they're always searching for it. But it's not something you find, it's something you work for. I want love. I want a guy who looks at me twenty years down the road and thinks I'm cute with my hair turning gray and my wrinkly face. Romance is this …" I lean down and kiss him, "… feeling in your chest."

His hand comes up, tangling in my hair, and then he pulls me back to his mouth. He kisses me reverently and I feel it in my toes. "Romance isn't bad."

"No," I agree. "It's not, but love makes your heart race and it is a simmer that doesn't ever fully go out."

Our eyes stay on each other's. My chest is tight as we both are silent, but I feel like he's saying something anyway. Before I can search too deep, he releases me. I sink back against his chest, not wanting to think about what that was.

Michael clears his throat. "Okay, so brother, work, and parents are covered. What else should I know?"

"Hmm." I use this time to compose myself. "I'm a Scorpio, I like horribly cheesy Christmas movies, I love guys who rescue girls with trees."

His laughter vibrates against my skin. "I like girls who need rescuing."

"Ahh, so you're a Romeo type?"

"I'm not sure I'm a type at all."

"Everyone is a type," I tell him.

Then I sit up and study him. Now that my libido is a little in check, I look at Michael as I would a client. How would I match him? Maybe this is the approach I should take on dating. Leave the emotions and that lusty goodness out and start to be analytical, the way I would if I were helping a client.

This thought has merit.

"Why do you look like you're about to dissect me?"

I grin. "Would you let me try?" And then I realize that he probably isn't thinking the same meaning as I am. "I mean, let me look at you not just as the guy who gave me not one but two fantastic orgasms, but as a potential match for someone."

"I'm going to regret this."

"Probably, but it'll be fun."

"You know, you're the second woman today who has tried to set me up." Michael shakes his head.

"Really?"

"Yeah, my sister, Laura—that's whose house I was supposed to be at—said there was some girl coming that was"—he air quotes—"just perfect."

"No way!" I laugh. "Willow, who, err, interrupted us earlier, was trying to do the same. She wanted to drag me to some work party of her fiancé, Reid."

Michael looks at me a little funny, like he just smelled something weird. "Reid? You said—you said Willow's fiancé is named Reid?"

"Yes." I cock my head to one side, recalling something he mentioned a moment ago. "And did you say your sister's name is Laura?"

"Yeah."

Chills sweep down my arms, although I'm not cold. "Is your …" I clear my throat, thinking back to what Willow said. "Is your sister's last name Thompson, by any chance?"

"It is." Michael swallows and sits up a little straighter in bed. "Is this Reid guy's last name something Italian?"

"Fortino," I whisper. We stare at each other, our eyes going wide. I almost expect the music from the Twilight Zone to start playing.

"Oh my God." Michael blinks, leaning back against the headboard. "I don't fucking believe it."

"Me neither." It can't be … can it?

"Are you thinking what I'm thinking?" he asks.

"That we were both supposed to be at the same party tonight so that we could be set up … with each other?" Even as I speak the words, it strikes me as too coincidental. Too unbelievable. Too insane.

Michael shakes his head. "It's fucking crazy. But I think it's true. My sister works with Reid. And she said his fiancée was bringing a friend who'd be perfect for me."

I start to laugh. I can't help it—this entire night has been so ridiculous and fun. "And Willow said I had to go to this party tonight to meet the little brother of this Laura woman who works with Reid."

"Christ." Michael runs a hand through his hair.

"I guess we saved them the trouble," I wheeze. "Who'd have thought?"

"Right?" Michael laughs too, a deep, joyful sound that warms my insides. "I can't believe it. My sister was right about something." He pulls me onto his lap so I straddle his legs.

"They're all going to flip out," I tell him. "Willow especially. She'll try to take credit somehow."

He wraps his arms around my waist. "So will my sister. But I didn't need them to find a perfect girl. I found her all on my own."

I grin. "Stuck in a doorway with a Christmas tree. God, it sounds like a Hallmark Channel holiday movie, doesn't it? We had our very own meet cute!"

"Do Hallmark Channel movies have sex in them?"

"Not onscreen." I giggle. "It's more like behind closed doors."

"Your door is closed." He flips me onto my back and covers my body with his. "And I'm very interested in a happy ending right now."

"Me too." We kiss, and I wonder if I'll ever get enough of his sexy mouth on mine.

I wonder if this is the start of something as good as it feels. I wonder if someday we'll be telling our meet cute story to our children and grandchildren—maybe it will be the one we tell every single Christmas as we put up the tree. And I wonder if it's possible to fall for someone so fast, because as he moves inside me again, I feel myself spinning head over heels. I never want it to end.

Of course, I don't *say* that to him.

But later, as we're saying goodbye at my door, I tell him that tonight feels like an unexpected gift.

"For me too," he says. He kisses my forehead. "And I, for one, would like to open it again tomorrow night. And maybe even the night after that."

"Really?" My toes tingle, and I can't keep my smile from getting bigger.

"Really. I don't know what you did to me tonight, Harlow North, but I'm under your spell. And I'd like to stay there for a while."

I lift my shoulders. "You know where to find me."

And he does—the next night, and the next night, and the next. In fact, we don't spend a night apart for the following year and a half, and two years to the day after he came to my rescue in the lobby, I walk down the aisle and become his wife.

We celebrate our first Christmas as Mr. and Mrs. West in our own home, where Michael is in charge of getting the tree in the stand, I am allowed to bake but not sing, and we laugh about how destiny wanted us together so badly, it left us no room to mess up.

Christmas miracle? Maybe.

But one thing is for sure—we were always meant to be.

THE END

We hope you enjoyed this fun Christmas story set in the Imperfect Match world!

If you loved this story, be sure to check out our other co-authored stories, *Imperfect Match* and *Hold You Close*!

about the authors

Corinne Michaels is a *New York Times, USA Today*, and *Wall Street Journal* bestselling author of romance novels. Her stories are chock full of emotion, humor, and unrelenting love, and she enjoys putting her characters through intense heartbreak before finding a way to heal them through their struggles.

Corinne is a former Navy wife and happily married to the man of her dreams. She began her writing career after spending months away from her husband while he was deployed—reading and writing were her escapes from the loneliness. Corinne now lives in Virginia with her husband and is the emotional, witty, sarcastic, and fun-loving mom of two beautiful children.

Connect with Corinne:
Facebook: https://bit.ly/1iwLh6y
Instagram: https://bit.ly/2L1Vzo6
Goodreads: https://bit.ly/2N1H2Gb
Amazon: http://amzn.to/1NVZmhv
Bookbub: https://bit.ly/2yc6rss

Stay up to date with Corinne and sign up for her mailing list:
corinnemichaels.com/subscribe

To sign up for monthly text alerts: Text CMBOOKS TO 77948
US only due to carrier restrictions

USA Today bestselling author Melanie Harlow likes her martinis dry, her heels high, and her history with the naughty bits left in. When she's not writing or reading, she gets her kicks from TV series like VEEP, Game of Thrones, and Homeland. She occasionally runs three miles, but only so she can have more gin and steak.

She lifts her glass to romance readers and writers from her home near Detroit, MI, where she lives with her husband, two daughters, and pet rabbit.

Connect with Melanie:
Facebook: https://bit.ly/1RiTP7z
Amazon: http://amzn.to/1NPkYKs
Bookbub: https://bit.ly/2yfljWR
Pinterest: https://bit.ly/2m60beu
Instagram: https://bit.ly/2ubxh19
Website: www.melanieharlow.com
Stay up to date with Melanie, sign up for her Mailing List:
www.melanieharlow.com/subscribe

also by the authors

Co-Written Novels

Hold You Close

Imperfect Match

books by
CORINNE MICHAELS

The Salvation Series

Beloved

Beholden

Consolation

Conviction

Defenseless

Evermore: A 1001 Dark Night Novella

Return to Me Series

Say You'll Stay

Say You Want Me

Say I'm Yours

Second Time Around Series

We Own Tonight

One Last Time

Not Until You

If I Only Knew

The Arrowood Brothers

Come Back for Me

Fight for Me

The One for Me

Stay for Me

Willow Creek Valley Series (Coming 2021)

Return to Us

One Chance for Us

A Moment for Us

Could Have Been Us

Standalone Novels

All I Ask

books by

MELANIE HARLOW

The Frenched Series

Frenched

Yanked

Forked

Floored

The Happy Crazy Love Series

Some Sort of Happy

Some Sort of Crazy

Some Sort of Love

The After We Fall Series

Man Candy

After We Fall

If You Were Mine

From This Moment

The One and Only Series

Only You

Only Him

Only Love

The Cloverleigh Farms Series

Irresistible

Undeniable

Insatiable

Unbreakable

Unforgettable

The Bellamy Creek Series

Drive Me Wild

Make Me Yours

Co-Written Books

Hold You Close (Co-written with Corinne Michaels)

Imperfect Match (Co-written with Corinne Michaels)

Strong Enough (M/M romance co-written with David Romanov)

The Speak Easy Duet

The Tango Lesson (A Standalone Novella)

inked fantasy

CARRIE ANN RYAN

chapter one

"Jack"

I CAREFULLY LIFTED THE LOWBALL GLASS TO MY LIPS, LETTING THE SMOKY aroma of the whiskey settle onto my tongue as I finished my sip. As I set the glass down, I looked around at the high-end bar, noting the people surrounding me. Nobody should recognize me here, not when they were all focused on their own lives. Their own desires. Tonight wasn't about who they were or what they wanted from me.

No, tonight was about pleasure and an evening that I hoped the person I was set to meet would never forget.

I took another sip and nodded at the bartender. The man nodded back and handed over my check.

"Just one for you, sir?"

I gave him a small smile, shaking my head and put down cash. No names, not for now.

"I'll be meeting someone soon, and I wanted to make sure I settled the bill."

The bartender frowned, tilting his head as he studied my face. "We could have added it to your bill at your table. You didn't need to worry yourself."

I just shook my head. "No, I don't mind. Now, by any chance, have you seen a woman with a white rose in her hair?"

The bartender's gaze widened for a second, and then he smiled as if he were in the middle of the game with me. *With us.* "No, but I'll keep on the lookout. A blind date?"

My lips twitched into a small smile again, and I took another sip of my whiskey. "You could say that."

"Okay," he said, looking as if he were more intrigued than ever. "That sounds like a story. And I do believe your date has arrived," he said, his eyes widening marginally as he looked over my shoulder.

I turned, my glass in my hands, and stared at the woman with dark hair and light eyes. She had on a black wrap dress that clung to her curves and made me want to pull delicately on the strings at the side. I wanted to see what would happen when the dress fell off her shoulders and pooled down at her feet.

There were many things I wanted to see happened tonight, and if I were lucky, I would be trying every single one of them. In vivid and intricate detail.

I downed the rest of my drink, not taking my eyes off of the white rose in her hair, and set the glass next to me on the polished wood of the bar.

"Thank you, Trevor."

Trevor, the bartender, cleared his throat. "You're welcome. Do you know where your table is, sir?"

"No, but I can ask the hostess. She said my table would be ready whenever my date arrived."

"If you're sure. Enjoy your evening, sir."

"I'm counting on it," I said, not bothering to look back at Trevor. No, my eyes were for the woman in front of me.

Jane.

At least that was the name that she had signed her texts with.

I could use Jane as her name for the evening. A perfectly normal name, for a perfectly pleasant woman, at least according to her texts.

But there was nothing normal or nearly pleasant about the goddess in front of me.

And I couldn't wait to get to know this Jane.

I prowled toward Jane, and her gaze went to the rose in the pocket of my jacket. Her eyes darkened for a minute, and then she met my eyes, a smile playing on her face. I stood in front of her, then inhaled the hint of her floral scent. Nothing overpowering, just a tease as to who this woman could be.

"Jack?" she asked, her eyes dancing.

"Of course, I love the rose," I said, and I reached out and slid my fingers delicately through the end of her hair, careful not to jostle the rose, but needing to touch her.

This Jane, this stranger.

She cleared her throat, danced from foot to foot on her tall heels. "Well, should we see the hostess about our table?" Jane asked, her voice a little breathy.

I licked at my lips and nodded. "They told me it would be ready as soon as you arrived. We won't have to wait."

"Oh, that's good. I mean, not that I mind waiting, but it would be nice to sit down. I'm not that great in heels," she said, laughing a bit before looking down at her feet. She wore sky high fuck-me heels and seeing that made my cock ache. I swallowed hard, willing myself to slow down.

I needed to slow down.

"They do wonders for your legs. But don't worry, I do not want you in pain."

I turned as the hostess came to us, a smile on her face. "Mr. Smith?" she asked, and I nodded, a smile playing on my lips.

"My date is here, as you can see, we're ready when you are."

"And we're ready here, your table is near the waterfall as you asked. Follow me, and I'll lead you to your table. Your waitress will be Corinne, and she will go over the specials with you as well as the wine list. We do have two new wines tonight that our chef and sommelier are really excited about." Our hostess continued to talk as she led us to the table, and I looked down at Jane, unable to keep my eyes from her. She was beautiful and looked like she smiled often, and yet had a side to her that maybe others didn't see.

I couldn't wait to get to know this woman tonight and see where we ended up.

"Here you are, have a lovely evening," she said, as I moved to one side of the table and held out Jane's chair. "Here you go," I said, and she gave me a small look, shook her head as a smile played on her face, and sat down.

"What was that for?" I asked, keeping a smile down for myself.

"You're acting like such a gentleman."

"And you don't think I can be a gentleman?" I asked, raising a single brow.

"I'm sure sometimes you could play at one, but I'm already enjoying tonight. Thank you for making me feel like a princess."

"I was thinking goddess earlier. And my acting the gentleman is what tonight is supposed to be about. Having fun, no names, just us, an evening for whatever we want."

Jane smiled and leaned back ever so slightly. The action caused her breasts to rise as she took a deep breath, and I did my best not to focus on that.

"I'm glad that my friends were able to help me get out tonight. It's been far too long since I've been out to dinner with a handsome man."

"I do believe that was my line, although I was going to say something about your beauty."

"You don't need to butter me up," she said, laughing, and I shook my head, laughing right along with her.

"You are beautiful, but sometimes I'm not great with words."

She tilted her head at me, stared. "Do you think that?"

"Sometimes. It depends on if the words are important or not."

"That's a good answer," she whispered, and the waitress came to speak about specials and wines.

"The sea bass sounds wonderful, honestly," Jane said as the waitress finished, waiting for our drink order. "I know this is just for drinks, but my mouth is practically watering at the sound of the Chilean sea bass."

"It does sound delicious, although the filet that she spoke of, the one that is smoke rubbed? That also sounds divine."

Corinne nodded between us, a small smile on her face. "You can't go wrong with either, and I have a lovely wine pairing for each."

I met Jane's gaze and smiled softly. "What do you say we each order one, and I'll let you have a bite. Just a taste."

I could see the waitress blush near me out of the corner of my eye, but it was the delicate pink of Jane's porcelain skin that enraptured my gaze.

"I think I can do that," Jane said, clearing her throat. "I guess I'll take the sea bass."

"And I'll take the filet, medium rare?" I asked, and Jane nodded.

The waitress left after taking our order, and I leaned back in my chair, looking at Jane and wondered where we would go tonight.

"So, Jane, what is it you do?"

Jane shook her head. "I thought we weren't supposed to ask questions like that? That way, we would never have to lie," she said, and I sighed.

"Maybe. Or maybe the story is just the beginning."

She laughed softly at that and took a sip of her water. "Or maybe you don't want to tell me anything about you so that I can make a big story about me. How about this?" she asked as she settled into her chair. "My name is Jane, at least for the evening. I'm here because I haven't been out of my home in so long, I think I've forgotten what the outside world looks like. I was told I would have a lovely evening with a wonderful man, one who I have texted often this week, and I would have as much fun as I desired." A pause. "Anything I desired."

I cleared my throat as the waitress set our glasses of wine down, as well as the breadbasket. She left in a hurry, seemingly aware that she had interrupted something. However, Jane and I were in public, and if I wasn't careful, I was going to toss her on top of this table and have my way with her.

With the look in Jane's eyes, she had the same thoughts.

"I was told," I began, "that tonight would be any fantasy you desired."

"And now you sound like a gigolo," she laughed, and took a sip of her wine. "Oh, that's amazing. Crisp."

I took a sip of mine and nodded. "A little oaky, I like it."

"So, you're not a gigolo?" she asked, her eyes dancing with laughter.

I smiled, set my glass down. "Not even close. But I can pretend for the evening if you'd like?"

She shook her head, her cheeks bright red. "No, I would just like you to be you, Jack."

I swallowed hard, and looked into those eyes, and knew if I

weren't careful, this evening would unravel, and my secrets would come to light.

Instead, I lifted my glass to hers, and she did the same. "To tonight. A night of fantasy. Of the only promise worth making."

She smiled, her eyes going dark. "To tonight."

And we each took a sip of our wines, and I knew the evening had just begun.

chapter two

"Jane"

I SIPPED THE LAST OF MY CHOCOLATE MARTINI AND LET THE SUGAR AND sweetness settle over my tongue. I loved all things sweet. It was an addiction, and I didn't mind. It was *my* addiction.

An addiction I knew that could rival the man in front of me if I weren't careful.

"Are you ready to go upstairs, Jane?" Jack asked, and I swallowed hard, then licked my lips.

"Forward, aren't you?"

Jack's eyes crinkled at the corners, the fine lines there deepening. "I thought we both had an understanding of exactly where this was going. Was I wrong?"

I set my glass down and dabbed at my mouth with my linen napkin before setting it on the table. "I think we both know where this is going, and I didn't say I disliked the forwardness."

Jack smiled, and it lit up his face and seeing that tugged at something me. I ignored that tug. That wasn't for tonight. No, tonight was about mystery and finding out exactly who I could be with this man, in this moment, and under these circumstances.

Tonight was about fantasy and fun.

I reached out for my small jeweled clutch and looked up at the man who couldn't stop staring at me.

"I'm ready when you are," I said, purring. I wasn't great at flirting, wasn't great at the role of the seductress, but it was fun to play. And after all, tonight was only about play. Tomorrow the carriage turned back into a pumpkin, my shoes would turn to slippers, and my form-fitting black wrap dress would turn into yoga pants and a tank top. My hair would fall from its curls, and I would pile it on the top of my head. I'd take out my itchy contacts, slide on my glasses—after

I scrubbed my face free of makeup and put on an anti-swelling mask and under-eye ointment.

That was the true me.

But Jane...Jane could be whoever she wanted to be.

Jack stood up, held out his hand, and I slid my fingers along his. "Come on then, the night's only beginning."

I clenched my thighs together for just a moment, aware that anyone looking at us would know exactly what we were about to do. But it's what I wanted, same as Jack, for us to be in our own world, while the rest might look on, but not matter in the end.

I wrapped my arm around his as I stood, and the two of us made our way through the lobby of the five-star hotel and to the elevators into the back. Jack used a special key on the private elevator, one that not every patron would have.

"The penthouse?" I asked, surprised, even though I shouldn't have been.

"You said in your texts you wanted tonight to be special, and I am loath to not provide."

"You sure do sound like a male escort," I said with a laugh, ignoring the look from the woman in pearls as she walked past us.

Jack winked over my head, and I held back a grin. "You keep saying that so loudly, and people are going to think you paid for the night."

"How do they know you're not the one who paid for me?" I teased, surprising myself. Jack threw his head back and laughed, looking like the most interesting and attractive man I had ever met in my life.

And I couldn't wait for what happened next.

We walked into the elevator as the doors opened, and I swallowed hard, my palms going damp. The elevator doors closed, and I bit my lip, not knowing what would come next, the anticipation heady. Jack slid his hand over my hip and squeezed, and I turned into his hold.

"Jack?" I asked, and in answer, he pressed his lips to mine. My mouth parted, and I groaned into him. He slid his other hand around me, gripping my ass, pushing me into his hard erection. I moaned, practically climbing up him like he was a tree, and he deepened the kiss, tangling his tongue with mine. He moved, my back pressing against the walls of the elevator, my arms above my head as he ran his hands up my side and cupped my breasts.

"I can't wait to strip you out of this, but there won't be enough time." He kissed me again and then pulled away, righting my dress before he did the same to his clothes.

The doors to the penthouse opened as soon as he straightened, and I nearly fell, my knees weak. Jack seemed to realize that, and he gave me a worrying look before gripping my elbow.

"I'm fine," I whispered.

Jack met my gaze and held his hand on the door to the elevator so it wouldn't close again. "Are you sure? We can stop this right now."

"That's exactly what I don't want. Come on, let's continue. You said the night was only beginning. We can't end it now."

Jack searched my face before nodding tightly. And then he led me into the penthouse suite.

My jaw dropped, and I looked around, stunned. "I didn't even know this was here."

Jack shrugged and looked for all the world like he did this every evening. I knew for a fact he didn't, but him playing the role made me smile. The floors were made of marble, the walls textured with antique wallpaper and faux that made it look as if it were a palace, rather than a hotel room in downtown Denver.

"Is that a piano?" I asked, and blinked.

Jack grinned. "A baby grand. I think they were sad they couldn't fit a full grand in here."

"Oh, how horrible, *only* a baby grand." I smiled.

"Too bad I can't play," Jack said, laughing.

"We could always pretend. But I feel like we would both end up hurting our ears in the process."

"Too true. Now, there's a full bath here in the guest area, but there's also the master bath in the back, one with a waterfall, and a full five-headed shower."

I blinked. "Five heads as in to get all angles, or for five different people enjoying it?" I asked, laughing.

Jack grinned. "I'm not sharing you, so we're just going to have to deal with the two of us."

My brows raised. "So, we'll be taking a shower together?"

"Maybe. There's a bench in there. I'd like to try."

I blushed and cleared my throat. "Sure of yourself, are you?"

"You knew precisely what tonight was for when you showed up," he growled, and yet his voice was soft at the same time. I couldn't help but breathe hard and try to catch up.

"So, there are the showers," I said, clearing my throat after a moment. "And you said a guest area?"

Jack smiled. "There are two guestrooms, along with their own foyer and sitting area. This is the main sitting area, but let me take you to the master bedroom."

I shook my head, looking at all the opulence and wondering why it was needed. "I would have been fine with a single bed, and maybe a desk." I blushed as I said it.

Jack looked at me and chuckled deeply. "That's good to know. But I wanted to show you, as my sister would say, the sparkly."

"So, you have a sister?" I asked eagerly, leaning forward with a smile on my face. This was the game, and I was having too much fun with it.

Jack frowned. "I shouldn't have said that. No details tonight. Right?"

I shrugged. "At least for now. We'll see what happens later."

I knew I wasn't good at this, and I would probably spill everything, break the fantasy. But, for now, I wanted to have fun. And here we were.

Jack led me past a dining room that had an actual chandelier and a small kitchenette area until he reached two double doors.

"Are you ready?" He asked.

"I'm exhausted from walking through this room already."

He grinned and then opened the double doors.

My mouth dropped open, and I swallowed hard. There was a

bed in the center, raised slightly, and it looked larger than a king. There were sitting areas to my left and to my right, along with a balcony on the opposite end. I knew the one door was probably a closet area, or maybe another sitting area, or perhaps even an office. The other looked to be the bathroom, all marble and chrome, and I didn't know where to look.

"This is ridiculous," I said with a laugh.

"Pretty much," Jack said grinning. "But it's ours for the evening."

"I have no words," I whispered, and Jack turned to me and leaned forward.

"I don't think there needs to be any. Other than are you ready for the evening?"

"Always."

"Good," he said, and then his mouth was on mine again. I moaned into him, and he wrapped his arms around me, sliding his hands down my sides. He moved again, cupping my ass as he spread my cheeks apart while pressing himself into me. I writhed against him, needing more. When he trailed his lips down my neck, I shivered in his arms. His fingers went to the tie at my side, and I licked my lips. He met my gaze and then undid the bow. My dress fell to the side slowly, the fabric gently caressing my skin as it parted.

I gasped, the sensation too much, even just from that bare moment in his look. He licked his lips and then trailed his gaze over me, as if needing to sate himself in the view. I felt as if I could feel every single caress of his vision, and I couldn't stop my moan. He smiled, and then reached out, his thumb gently sliding along my nipple.

"Black lace, it suits you."

I blushed. "Not usually."

"I'm pretty sure everything suits you…Jane," he whispered.

He slid his hands down my sides, his knuckles along my belly, and then traced the lace of my thong around my hips.

"Beautiful," he whispered, and then he leaned forward and licked along my collarbone. I shivered, my knees going weak, and he pulled away again before moving me toward the bed.

"I can't have you fainting on me."

"You sure feel high and mighty of yourself," I teased.

"I can't help it. You seem to do that to me," he whispered, and then he kissed me again.

I shivered in his hold, and then let him stand me next to the bed. It's so high that my ass barely touched the top of it.

"Will this work for you?" he asked.

I nodded. "Yes," I whispered.

"Good." And then he tugged the rest of my dress off, the silk pooling at my feet. I stood on my tiptoes in my heels, and he knelt in front of me, sliding his hands down my calves. It sent shivers up my body, and I did my best not to groan again.

"Let me take these off you. I don't want you to be in pain," he whispered.

"I can handle the heels."

"But I need you to have all of your energy for what I'm about to put you through," he whispered, and so I let him untie the straps at my ankles and slowly slid my feet out of my heels. My ankles quit their protesting, as I gradually set my feet to the ground, and then he was there, nibbling up my thighs, and sending quick kisses that nearly had me coming right there.

He smiled and then pressed a sweet kiss over my center.

"Jack," I whispered, doing my best to remember his name.

"Yes, Jane?" he asked, his voice soft, a throaty purr against my pussy.

"Keep going," I whispered.

"As my lady commands." He unhurriedly tugged the lace off my hips and tossed it aside after I stepped out of my thong.

"Beautiful," he whispered, I was falling into temptation, past nearly falling, and going full straight down the rabbit hole.

He kissed me again and stood up, reaching around me to undo the clasp of my bra. I let the lace fall and sucked in a breath as he lapped at my breasts, using his free hand to squeeze my breasts, gently, and then firmer. He plucked at my nipples and then slowly trailed his hand down my belly to my core. He speared me with two fingers, at the same time sucking on my breast. I came, so quick to the trigger that I nearly fell, and I felt like I had never come so hard, so quick before. Maybe I had, but I couldn't remember. The only thing that mattered was the man holding me, making me feel like he would never let me go.

Jack lifted me up into his arms, cradling me to his chest, where he kissed me again, and I leaned into him, smiling sleepily.

"Enjoying yourself?" He whispered.

"That was amazing," I gasped, and then he slowly slid me into bed, and I nuzzled into the comforter.

"But what about you?" I asked, looking up at him.

He trailed a finger down my cheek. "Rest, you'll need your energy."

And at this throaty growl of his voice, I closed my eyes and drifted off, knowing as soon as I woke up, the night would be far from over.

chapter three

"Jack"

I PULLED JANE INTO MY ARMS A LITTLE BIT TIGHTER, GRINNING AS SHE nuzzled into me. She was all smooth curves and soft skin against me. After she had fallen asleep, nearly passing out from her orgasm, I'd made sure she was comfortable, stripped out of my clothes, and curled around her naked. I couldn't help it. I needed to be skin-to-skin.

And after all, this was Jane. This is what we wanted.

I studied her face, the strong lines of her cheekbones, the little tilted uptick of her nose at the end. She had long lashes, and her makeup was still pristine. I knew who had done her makeup for tonight and they would have made sure it would stay on, though I knew it might not once we took our shower.

If we got there. Right now, though, I was completely satisfied laying here with Jane in my arms and pretending the rest of the world didn't exist.

In the morning, we would go about our responsibilities, and we would leave Jack and Jane behind. It was what was needed. Jack and Jane may never meet again, but they would have this evening.

Jane's eyes opened, and I smiled down at her. "Hello, sleepyhead," I whispered.

"L—Jack."

I shook my head and tapped her on the lips in warning. "Are you ready?" I asked, my voice a growl.

Her eyes widened, and she swallowed hard. "Always." I kissed her hard, delving my tongue against hers. She groaned, raking her nails down my back. I shifted above her and cradled myself between her legs and reached for the condom.

Her eyes widened, and I smiled. "I need to protect you, Jane," I whispered.

"Oh," she said, and I kissed her again, before kneeling between her thighs. I rubbed along her clit, along her swollenness, and smiled. "You seem ready for me already. So greedy after two orgasms."

"I can't help it when it comes to you, apparently."

"You can't help to come when it comes to me," I teased.

She rolled her eyes. "That was a ridiculous joke."

"Well, I am ridiculous. Sue me." She snorted, and I leaned down to kiss her again, before slowly rolling the condom down my length.

"Are you ready?" I asked.

"You need to stop asking me that or I'm going to have to take care of the problem myself," she said before reaching out, not to touch herself, but instead gripped the base of my cock over the condom. I nearly passed out but told myself I was stronger than that.

Clearly.

I grinned, then positioned myself at her entrance. "I thought I would be a little more suave."

She squeezed me again. "Let's see exactly how you can work it, Jack," she teased, and I winked before I slid inside, deep with one thrust.

She let out a shocked gasp, and I froze.

"Jane?" I asked.

"I'm fine, I just, wow…I was ready, and yet still wow."

I chuckled, my cock twitching deep inside her. "I'll take that as a compliment," I said.

"If you begin to move, we can call it a compliment," she said, squeezing her inner walls. My eyes crossed, and I swallowed hard, before I lowered my head, kissed her again, and began to move. She wrapped her legs around my hips, and I slowly worked my way in and out of her, nearly shaking and already sweat-slick at just the beginning of our evening.

She moaned, meeting me thrust for thrust, both of us moving like we had done this a thousand times before. But this is Jack and Jane's first, something that just helped the moment.

I rolled over to my back, needing to see her, and she hovered over me, a smile on the face.

"Jack," she whispered.

"Jane," I reached out, cupped her breasts, flicked my thumbs over her nipples. "Dear God, you're beautiful."

She trailed her fingers over the ink on my chest and arms, and then through my beard.

"Jack," she whispered, and that was all she needed to say. She put both hands on either side of my head and rode me, rocking her hips like a seductress, a siren that called my name.

I thrust up into her again, and her eyes went dark, her mouth parted, and she let out a little oh, and then she came. Her body flushed. Her nipples going even darker, harder. I followed her, my balls growing tight, and I came, my body shaking. Both of us were sweat-slick, holding one another, and she collapsed on top of me. I held her close, sliding my hands down her back.

"Wow," she whispered.

"Just the beginning," I muttered.

"I think we're getting a little too old to call that just the beginning."

I laughed and slapped her ass. She looked up at me, shocked. "Jack!"

"I think you liked that," I muttered. "Shut up," she said, not denying.

"It may take me a little longer than when I was younger, but I still want to try that shower. And maybe that chair."

"It's a hotel, who knows who's had sex in that chair."

I was still deep inside her, and both of us shuddered, laughing. This is what I had wanted, sex, fantasy, and comfort. Perfection.

"In the shower. After a minute. Let me hold you."

She smiled softly, her body going liquid, and she lowered herself on to me. And I held her.

My Jane.

At least for the night.

chapter four

"Jane"

My phone buzzed and I groaned, rolling from the man's arm that was wound tightly around me.

He grumbled something under his breath, and I smiled softly before reaching for my phone.

Aaron: *I figured you should get a text for checkout time. You have two hours. Enjoy your morning.*

I looked at the clock, and my eyes widened. Not only had I slept in my contacts and my makeup, even though it was probably running down my face after the shower sex that we had had, I still could not quite believe it was already nearly eleven.

My fingers quickly went to my phone.

Me: *Thank you! We're still in bed.*

I flushed and could not believe I was texting my brother-in-law about being in bed.

I can practically hear Aaron's laugh from here.

Aaron: *Have fun. Glad you guys had a good night. But I don't need any details. Madison says she does. I don't want to know.*

I laughed, said my goodbyes and thank yous, after checking on his charges, and set my phone down.

"Was that my annoying brother?" the man in my bed asked, his voice low and a little grumpy.

I smile. "Yes, just making sure we didn't overstay our welcome."

"Well, what time is it?"

"Nearly eleven."

Liam Montgomery sat up, his eyes wide. "What?"

I laughed at my husband and leaned forward and kissed him hard on the mouth. "I think midnight has struck, or maybe it was three in the morning when we finally went to sleep. Jack and Jane are gone, but I'm here."

Liam tucked my hair behind my ear and kissed me again. "I love you, Arden. Arden Montgomery."

I sighed at the name, loving the fact that my husband was so sweet, and all mine. All hardness and inked flesh that I could get my hands on. Mine, mine, mine, mine.

"You sound like a seagull from that movie with the fish," Liam said, laughing.

My eyes widened. "Did I say that out loud?" I asked, laughing.

"Pretty much. But, I kind of like it."

I leaned forward and kissed him again, and he groaned. He reached out and cupped my breasts, and I pulled away. "Hey, I wasn't done," he grumbled.

I shook my head. "We should get ready for the day. I can't show up to your brother's house looking like this." I pointed to my bedhead and whatever makeup I still had on my face, and Liam just shrugged. "They know what we were doing last night."

I blushed and shook my head vigorously. "They better not know everything, Liam Montgomery."

"You know, as much as I enjoyed being Jack last night, there's nothing better than hearing you call me by my given name, first and last."

I licked my lips. "I was thinking that I love being called Arden Montgomery. Look at us, no longer in fantasy."

"It was fun while it lasted, but I still got to say, this penthouse? You and that fucking hot dress and those fuck-me heels? Amazing night. But I also love cuddling with you on the couch while we watch movies and read books."

"Sometimes you just make my heartache," I whispered, tears falling down my cheeks.

Liam frowned and wiped the wetness from my skin. "No crying. Tonight's a good night. Last night was a good night. And this morning is even better."

"I know. I love you so much."

"And I love you, too. And, I want to go home," I whispered.

Liam's gaze met mine, and he nodded. "I'll go use the guest bathroom to get ready, because I know if I go in with you, we're going to take a little time."

I blushed. "Probably. There were three benches in there, and we only got to use two."

He growled, kissed me hard on the mouth, and hopped out of bed. I couldn't help but watch his ass as he moved away. After all, my husband had a great ass.

And I couldn't help it. He was naked. What could I say?

I rolled out of bed, stretching. I knew I'd be sore, but that was fine.

It was a great night off, but we had responsibilities at home, and I just needed to be there.

I showered, ignored the fact that I looked like Beetlejuice. I quickly blew dry my hair. Mostly because if I didn't, it would be a complete rat's nest, and I didn't have all of my curly hair products with me. I had wanted to travel light, although I wasn't completely Jane. Jane would have a single toothbrush and call it an evening. Arden had an entire suitcase.

I couldn't help it. I needed to be prepared.

I met Liam in the living room of the penthouse and looked around. "This is ridiculous," I said.

He shrugged, his cheeks going red slightly.

"I made a shit-ton of money as a model, and I make decent money in my current job. I'm allowed to every once in a while spoil you."

"Maybe," I said with a laugh. "But this is a little ridiculous."

He shrugged. "Very much so."

I looked around again. "Though we could maybe fit the entirety of the Montgomerys in here," I said, teasing.

"There's far too many of us for that, and I'm not footing the bill for that," he said and laughed. He kissed me hard again and then took my suitcase. "Come on, my wife, let's head home." He put both suitcases in one hand, squeezed my hand, and led me out of the penthouse.

Once in the sunlight that peeked through the car window, we were no longer any remnants of Jane and Jack. Just Liam and Arden.

A married couple—the first of Liam's siblings, and mine—and happy.

I had met Liam when I had been at one of my lowest points. Where I had thought that death would be welcome because the pain of living had been almost too much. I was still sick. I still had flare-ups. I still was in the hospital more than I'd like to admit. But I wasn't alone. Not that I had ever really been alone, because my brothers had always been there. But now they could focus on their wives and their children because Liam would always be there. Along with his family.

We had all grown leaps and bounds over the past few years, and I still couldn't quite believe that I had landed Liam Montgomery. The love of my life.

He looked over at me then, his aviators showing my reflection, and I knew he could see my heart in my eyes.

I couldn't help it. I didn't hide it from him.

He brought our clasped hands to his lips and kissed the back of my hand.

We pulled into Aaron Montgomery's driveway as the front door opened.

Jasper, my white Siberian Husky, practically leaped out of the doorway, barked happily, and sat patiently, even though he was shaking, on the grass waiting for us. Liam parked, and I jumped out of the car, all thoughts of pain from my lupus gone from my memory.

I knelt, hugged Jasper tight, and kissed the top of his head. "There's my baby boy."

I looked up as Lake came toward us, her hair piled on the top of her head, and her chin lowered just a bit.

"Mom?" Lake asked, and my heartbeat sped and felt like it grew five sizes.

"Hey there, baby. Did you have a good night with your Uncle Aaron and Aunt Madison?" I asked and opened up my arms.

My daughter, of only a few months, ran into my arms. I hugged her tight, inhaled that sweet scent that was all Lake, and held back tears.

"Hey, Dad," she said as she pulled away and held Liam close.

I heard Liam's breath catch, and I knew he was ready to sob right along with me. She had only started calling us Mom and Dad two weeks ago. We had been Liam and Arden during the foster process. And as the adoption had become final, we were still getting our bearings.

But our ten-year-old daughter, Lake, was the light of our lives.

I knew that while the rest of the Montgomerys were slowly breeding an entire generation that would rival the originals, Lake might be our only child. And that would mean the world to me.

I had fallen in love with this little girl from the moment I had seen her, and I had nearly cried myself to sleep in tension and stress every night until the adoption papers had finally been signed. But now we were a family, the four of us with Jasper, and I couldn't believe that this was my life.

Aaron and Madison stood in the doorway, giving us a piece of privacy, even if we were in the middle of their yard. Madison was crying, leaning against Aaron. My brother-in-law was also crying.

We were a bunch of softies, and I loved it.

I looked up at Liam, my Jack for the evening, but my husband forever, and I smiled.

Last night had been a night to be wrapped up in fantasy and bliss. But fiction could tangle with real life.

And as I held my daughter close, my best boy puppy leaning hard into my side, and Liam holding us all, I knew that my reality was far richer than any fiction I could ever imagine.

Thank you so much for reading **INKED FANTASY**

I love the Montgomerys. I truly do. And these Boulder Montgomerys are so amazing and dare I say…bolder. Yes, I've been making that joke to myself while even writing hard topics.

As someone with an autoimmune disease, writing Arden's romance was a bit personal, but finding her HEA was perfect. Liam? Liam is a Montgomery. His personal journey into figuring that out is what made him a Montgomery.

As for who is next? Ethan is next though he's not going to go about it the usual away. I cannot wait for you to read his story.

Bristol and Aaron will be getting their stories as well!

And how about those Brady Brothers? You guessed it, I fell in love. I didn't mean to. But now they are getting a series of their own in the Promise Me series!

And if you're new to my books, you can start anywhere within the my interconnected series and catch up! Each book is a stand alone, so jump around!

Don't miss out on the Montgomery Ink World!
•*Montgomery Ink (The Denver Montgomerys)*
•*Montgomery Ink: Colorado Springs*
(The Colorado Springs Montgomery Cousins)
•*Montgomery Ink: Boulder (The Boulder Montgomery Cousins)*
•*Gallagher Brothers (Jake's Brothers from Ink Enduring)*
•*Whiskey and Lies (Tabby's Brothers from Ink Exposed)*
•*Fractured Connections (Mace's sisters from Fallen Ink)*
•*Less Than (Dimitri's siblings from Restless Ink)*
•*Promise Me (Arden's siblings from Wrapped in Ink)*

If you want to make sure you know what's coming next from me, you can sign up for my newsletter at www.CarrieAnnRyan.com; follow me on twitter at @CarrieAnnRyan, or like my Facebook page. I also have a Facebook Fan Club where we have trivia, chats, and other goodies. You guys are the reason I get to do what I do and I thank you.

Make sure you're signed up for my MAILING LIST so you can know when the next releases are available as well as find giveaways and FREE READS.

Happy Reading!

The Montgomery Ink: Boulder Series:

Book 1: Wrapped in Ink

Book 2: Sated in Ink

Book 3: Embraced in Ink

Book 3.5: Moments in Ink

Book 4: Seduced in Ink

Book 4.5: Captured in Ink

about the author

Carrie Ann Ryan is the *New York Times* and *USA Today* bestselling author of contemporary, paranormal, and young adult romance. Her works include the Montgomery Ink, Redwood Pack, Fractured Connections, and Elements of Five series, which have sold over 3.0 million books worldwide. She started writing while in graduate school for her advanced degree in chemistry and hasn't stopped since. Carrie Ann has written over seventy-five novels and novellas with more in the works. When she's not losing herself in her emotional and action-packed worlds, she's reading as much as she can while wrangling her clowder of cats who have more followers than she does.

www.CarrieAnnRyan.com

the *inevitable*

NIKKI ASH

chapter one

Sierra

"CHICKEN SALAD, EXTRA EGG, EXTRA TOMATO, AND AN additional ranch dressing on the side and… a refill of your sweet tea, extra lemons." I set the salad and drink down in front of my customer. "Can I get you anything else?" I ask out of habit, immediately regretting my choice of words.

He opens his mouth, a sly smirk quirking at the corner of his lips, but before the words can spill out, I raise my hand because I already know what he's going to say. For the past week, he's shown up here and sat in the same spot, ordering the same drink and salad while making the same request. *Go out on a date with me.*

And every day, despite how badly I want to do just that, I've given him the same answer: *No.*

"Besides me."

His sexy two-dimpled grin splays across his face. "Well, if you're still off the table, then I'm good." He grabs the ranch dressing and pours it over his salad.

"I'm still off the table," I reiterate yet again. Technically, I'm very much available, just not to him. Because when he walked in here on that first day and our eyes met as he sat at the bar, I immediately felt something course through my veins. Like fireworks waiting to be set off on the Fourth of July, they'll all shoot off with one spark, beautiful and dazzling, and explode in the sky. But what happens once they burn out? When the colors fade into ash, and we're left with only the aftermath?

Even though I have no doubt those sparks would be worth chasing, knowing the destruction they'll leave behind means I can't risk it.

The first time Kolton spoke to me, and those damn dimples popped out of his cheeks, I knew he would be bad for my heart. I went into self-preservation mode the best I could, locking away my organ in an attempt to protect it. But Kolton isn't making it easy on me. Every conversation, every joke, and every shared laugh cracks my shield a little more. I know it's only a matter of time until my heart is exposed, and I'll have no choice but to either flee the country—okay, maybe that's a bit dramatic—or give in and say yes to him, risking everything I've worked hard to protect over the past several years.

"Maybe so," he says, mixing his dressing in with the salad. "But I can feel you caving."

I bark out a laugh, refusing to let him know he's right. "How so? I'm pretty sure we had damn near the same conversation yesterday and the day before… and the day before that." Usually, I'm not behind the bar. For the past couple of years, I've managed The Orange Sunrise, an upscale restaurant-slash-bar in downtown Carterville. But last week, I caught two of my employees stealing and was forced to fire them, leaving the bar unattended.

"True," he agrees. "But today, you got my food without me even having to order it… a sign that you're paying attention to my wants and needs. And when you turned me down, you smiled this time instead of glaring at me. Sierra, you're caving, and soon, you're going to give in to what's brewing between us."

Jesus, he's right. I am paying attention. And he is getting to me. That force field protecting my heart simply isn't strong enough to withstand his charm. What about him urges me to let my guard down?

I release a completely unladylike snort because you know… fake it till you make it. "For a man who's been turned down a half dozen times, you seem quite sure of yourself."

"I don't hear you denying there's something between us." He points his fork my way. "I've been turned down five times, but I won't let that stop me. I can feel it…" He leans in, and without thought, as though a rope pulls me toward him, I do as well. "The sexual tension is so thick between us that it'll be worth the effort because when you give in, this thing between us will explode."

His words roll off his tongue like the sweetest yet scariest promise, reminding me of when I was younger and would use drugs as an escape. When I was high, I was on top of the world, but the minute it ended, and I crashed, it left me in a puddle of pain and regret. And that's what he could easily become to me… a drug. The high would be incredible, but the crash… it would no doubt destroy me.

"Besides," he adds, unaware of how my heart pounds behind my rib cage. "It's inevitable." He stabs the greens with his fork and shoves a bite into his mouth.

I count to five, needing to get my feelings under control. Every day he shows up here, he gets more personal, revealing more of himself. And with every word he speaks, he makes it harder for me to resist him.

"Inevitable, huh?" I choke out, grabbing the washcloth to focus my attention on something else other than him.

"As inevitable as the sun rising in the east and setting in the west."

"How very poetic of you. Is that what you teach? Poetry?"

I've seen his university badge, so I know he works there.

He chuckles.

"What?" I glance up from wiping down the already clean counter.

"You just proved my point. You're caving."

"How so?"

"You're asking me questions. Trying to get to know me."

"More like it's slow and I'm making conversation with the only person sitting at the bar," I retort.

"Whatever you have to tell yourself." He takes a sip of his drink. "But to answer your question… No, I don't teach poetry. I teach psychology. I've almost completed my master's in clinical psychology."

"You want to be a psychologist?" After my parents died, the state required my sister, Blakely, and me to see one. I hated her because she was condescending and lacked empathy. It's one of the reasons my sister is in school to become a guidance counselor. She wants to help guide kids in a positive way.

"I'm actually hoping to get a full-time teaching job at the university. But I'd love to volunteer at various mental health facilities.

Therapy saved my life, and I want to help others the way it helped me."

Thankfully, a customer sits down at the other end of the bar. I excuse myself to greet her, and from there, the evening picks up. A steady flow of customers keeps me busy—between running the bar with one other person and managing the restaurant—and when I finally get a chance to check on Kolton, he's not there.

"Can you grab a bottle of Johnny Walker black label from the back?" Wilma asks. "We're out of it up here."

"Sure."

I'm halfway down the hall, my eyes trained on my phone, reading a text from my sister, when I run into a… wall? "Oomph." I stumble backward, my feet losing their balance, and am mentally preparing myself for the fall when powerful hands grip my waist and keep me upright.

My vision adjusts to the darkness, and I find the wall isn't a wall at all, but Kolton. He must've been coming out of the men's restroom.

"Shit, are you okay?" he asks, his voice filled with concern. "I was looking at my phone and didn't see you." His eyes lock with mine, and the sudden heat of his stare fills me with liquid lust.

"I was too." My words come out breathy, our proximity messing with my head. Usually, I have the bar to serve as a barrier between us. But now… nothing's between us. It's just Kolton and me in a dark hallway.

His fingers dig into my sides, his front flush with my own. My chest brushes up against his, and I can feel my nipples, sensitive with desire, pushed up against his muscular torso. Our faces are close. Too close. He's a head taller than me, but in my heeled boots, I'm close enough that I can reach up slightly and lay a soft kiss to his chiseled jawline, working my way to the corner of his mouth before giving his lips my attention…

As if he can sense what I'm thinking, he groans softly under his breath. "I want to kiss you so fucking badly."

"Then do it," I whisper. "Kiss me."

"Go out with me."

And just like that, the moment is broken. I back away, sucking in a breath of air that isn't filled with Kolton's scent. "I can't."

Without waiting for his response, I turn my back on him and disappear down the hall into the storage room. In the darkness, I take a moment to get my breathing—and libido—under control, and then I grab the bottle I need and head back out.

When I return to the bar, all that's left of Kolton is his signed receipt. Wilma must've given him his bill.

"He couldn't keep his eyes off you," Wilma says, glancing over my shoulder. "When I brought him his bill, he looked like a sad puppy that I wasn't you."

"It's not happening..." *Then maybe you shouldn't have told him to kiss you...* I'm going to chalk that up to temporary insanity.

I have no intention of giving him a chance to break my heart. Thanks to my sister and my beautiful nephew, I'm on the right path, and I refuse to ever go back down the path of destruction. I prefer to date men who won't destroy me. The ones I'm safe from giving my heart to.

"Have you seen the man?" Wilma waggles her brows. "He's fine as hell."

There's no denying he's a good-looking man. With his floppy brown hair he keeps swept under his gray beanie, his mesmerizing brown eyes look at me as if he can see straight into my soul, and when he gets comfortable and rolls the sleeves of his dress shirt up... Holy shit! Between his muscular forearms and the ink donning them, my insides become a freaking inferno. Nothing is hotter than a man who can wear a suit like it was made for him while hiding the bad boy underneath. Too bad I won't ever get the chance to experience either. My mom had a man like that once—my dad—and it killed her... literally. No way am I following in those footsteps.

chapter two

Kolton

"You're home late," my brother says as I walk through the door of my apartment, shedding my coat and suit jacket along the way. "Actually, now that I think about it, you've been getting home late a lot lately." Keegan crosses his arms over his chest and quirks a single brow. "You have a secret nightlife I don't know about?"

I set my briefcase on the coffee table and drop onto the couch. "Wasn't aware that you staying here temporarily meant suddenly becoming my parent. Do I have a curfew, too, Dad? Am I grounded?"

"Ha-ha. Seriously, though, what gives?" He sits across from me on the other couch and props his shoe-clad feet on my table. I eye it in annoyance, and he laughs, removing his feet.

"How much longer are you going to be crashing here?"

"Not sure." He shrugs. "Stop deflecting."

I sigh, knowing he won't give up. My brother knows me too damn well. A downfall to being in each other's lives for almost twenty-five years—you get to see every part of the other person.

"There's this woman…" I begin, barely getting the words out before Keegan hoots.

"Oh, shit! Seriously? Took you long enough to get back in the game."

"Well, I'm not exactly back in." I release a harsh breath. "More like sitting on the sidelines and begging to get put into the game."

Keegan laughs. "She turned you down?"

"Five times."

He scoffs. "What the hell is wrong with you?"

"She told me I'm ugly," I joke.

He cracks up. "That can't be true. I happen to know you're a sexy-ass specimen of a man." He waggles his brows, and I throw my pillow at him. "But that's not what I meant. What the hell is wrong with you that you asked out the same woman five times? You didn't get the hint the first four times she said no?"

"I know… I know I should let her go, but you're not there. You should see the way she looks at me when she doesn't think I'm paying attention."

I lean forward, my elbows landing on my knees, and scrub the sides of my face in frustration. "And the way she smiles when she doesn't know I'm watching her. She has the most beautiful smile, but there's something about it that's just the tiniest bit sad…"

I close my eyes, replaying the way her heart-shaped lips purse when she tries to hold back her smile. "Something about her has me drawn to her, has me wanting to reach inside her and find out everything there is to know about her." And then tonight, when we ran into each other, and I kept her from falling… When she looked at me and told me to kiss her? Fuck! I should've done it. I should've kissed her. But I didn't because I want more from her, and I knew if I kissed her, she would regret it, and then I wouldn't stand a chance.

"Jesus, man," Keegan says. "I haven't heard you sound this passionate about anything since…" He flinches, his words trailing off, not wanting to finish his thought.

"Since I killed Keith," I finish for him, needing to say the words out loud.

"Will you stop that shit?" Keegan hisses. "You didn't kill him. That piece of shit did."

My family loves to baby me, but I refuse to take the coward's way out. I can't change what happened, but I won't pretend my choices and actions weren't what led to the moment that ended our brother's life. The only way to truly move forward is to admit the truth and deal with it.

"We'll agree to disagree." I shrug. "I don't know. Maybe it's for the best that she's not interested. I have a shit ton of baggage and—"

"Stop," Keegan barks. "You want to blame yourself for Keith's death? I can't stop you, even if I don't agree with it, but I refuse to sit here and listen to you be self-deprecating. You've punished yourself for long enough, and you deserve to be happy. So if you think she'll make you happy, I say go for it. Keep at it until she agrees to go out with you." He laughs and stands. "Or until she calls the police and gets a restraining order."

I slowly raise my middle finger, silently expressing how I feel about his comment.

"No, thanks," he quips. "You might be hot, but you're still blood."

"What can I get you?" a raven-haired woman standing on the other side of the bar asks.

"Umm…" I glance around, hoping to locate Sierra. "I was wondering if—"

Before I can finish my sentence, the woman present in all my thoughts and fantasies walks out from the back. She's dressed in her work uniform: tight black dress slacks and a collared shirt with the restaurant's logo in the left corner. Her purse is strewn over her shoulder as she strolls in her black heels toward the door.

"I've changed my mind," I call back to the bartender while I spring from my seat and chase after the gorgeous brunette.

"Hey, Sierra! Wait up," I yell, catching up with her.

Her steps momentarily falter, and her eyes quickly widen, just before that wall she's an expert at erecting flies up.

"I'm off, but Monica is running the bar. She can take your order." She doesn't stop walking.

"Unless you're on the menu, she can't help me." Cheesy as fuck, I know, but at this point, I throw that shit out to get her attention. Like a five-year-old boy who messes with the girl he likes at recess.

I know it works when she snorts under her breath, then covers her mouth and nose to cover it up—too late. "I really have to get going," she says. "The bus will be here in a few minutes, and unless I want to wait an hour for the next one, I need to grab it."

"Get a drink with me." I rush forward and block her path. "Please. Just one drink."

She stops in her place. "I'm not looking for a boyfriend."

"Who said anything about being your boyfriend?" I joke. "I just asked you to get a drink with me. If I buy you food, will you assume I'm going to ask you to move in with me? Oh, shit." I widen my eyes in mock surprise. "If I throw in an appetizer, will you expect me to propose?"

The cutest fucking blush creeps up her neck and cheeks. "I… I didn't…"

"I'm just messing with you." I step toward her. "In all seriousness, I have every intention of becoming your boyfriend one day." Her eyes bug out in shock. "And one day, you will move in with me… Or I can move in with you." I shrug. "And then, when I know you're going to say yes, I will most definitely propose."

"Kolton!" She gasps.

I ignore the beginnings of her freak-out. "You and me… it's inevitable. But don't worry. I'm okay with taking things slow… for now." I playfully wink. "All I want to do is take you somewhere to buy you a drink and have a conversation. So, what do you say? One drink? Anywhere you want."

She sighs, and her face dips, her gaze dropping to the ground. She's thinking, contemplating. I'm wearing her down…

"Please," I murmur, moving into her space.

Her hair is fanned over her face, so I lightly pinch her chin, forcing her to look up at me, so she can no longer hide behind her curtain of hair. "If you really want me to stop pursuing you, I will, Sierra. But I don't think you want me to stop. I think you're scared of what you feel between us, and I get it because I am too. I've never felt the instant connection with anyone the way I feel it with you."

She sucks in a harsh breath, and a wayward strand of hair falls over her eye. I use it as an excuse to touch her by tucking it behind her ear. As my fingers glide down the side of her face, she shivers.

"Kolton," she breathes, leaning her face into my palm and closing her eyes. "I don't know what to do."

"You take a deep breath, you open your eyes, and then you agree to have a drink with me."

She swallows thickly, then does what I say. "Okay. One drink." She steps backward slightly, out of my reach, and my hand drops. I want to pull her back so I can touch her some more, but I can tell just agreeing to have a drink with me was hard for her. I need to remember to take shit slow so she doesn't feel overwhelmed.

"Do you want to walk to someplace close, or do you trust me to drive us somewhere?"

She glances around. "You'll need to give me a ride home anyway, so I guess we can drive somewhere. Just… if you're planning to murder me, can you at least leave my body somewhere the police can find it so my sister will know I'm gone?"

I chuckle at her dry sense of humor. "I promise."

I guide her around back to the parking lot and over to where I parked my bike. I only have one helmet, but we won't be going far, and technically, they're not required here.

"Wait, you drive a motorcycle?" she says, coming to an abrupt halt when we arrive at my bike.

"Is that a problem?" I grab my helmet and hand it to her.

"No… I don't know…" She groans. "It's just…I dated my fair share of bad boys in high school, and it never ended well. And the past couple of years I've tried to become someone better… Someone my sister and nephew can be proud of and—"

"Whoa there. That's a whole lot of stereotyping and assumptions in one breath. Yes, I have tattoos. Yes, I drive a motorcycle, but I'm also in college getting my master's, and I'm a mama's boy through and through. Sometimes riding a bike is just that… the love of riding."

Her face falls. "Shit, I'm sorry. Are you sure you want to get to know me? I can't imagine what you know of me so far is all that amazing."

"So far, the little bit I know about you is enough to make me curious. And I imagine, once you actually let me in, it's only going to lead to me wanting to know even more."

Her lashes flutter, and her caramel-colored eyes meet mine. "You sure you're not a poetry major? Because you definitely know how to spit out some beautiful words."

I snort out a laugh. "I'm not usually this romantic," I admit. "Actually, I'm pretty rusty in that department. But you seem to bring it out in me." I swing my leg over the side of my bike. "Now, how about you throw your purse into the saddlebag, put my helmet on, and we go for a ride, so I can romance you into agreeing to spend your life with me?"

This time, instead of freaking the hell out at my antics, she laughs. After doing as I said, she hops onto the bike behind me and snakes her arms around my waist, pressing her soft breasts into my back.

"All right, Romeo, I'm ready to be romanced."

"Doesn't he commit suicide at the end of that play?"

"Yep, they both did. Isn't that how romance goes, though? You either live happily ever after or you crash and burn."

I take off out of the parking lot, and Sierra's grip on me tightens. This bike was my brother Keith's. He had it custom made and left it to me in his will. At first, after he died, I didn't want to touch it, but after I got my shit together, I figured what better way to remember him than to ride the one thing he loved. Until now, I've never had a woman on the back of the bike, and I can't help but feel like maybe there was a reason for that. Because the way Sierra's body fits against mine, it's as if she was made for riding on the back.

I take us the long way through town, enjoying the cool breeze and her holding me tightly. A couple of times, I glance back and find her eyes bright, glancing around, her brown hair whipping around her face. In all the times I've gone into The Orange Sunrise, I've never seen her look as carefree as she does on the back of my bike.

When we pull up to a coffee shop my mom loves and frequents, Sierra yells over the engine that she loves this place. I turn off the bike, and she hops off. I watch as she pulls the helmet off and shakes her hair out, and I swear to God no woman has ever looked so goddamn beautiful. With her face flush from the cool air and her hair windblown, she's a fucking wet dream.

"What?" she asks when she catches me staring. "Is my hair a mess?"

"It's perfect." I swing my leg over the side and stalk toward her. "You're perfect." I cup her cheek with my palm, needing to touch her yet wishing I could kiss her.

"You barely know me," she mutters, not realizing that even though she's tried to put a wall up, I've spent the past several days slowly chipping away at it, breaking away every bit I can get my hands on.

"I know you have a sister and a nephew who mean the world to you. You would do anything for them, including working too many hours at a restaurant you don't love and that doesn't appreciate you. You have dreams to one day own your own restaurant, but right now, your goal is to help your sister get through college because you feel you owe her that much. Your parents aren't around, and you don't like talking about them. You prefer vanilla cake over chocolate, which is crazy since chocolate blows vanilla away… You love Cherry Coke and french fries with cheese. You had a rough go of it in high school, and you're trying to make up for it in your twenties. Your favorite color is pink and—"

"I *never* told you my favorite color!"

"No, but it's obvious. You've come to work with your nails painted three different colors, and all of them were shades of pink. The necklace you wear every day has a pink heart on it, and your cell phone case is glittery and pink."

"Holy shit!" She shakes her head, eyeing me speculatively. "I can't believe you got all of that out of me. You really are a therapist in training."

"No," I say through a laugh. "I'm a man interested in a woman, which means I listen and pay attention."

Her features soften slightly. "There you go again with all that poetry."

"C'mon, beautiful." I take her hand in mine, loving the way my hand engulfs hers. "Let me buy you a cup of coffee and convince you to let me take you out."

After we order our coffees, I steer us outside and around the back. There's a park that butts up to the coffee shop, complete with a walking trail, picnic tables, and a pond filled with ducks.

We walk along the perimeter, drinking our coffees in silence until we get to the area with the picnic tables. Sierra hops up on one, and I join her, leaning against the side of it.

Her phone goes off, and she pulls it out. Whoever it is makes her sigh in frustration. She types rapidly for several seconds before she clicks her phone back off and shoves it back into her pocket.

"Everything okay?"

"Yeah." She sighs. "Work… You were right. I hate my job… Actually, I don't hate my job. I love it. I love everything about the restaurant business: the menus, the ambiance, the guests. I just don't love the owner. When I first started working there, her father owned the place. He was so passionate and dedicated to making sure it was run right. Then he died of a heart attack, and his daughter took it over. She knows nothing about the restaurant or hospitality industry. She makes horrible choices and refuses to listen to me. The place is going under, and it breaks my heart to see it happen. I wouldn't be surprised if the restaurant closes by the end of this year. And then I'll be out of a job and looking for somewhere else to work… having to start all over again."

"What is it you want to do?"

"My dream is to own my own restaurant."

"Have you thought about buying it from her?"

Sierra laughs humorlessly. "With what money?"

"Take out a loan."

She takes a sip of her coffee and stares out at the pond. "My sister is hoping to get into a master's program, and her financial aid will end. She'll have to take out loans, so I'll be the only one bringing in any money. Even if I could somehow get approved for a loan, now isn't the time to be taking risks."

Her eyes shine with unshed tears, and my heart feels as though it cracks, but I don't say anything because I know this is hard for her. She most likely didn't mean to let all that out, and she's trying to wish away those tears because she thinks they make her appear weak even though she is quite the opposite.

As I suspected, a second later, she blinks several times and takes in a deep breath. "It's for the best," she says with false confidence. "Being a restaurant owner is a lot of responsibility, and most fail. I would probably fai—"

I turn to face her, stepping between her legs, and cover her lips with my fingers. "Do not finish that sentence. You would not fail. Maybe now isn't the right time, but one day it will be, and you will get that loan and buy or open your own restaurant, and it will be a success because I can see your drive when you're working and hear your passion when you talk about it. You want it, and you will stop at nothing until it's a success."

Sierra releases a harsh breath, and the warmth tickles my flesh. She darts her tongue out to lick her lips, and her tongue grazes the pads of my fingers. When she realizes what she's done, her eyes go wide.

I drop my hand but remain close to her.

"Go out with me." I cup her face in my palm. "Please."

chapter three

Kolton

"Who are you all dressed up for?" Keegan jibes when I walk out of my room dressed in jeans, a white collared shirt, and a pair of brown leather Sperry boat shoes.

"Sierra agreed to go on a date with me."

"Nice," Keegan says, waggling his brows up and down like an immature high schooler. "Want me to make myself scarce tonight so you have the place to yourself?"

"I don't think that'll be necessary. She's making me meet her at the restaurant instead of picking her up. I think it's her way of taking things slow." Even though I had driven us to the coffee shop and then driven her home, she insisted she meet me at the restaurant. She said if the date doesn't go well, she doesn't want it to be awkward. It was the stupidest thing I've ever heard—and I knew she was just saying it because she's nervous—but I agreed. Honestly, I would agree to almost anything to get her to give me a chance.

My phone dings with a text, and I pull it out to see who it is. The second I see Sierra's name, my heart drops. *Fuck, she's probably getting cold feet and is going to cancel…* It took some serious convincing on my part to get her to go to dinner and even more convincing to get her to give me her number. The woman definitely isn't making it easy on me, but I'm up for the challenge. What's that cliché as fuck saying? Nothing worth having comes easy? She's worth having, so if it takes some hard work, then so be it.

Sierra: Change of plans. Meet me at my place.

"Everything okay?" Keegan asks.

"Yeah, Sierra just texted me to pick her up."

"You sure you don't want the place to yourself?"

"Nah. Even if it were possible, I'm not about to rush it with her. She's skittish about dating as it is. I don't want her to think I'm just trying to get in her pants."

When it's time to pick her up, I drive over to her place. Since both of our apartments are situated right off the university campus, it only takes a couple minutes.

I park and jog up the flights of stairs, knocking when I get to her door.

A second later, the door swings open, and standing there is Sierra dressed in a flowy, low-cut top and skintight jeans. Her pink toes are peeking out of high as hell heels.

"Wow," Sierra says, "I didn't see it before because I wasn't looking for it, but damn, you look just like my nephew."

Her statement takes me by surprise, and I'm unsure how it's relevant to our date. "Am I missing something here?"

"Who are you?" Sierra asks, ignoring my question. "Keegan or Kolton?"

My eyes widen, then my lips curl into a grin, wondering how the hell she knows my brother. There's no way they've slept together. He barely has time for women, and he would've recognized her name. "I'm Kolton."

"Why did you lie to me?" someone asks. I turn my attention to the other woman standing by the door. I didn't notice her because I was completely focused on Sierra. *Why does she look so familiar?* Maybe it's because she and Sierra share similar features: brown hair, caramel eyes, pert nose… This is obviously her sister—but I don't think she's ever mentioned her name.

"About what? When?" I ask, confused as fuck. I came here to go on a date with Sierra, and suddenly, I'm getting grilled with questions.

"When you slept with my sister!" Sierra bellows. "And don't try to act like you don't remember her. You tried to get her attention earlier." *What the hell is going on?*

"I didn't sleep with her," I say, my gaze locking with Sierra's. "I don't even know her."

"Is this a game to you?" her sister asks, hurt and confusion filled in her tone.

"You think you slept with me?"

"I think I slept with *Keegan*," she volleys.

Oh, shit... What has my brother done? "And you think I'm Keegan?"

"Do you have a split personality disorder?" she asks, making me laugh.

"I think I know what the problem is, but it would probably be best if I show you." I doubt she'll believe me unless she sees it for herself.

I pull out my phone and call my brother.

"What's up?"

"I need you to come here."

"Where?"

"To Sierra's place. Don't ask questions. Just come." I rattle off her address and then hang up.

While we wait for Keegan to arrive, the women step outside, then close the door behind them. Sierra refers to her sister as Blakely, and I damn near choke on my own saliva. Holy shit! There's no way this is a coincidence. My brother met a woman years ago on spring break named Blakely. He talked about her for months, upset that his phone got fucked up, and he lost her number.

We stand in awkward silence until Keegan rolls up on his skateboard a few minutes later, then runs up the steps. The second he comes into view, Blakely gasps at the same time Keegan's face splits into a grin.

"Jailbird," Keegan says. "I knew that was you earlier."

"Keegan?" she asks, clearly in shock.

"I see you've met my brother Kolton."

"You didn't tell me you had a twin brother," she mutters.

Yep, that's right. Keegan and I are identical twins. Hence, why he thinks I'm so hot. It's always been an inside joke between us.

Keegan and Blakely chat back and forth, getting caught up, until the door opens and out walks some guy. Blakely makes introductions—Brenton is a friend of hers, who, I have no doubt by the way he's looking at her, has the hots for her. Even if it seems she doesn't feel the same way.

There's an awkward lull in the conversation, and then Keegan says, "Was… is that kid yours?" And that's when I remember her. She was walking across campus with Brenton and a little boy, who must've been her son. She tried to talk to me, but I had no idea who she was. She had assumed I was Keegan.

Blakely's eyes go wide at Keegan's question, and she immediately looks nervous. "Is Zane okay in his room?" she asks Brenton.

"Yeah," he replies. "He's playing with his Legos. I came out here to make sure everything is okay. You've been out here for a while."

"Can you go check on him?" she asks. "I think I should talk to Keegan alone."

Brenton opens his mouth to argue, but Blakely speaks first. "Please."

"What about them?" he asks, pointing at Sierra and me.

"Sierra," Blakely says, turning to her sister.

"We're actually late for our date," I mention, glancing at the time on my phone. I have no idea what's going on, but Keegan will fill me in later. "I can probably get us in for later, though."

"That's not happening." Sierra scoffs, confusing the shit out of me. "We're practically family." She cackles, and Blakely smacks her arm.

Practically family? What the hell is she talking about?

"Really?" Blakely glares at her sister.

"Sorry." Sierra shrugs.

"Can someone explain what the hell's going on?" Keegan asks, obviously as confused as I am.

"I'll watch Zane," Sierra says to Blakely, "and you can go talk to Keegan."

Shit, there goes our date…

"Do you really think it's wise to be alone with him?" Brenton asks Blakely.

I can practically feel the sudden tension rolling off my brother.

Locking eyes with him, I give a subtle shake of my head. Whatever is going on, he needs to keep his cool.

Blakely and Brenton go back and forth, arguing over whether she should be alone with my brother. I'm about to speak up when Blakely smiles, and says, "You haven't murdered anyone in the past four years, have you? Gone to jail for anything?"

"Nah, Jailbird," Keegan replies with a laugh. "No murders, no arrests. How about you? Have you kept yourself out of jail? Paying for everything at the store? Attending all your classes?"

Sierra laughs. "You told him about the time we shoplifted and when you got caught skipping?"

Wait, what?

Blakely rolls her eyes. "I was making sure he wasn't going to rape and murder me, and it backfired."

"You've been arrested?" I blurt out.

"We were bad teenagers," Sierra says with a shoulder shrug and a smirk. "Now, we're responsible, law-abiding adults."

"That's good to know," Keegan jokes. "So, you wanted to talk?" he says to Blakely.

"Yeah." She nods, and her smile disappears. "Brenton, you can go," she tells him. "I'll call you later."

"You sure?" he asks, sounding whiny as fuck. Poor guy, he has it bad.

He takes off, leaving the four of us. Blakely suggests to Keegan they go for a walk and talk, and then Sierra says she's going to head in with her nephew.

Before she can open the door, I snag her wrist gently.

"This isn't over," I tell her. There's no way I'm letting her bail on our date.

She doesn't say a word. Instead, she just slips inside.

The second I'm back home, I send her a text: **When am I getting my rain check?**

I wait several minutes, but of course, my text remains unread.

"You're not going to believe this shit," Keegan says a couple of hours later when he walks through the door with a huge grin on his face.

Sierra still hasn't texted me back, so I'm cranky as fuck. "What?"

"Zane, Blakely's son… he's my son."

He drops onto the couch. "I can't believe it, man. I'm a fucking dad."

Well, shit, now it all makes sense. Sierra's earlier comments… *"You look just like my nephew… We're practically family."* Because she knew Keegan was the dad, which makes me Zane's uncle.

Oh. Fucking. Well. If she thinks that's going to stop me from pursuing her, she's got another thing coming.

chapter four

Sierra

During my entire shift, I keep one eye on the entrance, waiting for Kolton to walk in. Yesterday was a shock, to say the least. My sister, who has dreamed of the day when she would find her son's father, has found him. And of course, he's none other than Kolton's identical twin brother. Because apparently having one of those sexy men in the world isn't enough, God graced us with two of them.

I've been avoiding his texts since yesterday, trying to decide what I'm going to do. I always told myself I wasn't running from love. I've just never come across the right guy. But the second it hit me that Kolton could be the one, I did exactly that. I ran. And now I have to figure out if I'm going to continue to run, or if I'm going to give us a chance because it's not fair to keep stringing him along.

As if the thought of Kolton has summoned him, he appears at the door, sauntering my way with purpose. Today, he's dressed in a navy-blue button-down shirt with his sleeves rolled up and a pair of black slacks that fit his muscular thighs. Maybe if I had teachers like him in high school, I would've considered taking the step toward higher education.

"If you want me, you can have me, Sierra. You just have to say the word." His words knock me into reality.

"Excuse me?" I splutter.

"You're practically undressing me on the spot." He smirks playfully, then leans over and runs his thumb along my chin. "And drooling."

"I am not!" I shriek, grabbing a coaster and placing it in front of him.

"Oh, you were, but I'll try to keep my clothes on in front of all these people. What's underneath is for your eyes only."

I groan, hating that I don't hate him at all. "What can I get you?" I ask, making him smirk.

Dammit! I keep setting myself up for this shit.

"Other than me," I add.

He chuckles. "I'm done with these games. I want you to go on a date with me."

"It's not happening. We're family."

I know. I know. Stupid excuse. But it's all I've got to keep him at arm's length while I figure out my feelings toward him.

"We're not family. But I am excited to officially meet my nephew." A genuine smile graces his lips. "Keegan is meeting him today. He and Mom went shopping for Zane earlier. The guy is on cloud nine."

My heart soars for my nephew and sister. This reunion could have gone in so many directions, and I'm thankful it went in the one that means Zane will have a loving, caring father, and my sister will have a partner to parent with.

"He's an amazing kid," I tell him. "Smart and adorable and funny."

"Of course, he is," he quips. "He's a Reynolds."

I roll my eyes. "Salad and iced tea?"

"Yep, with a side of you, please."

"It's not happening."

"Oh, it is. And the sooner you accept that, the sooner we can move forward… together."

He pulls a bunch of papers out of his briefcase and sets them on the bar top. "Do you mind if I grade my papers here?"

"I don't care." I shrug. "But wouldn't you want to do that in peace and quiet at your house?"

He shakes his head. "I'd rather do it with the backdrop of you."

I shake my head and walk over to the computer to place his order, trying not to seem affected by his words, when the truth is, I'm very much affected. For years after my parents died, I kept everyone at arm's length, not wanting to risk my heart getting broken. I watched my mom's heart get torn to shreds little by little, bit by bit, all in the name of love, and I swore I would never allow that to happen to me.

But the second I heard my nephew's heartbeat on the monitor, it was as if my chest was cracked open, and my heart was on display for the world to see. Which was fine since my entire world consisted of Blakely and Zane—and I knew they would never hurt me.

But now Kolton wants in, and I have no doubt, if I give him my heart, he has the capability to destroy it the same way my dad destroyed my mom. And I have to decide if I'm willing to take that risk.

The evening flies by. Kolton hangs around, grading papers, and when I'm not busy, we chat. When the final customer pays his check and leaves, I glance over at Kolton, who's still nursing his iced tea.

"You ready to go?" he asks, standing when I come around the bar to lock up. The staff has all cashed out and shut down their stations, and Kolton and I are the only ones left.

"Yeah."

He hands me his helmet, and I reluctantly put it on my head, knowing it's going to ruin my hair.

"What's wrong?"

"These helmets are clearly not made for women."

He chuckles. "No, probably not, but you still look sexy as hell with it on."

The ride to my apartment complex is quick, and when I get off the bike, I expect him to ask me out, so I'm shocked when he walks me to my door like a gentleman, kisses my cheek, and tells me he'll see me soon.

When I walk inside, Blakely is still awake, studying. She gushes about her evening with Keegan and how well it went telling Zane he's his dad. He also mentioned he wants to get to know her as more than Zane's mom. After we chat for a few minutes, I jump in the shower and drop into bed exhausted. When I plug my phone in to charge it, I notice a text from Kolton.

Kolton: Good night and sweet dreams.

I usually ignore his texts, afraid to open that door, but tonight, I reply: **Good night.**

The rest of the week feels as if it's in fast-forward. I'm working every day—between managing the restaurant, manning the bar, and running interviews. Kolton shows up every day, but he no longer asks me out. He eats and drinks and grades papers. When I'm not busy, we chat about everything and nothing. I have to admit I miss his flirting, but I also enjoy getting to know him without feeling like there's an agenda.

By Friday, I'm convinced Kolton is over asking me out, and the only reason he continues to frequent The Orange Sunrise is for its iced tea and salad.

But then, right after my sister asks me to join her on Saturday to meet Keegan's parents, a text comes in from Kolton, making it clear where he stands.

Heard you're joining us for lunch. If it were up to me, you'd be coming as my girlfriend and not as my brother's baby momma's sister, but I still look forward to spending the day with you nonetheless... Next time, though, you'll be visiting as mine.

Me: I *think* that was romantic... in a creepy sort of way.

Kolton: Are you saying you miss my flirting?

Me: ....

Kolton: I'll take that as a yes.

So, he has been making it a point not to flirt with me.

I set my phone down, but then my curiosity gets the best of me.

Me: Why haven't you been flirting?

Kolton: Wow, so you really do miss it, huh?

Me: That's not what I asked.

My phone suddenly rings, and Kolton's name flashes across the screen. "Hello?"

"You okay?"

"Um... yeah."

"Just checking. It's hard to tell through text. You seemed very distraught over me not flirting with you all week."

"Hardly. I was just wondering what changed."

"I was waiting for you."

"For me?"

"To realize you miss my flirting."

Motherfucker... Of course! He used reverse psychology... because he's a freaking psychology major.

"I'm hanging up now."

"No, wait," he says through a laugh, but I don't. After hanging up, I go one step further and turn my phone off. Let him psychoanalyze that!

It's Saturday morning, and the five of us are piled into Keegan's truck on our way to meet their parents. Blakely is droning on about how nervous she is to meet Keegan's parents while he reassures her everything will be fine. I shouldn't be nervous since I'm only coming along as moral support for my sister, but I can't help the anxiety attacking my belly. I'm about to meet Kolton's parents. I haven't been around any parents in years. After ours died—and shortly after our grandma died—we were put into foster care. One woman was nice, but she was more like a roommate than a mom... From that moment forward, it was Blakely and me against the world.

"Mom will be so happy to have Zane there. She won't care about anyone else," Keegan promises her.

"And add to that Blakely and Sierra." Kolton snorts. "She always says she wishes she'd had a daughter. Now she's getting two-for-one."

He looks over at me and winks, and my heart bottoms out in my stomach. Has Kolton told his parents about me? If he hasn't, will I be disappointed? Will they think I'm good enough for their son?

My thoughts are still running rampant when we pull up to the most adorable gray and white house. It's nothing like the over-the-top home Blakely and I grew up in... and I love it.

I unbuckle Zane from his booster seat and then climb out, taking it all in. In the front of the house there are flower beds containing beautiful multicolored flowers spread out across the front of a cute wraparound porch with cozy-looking rocking chairs. The entire scene in front of me screams homemade apple pies and family dinners, and it warms my icy heart.

Distracted by my thoughts, I don't notice Kolton come up behind me until his lips graze the outer shell of my ear.

"You must be exhausted," he murmurs.

"What?" I ask, snapping my gaze from the house to him. "Why would I be exhausted?"

Kolton smirks devilishly, and I know whatever he says next will be something flirty. "Because you were running through my mind all night."

I can't help the snort-laugh that bubbles out of me. He has got to be the cheesiest guy I know, and somehow it only adds to his charm.

He takes my hand in his and guides me into his house. When we enter the house, the sweetest woman comes rushing over to us. She makes a beeline straight for Blakely and envelops her in the warmest motherly hug.

"My son has told me so much about you. I'm so happy I get to finally meet you." She pulls back slightly to assess Blakely. "You're gorgeous." She smiles sweetly, then glances over at me. "You both are." Barely releasing Blakely, she says to me, "Come here," and pulls me into their hug. My insides melt at her touch, not realizing how much I've craved this. Even when our parents were alive, our mother never hugged us like this.

"I hate what happened with you and Keegan," she murmurs to Blakely. "Him losing your number and you girls having to take care of my grandson alone all these years."

Tears prick my sister's eyes, but I try to remain strong.

"It's okay," Blakely tells her.

"Well, I can promise you that you will never be alone again. You have all of us now. I'm so excited to be a grandma," she gushes. "Anything you need, you just let me know."

"Thank you, Mrs. Reynolds."

"Oh, no! You call me Larissa, or Mom, whichever." She winks. "And this here is my other half." She waves her husband over.

"I'm Paul," Keegan's dad says with a friendly smile. He looks like an older version of Keegan and Kolton, right down to the dimples. "It's very nice to meet you." His eyes meet mine. "Both of you."

The early morning turns into afternoon as we eat and talk and laugh the day away. After lunch, the guys go fishing while Blakely, Larissa, and I go shopping. The entire day I can see the emotions splayed across my sister's features. She doesn't know what to do or how to act. This is new for both of us. But I can see in her eyes that she's so damn happy. Zane not only has a mother and a father, but he now has an entire family, which only solidifies my decision. Kolton and I can never be anything more because if, or when, it doesn't work out, everything would be awkward. My sister and nephew deserve to have this family, and I won't be the reason they risk losing it.

Later, when we get home, I send a text to Kolton before I lose my courage: **I'm sorry, but we can't be anything more than friends. We're family now, and that's the way it has to stay.**

He sends a response back immediately: **If I believed for a second you really felt that way, I would accept that, but I know you're scared. Sorry, Sierra, but I disagree. We can and will be more… It's only a matter of time.**

chapter five

Sierra

"I'M RUNNING OUT TO GET COFFEE. WANT ANYTHING?" I ASK Monica as she throws her apron around her waist, ready for the start of her shift.

"Nope! I'm good."

"All right. I'll be back!"

"Or you can go home and start your weekend early."

That sounds nice… but at the same time, I need to get a bunch of stuff done before I'm off for the next three days.

I rush out of the restaurant, needing my caffeine fix, and run straight into Kolton.

"What are you doing here?" I ask, not confused that he's here—he's been here every night this week—but that he's here this early. He usually arrives in time for dinner and stays until closing, then insists on giving me a ride home.

"I have Fridays off. I usually spend the day doing schoolwork or grading papers. My brother told me you were working this morning… Are you off already?"

"I'm taking a coffee break."

"How long do you have?"

"Technically, however long I want… I'm not on the schedule to-day. Why, what's up?"

"I want to talk to you." He walks over to his motorcycle and pulls something out of the saddlebag. "For you," he says, handing me a helmet—this one is different from the one I wore the other night. It's lighter and has a cute black and pink design on the back.

My heart swells behind my rib cage, and I know I'm screwed. "Did you buy this for me?"

"Of course. You're going to need your own helmet since I plan to have you on the back of my bike every chance I get." He nods toward the helmet in my hand. "The guy said women prefer that design because it's easier on their hair."

He gets on his bike, leaving me momentarily frozen. I mentioned to him that the helmet ruined my hair, so he went out and bought one that wouldn't. Jesus, this man is something else. How am I supposed to resist him when he says and does all the right things?

After a few seconds, I hop on, pushing my helmet on my head and wrapping my arms around him. We head east, riding in silence and enjoying the view around us. About thirty minutes later, he turns on to Ocean Ave, the road that runs north and south along the Atlantic Ocean. The breeze from the ocean picks up, and I snuggle closer to Kolton, trying to get warm. He smells clean with a hint of sweetness, like laundry detergent mixed with vanilla.

Eventually, he pulls into a deserted parking lot that overlooks the beach and parks his bike, turning the engine off.

"It's beautiful out here." I inhale a deep breath, feeling immediately rejuvenated. Something about being at the beach, smelling the salty air, and listening to the crashing waves instantly calms my nerves, making me feel like a new person.

"Yeah, it is," Kolton agrees. "I like to come out here when I need somewhere to be alone and think."

"About what?" I ask, wanting to know more even though I shouldn't.

He slides off his bike and takes my hand to help me off. With our fingers intertwined, we walk down to the water. It's a cloudy day, the norm here in Florida, but the sun is shining enough that it probably won't rain until later.

Kolton drops to the ground and pulls me down with him so we're sitting side by side. After sitting like this for a few minutes, he finally speaks. "A few years back, my older brother Keith was killed… and it was my fault. I was young and dumb, and my actions led to my brother's death." He releases a shaky breath, and I swallow down my shock, waiting for him to continue.

"Afterward, I took off, left the country to study abroad. I couldn't be around my family, couldn't handle the weight of knowing they all lost someone they loved because of me. I was only gone about a year before my brother convinced me to come back. Our mom was missing me, and he was pissed that my leaving meant she lost two of her sons. So, I returned. It was hard to be back at first and face everyone… When it would get to be too much, I would hop on my bike, which was Keith's, and go for a ride. I ended up here one night and spent hours staring out at the water. It felt as if all that weight I was carrying ran into the water and was washed away."

"I feel the same way. When we were little, our parents used to bring us here every year for vacation. No matter what was going on, once I was at the beach, with my toes in the sand and the sun beating down on my face, it was as if everything else momentarily faded away."

Kolton takes my hand in his and brings it up to his lips, placing a kiss on my knuckles. When he lowers our hands, he keeps our fingers locked together.

"I lost my parents," I admit. "When Blakely and I were teenagers. We were in a car accident, and by some miracle, even though both our parents died, we survived. It's not the same as what you went through, but I just want you to know in my own way, I kind of get it." Kolton squeezes my hand. When I glance over at him, he's staring out at the water, deep in thought.

After a few minutes, he speaks. "Since I've returned, I've been on a mission to prove myself. To prove that my brother's death wasn't in vain… To prove that, even though nothing I do will bring him back, I'm living up to what he would've wanted for me. I'm in school, getting my master's. I've been working hard on my relationships with my parents and Keegan, but somewhere along the way, I didn't focus on me. Maybe it's because I didn't believe I deserved to be happy, or I was directing my attention on other stuff… I don't know."

His eyes meet mine, and at this moment, I've never felt so in sync with another person as I do with Kolton. I feel everything he's saying down to my core. And because of that, without second-guessing myself, I give him a piece of myself I've never given anyone else—not even Blakely.

"My parents were twenty years apart in age," I begin. "My mom was seventeen when she met my dad. She was an orphan, never had any kind of real love, and he offered it to her on a silver platter, so she took it. In his own weird, twisted way, I know he loved my mom, but he also loved to be in power, to control things and people, and my mom was easily controlled.

"Growing up, to someone standing on the outside, Blakely and I had the perfect life. The huge house, expensive clothes...Our father ran a successful company. We went to a prestigious private school. Our mom attended charity brunches while we were in school and followed him around all over the globe when he needed her to. She was the perfect trophy wife while we were raised by nannies.

"But in reality, it was all a façade. Our dad made bad decision after bad decision. He ran up debt and took risks he shouldn't have. He was involved in illegal activity that, we found out later, he would've been sent to jail for. He kept our mom on a short leash, and when she misbehaved, he hurt her..." I shiver, remembering walking out of my room to get a drink and overhearing him yell at her just before he slapped her across the face. That was the first time I saw him lay his hands on her—and it wasn't the last.

"My mom should've left him, but she was so freaking in love with him... or maybe she was in love with the idea of him, I don't know. Either way, in the end, when he knew his life was about to go up in flames, instead of protecting us from the heat, instead of protecting *her*, he threw us straight into the fire. He found out she was going to take us and run, and he drove drunk, flat out saying he wouldn't live without her, right before he plowed us into a pole, killing them both."

Kolton sucks in a sharp breath. "Jesus, Sierra, I don't even know what to say..."

"There's nothing to say. Just like there's nothing I can say about your brother's death. We can say we're sorry, but we both know that word is useless. It doesn't change anything. Horrible things happen that are out of our control, but it's how we react to them that defines us. And how I handled shit after my parents died was horrible. I pushed my sister away and made her feel as if I didn't love her anymore. We were best friends, and I abandoned her. I was so hurt by what happened… afraid to love again… to be vulnerable. My mom gave my dad everything. Every bit of her. She made him her priority even though she had us, and in the end, her love and devotion to him killed her."

"Sierra—" Kolton starts, but I cut him off, needing to get it all out.

"When Blakely found out she was pregnant, she was terrified. And the day we heard Zane's heartbeat, I realized how badly I messed up. I didn't even know about Keegan. She should've been able to come to me, but she didn't. She considered giving Zane up because she didn't think she had any other choice, and my heart broke. I vowed that day to make it up to her. All the years I spent pushing her away, I would make it right."

"And that's why you work at a restaurant you hate, to pay all the bills so your sister could keep Zane and get her degree."

"Yeah," I breathe, staring out at the ocean. "It's more than that, though. Blakely never gave up on me, and now it's my turn to be there for her. And if I date you and we don't work out, I could risk her happiness. Did you see how ecstatic she was to give Zane more family?"

"I understand how important your sister is to you because I feel the same way about my brother, but it doesn't mean you can't find your own slice of happiness."

"True…" I turn my head to look at him. "But it can't be with you. I feel the connection between us, the spark, the chemistry, and I don't want to end up like my mom. She loved my dad with all of her being, and in the end, her love for him killed her."

Kolton reaches over and pulls me onto his lap, so I'm straddling his thighs. With both hands, he cups the sides of my face. "I know firsthand how easily a single choice can affect someone else's life, and I would never purposely put you in danger. If you give me your heart, Sierra, I promise to always protect it, handle it with care, and provide the love it needs to thrive. After my brother died, I didn't think I deserved to find love or be happy, but then I walked into that bar. With just one look at you, I knew I needed you in my life. The way you danced behind the bar reminded me of how carefree my brother was, and when your eyes glittered with mischief, I swear, it was as if he sent you to me."

"Kolton." I gasp. "You can't say that. I can't possibly live up to those expectations..."

"It's the truth, and the only expectation I have is for you to give us a chance. To see if things can be as good as I believe they can be."

"And if it doesn't work out between us?"

"You have my word that no matter what happens, I will make sure our families are never affected." He glides his hands down the curve of my neck and across my shoulder to land on my hip. "Please, just give us one chance. We've both been through hell, and we deserve to find a bit of happiness, especially since your sister and my brother have found it."

Well, hell, how do I say no to that? "Okay, I'll give us a chance. We'll start with one date and see where it goes from there. When?"

Kolton's face splits into the most gorgeous two-dimple grin. "Tonight, so you don't have time to back out."

I laugh. "We're already out." I run my hands up his shoulders and snake them around his neck.

"No way." He shakes his head. "I want a real date. One where I pick you up and take you out."

"Fine. Tonight it is. I'm watching Zane for Keegan tomorrow night. He's taking Blakely away for the night."

"Perfect." He moves his hands around to the globes of my ass and lifts us both into a standing position. "Better get you back to work. You've taken a helluva break."

"Actually, you can take me home." I pull out my phone and text Sonora—the owner of The Orange Sunrise and my boss—to let her know I won't be back in.

The ride home is different than the other rides we've taken, and I know it's because there's been a shift between us. I've given in, and by doing so, I've lowered the wall I had erected. In turn, Kolton feels less tense, as if my agreeing to go out with him has relaxed him.

Like the gentleman he is, he walks me to the door when we arrive at my place. Only, instead of saying goodbye, he gently pushes me against the wall. With one hand next to my head and the other gripping my hip, he leans in and brushes his lips against my cheek.

"You won't regret this," he murmurs into my ear, causing a shiver to race up my spine. "I can feel it. It's going to be so damn good."

He kisses the shell of my ear and then backs up. "I'll see you in a few hours."

chapter six

Kolton

"WHAT'S SO IMPORTANT THAT YOU COULDN'T TEXT ME OR tell me over the phone?" Keegan asks when I walk through the door. I've been meaning to talk to him about something, but he's been at Blakely's more than he's been home lately.

"We need to talk." I drop my briefcase on the couch and sit at the table where Keegan types away on his laptop.

"Yeah, I gathered that. So, what's up?"

"I ran into Blakely and that asshole Brenton the other day… He had her pinned against the wall."

Keegan's head snaps up, giving me his full attention. "In what way?"

"Like he was threatening her or some shit. I couldn't hear what was being said, but Blakely looked scared. She tried to play it off, but I got a weird vibe. Something isn't right."

"No, it's not," Keegan agrees. "I just need a little more time, and that fucker is going down."

"Good. That guy is bad news."

"I heard about your date tonight." Keegan smirks, changing the subject. "She finally gave in, huh?"

"Yeah, now I just need to find a way to keep her."

"I'll be staying at Blakely's tonight, so you have the place to yourself."

"I already told you I'm not going to rush shit."

"Yeah, yeah. Anyway, it'll be empty. Just make sure she's home by early afternoon tomorrow. She's watching Zane for me so I can take Blakely away." He waggles his brows and stands. "I just came home to handle a couple of things. I'm heading back over to

Blakely's. Guess I'll see you later." He winks, and I chuck a pillow at his annoying ass.

I spend the afternoon attempting to grade papers, but eventually, I give up when the only thing I can think about is Sierra and what I'm going to do for our date tonight. I could take her to the same restaurant I had reservations at the night Keegan found out about Zane, and she bailed, but that feels like bad luck.

No, I need something different—special.

And then an idea hits.

chapter seven

Sierra

I'M IN THE BATHROOM, APPLYING THE LAST TOUCH OF MAKEUP TO MY face, when the sound of someone knocking reverberates through the small apartment. *Shit! Is it already six o'clock*? A few moments later, Zane squeals in delight. Words are spoken, but they're muffled, and then the pitter-patter of his feet gets louder and louder until he ends up in the bathroom with me.

"Uncle Kolton's here," he says, stopping in front of me. "He said he's taking you on a date." His nose scrunches up in disgust. "Are you going to kiss him like Mommy kisses Daddy?"

"Mayybbbeeee," I taunt.

"Ewww. Kissing is gross! Girls have cooties!"

"What?" I gasp. "Are you saying I'll give you cooties if I kiss you right now?"

I widen my eyes, and Zane shrieks, knowing what's coming. Before he can dart out the door, I pick him up by his waist and pull him into my arms, raining kisses all over his face.

"Auntie Sierra, stop!" he yells through his giggles as I walk us out to the living room, not stopping my assault on his face until we arrive.

When we reach the living room, I drop him to the ground, stifling my laughter at all the lipstick kisses I left all over his face that he doesn't know about.

"Yuck!" Zane complains, wiping his mouth, the only spot I didn't actually kiss. "Uncle Kolton, you better be careful. Girls have cooties."

"Hey," Blakely says, mock hurt in her tone. "I don't have cooties."

"I know that," Zane agrees. "Because you're not a girl. You're a mom."

Kolton and Keegan both chuckle under their breath.

"I'll be careful, bud," Kolton says, "but if she tries to kiss me, I might have to risk getting cooties."

Zane gives him an incredulous look as if he can't believe Kolton would even consider such a thing. "I'm gonna watch the *SpongeBob* movie with my daddy and mommy." He shrugs and heads over to the couch to get comfortable.

"All right," Keegan says, his tone serious. "Curfew is eleven. No drinking and driving, and remember... no glove, no love." He whips a condom out of his pocket and throws it at Kolton.

"Oh my God, Keegan!" Blakely smacks him in the chest. "Go make us some popcorn." She pushes him toward the kitchen. "Have fun, guys!"

"But not too much fun!" Keegan calls back as they disappear.

Once they're gone, my attention turns to Kolton. He's dressed in a forest green, short-sleeved collared shirt that shows off the ink on his forearms and biceps, a pair of nice blue jeans, and black dress shoes. His wrist holds a chunky silver watch. He's shaved since I saw him earlier, leaving only enough to be considered a five o'clock shadow, and when he steps closer, I smell a light scent of vanilla mixed with woods.

"You look beautiful, Sierra. Fucking gorgeous." His words are softly spoken, so Zane can't hear. "That dress..." He rakes his eyes down my body, sending goose bumps along my flesh. "I think I made a mistake."

"What? Why?" I breathe. He asked for this date over and over again, and now he's not sure? I don't understand. Is it what I'm wearing? I glance down at myself. I went with a pale pink floaty dress and a pair of knee-high suede boots since I wasn't sure if he would be picking me up on his motorcycle.

"I wanted you all to myself, so I planned to take you back to my place, but seeing you dressed like this with your makeup and hair done... It feels like it's a damn waste not to take you out and show you off." He runs his fingers along the edge of my dress where it meets my collarbone, and the area between my legs clench in sudden need. It's been a hot minute since I've been looked at and appreciated like Kolton's doing right now.

"C'mon, Romeo." I hook my arm in his. "I promise you this dress will *not* go to waste."

As suspected, Kolton drove his bike over here. He climbs on, and I follow. Because the bottom of my dress is flowy, I'm able to sit behind him without exposing myself to the entire town of Carterville. But when Kolton takes off, and his hand lands on the exposed flesh of my thigh, I couldn't care less about the town or the people or anyone besides Kolton.

With my body up against his, my center rubs against his lower back, causing friction. The sensation causes my nipples to pebble through my thin bra and dress, and I tighten my legs, wondering if Kolton can sense how turned on I am.

All too quickly, we arrive at his place. He places his hand in mine to help me off the bike, and the sparks between us flow like a live electrical current.

"This is it," he says, closing the door behind us. "I made dinner. Are you hungry?" My eyes meet his, and I know he's feeling what I'm feeling. The thick sexual tension. The desire to touch each other. The need to be close to each other. But this is only our first date. You don't have sex on the first date, right?

"I'm starving," I say, my voice breathy.

His brows rise, understanding my double innuendo. "Good. I am too." Lacing our fingers, he walks us to the dining room. The lights are dim, and table is set with beautiful-looking china. In the center, he turns on two electric candles to illuminate the room along with a bottle of wine.

He releases my hand and uncorks the wine, pouring us each a glass. "To our first date," he says with a sexy grin, making my insides turn to mush.

"To us," I agree. We clink our glasses, and he throws his back like a shot, his Adam's apple bobbing as he swallows. A fantasy of me licking down each ridge of his throat and sucking on his flesh hits me hard.

It suddenly feels hot in here, so I down my own glass and grab the bottle to pour myself some more.

"You okay?" he asks, his tone more knowing than concerned.

"Yeah," I breathe. "Just… hot." I lift my hair to emphasize my point, but since the burning ache comes from inside me, it does nothing to put the flames out.

Kolton steps closer, and the air thickens, making it hard to breathe, to function, to think clearly. "I can see the look on your face," he murmurs. "The flush creeping up your neck… I can see the way your squeezing your thighs together… And if I were any less of a gentleman, I would act on it. I would pull that dress up to your waist and pull your underwear down your thighs, and then I would ravish every inch of your body until you begged me to make you come. But I didn't bring you back here to fuck you, and if I do just that, you're going to think I did. And like I told you before, Sierra, I want you long term. Not for the night or the weekend… I want you forever. So, instead of letting my dick call the shots, I'm going to grab our dinner warming in the kitchen, and we're going to eat and talk."

"Okay," I say, swallowing thickly. He turns to leave, but before he does, I grab his arm, making him turn back to look at me. "But let's say I wanted to think with my pussy…"

Kolton groans. "Sierra…"

"Would you fuck me?" I wrap my arms around his neck. I don't know what the hell has gotten into me, and I really don't care. Maybe it's stupid, and maybe it's crazy, but with Kolton, it feels right. I've spent the past five years focused on Blakely and Zane, hooking up with guys I knew I didn't have a future with so I wouldn't have to worry about catching feelings. But with Kolton, I know he's the one. It's the reason I've pushed him away. I was scared. But I'm not anymore. I want him now.

In me, on top of me, all over me.

"Would you take me right here on the table? Make me scream your name?"

Kolton's answer is to lift me into his arms and lay me on top of the table. The china clinks, and some of it might even land on the floor, but neither of us cares enough to look.

His mouth crashes against mine, his tongue plunging past my parted lips, capturing and swirling with my own. My legs wrap around his waist, my center grinding against his already growing erection.

"Fuck," he hisses against my mouth as I reach for his pants, unbuttoning and unzipping them. I push his briefs down and feel his dick spring free.

"Sierra," he moans, breaking our kiss when I wrap my fist around his shaft and stroke it up and down. "It wasn't supposed to happen like this." He runs his thumb along my swollen lips. "I was supposed to wine and dine you. Convince you to go on a second and third date with me."

"Didn't you say what's between us is inevitable? That we're forever?"

"And you said you were scared."

"And I am," I admit. "But I also feel it... what you feel. And I'm done living my life in fear." I latch onto his shirt and tug him toward me so our bodies are flush with only my hand wrapped around his dick between us. "If we crash and burn, then at least I can say it was a hell of a ride."

He stares at me for a long beat, and I wonder if he's going to push me away and tell me we're going too fast. I hold my breath, hoping he does neither.

"It will definitely be a hell of a ride," he growls. "But nobody is getting hurt." His mouth fuses with mine. He bites, sucks, and nibbles on my lips.

We're all teeth and tongue.

Hands touching and caressing.

Needing and wanting.

As if neither of us can get enough.

He pulls my dress up my body and unlatches my bra, exposing my breasts to the cool air. He wraps his lips around my nipple, and his tongue lashes back and forth across the hardened tip. Bolts of electricity spark inside me as if he has a direct line to my clit.

"Kolton," I moan, pumping his cock harder. Squeezing it in desperation.

He kisses his way down my middle, and when he gets to my belly, I lose my connection with his dick. He presses an open-mouthed kiss to the top of my silk-covered mound before he tugs my panties off, dropping them onto the floor.

"I need to taste you," he murmurs, licking his lips as he spreads my thighs wide open.

He drops to his knees, and his eyes glint in the darkness. His thumb and middle finger spread my folds open, and his forefinger strokes my center up and down, teasing my clit. "I bet you taste better than what I made for dinner." He looks up at me. "What do you think?"

I'm not sure if I'm supposed to respond, but it doesn't matter because when the flat of his tongue lands on my center, I'm rendered speechless. My hands fist the edge of the wood table as Kolton devours my pussy like a starved man. He works me up, licking and sucking on my clit, bringing me to the brink of my orgasm before his mouth leaves my pussy.

"What the hell!" I hiss, my chest rising and falling in quick succession.

"I was right. You taste fucking delicious." Standing, he reaches behind him to pull his shirt over his head. As it rises, each of his cut abs makes an appearance until he's displayed his entire upper body. He's all ink and muscle and—

Holy shit! He drops his pants and briefs, and his dick juts out. Thick and veiny with a tiny bead of pre-cum dripping out of the mushroom tip.

"My turn," I breathe, not even caring that I never got my orgasm as I slide off the edge of the table and drop to my knees. I lift his shaft and run my tongue along the velvety smooth flesh. When I get to the top, I lick the saltiness away, swirling my tongue around the angry head, and then take him all the way into my mouth until he bottoms out in the back of my throat. I do this several times, getting his dick nice and wet. He's hard as steel, and I can practically feel him throbbing in need.

Just as I'm taking him back into my mouth, he fists the back of my scalp. I think for a second, he's going to face fuck me, and right now, as turned on as I am, I probably wouldn't mind.

But instead, he gathers my hair and gently pulls my mouth off him, bringing me to a standing position.

"As much as I enjoy your pretty lips wrapped around my dick, I need to be inside you." He lifts me back onto the table, pushes my legs apart, and pulls me to the edge. He reaches down and grabs the condom his brother jokingly gave him and rips it open with his teeth. He rolls it over his shaft and then grabs my thighs, hauling my legs over his forearms.

His lips capture mine as he drives into me hard and deep. We're so close I can feel his heart beating erratically against my own. As if we've become one in every way possible.

His thumb finds my clit, and with a few strokes, I detonate, my climax hitting me hard and fast. Kolton moans into my mouth, and even though he's wearing a condom, I can feel when his orgasm hits him and his warm seed fills the rubber barrier.

Our kiss ends, and he drops his face into the crook of my neck, trying to catch his breath. "You realize what you just did, right?" he asks, lifting his head to look me in the eyes.

"What?"

"You solidified everything I already knew. How good we would be together… How amazing you would feel." He presses his mouth to mine in a quick yet punishing kiss before he pulls back, leaving my head spinning. "You know what this means, right?"

"No… what?"

"You're mine."

chapter eight

Kolton

"IS THAT BOX FROM DUNKY DONUTS?" ZANE ASKS, HIS EYES lighting up.

"Yep." I open the box, just long enough for him to get a peek before I close it. "Go grab some plates."

He rushes into the kitchen, giving me enough time to drop the box on to the table and pull Sierra into my arms for a kiss. "Fuck, I missed you," I mutter against her lips.

"It's only been a few hours." She giggles, peppering me with several quick kisses before stepping back.

"A few hours too many," I whine, fully aware I sound like a child. But in my defense, after spending the night before with Sierra in my bed and me in her all damn night, it was hard to spend last night alone. But she was watching Zane and didn't feel it was appropriate for me to spend the night, so to respect her wishes, after we finished watching *SpongeBob* for the second time, I took off, leaving her to put Zane to bed.

She rolls her eyes. "We spent the night on the phone."

"Yeah, we did." I grin, remembering the phone sex we had. It was hot as fuck, but not the same as the real thing.

"Got 'em!" Zane yells, thrusting the plates at me. "Can I have three?"

"You can have one," Sierra says, opening the box so he can choose the one he wants.

"I'll grab the milk," I offer.

As the three of us sit at the table, eating donuts and drinking our milk, I can't take my eyes off Sierra. She talks and jokes with Zane, laughing and smiling the entire time. She's so attentive and patient with him. My mind goes to what it would be like to have a baby with her, to create a family together.

"What?" she asks when she catches me staring.

"I think I'm falling in love with you." I didn't mean for the words to come out, but fuck it, she already knows I'm obsessed with her.

A blush creeps up her neck. "Kolton…"

"Can I do my puzzle?" Zane asks.

"Yeah," she tells him, her eyes never leaving mine. "Go wash your hands first."

He jumps off the chair and runs down the hallway, leaving us alone.

"I mean it," I say, edging closer into her personal space. "I know it's too soon, but I can't help how I feel."

"I feel it too," she admits. "I'm falling in love with you too. And that should scare the hell out of me, but it doesn't."

"Auntie Sierra! I can't pump the soap," Zane calls out.

Sierra leans over and presses a soft kiss to the corner of my mouth before she gets up to go help Zane. I clean up the mess, and when I go back to check on them, Zane is on the floor in his room, dumping his puzzle out.

"C'mon, Uncle Kolton," he says. "We have to put the million trillion pieces together to make SpongeBob!"

We're putting the last pieces of the pineapple together when the door opens.

"Blakely and Keegan must be back," Sierra says, standing. "I didn't think they were returning until later."

"Go tell them I only have two pieces left," Zane says, his tongue sticking out of the side of his mouth in concentration.

We head out to greet them, and maybe it's brotherly intuition, but something feels off… tense… between them.

"You're back early," Sierra says when we get out to the living room.

Blakely eyes me curiously.

"I didn't spend the night," I tell her, wrapping my arm around Sierra. "Just brought breakfast over. I hope that's okay."

"This is just as much Sierra's home as it is mine," Blakely says with a forced smile plastered on her face. "Of course, you're welcome here."

There's a knock on the door, and Keegan answers it. "Yeah?" he asks, his voice filled with contempt.

"I'm here for Zane," a masculine voice says.

"For what?" Keegan asks.

Brenton steps around him and enters the apartment. "It's the last Sunday of the month." When Blakely looks at him confused, he adds, "Home Depot day."

"Yes! Home Depot day!" Zane yells, running out, fist-pumping the air, and then darting back into his room. A minute later, he comes back out, holding a bright orange apron in his hand. "I'm ready!"

"Ready for what?" Keegan asks, confused.

"On the last Sunday of every month, Brenton takes Zane to Home Depot for their craft day. They make stuff out of wood. Sierra and I usually go get our nails done," Blakely explains.

"Like hell he is," Keegan hisses, turning toward Brenton. "You're not taking my fucking kid anywhere."

Oh shit, this isn't going to end well.

"Daddy, you said a bad word!" Zane giggles, having no idea his dad is about to beat the shit out of his mom's friend.

"Sorry, bud," Keegan says. "Why don't you go play in your room while Mommy and I talk?"

Zane's face falls, but he does as his dad says and goes to his room.

Once he's out of earshot, Keegan and Blakely get into an argument about Brenton taking Zane. Blakely doesn't understand why Keegan isn't okay with it, and Keegan can't explain it to her. I keep my mouth shut the entire time, staying close in case Keegan loses his shit and tries to hit Brenton. I wouldn't blame him, but it would fuck everything up that he's worked his ass off for.

"Fuck this!" Keegan yells, getting into Brenton's face. "Anything happens to Zane, and I'm going to hunt you down and kill you."

"Keegan!" Blakely yells. "Stop it!"

Keegan pushes past Brenton and stalks out the door. Before Blakely can chase after him, I stop her. "Let him go. He just needs to calm down."

I follow him, catching up to him just before he takes off in his truck. "You need to chill the hell out."

"Fuck that!" he barks. "That asshole doesn't belong anywhere near my kid or girlfriend."

"And you're going to make sure that doesn't happen, but in order for you to do that, you need to calm down. Keep that shit up, and you're going to fuck everything up."

He releases a harsh breath. "Dammit, I know you're right, but… fuck!"

"Remember the endgame."

He nods once. "Yeah."

"You going home to calm down?"

"Fuck, no, I'm going to follow his ass."

"Figured." I chuckle, knowing my brother too damn well. "Just don't get caught."

Not wanting to face Sierra right now, I get on my bike and head home. She'll assume I went home with Keegan, which is for the best.

I'm home for about twenty minutes when a text comes in from Sierra: **Blakely is upset. I didn't have a chance to say goodbye. I'm sorry. I know we were planning to hang out today, but I need to be here for my sister. <sad face emoji>**

Me: It's okay. It's a shitty situation.

The next two days are spent with my brother freaking the hell out over the fact that Blakely isn't talking to him. Not wanting to risk being put in a bad position, I keep it neutral when Sierra texts bitching about the situation. It's late, probably ten o'clock, when there's a knock on my door. I'm grading papers and have lost track of time. Having no clue who it could be since Keegan has a key and my parents would call first, I get up to answer the door.

"Who is it?"

"Sierra." Sierra… I swing open the door and find her standing on the other side in a pair of tiny cotton shorts and a matching hoodie. Her hair is up in a messy bun, and her face is free of makeup. She looks gorgeous… and like she just woke up.

"Everything okay?" I open the door wider so she can walk through.

"Yeah," she says, wrapping her arms around me as I close the door behind us. "Keegan showed up tonight. Blakey wasn't home, so he waited for her. They must've made up because the last I heard was her screaming his name before I snuck over here." She leans on her tiptoes and kisses me. "I was thinking we could have a sleepover of our own."

"You sure as hell don't have to tell me twice." I scoop her into my arms bridal style and walk us to my bedroom, dropping her onto the bed. She shrugs out of her hoodie, leaving her in only a tiny tank top and shorts that could be considered underwear.

"Kolton, get over here." She runs her fingers over her belly and lifts her shirt up and over her head, exposing her pert breasts.

I spring into action, pulling my shirt over my head and dropping it onto the floor. I climb onto the bed and spread her legs, situating myself between them. Starting at her feet, I trail kisses along her smooth flesh, inhaling her soft, sweet scent. I make my way up one leg and then switch to the other. The entire time she wriggles in her place, moaning softly. I have no doubt she becomes wetter with each kiss I place on her body. I glance up, and her eyes are hooded over with lust, her hands kneading her breasts, her fingers tugging on her nipples.

When I get to the top of her thigh, I yank her shorts down. She's wearing a thin, light-pink cotton thong, and I can tell she's neatly trimmed through the material. I pull them down as well, so she's completely bared to me, and press an open-mouthed kiss to the top of her pussy, inhaling the sweet signature musk of her arousal.

"Fuck, Sierra. I could live between your legs for the rest of my life and die a happy man."

I spread folds open and insert a single finger to gauge how turned on she is. My digit glides in with ease as her juices coat my skin. I pull it out, then insert two—this time, pushing them in deep until my fingers disappear inside her. Sierra moans in pleasure, squeezing her legs against my shoulders.

"Kolton, I need you," she whines.

"Shh… I'm admiring your perfect pussy." I pull my fingers back out once more, making her huff in annoyance, then insert three fingers, filling her up.

"Oh God, too much." Her head whips from side to side.

I remove my fingers once more and spread her legs wide. Her wetness drips down onto the bed. Which makes me wonder…

"Hey, Sierra."

"What?" she asks, popping her head up slightly.

"Has anyone ever fucked you… here?" I drag her juices downward, circling her puckered hole.

"No," she breathes, a slight blush creeping along her neck.

I wet the area and push my finger past the first ring of her ass, and she groans in pleasure. "More," she begs. "I need… more."

Slowly, I push it all the way in, sending her ass off the bed. I'm fucking entranced by everything that is this woman. I can't take my eyes off her.

With one finger in her ass, I push the other into her pussy. She's tight and wet, and I wish to fucking God my dick was in one of those holes. I finger-fuck both her holes until she's screaming my name, writhing under my touch. Never letting up until she's come down from her orgasm.

"Holy shit," she groans, grabbing my head and tugging me up to her face. My fingers, no doubt covered in her orgasm, slip out of her. "I'm going to need you to fuck me now," she demands, her voice filled with a fiery passion.

Her fingers thread through my hair, and she tugs me down to her. My palms land on either side of her head, caging her in, and our mouths collide in a passionate embrace. Our kiss isn't stemmed from want but from need. I need Sierra in every way, the same way I need to breathe. She's quickly become an integral part of my life.

Our kiss heats up, becoming an inferno of lust and desire. Her legs wrap around my backside, and her warm pussy grinds against my erection. I break our kiss, wanting to taste other parts of her—the shell of her ear, the delicate area just underneath. My tongue glides down the curve of her neck, sucking on her pulse point before nipping her collarbone.

I take her breast into my mouth, pulling on her nipple with my teeth. When she gasps, I release it, licking away the sting of the pain and loving the way her body reacts to mine.

While I give her body attention, licking and sucking and laving at her perfect tits, her hands find my shorts, pushing them down and wrapping her fingers around my shaft. The feel of her stroking my dick sends bolts of electricity through my body.

"I need you," she breathes, sitting up and pushing me onto my ass. She climbs onto me so we're both sitting up, our bodies connected in almost every way. She uses my shoulders to lift, and then she lowers herself onto me, sucking my dick into her heat, inch by inch. She's tight as fuck in this position, and I have to count to five in my head so I don't blow my load before she finds her second release.

She continues to use my shoulders as leverage, bouncing up and down on my dick. I grip the curve of her ass with one hand and find her clit with the other. As she rides me, I rub circles against her clit, using her wetness to create friction.

"Oh God, yes!" she screams. "Right. Fucking. There."

Her body tenses like a stretched bow awaiting release, and then she lets go, exploding around my dick. Her body trembles, her clit throbs, and her head gets thrown back as she rides out wave after wave of pleasure—the sight sending me straight over the edge along with her.

Nobody has ever affected me the way Sierra does, and when I'm with her, all common sense flies out the window, leaving only my need for her.

"I love you," I murmur against her lips, "so fucking much."

chapter nine

Sierra

He loves me… Kolton Reynolds loves me. But does it count when a man says it during sex while he's coming deep inside you?

Oh, shit!

He came inside me.

"Pull out quick!" I screech even though I'm the one on top.

I scramble off him as he looks at me like I'm crazy. "You came inside me."

He tilts his head to the side in confusion. "I'm not on birth control." I had an IUD since the pills make me feel sick, and the shot gives me horrible acne, but I had issues with it, and they had to remove it. Since I wasn't actively having sex, I took a break from all birth control.

It takes Kolton a second to understand what I'm saying, implying, and once he does, I expect him to freak the fuck out. So, I'm taken aback when a huge shit-eating grin spreads across his face. He pushes me onto my back and spreads my thighs.

"Are you telling me that what we just did…" He thrusts a finger into me, making me moan. "Me coming in you…" He leans over me until our faces are only inches apart. "Could lead to you carrying my baby?"

I nod in shock.

His smile grows wider. "I hope it does."

"Kolton!" I smack his shoulder. "Have you lost your damn mind?"

"Maybe," he says, his features sobering. "But for the first time since my brother died, I'm feeling again. You've woken me up, Sierra, and I never want to go back to the shell of a man I was before."

He presses a chaste kiss to my lips. "I meant what I said. I love you. I don't give a shit that it's only been a short time. I know you're the one for me, and if what we've done leads to you being swollen with my baby, then good."

What he's saying should send a signal to my brain, telling me to run fast and far, but the only thought that enters my head is the image of me pregnant with Kolton's baby. Giving birth to our little boy or girl with him by my side. Creating a loving family with him.

It should scare me, but it doesn't. Instead, it leaves me wanting more.

"Where are we going?"

"It's a surprise."

I roll my eyes, acting as though he's annoying even though deep down, I'm excited. It's Valentine's Day weekend, and Kolton surprised me with a long weekend away. He even called my boss and asked her to ensure I was off. I'm shocked she agreed, but it shouldn't surprise me. Kolton is a charmer.

"We're on I-4," I point out, "which means we're going to Orlando."

He chuckles. "You're right, we are, but what are we doing there?" He quirks a brow up and glances over at me.

"Hopefully going somewhere with a bed, so you can fuck me." I run my fingers across his leg and over his crotch, making him chuckle. We've been together for a month now, and the heat between us hasn't cooled at all. When I'm not working, I'm with Kolton, and he's either wooing me or making love to me. I haven't been home much lately, and I haven't spent as much time with Blakely and Zane as I usually do, but I don't feel too bad because I'm with Kolton the same way Blakely's with Keegan.

"That'll definitely happen," Kolton says, scooping up my hand and lacing our fingers together. "But first, I have a little surprise for you that I think you'll enjoy." He gnaws on the corner of his bottom lip, suddenly looking nervous. "At least I hope so."

A little while later, we arrive at the Gaylord Palms, a fancy resort in the heart of Orlando. I've been here before with Blakely and Zane to see their annual Christmas exhibit, but we've never spent the night.

After we get checked in, Kolton asks the woman where the conference is being held. She hands him a sheet of paper and draws some directions for him before giving him our keys.

"We have a few minutes to freshen up, but then we have to head out," he says. "We have somewhere we need to be. Wear something nice." He told me to make sure I included a few nice outfits, but I had assumed it was to go out to dinner—yet it's only ten in the morning.

We step into the room, and it's gorgeous, but what's really cool about it is that the balcony leads to an atrium that makes it feel as though you're outdoors.

I grab a pair of dress pants, a flowy top, and my heels and get dressed in the beautiful bathroom. When I come out, Kolton is wearing a pair of charcoal gray dress slacks that hug his ass, a black long-sleeve button-up, and dress shoes.

With his hand in mine, we walk to the elevator and take it to the first floor. Then we head to the left and walk for a while. The signs point to the convention center, and I remember Kolton asked the woman at the front desk about the conference.

And then I see a sign: The International Restaurant and Foodservice Show.

"Kolt..."

"Surprise."

"What are we doing here?" I pull him to the side. "I'm not a restaurant owner."

"No, but one day you will be. I read about this show. It's where all the top restaurateurs come to discuss the business. Independently owned, franchises... You name it. A guy I know from school who teaches business had some extra tickets. I figured it would be fun. Remind you of what you want, what you can one day have."

Oh, my heart... Tears prick my eyes, making him misunderstand.

"We don't have to—"

"No," I choke out, wiping away a tear. "I want to. This is so thoughtful of you." Even if the chance of me ever buying or starting my own restaurant is equivalent to one winning the lottery. It feels good to have someone think about me… to put me first.

We spend the day meeting a plethora of people in the hospitality industry—from liquor vendors to interior decorators. When the conference ends for the day, I walk away with enough contacts and information to have a great start to opening my own restaurant if I had the money. It also made me see and understand all the ways Sonora is messing up with The Orange Sunrise. It's too bad she didn't attend this conference.

"All right, I think I'm switching from psychology to opening a bar," Kolton says as we walk out of the conference and back to our room.

"It's kind of the same thing," I joke. "All those people drinking at the bar tend to tell their life stories once they're drunk."

Kolton chuckles. "Some even end up falling in love with their bartender." He throws his arm around my shoulders and kisses my temple.

When we get inside our room, he says, "We have reservations for dinner at—"

But before he can finish, my mouth closes over his, desperate to show him how much I appreciate his thoughtfulness this weekend. "We can eat dinner later. Right now, the only thing I'm hungry for is you."

chapter ten

Kolton

"Jesus, these kids can't write for shit." On another paper, I note that the student needs to take time to visit the writing center and then move it to the graded pile. As I'm grabbing the next paper from the pile, my phone rings out in the quiet room. Since Sierra is babysitting Zane today, I'm not expecting it to be her—our nephew is great at keeping whoever he's with busy—so I'm not surprised when Keegan's name appears on my caller ID.

"What's up?" I ask, standing to pour myself another cup of coffee so I can get through the rest of the papers.

"It's over. We found him, and he's behind bars."

"*Him*, as in…"

"Miguel. Turns out he was connected to Brenton. He's been here, right under our nose, the entire time."

I exhale a breath of relief. I've been waiting to hear those words from Keegan for too damn long.

"There was one minor snag," Keegan adds, his tone weary. "Blakely was there when it all went down. She knows I'm an undercover narcotics officer."

Oh, shit… That is not how he wanted to tell her. "How is she?"

"Pissed as fuck. And I don't blame her." He sighs. "I just dropped her off at home. She wants nothing to do with me."

"Just give her time. You were in a shitty position and did the best you could. She'll come around."

"Yeah, I hope so. I need to go back to the station. There's a shit ton of paperwork that needs to get done."

"Does this mean you're moving home now?" Keegan was only living here to play the part of a college student. He actually owns a nice-ass house elsewhere.

"Yeah, I'll be back tonight to pack my shit."

"Hey, Keegan…"

"Yeah?"

"Thank you."

"You're welcome." We're both silent for a beat before he adds, "Blakely doesn't know the whole story… or really any of it. Can you let me tell her, please? I would rather it come from me. I had to keep it all a secret so I didn't compromise the investigation."

"Of course."

We hang up, and I call Sierra, knowing she's going to pissed. She and Blakely are two sides of a coin. And even though I technically never lied to her—and I made sure I didn't—omitting the truth is still lying. When she doesn't answer, I send her a text that I need to talk to her. She doesn't reply.

I consider going to her place, but I don't want to push too hard, so instead, I try to finish grading the papers, which ends up taking twice as long as it normally would since I can't focus for shit. The longer my phone call and text goes unanswered, the deeper the sinking feeling in the pit of my stomach goes.

Just when I'm about to say fuck it and go to Sierra's place to explain my side, my phone rings.

"Please, let me explain," I beg when I answer her call.

"Explain that your brother is an undercover cop who was investigating Brenton, and instead of telling my sister, he let her continue to hang out with him and put her and Zane in harm's way? I already know."

"There's more to it than that."

"You and Keegan lied and kept important shit from us," she says, her voice resigned. "That's exactly what my dad did, and it's exactly what I was afraid of happening to me." No. No. *No, No, No…*

"It is not the same thing."

"My sister could've had Zane taken away!" she yells, her voice filled with heartache. Heartache I inadvertently caused. "And for what? So your brother could catch a drug dealer? He put his job above his family, just like our dad did, and you sat back and watched it all happen!"

"No. Keegan was watching them. He was following them everywhere. He never would've let anything happen to them. Please, you have to trust me."

"It doesn't change the fact that you lied and kept things from me, and now, I can't trust you," she says, her voice cracking with emotion. "I don't know what'll happen between Keegan and my sister, but as for us… we're over."

She hangs up on me, and I want to call her back, beg her to listen, to see reason. I want to go over there and make her understand why he did what he did. But I can't do any of that until Keegan talks to Blakely.

Shit! I slam my phone on the table. Will the domino effect of my choices back then ever come to a stop?

"How are things with you and Sierra?" Keegan asks at breakfast three days later.

"Not good. I can't really do much when I can't tell her the entire story."

Keegan flinches. "Shit, I'm sorry. I didn't even consider that. Look," he says, taking a sip of his coffee. "If you want to tell Sierra, you can, but if you can ask her to please let me tell Blakely, I would appreciate it."

"Thanks," I say, standing and patting him on the shoulder. "I'm not sure if she'll even hear me out, but I appreciate it."

"Brenton got out on bail. I'm going to head over to campus to make sure he doesn't fuck with Blakely."

"He shouldn't even be on campus."

"Doesn't mean he won't be."

Ten minutes later, my brother and I arrive on campus and walk toward the psychology building when I spot none other than Brenton and Blakely in a heated argument in the quad.

"Fuck!" Keegan yells, ready to charge over and lay Brenton out.

"Stop! Let me handle it. You don't want to take a chance of getting into it with Brenton and fucking up the case. Call for backup."

"They're already on campus." He yanks out his phone, no doubt to give them the location of where we are while he steps into the shadows so nobody sees him.

I stalk over to Brenton and Blakely. "You need to get the hell away from her right fucking now," I yell at Brenton, who's now in Blakely's face.

"I was just talking to her," Brenton says.

"And now you're not." I step between them. "Walk away."

"The only place I'm walking to is class," Brenton points out.

"Actually, you're not. You obviously haven't checked your email. You've been withdrawn from your classes and expelled from this university."

"You can't fucking do that!" Brenton roars, making Blakely jump in fear.

"It's already been done. If you want to argue about it, speak to the dean." I take Blakely's hand, needing to get her away from Brenton before Keegan flips his shit. "Let's go," I murmur as we round the corner to where Keegan and two other officers are standing.

"You were here the whole time?" she asks Keegan.

"Of course," Keegan says. "But I know you want your space." He shrugs. "I told you you'd be safe no matter what and that someone would be on you."

"Thank you."

I'm distracted the entire time in class, but I still somehow manage to get through the lecture. Once class is dismissed, I head out to The Orange Sunrise, needing to speak to Sierra since Keegan is okay with me telling her everything.

chapter eleven

Sierra

I feel him before I see him. Kolton. The man I've fallen in love with. I've been thinking about him every second of every minute since I hung up on him. The tiny hairs on the back of my neck rise, and my belly tightens in anticipation as I watch him walk over to where I'm standing at the hostess stand.

"I can't wait any longer," he says. "I've tried to give you your space. I get it. The entire situation sucks, but I can't just let you walk away. Not like this… hell, not ever."

Kolton's jaw tightens, and his eyes shine with unshed tears, and it's then I see how badly he looks. Dark circles under his eyes, his normally tan complexion pasty. He's been suffering right along with me.

"Paula, please make sure you keep all takeout receipts tonight. I'm heading out. If you need anything, Sonora will be in soon."

Like everyone else does when I mention Sonora, she rolls her eyes. "See you tomorrow."

I grab my purse from behind the hostess stand and walk outside with Kolton following. Not wanting to have this conversation on the streets, I walk over to his bike. "Want to go to your place and talk?"

"Yeah," he says, his voice cracking.

The ride to his apartment is quick, but as I sit behind him with my arms wrapped around his torso and my face nestled against his back, I wish we could ride for longer.

We walk inside his place, and it looks different… I can't quite place it.

"Keegan moved out, so his messy ass shit isn't all over the place," Kolton says, answering my unspoken thoughts. "He's planning to ask Blakely to move in with him." He sits on the couch and scrubs his palms over his face.

"I doubt she'll be on board with that." I sit across from him on the loveseat.

"With Brenton out on bail, he's hoping she'll put aside her hurt and do what's best for her and Zane's safety. Brenton's already approached her once, and I had to intervene."

"What?" I shriek. "When? She didn't tell me."

He sighs, exhaustion evident in his features. "This morning... But I don't want to talk about them. I want to talk about us."

"I don't know what there's to talk about. You lied and hid shit, and I can't be with someone like that. You knew about what my father did, yet—"

His eyes lock with mine. "That's such bullshit!" he barks, making me jump. He cuts across the area to where I am, kneels in front of me, and frames my face with his palms. "It's not fair for you to compare what happened to what your dad did. You said it yourself when the fire caught, he threw you guys into it. Keegan, on the other hand, was in that fucking fire doing everything he could to fight it so Blakely and Zane wouldn't be touched. He's been fighting that fire for fucking years."

"Years?" I knew Brenton sold drugs in high school, but why would it have taken Keegan that long to put him away?

Kolton sighed. "There's something you need to know, but I need you to keep it between us until Keegan speaks with Blakely. He wants to be the one to explain it to her."

"Great. More secrets. If you're not supposed to tell me, then don't." I stand, and Kolton stands with me. "I don't know why I even came here." *Liar! You came here because you love him and miss him and need him to make it right because even though what he did was wrong, you can't imagine your life without him.*

"Sierra." He grabs my hips and tugs me toward him. "You came here because you love me, and despite how hurt you are, you know that whatever happened was done to protect you and your sister and Zane. You can try to push me away to protect your heart, but you know I would never do anything to hurt you."

Jesus, it's like he has insight into my head and heart...

One of his hands glides up my side and cups my cheek. "I love you so goddamn much, and even though I hate how you and Blakely found out, I wouldn't change a single thing because what Keegan did was to protect the three of you." He swallows thickly. "And..." Tears well up in his eyes and then tip over, racing down his face. "He did it for me too."

My heart tightens in my chest. I don't understand what he means, but I can feel it in his words and in the way he's touching me. In the way he's looking at me. How upset he is over all of this. He means what he's saying, and he's right. He's not my father. He's nothing like him, and it's not fair to compare Kolton to him.

"I'll tell you everything..."

"No," I breathe. "I... I trust you," I choke out. "I was shocked and scared, and I felt so damn stupid. But you're right, you aren't my father. Neither you nor Keegan are. And yes, I do love you. So, even though I'm upset, I'm not going anywhere. I want to be with you. Whatever the reason Keegan did what he did, and your family supported him, I believe you. That it was done, not to throw us into the fire, but to save us from it."

Kolton sighs a breath of relief, and then shocks the hell out of me with his next words. "Move in with me. I don't want to be without you. I don't want to wake up or go to bed without you. I want to spend my life with you. I wanted to ask you weeks ago, but with Keegan here and everything going on, I didn't want to ask you while hiding shit from you."

"Technically, you're still hiding things from me," I sass.

He nods. "Only because you don't want to lie to your sister. Otherwise, I would tell you everything now."

"I want to move in with you." Kolton's eyes go wide in surprise. "But I need to speak to Blakely first and see how she feels. If she doesn't forgive Keegan—"

"She will," Kolton says. "I know she will. They love each other, and when you love someone like that, you don't throw in the towel that easily."

I nod in agreement. "I can't move out if she isn't taken care of. I pay the bills, so she needs me."

"You can keep paying them." Kolton presses his lips to mine. "I'll take care of everything. In May, I'm graduating, and if all goes as planned, I'll be working at the college full-time. I can afford to pay our bills. I just want you in my bed with me every night."

"I want that too," I murmur against his mouth. "I just need a little time."

"Off work today?" Blakely asks when she and Zane walk through the door. I was technically off, but like always, I had to go in and take care of shit. I considered going back after Kolton and I talked, but instead, I came home so I could wait for Blakely.

"Yeah, I spoke to Kolton. He said Brenton approached you. How are you doing?"

"I'm okay." She pauses and glances at Zane. "Hey, sweetie, go potty and get ready for your nap, please."

"Okay, Mommy!" he says like the good boy he is, before running down the hallway.

"I can't believe he actually thought he'd apologize, and I'd forgive him," Blakely says once Zane is out of earshot, referring to Brenton.

"I can't believe he was doing that shit right under our noses." I huff. "I feel as stupid as you do. You know he used to sell when we were in high school?"

"What? No, I didn't know that."

"Yep, but I just thought it was him being a stupid teenager. I never thought he would continue."

"He thinks I'm going to come around, but it's not happening."

"Kolton mentioned you and Zane moving in with Keegan. He said it would be safer."

"What else did he say?"

"That's it. He wanted to explain the entire story, but he said he can't until Keegan speaks to you. They feel you deserve to know the truth first." The truth is, he wanted to tell me, but I wanted to wait. Blakely deserves to know the truth first.

"I was thinking about talking to him," Blakely admits. "To at least hear him out."

"I won't tell you what to do, but I think that would be a good idea."

"And if we moved into Keegan's place, would you move with us?"

Shit! I wasn't planning to say anything about Kolton asking me to move in with him yet, but I can't lie to her... I won't.

"S?"

"I was..." I take a deep breath, trying not to appear too excited. I don't want her to base her decisions on me. "I was actually thinking I could move in with Kolton."

Blakely's eyes bug out. "He asked you to move in with him?"

"He did. He said the only reason he didn't ask sooner was because of everything going on, but now that it's done, he wants me to move in. But I told him I had to speak to you first."

"I would never keep you from moving in with him," she says softly.

"Are you upset?" I stand and walk over to her. Blakely and Zane will always come first. If she doesn't want me to move, I won't.

"No... I guess I'm just a little sad. It seems like everything is changing. I just learned Keegan is a cop, and now you're talking about moving in with your boyfriend. Brenton was my best friend for years, and now he's being cut out of my life. It's just a lot to take in, you know?"

"I know."

"Mommy! I'm ready for bed," Zane yells, making Blakely and me laugh.

"I wonder if all kids love to nap the way Zane does."

"I doubt it," I tell her. "Watch, you'll have another kid one day, and he or she will despise naptime, and you'll never have a moment to yourself."

"Wow, you're not only knocking me up, but you're cursing me. Thanks." She stands to go tuck Zane into bed, and there's a knock on the door.

"I'll grab it while you tuck him in," I offer, already heading to the door.

I open it up and find Brenton standing there, only before I can yell at him and tell him to go fuck himself, an officer steps between us. "Sir, there's a restraining order." The officer hands him a piece of paper. "If you come within fifteen hundred feet of Blakely, Sierra, or Zane Jacobs, you will be arrested. This is your one and only warning."

"This is bullshit," Brenton hisses, but does as the officer says and walks away.

"Thank you," I tell him.

He nods once. "Someone will always be here to make sure you're safe."

"Who was it?" Blakely asks as I close the door.

"Brenton."

"What? He came here?"

"Yeah, but he only made it to knock on the door before a police officer stopped him and made him leave."

"I think maybe I should take Keegan up on his offer to move in there with Zane."

"I think so too," I agree. Even if they can't make it work, I know Keegan will keep them safe.

"I'm going to speak to Keegan today. Let him explain. I don't know where we'll stand afterward, but at least that way you and Kolton can move forward."

I wrap my arms around her and give her a hug. "I'm not going anywhere. Not until everything is figured out."

chapter twelve

Kolton

KNOCK. KNOCK. KNOCK.

I jump up and sprint to the door, hoping like hell it's Sierra. She texted me earlier that she was watching Zane so Blakely and Keegan could talk. Then, a few minutes ago, Keegan sent me a text that said he told Blakely everything, and they're okay. I was dying to text Sierra to ask her to come over to talk, but I didn't want to appear *too* crazy.

"Hey," she says when I open the door.

"Hey."

"My answer is yes."

"Yes?" I quirk a brow up, confused.

"I'll move in with you." She steps inside, and I close the door. "I needed you to know that before we talk. No matter what you have to say, I need you to know that I'm one hundred percent in."

We sit on the couch, and as much as I want to pull her onto my lap, I refrain, needing to tell her everything. But before I can start, as if she can sense what I really need, she edges closer and then climbs on to me, straddling my thighs.

"Talk to me, Kolton. Tell me everything."

I close my eyes, taking a deep breath, then open them, ready to tell her the entire truth. "When I was nineteen, and in college, I did the stupidest thing someone could do. I was struggling to keep up with my classes, and I went in search of drugs to help."

I search Sierra's face for judgment, but she doesn't give anything away as she waits patiently for me to continue. "A friend of a friend referred me to this guy, Miguel. He sold all types of shit, including pills he swore would help me stay awake and focus. One pill turned into several, and soon, I was addicted, relying on them to help me function. I didn't know it at the time, but my brother Keith was a narcotics officer investigating an influx of drug dealing on campus…"

Sierra's arms snake around my neck, and I grip her hips, needing to feel her to keep going. "I was buying another bottle from Miguel when Keith approached. Miguel took one look at Keith's badge and pulled a gun on him. Shot him dead right there."

Sierra gasps, and her hold on me tightens.

"That's right. I was buying drugs from the man who killed my brother. Everyone went into panic mode, and Miguel got away. Keegan became a narcotics officer, determined to follow in Keith's footsteps. A few months back, there was a whisper that the dealing was happening again. Keegan was brought in undercover as a college student to catch the guy."

"Brenton," she breathes.

"Yep, he was selling. Only, he wasn't doing it on his own. The man running the operation was his ex-stepfather… Miguel Sanchez."

"Oh, my God!" Tears prick Sierra's eyes.

"Keegan not only brought Brenton down, but he also brought down our brother's killer," I choke out. "It won't bring him back, but…"

"But your family will at least have some closure."

I nod. "Yeah. I can't bring him back, but at least I could give them that. I went in and identified it was him."

"Oh, Kolton. I can't imagine that was easy for you. Having to see that piece of shit."

"It was the hardest thing I've ever had to do, but something I deserved because it was my fault…"

"Stop it," Sierra demands. "That man choosing to kill an officer was not your fault."

"If I hadn't been buying from him—"

"You can't live like that. It's unhealthy. But I get it," she says. "When my parents first died, I used to blame myself. I overheard my dad hurting my mom so many times, yet I never told anyone. I used to think, what if I would've told someone: a teacher or another parent. Or what if I would've told my mom I knew. Maybe she would've left him sooner… But eventually, I realized that there was no point in wondering what-if. We all make choices, and many of them are mistakes, and most of the time, we get a chance to right them."

"But sometimes, our choices are deadly."

"Yeah," she agrees. "But in our case, they weren't our choices. My dad chose to put us in the car and drive drunk, and Miguel chose to pull that trigger. They don't deserve to be let off the hook. They made those choices, not us."

I lean forward and nuzzle my face in Sierra's neck, so fucking thankful for her. "You're perfect," I murmur. "Don't ever leave me, please. I need you. Forever."

"I'm not going anywhere," she says, lifting my face and kissing me hard. "It's like you said. You and me… we're inevitable."

epilogue

Sierra

Five Years Later

"HOLY SHIT." I STARE DOWN AT THE TEST, THEN LOOK UP AT MY sister. "Tell me I'm reading this wrong."

Blakely laughs. "Sure, you're reading it wrong… and so am I."

My head pops up. "You're…"

She nods. "Yep."

"Babe!" Kolton yells from outside my back office. "Get out here. We need to celebrate! I ordered some apps and drinks."

"I'll be right out," I yell back even though the last place I want to be is out there, in my new restaurant, smelling all that food and not being able to have a single drink.

Blakely giggles. "I can't believe this is happening… again."

"That's what we get for marrying brothers."

We both walk outside to find our families sitting at the table. Kolton and Keegan are each nursing a beer while Zane plays a game on his phone.

"Mom! Can I borrow your phone?" Colby, Kolton's and my four-year-old son, asks. "Mine is dead."

"Mine is too!" Finn, Blakely and Keegan's son, who is also four years old, says.

That's right. A couple of months after I moved in with Kolton, and Blakely moved in with Keegan, we both found out we were pregnant and due the same week. Neither of our guys knew, but they found out at the same time when they both proposed together.

Six months later, we were married on Cocoa Beach alongside each other, and three months after that, we both gave birth to our little boys only three days apart.

"There she is," Kolton says, wrapping his arms around me. "That article in *Foodie* is amazing! And the critique was right on all accounts."

I smile, replaying the article in my head. When I found out a food critic had stopped by anonymously, I freaked out. What he wrote and published could make or break me. But Kolton told me it would be okay. What I've built here is solid, and I had nothing to worry about. The article came out today, and he was right. The critic loved the restaurant and gave it three Michelin stars, the highest compliment a restaurant can receive.

I'm so proud of what I've created, but I'm also scared. It took four years of saving to come up with enough down payment for a loan to open my own restaurant. I decided to buy one that was failing and resurrect it. I couldn't do it with The Orange Sunrise since it closed less than a year after I predicted it would. I had just given birth and wasn't in a position to save it.

I'd busted my ass for almost a year getting the restaurant ready, and for the past six months since it opened, I've been working even harder to make it a success… only to find out tonight that I'm expecting again. I knew it was a possibility, but I kind of thought it would take a little longer than a month for it to happen. Don't get me wrong, I'm excited, but I have no clue how I'm going to juggle running a new restaurant, raising a four-year-old, and being a wife while baking another little one in my oven.

"We have shots," Keegan says, handing one to Blakely and me.

"To Sierra," Kolton says. "For following her dreams." He leans over and kisses my cheek. "I knew you could do it, baby. I'm so damn proud of you."

The guys both throw back their shots and then look at Blakely and me in confusion when neither of us does the same.

"What's wrong?" Keegan asks Blakely.

"I'm pregnant," she blurts out.

"What?" His entire face lights up. "Are you serious?" He stands and pulls her into his arms. "Hell yeah! That's what I'm talking about." He releases her and glances at his brother. "Looks like you owe me a hundred bucks."

"For what?" Blakely asks.

"I knocked you up first." Keegan shrugs.

"You bet on which one of us would get pregnant first?" Blakely laughs, smacking her husband in the chest.

"The other night while we were watching the game, Kolton mentioned they were trying again, and I told him we were too, so we made a friendly wager… Whoever's sperm was stronger wins."

Blakely snorts out a laugh, glancing at me knowingly.

"I'm pregnant too," I announce.

Kolton's eyes go wide before a shit-eating grin spreads across his face. "You're pregnant?" He looks from me to Blakely and back to me again. "You're both pregnant."

"Yeah," I tell him, rolling my eyes playfully. "We're both pregnant."

He fist pumps the air before he pulls me onto his lap. "I'm so fucking excited," he murmurs into my neck, kissing the sensitive spot beneath my ear. "I can't wait to see you growing my baby again."

"I'm a little scared," I admit. "Do you think maybe we're taking on too much?"

Kolton pulls back slightly, his eyes meeting mine. "We've got this, Sierra. You and me together… we can handle anything." The moment his mouth connects with mine, my entire body visibly relaxes. He's right. We've got this. Not a single day has gone by that Kolton hasn't been my partner in all things. Supporting and encouraging, standing by my side.

"So…" Keegan starts, making Kolton and me look his way. "Which one of you is further along?"

Want to read Keegan and Blakely's story?
You can find them in *Fool Me Once*.

Keep in Touch with Nikki Ash
Facebook | Twitter | Instagram | Goodreads
Amazon | Website | Nikki Ash's reader group

Would you like a free book?
Join my newsletter today and get *Finding Our Tomorrow*

about the author

Nikki Ash resides in South Florida where she is an English teacher by day and a writer by night. When she's not writing, you can find her with a book in her hand. From the Boxcar Children, to Wuthering Heights, to the latest single parent romance, she has lived and breathed every type of book. While reading and writing are her passions, her two children are her entire world. You can probably find them at a Disney park before you would find them at home on the weekends!

Reading is like breathing in, writing is like breathing out.
—Pam Allyn

christmas at the white house

K.A. LINDE

chapter one

The Rose Garden

The White House Rose Garden bordered the Oval Office and West Wing. The First Lady's pride and joy side by side with her husband's greatest achievement.

I'd always thought it was outdated that the woman got the garden next to the greatest office in the world. But that was before I'd stepped into those shoes. Before I'd realized the significance of the garden and how essential standing by my husband as Brady ascended to that office would be.

Now, I walked the length of the small lawn. The roses were no longer in bloom. The crabapple trees had lost their leaves, set to flower pink again in the spring. The grass was still green under my feet. But it didn't feel like home, like North Carolina winters.

I wrapped the peacoat tighter around myself as the DC breeze cut crisp into the garden. One more circuit, and then I'd go inside. The kids would be wondering where I was to tuck them in if I stayed out much later.

Still, I walked around the garden one more time. Soaked up the presence of all the incredible women before me. Brady was doing good work here, necessary work. It was hard not to think that I could be doing more. Not that anyone in Congress or the public agreed. Everyone was hypercritical of a First Lady with opinions. As if the reason the president had fallen in love with me wasn't because I was the most opinionated person in the room.

A smile touched my lips. Easier times.

Impossible to believe that. At the time, it had felt catastrophic. Every day a new pain, a fresh wound. But the campaign had hardened us, brought us together rather than apart, and now, we were here.

Currently, it was just asinine things that set people off. What suit

I wore, what designer had dressed me for an event, the ridiculous Christmas decorations debacle. I hadn't even *actually* designed them myself. But somehow, they were all wrong.

I rolled my eyes. I wished that I were still allowed a snippy response to the bullshit misogyny. Wouldn't it be better if I was focusing on education policy? I had a PhD for Christ's sake!

"You're pacing again," a voice called from the steps of the Oval Office.

My husband stood, resplendent in a black suit with a crisp blue tie. As handsome as the day that I'd set eyes on him. His hair was still dark, though going salt and pepper at the temples in a way that I hadn't realized would make me love him even more. We'd lived those years together. Always together.

But it was the deep, dark eyes and the perfect lips that smiled at me just right that had me melting where I stood.

I *had* been pacing, leaving little high-heel divots in the lawn. Aerating. Though the garden staff would surely disagree.

"You do it, too," I said with an arched brow.

"I learned all of your bad habits."

Brady stepped down the stairs and strode across the lawn like he owned it, which he did. He owned the whole damn world at this point. He'd gotten everything he'd ever wanted. We'd clawed our way to this spot. This very spot on the White House Rose Garden lawn, and it hadn't gotten any easier.

At least our relationship always been secure. I'd never, ever doubted his love for me. Even if journalists sure did.

An arm came around my waist. His other hand tilting my face up to look at him. That face. God, it wasn't fair the way men aged. More gorgeous every year.

"What are you worried about?" he asked.

"Everything."

His lips dipped down to mine. Desire shot straight through me. Heat and passion. I remembered days where we had done nothing but have sex at the lake. No responsibilities. Nothing else to occupy us, but the feel of his body against mine.

"We'll get through it."

We would. As we always had.

"I know."

He kissed me again, long and deep. His fingers dug into my hips. His tongue opened my mouth to him. I released a breath as he claimed this kiss, claimed me as his. Just as I always had been.

"Brady," I moaned. "We're in the Rose Garden."

He laughed against my lips. "So?"

"I'm pretty sure someone is watching us on a security camera."

"So?" he repeated.

I chuckled, sliding my hands up his suit and playing with the back of his hair, which he always cut super short now. No more time for it to grow out. Always perfect for the public. Our first year almost complete, bungles and all, and already, he was prepared to say good-bye to propriety and fuck me in the Rose Garden.

I really should oblige.

A throat cleared behind us.

Brady released a breath, as close as he could get to a sigh, and closed his eyes. He straightened and released me, turning to face his chief of staff, Alexandra McKinney. She'd been a huge asset throughout his presidential campaign, and she was now the first Black woman to be the president's chief of staff. I admired her greatly. Though I wasn't particularly pleased with her right at this moment.

"Sir, your presence is required in the Oval Office."

Brady nodded. "Of course. Congress again?"

"Yes, sir. They want to discuss the budget before the year is up."

"Of course they do." He pressed a final kiss to my lips.

"Good to see you, Liz," Alexandra said.

"Bad timing," I said with a wink.

"It always is."

"Will this take all night?"

"Let's hope not," Brady said as he crossed the lawn to where Alexandra was standing.

They immediately began discussing whatever the new budget emergency was, and it was as if I'd disappeared entirely.

The door to the Oval Office closed, and I was once again alone in the Rose Garden. Brady's legacy was set, but mine was still in question. What was I going to do during this presidency? What would these old white men let an educated woman do?

I was tired of asking for permission. I would no longer sit idly by.

Brady would support me. He always had. Even when I'd been the innocent twenty-something. I wasn't that girl anymore.

I pulled out my phone and started to sketch the education policy I'd been dreaming of. It was too important to put off. The presidential honeymoon was over. It was time to bring in the big guns.

chapter two

Birds of a Feather

My brain was still in a manic fog from the policy I'd been crafting as I took the White House stairs up to the third floor. It was past Jacqueline's bedtime, but I was unsurprised to find her in the children's study with her older brother, Jefferson. She adored him even if her presence sent him over the edge more often than it soothed him.

"Jackie, aren't you supposed to be in bed?" I asked with an arched eyebrow. A "mom look," as Jefferson called it. I'd learned it really quickly with his devious behavior.

"But, Mom!" my six-year-old daughter cried, somehow dragging the one syllable word into two—*muh-om*.

"No buts. Your father is working late, and it's almost Christmas. You wouldn't like Santa to skip the White House this year, would you? On our first year?"

"No," she grumbled.

"I didn't think so."

"Yeah, he's going to give you coal," Jefferson said.

Jacqueline stuck her tongue out at him. "He is *not*."

"Is so!"

"Is not!"

"Is so!"

"Okay," I said, getting between them, "that's enough. Santa isn't bringing anyone coal. We've all been good. And Jackie is going to be good by getting into bed." I pointed at my ten-year-old son. "And you're next, bud."

"I'm so much older though, Mom," he said with a grin that I was sure he'd inherited from the Maxwell bloodline. "I should get to stay up later than Jackie."

"You already do stay up later."

"But, Mom, look at it this way: Jackie got to stay up a half hour later. But I'm older, so I should get to stay up a proportionate amount more. So, I should get to stay up an extra hour."

I narrowed my eyes at my freakily brilliant son. "Who is teaching you words like *proportionate*?"

"Alexandra."

"And who is teaching you negotiation skills?" I asked.

He grinned devilishly. "Daddy."

"That's it. You're banned from the Oval Office."

Jefferson rolled his eyes, and I snapped my fingers at him. "Did you just roll your eyes at me?"

"Ooh, you're in trouble now," Jackie said with a maniacal giggle.

"No!" he yelled.

"Are you yelling?"

"No!"

"Daddy is working late tonight, and I just don't have time for this. I'm going to put Jackie to sleep. You'd better have finished your homework because you're next."

He grumbled, "All right. Fine."

I herded my equally precocious daughter down the hall and into her bedroom, which we had redecorated with swaths of black and hot pink. The child only liked those colors at the moment and had balked at living in a place that was dressed up like some nineteenth-century ball. I really didn't blame her. I was still getting used to the White House quarters…and lack of privacy.

Even though the White House had been our home for almost an entire year, it still felt like this foreign entity. There were all these noises I wasn't used to and people bustling about. Not on the second and third floor, but I could *hear* them below. Little mice crawling around.

I loved that the White House was the people's house. That we had it open to the public, like it always should be. But sometimes, I just wanted to disappear into the North Carolina wilderness, where nothing but the lake and the cicadas could reach us.

"Mom, will you sing me that song?" Jackie asked as she crawled into her bed. Black sheets, hot-pink comforter, mixed pillows.

"Of course. Which one?"

"The one you sing to Daddy."

I smiled at my sweet girl, and then I started to sing "All of Me" by John Legend, the words a lullaby as Jackie closed her eyes and fell into a slumber. I didn't even get halfway into the song before she was out like a light. Going to bed a half hour later was a big deal for her without a nap.

I kissed her head and then found Jefferson buried in his books. He was off the charts in terms of intellect, and finding tutors to keep him interested was beyond a problem. He was outpacing anything a ten-year-old should be capable of. We were excited for him and also terrified at the pace.

"Are you finished?"

He tucked the engineering text he'd been reading under his arm. "I'll just read this before going to bed."

I brushed his hair off of his forehead. "Just this once. Don't tell your dad."

He beamed as if he'd won a prize. "Yay! Thanks, Mom!"

I followed him into his bedroom, which was the opposite of Jacqueline's in every way. He reveled in the old weirdness that the White House had. He liked the odd baubles and wanted the antique drapery and sheets. He was old school to Jackie's modern. I loved their duality.

He climbed under the covers, setting the textbook off to the side.

I pressed a kiss to his forehead. "I love you, bud."

"I love you, too, Mom."

"Thirty minutes. If I come in here and find you still reading after that, then no more books in bed."

"Ugh," he groaned. "Fine. A half hour."

"Sleep well."

He quickly opened the book to where he'd left off, burying his nose in the text. He wanted to get the full thirty minutes in.

I smothered a laugh and left him to it. I was sure he'd go longer than thirty minutes, but it was hard to care when he loved reading this much.

With a yawn of my own, I headed back down to the second floor, where my bedroom with Brady was as well as the kitchen and private dining room. It felt empty, padding the length of that hallway down to our bedroom without him.

A year in, and I still wasn't used to Brady not sleeping next to me every night. He always ended up in bed with me, but sometimes, he got in after I was asleep and was gone again before I woke up. Trying to fix a fractured nation.

I got ready for bed alone, taking my long blonde hair out of its careful twist. I changed out of my pantsuit and heels and into a matching set of navy silk pajamas that had been a gift. My initials—EM—were embroidered on them. Elizabeth Maxwell. The name still felt delicious when I thought about taking Brady's name.

I crawled into the enormous turn-of-the-century bed and decided against picking up the holiday romance I'd been reading for fun in favor of my policy proposal. My iPad was charged, and I returned to what I'd been working on, feverish with the intent to get this right.

When I looked up again, I had a firm proposal in place. I sank back into the pillows, releasing the tension from my shoulders. I really had something here.

It was past midnight. Brady still hadn't returned from work. I should just go to bed, but I had too much energy to turn in for the night. I needed to see him. I slid on a pair of slippers, tucked my iPad under my arm, and headed for the Oval Office to see the most powerful man in the world.

chapter three

The Oval Office

Alexandra looked up from her desk when I appeared in her office.

"Liz," she said with a knowing smile.

"Is he still occupied?"

"Always." She brushed back a tightly coiled curl from her forehead. "He's trying to get this all sorted by the morning."

"That's not going to happen."

"No, it isn't." Alexandra laced her fingers together in front of her and leaned her elbows on the desk. "What can I do for you?"

"Why don't you get some sleep?"

"Ma'am?"

I winked at her. "I've got this."

She contemplated my words for a moment before a smile crossed her face. She pushed her chair back and stood. "Take care of him. He's running on empty."

"I always do."

She touched my arm before passing. "I know you do. He's lucky to have you."

"Trust me, I know that."

She laughed easily and then disappeared from her office. I could have gone through Brady's secretary, but I'd wanted to check on him first. Alexandra always had a knack for knowing when he needed the break. If it had been as serious as it had been in the past, she would have stopped me. I would have gone back to bed. The world would have kept turning, and Christmas would be here soon enough.

But instead, she'd walked out and left me to my own devices. Better for me.

I knocked on the door that led into the Oval Office and heard a gruff response, "Come in, Alexandra. This'd better be important."

"I think it is," I said as I breezed into his office.

Brady's head jerked up at the sound of my voice. His eyes crinkled at the corners, and a wide smile split his face. "Liz, I figured you'd already be asleep."

"I probably should be. It doesn't seem like either of us has that luxury."

"And the kids?"

"Happily tucked away. Though I suspect Jefferson is reading that engineering text until he passes out face-first on it."

Brady laughed. "Can't fault him."

"You're training him to debate me," I sassed. "It's not as much fun."

"Training him? Never," he said, pushing aside the memo he'd been working on. "I just give him a gentle nudge."

"You want him to go into politics."

He lifted one shoulder. "Runs in the family."

"I think you're nudging the wrong one in that direction." I leaned against the desk, crossing my arms.

"Oh?"

"Jacqueline is the politician of the two. Jefferson wants to read his way through the world. He's the academic, if I've ever seen one."

He waved his hand. I knew how much he wanted Jefferson to follow in his footsteps, as he'd followed in his father's. But these were *really* big shoes to fill. I couldn't imagine my whip-smart, intellectual son wanting to compete for that attention. But he was only ten. Plenty of time to decide for himself.

"I don't assume you came here for this conversation," Brady said with a knowing glint in his eyes.

He reached out and pulled me behind the desk. He sat me down on the desk with his legs on either side of my body. I carefully set the iPad down.

"No, it's after midnight."

"I know. Always more work to be done," he said, slipping his hands up my legs.

"I've been up all night, working on a proposal."

"Hmm?" he asked as he kissed my knee.

I squirmed. "Brady, are you listening?"

He looked up at me with lust in his eyes. "All ears."

I rolled my eyes. A habit I was beating out of my children even though they had gotten the habit from me. "I worked on an education policy proposal. I think we can get it passed next Congress. It's really good. And I'm not just saying that."

"Mmhmm." He pressed my legs wider and began to trail kisses up my inner thigh.

"You're not listening."

"I trust your proposal is brilliant, Liz," he said, yanking my legs down and pressing my back down onto the desk.

I didn't know what papers I was lying on top of and frankly didn't care. I knew that look in my husband's eyes.

"It is."

"I believe you, but I'm a little busy now." He fingered the waistband of my silk pants and dragged them down my legs along with the black thong.

Then, the president sank onto his knees before me.

"And then I brought the president to his knees," I murmured.

He chuckled deep in the back of his throat. "Airplanes, baby."

I grinned, my heart warming at the words that had followed us through our entire relationship. I was the one who made his heart race. I was the one who made him feel whole. I was the one who made everything make sense. No matter what the world threw at us, we endured. And better than that, we thrived. We always had.

Other people had the happiest days in the beginning of their relationship and had no idea how to survive the darker times. But Brady and I had realized early on that we couldn't survive the dark times alone. Without each other, we were less, and we'd never looked back after that decision. We never would.

I was his *airplanes, baby*, and he gave me the stars.

chapter four

We Own That Desk

EVERYTHING WENT QUIET.

Yes, it was after midnight at the White House. There were still people meandering the halls. But thankfully, I couldn't hear a single one of them. For the first time in so long, we were alone and in silence.

"I've missed you," Brady said as he worked his way up my inner thigh once more.

His lips were hot on my skin, and I squirmed slightly at the touch, but I couldn't actually go anywhere. His large hand pressed my other leg open wide for him.

"Maybe you should come to bed sometime when I'm still awake."

He growled under his breath and nipped my leg. I yelped slightly.

"It might be nice, you know?"

"I have a job to do."

"Yes, you do," I said, coming up to my elbows to meet his gaze. "Me."

He arched an eyebrow before sliding me back flat. "I plan to take very good care of my wife."

I still swooned at the word. Twelve years we'd been married, and I loved when he called me his wife.

Then, his lips moved up to my center, and I swooned for a whole new reason. His tongue flicked out and licked my clit. I jumped at the first contact, but then he went to work. As diligent with my pleasure as he was with his official duties. I scattered papers and tried not to cry out. The last thing we needed was a security team bursting in on us.

"Liz," he breathed, "God, you taste good."

He slid one finger inside of me and then the other. I tightened around him, wanting nothing more than to have his cock instead of his fingers.

"And so wet," he drawled.

"Oh fuck."

"Was it the policy foreplay?" he teased.

I practically growled at him.

He laughed softly. "Do you think you could tell me all about your proposal right now, Mrs. Maxwell?"

"I probably could, Mr. President. Where would you like me to begin?"

"Oh, start at the beginning," he said as he moved his fingers in and out of me.

"Oh, just shut up and fuck me."

He didn't need to be told twice. The rumble of approval from my vulgarity was answer enough. He stood swiftly, shucking off his suit coat and draping it lazily against the back of his chair. I dropped to my feet before him, naked from the waist down, and removed my top as well. A chill swept through his office, making my nipples erect. Brady noticed because he paused in the removal of his shirt and stepped forward, pressing his body against mine.

His hand came to one breast, massaging the peak. His head dipped to take the nipple in his mouth. My head lolled backward as he sucked it into his mouth and then teased it with his teeth.

I reached for his suit pants. It was only half-fair that I was already naked and he was still in his pants. I jerked on the belt, yanked it free, and then undid his pants as well.

"In a hurry?" he said with a careful smirk.

I *was* suddenly in a hurry. I'd come here for policy reasons and to make my husband go to sleep. I should have known that he wouldn't be satisfied with either of those reasons. We'd never been able to keep our hands off of each other, and I hoped we never would.

"Want you."

My hand dipped into his black boxer briefs, and I found his erect cock waiting for me. He groaned, returning his lips to mine and kissing me fiercely as I drew my hand up and down the length of him.

"More," I told him.

I drew down his pants and boxers and then pushed him back down in his seat. Then, I settled on my knees between his legs.

He arched an eyebrow. "Well, this has never been done before in the Oval Office."

"You're filthy."

"I'm yours."

So, I took him like he was mine. I licked the tip before dropped my mouth down all the way around his cock. I ignored my gag reflex and went even deeper. Then, I added my hand, centering my focus on the tip again.

He buried his hands into my hair. He didn't exactly guide me up and down on him, but he couldn't help himself. He was a man in charge. He was used to being the person everyone looked to for answers. And even in the bedroom, he always demanded that. Even the times I was on top, he was in command. I wouldn't have it any other way.

He grew somehow impossibly bigger in my mouth. He was getting close. I could probably get him off with a few more strokes, but he stopped me.

"Need to get inside of you," he said.

I released him, still on my knees, looking up at my husband with need. "Yes," I gasped.

He brushed his thumb across my wet lips and then placed a kiss on them. I thought he might just pull me into his lap and let me sink down onto him, but he had other plans. Better plans.

He flipped me around, pushing me facedown onto his desk with my ass in the air. My breasts spread out all over state secrets. He toed my legs further apart and then drew a hand down my spine.

I shivered all over at the contact, the anticipation.

Twelve years ago, we'd fought over dominance. But we'd known each other for so long, knew the way our bodies moved and felt. I knew that he was as likely to throw me over his shoulder and toss me in bed as he was to let me ride him like a cowgirl.

And I knew that this between us was so much more than sex.

I knew it as he eased my tension with that one touch. And the way he smacked my ass because he liked to watch it bounce—bigger after two kids but he never cared. And as he leaned forward to press a kiss to my shoulder, I knew that he was the love of my life.

A hard man to live with. As dedicated to the public and our country as he was to me and our family. Some days, the country won. Some days, we did. There were never enough hours in the day. Never enough time together. I would steal every minute I could with him. Steal every last kiss and fuck and ass smack. I'd do it all because I knew we were doing the right thing. We were living these hard years together, where he was on top of the world, so that we all had a better life, going forward. And I did it with my entire heart.

I was just damn sure going to leave it better than when I had gotten here.

The country and our marriage.

His cock brushed against my opening, and I dug my fingers into the desk. Then, he thrust forward, taking me wholly in one movement. I gasped as he filled me up. All these years and two children later, and he was still so fucking big.

"Fuck," I breathed.

He grabbed my ass, squeezing the cheeks apart, and then slapped one cheek.

"Oh God."

Then he moved to grip my hips for leverage as he withdrew ever so slowly from me. I slammed my eyes closed, preparing for him and the thrust back. Which was as brutal and rough as I'd imagined it would be. My whole body jerked forward against the desk. I was probably going to be bruised on my thighs, and I had no complaints.

Brady moved in and out of me at a comfortable rhythm,. I could already feel my orgasm hanging so close to the edge. He'd kept me on the edge when he went down on me, and I'd gotten even hotter as I blew him. Now, with him inside of me, driving into me with so much force, I was set to release any second.

"Please, please, please, please," I begged incoherently.

"I do love when you beg."

He tensed at the same time I did. And then I unleashed, coming all over him and crying out louder than I should have. Brady roared, finishing with a hand on my back as he emptied himself inside me, collapsing forward.

"Fuck, Liz."

"I think you needed to be done for the night."

He kissed my shoulder. "I think you're right."

"Always am."

chapter five

Christmas Presents

I GROANED AS HE WITHDREW, AND WE BOTH TOOK OUR TURNS CLEANING up in the Oval Office bathroom. When I returned to his desk, he was back in his suit, as if nothing had happened.

I pouted as I reached for my pajama bottoms. "I like seeing you naked."

"We have a bedroom for that."

"You weren't saying that a few minutes ago."

He pressed his lips to mine. "Hard to think when you're with me."

I laughed. "Not anymore. You're busy too often."

"Am I shirking my husbandly duties?" he asked with an arched eyebrow.

"I wouldn't mind you performing them in here more often."

He shook his head and tugged me close again. "How did I get so lucky?"

"I don't know. Lots of groveling."

"I've never groveled in my life."

"You answered the right question that day," I told him.

"I sure did."

I turned away from him and pulled up the proposal on the iPad. "Here. Tell me what you think."

He skimmed it as he trailed kisses down my neck. He pushed the iPad up so he could keep reading. And then when he got to the end, he looked up. "You really came here about a proposal."

"Of course. Did you think I just wanted sex?"

"Didn't you?"

"Bonus." I set my jaw and waited. "Well, what do you think?"

"I think…it's brilliant. It's going to be a bitch to get through Congress." He met my gaze levelly. "But we'll do it together."

"With my name attached?"

"Better be."

I smiled widely and threw my arms around his neck. "This is the best Christmas present I could have asked for."

"Something is wrong if the gift you want most is education policy."

"Is it?"

"No, it's absolutely the reason I fell in love with you."

I beamed.

"But…would Christmas really be here without a real present?" He produced a small blue box Tiffany's box out of his desk.

"You didn't," I said.

"Of course I did."

I took the box from his hand and removed the white bow. I popped open the box and found a large ruby pendant encrusted with diamonds.

"Oh my God," I breathed as I pulled the long chain out of the box. "It's stunning."

"It's an antique Carolina ruby," he said as he slipped the necklace around my neck and let the ruby hang low between my breasts. "Now, you'll have a piece of home with you at all times."

"Brady," I whispered, moved by the gesture. I touched the stone. "It's perfect."

"Merry Christmas, Liz."

"Merry Christmas!"

I threw my arms around my husband, the president and most powerful man in America, content that we would survive these next few years in the White House. Not because of the ruby at my throat, but because I already had a piece of home with me at all times—my husband and two beautiful children. Together, we could do anything.

If you loved this short story with Brady & Liz, find out how it all started in *Off the Record.*
www.kalinde.com / books / off-the-record

"I'm in love with two men, but I can only marry one.
And today is my wedding day."
Hold the Forevers is an angsty love triangle like you've never seen before. It will keep you guessing who is the groom and who is objecting? Coming February 23rd. Preorder now
www.kalinde.com / books / hold-the-forevers

ctrl+alt+bang

J.D. HOLLYFIELD

Don't play games with a girl who can play them better

—Unknown

chapter one

Footsie is for fuckheads...

Melanie

I never considered myself a betting man. Or a man at all since I carry around breasts. Not cannons, but a nice rack of perky tits any man would be happy to snuggle between. Any man but my ex-boyfriend. And since I'm not a betting *wo*man either, I never would have wagered this shit would happen to me.

The big C-word: cheating.

By a big D-word: douchebag.

Enter Tad, my lazy, perpetually-trying-to-find-himself, loser ex-boyfriend, who, up until a week ago, was still my loser boyfriend. A guy who I allowed to change me from my normal spitfire self, to a meek, naive, well... just a pathetic human. And yes, I'm mentally kicking his balls in having to admit that.

Good ol' Tad had it made—an apartment he didn't pay for and a girlfriend who cooked and cleaned for him. His lifestyle consisted of lounging around in his old, smelly flannel pajama pants and talking to his online friends all day. Yeah. Real winner. And who's to blame? Most likely myself since I stayed with him for almost two wasted, pathetic years.

Let's take a minute to stroll down memory lane. When we met, he was great. A dreamer with so many aspirations that I fell instantly in love with him. A man without restrictions. The sky was the limit! Well, it turns out there were limitations all right. I was starting to think his true profession was making excuses. *It's not the right job, babe. I'm not feeling the vibes on that one, babe. Their dress code is out of my comfort zone, babe.* Nothing. Was. Right. Now, normal feisty me would tell him to get out of his smelly flannel pants and take anything that is offered. Get a fucking job! But since I was becoming a sucker with no backbone, I said to myself, who was I to push? He had so much passion, I couldn't dull his shine by forcing him into a career that wasn't meant for him. But for the love of God, I wanted him to be *something*.

Then, one day, it happened.

He came to me, the biggest, most enchanting smile on his face. He spun me around and around until we were both dizzy and out of breath from laughter. We fell to the ground, and he kissed me so passionately, my toes tingled.

Then he told me he'd found his calling. No, he found his *passion*. My boyfriend wanted to be a photographer. It didn't have the same ring as a doctor or lawyer—even a stable nine to five position that came with benefits and a salary.

A photographer.

As in, a person who's supposed to maybe understand lighting, exposure, oh I don't know someone who knows how to take a photo—basically a job that requires expertise. None of which Tad had. My smile strained while I asked simple questions. *Don't you need experience? Don't you need a camera? Don't you need money to start this hobby—I mean career?*

Tad had it all figured out. There was no talking him out of it. He just needed me on board. Mainly because I had to front him all the cash. Hello! Where were my friends and family when the alarms started going off screaming, *Don't fucking do it*! Oh, wait, they were there. I just ignored them all. So, what did I do? I cleaned out my savings and supported my man. Bought him the best camera out there because, of course, *he* insisted he needed to be able to run with the best. Spent countless hours setting up a business website and ordering business cards to flutter all over town.

I had faith in him. I was finally seeing the man I first met, showing such passion and drive—oh wait, he never had drive. Scratch that. But he was going to make it. And when that happened, not only would he pay me back—which he swore to do—maybe there would be a ring in the future.

The future…

Insert belly fucking laughs.

Asshole.

I'm getting ahead of myself, though. I can't start the shit-talking until I explain why I'm talking the shit.

Deep breaths.

Rewind six months. Tad was accomplishing exactly what he set out to do. He sat in front of the computer, researching and learning his way around a lens. I was his perfect muse, and I had to admit, the pictures he took of me weren't half bad. Before long, his business was booming. Almost overnight, he had clients interested in his services and his business was growing steadily.

Everything was panning out. I actually did see a ring in my future.

Insert unstable hyena laughs.

My mother always told me trust was the most essential asset in a relationship. Without it, you have nothing. That was Tad and me. I trusted him wholeheartedly, and he was my other half. My best friend. There was no reason *not* to trust him.

Until he gave me several. Long workdays. Late nights. The smell of perfume that wasn't mine. And I know because I don't smell like a cheap whorehouse. I didn't want to fathom that my boyfriend would cheat on me, not after everything I'd done for him. But when I got a call from my girlfriend, my suspicions were confirmed.

"Girl, he was at lunch with some total skank!" my best friend, Deanna, shouts.

"Maybe it was a client."

"They were playing footsie under the table. I almost barfed up my salmon. And that shit was expensive! You have to wait months to get reservations at Winnebago's!"

"I don't know, Dee…I feel like you're overreacting. Was this a liquid lunch? 'Cause sometimes you tend to—"

"Melanie, she was inspecting his teeth. What client inspects teeth? I don't even get the freaky with my dentist and he's hot! She was all up in that grill. If I hadn't been so grossed out, I would have missed their tacky nose kisses. He is cheating!"

No. Not my Tad. I couldn't believe it. I was just being paranoid. Stressed about work. Tired from missing him while he worked late; sometimes not even making it home. I mentally put my shades on to block all the neon signs trying to blind me. I mean, who wouldn't? No one wants to find out they're being cheated on—especially by a guy who practically owes them everything.

Asshole.

Wait, I already called him that.

Fucker.

Having faith, I kept my mouth shut, but this time took off the shades. I started to pay attention to his schedule. Stole peeks at his calendar and clientele. All women, by the way. No need to panic! It could have been a coincidence!

It wasn't.

It never is.

The inner voice of a woman's is strong—way stronger than my cheating boyfriend's dick, which I thought was suffering from erectile dysfunction. But that's a rant for another day. His dick was working fine—just not with me. When I got a call from Jenna, my other bestie, who happened to see Tad at—no shocker—outside of a dentist building, she filled in the final blanks for me.

"Did you know your sleazy boyfriend is currently massaging some slut's tonsils? I will rip his useless, flaccid dick off the next time I see him. I knew you should have dumped him the second he started in on that whole 'I'm just nervous' bullshit when you were trying to sack him. I mean, who lies to a girl about not having a working penis!"

"I don't know what you're talking about, Jenna."

"Bullshit. I talked to Deanna. You're in denial, and that loser is cheating on you. I just witnessed it! I'm at the dentist getting my Invisalign mold and saw him. He was in the back parking lot with some girl. She was atrocious looking, by the way."

"How do you know it wasn't just a friend or a client—"

"Melanie! They were kissing. Like disgusting teenagers."

Hmmm…sounds exactly how Tad kisses. "You sure it was him?"

"Jesus. Yes, I called out his name. When he turned, I threw my Yeti at

him. Hit him right in the forehead. I didn't get my cup back, though. Pissed about that."

"Hmmm..."

That was the only response I had. Maybe it was a calm before the storm reaction. Because what happened next was nothing short of theatrical. I finally listened to the screaming expletives in my inner voice and did the first thing that came to mind—revenge. After putting some pieces together, I started with his website, which I happened to have designed. The dumbass didn't change his login or password, so I was ablet to read the email after email of women propositioning him and him accepting. My boyfriend wasn't a photographer. He had turned himself into a goddamn gigolo.

Talk about a failed return on investment.

I drank myself into a stupor. Then I wrote down every dime I'd spent on him—from rent to dry cleaning his stupid flannel pants to his fake career. He didn't just owe me money. He owed me his life.

Okay. Before anyone gets worried, I didn't murder him. I'm a natural brunette and don't care much for the color orange. It really tends to drown out my pretty blue eyes. No, I let him live, but when I was done with him, he may have wanted me to end him.

I simply waited until he got home, played the perfect girlfriend, offered him a drink spiked with enough Viagra to take out a horse, and waited. And then I handcuffed him to the bed and watched him experience the most painful erection. He howled and cried. Begged me to uncuff him. Or at least give him a hand job. Instead, I used *my* fancy camera and made him *my* muse. Then, while he cried for me to take him to the ER because he swore his dick was going to explode, I emailed the pictures to every single person on his contact list.

Then I called his mother and told her to come collect her loser son and get him the fuck out of my apartment. I couldn't imagine how uncomfortable it was having his mom find him with a hard-on, but I couldn't have cared less. I was done.

Pats my own back.

Cries hysterically.

Assembles girl gang to pick up the pieces.

chapter two

Everyone should have a girl gang

Melanie

"Holy shit, show me the pic!"

"Ew, no! I don't want to see his hairy junk. I bet he has a nasty, overgrown bush," Jenna gags, while Deanna offers me a sympathetic smile.

"Sorry, no harry bush dick pic," I say, sipping on my dirty martini. Yep. Just what the doctor ordered. "Plus, I got rid of them all after I sent them to his mother."

Jenna spits her drink out, and Deanna yelps, wiping her face with her napkin. "Dude, what the hell?"

"Totally sorry, but you sent them to his *mom*? Savage!"

I guess I shouldn't mention that I also sent it to his grandparents. "Listen, guys. I really don't want to talk about Tad anymore. I'm just glad he's gone so I can move on." Three martini glasses go up to cheers. "I'm looking forward to some me-time. Maybe re-organizing my book—"

"Oh, hell, no!" Jenna startles me when her demanding voice cuts through my suggestion of house cleaning. I could really use a fresh wipe down. Spend the weekend re-organizing—"You are *not* going all Merry Maid on us. You're not getting any younger, and we know Tad did nothing for that poor vag of yours."

Deanna agrees with an "Mmm-hmmm."

"We are absolutely fucking thrilled you finally got rid of that jag-off. We've been waiting for this moment." Another nod from Deanna.

"Exactly what have you two been waiting for?" They're supposed to support me, not rub salt in my still fresh wounds by reminding me how much I suck.

"For you to finally get properly laid." My two friends nod in unison.

"I don't need to get—"

"Yes, you do," Deanna comments, hiding behind her martini glass. My mouth parts, and a dramatic *pfft* falls from my pouty lips. They aren't wrong, though.

"Honey," Deanna starts, her tone saccharine sweet, "when was the last time you had an orgasm? *With* another person. Vibrators don't count."

I don't like where this is going. It's none of their business. "I don't know! It's…been awhile. You know, Tad was very insecure about his—"

"Supposedly non-working dick?"

"Jenna!" I snap, trying to hide in my own martini as the old woman next to us scowls. The problem is, I honestly can't remember the last time I had sex—a good ol', skin on skin, tongues-in-dirty-places, sweat-inducing, exploding orgasm. I mean, there was that one time with Javier…my vibrator. I had just changed his batteries, and holy moly, what a difference a new charge can make!

"We're going to assume your silence is because you're practically a virgin again—"

"I'm not a—"

Jenna waves her hand to cut me off. "Trust tree. We're in it. There is no need to be ashamed that your most important asset has been taken advantage of. She needs to be used, sister! She needs to be petted, groomed, and stuffed with shit!"

"Jenna!" Deanna and I snap at the same time. Jenna turns her accusing eyes on Deanna.

"Oh, girl, don't get me started. I know what you did last summer when you and Kevin went to Cancun."

Deanna's face turns beet red. "I told you we had too much to drink."

"Yeah, cool. I normally take couples home and swing too—"

"It was a one-time thing!"

Jenna throws her head back and laughs. "You spent the entire week with them doing nasty things to each—"

"Guys! Jesus. Not the place," I say, cutting them both off. From the way Granny is eyeing me, we're about to be forced to take this conversation elsewhere. "Fine, you're right. I haven't had sex in a long time. I can't even remember the last time I *saw* a dick." Now that I think about it…

"Oh my god. What if I don't even remember what a dick looks like? If a dick came calling, would I even know? Would I be like, 'Wow! Hey, little buddy! What are you?'"

The horrid gasp from Granny has me shutting my yapper, whereas Jenna turns to Grandma and says, "Yeah, she needs dick bad."

Yep. We're getting kicked out.

The couple calls over their waiter, and after a long story I'm sure is about dicks, they change tables.

There's nothing left to say. I clearly need dick, and my friends know it. But I'm not as outgoing as Jenna. Or social like Deanna. I keep to myself. And I like it that way. I can't even fathom being out in the dating world again. "Maybe in the future I'll meet someone, but right now—"

"Shut it, prude. Sorry, that was your vagina talking through me. She wants you to shut up. Now, we have something for you."

Not good.

Last time Jenna had something for me, I hallucinated for three days in Mexico and woke up in a hotel bathtub wearing a flamingo costume.

"Deanna and I…" she squeals, making me more nervous. Shit, I have no interest in seeing dead people again. "We signed you up for this dating app—well…more like a sex app."

I choke on my olive. "What!"

Jenna goes on. "Yeah, girl. It's legit. Don't worry. I tested it out a few times to make sure. Lots of dick on it. Some great, some not so great dick, but dick. Lots of dick." Jenna snatches my phone and slaps the screen with her long nails. "There! I downloaded it and signed in." She points the phone toward me, and my head jolts back in confusion.

FitItIn?

"How…how do I already have twelve reviews?"

Jenna shrugs. "Like I said, I tested it out for you. You needed some sex reviews so people don't think you're bad in bed…or a serial killer. Now, you just have to go on the app, swipe left or right, pick a guy, and have him clean out the crawl space."

"Crawl space?"

"Yeah, your lonely vagina. I'm sure it needs a good cleaning. I can send you to my wax guy. He does amazing work."

Jesus. Maybe tripping would have been better. "I don't know about this. I can't really just have sex with someone without building a relationship first."

"Oh yeah? And how did that work out for you? Shit, I'm sorry. I didn't mean to rub the salt in, but, girl, we're just looking out for you. We want you to be happy. And you sitting around rearranging your book collection is not going to do it. *Trust me.* Although…I wouldn't mind a man doing some of the things in those books." I do own a ridiculous amount of top-notch romance novels from some of the best authors in the world. "Last girl's night, I started reading Bad Daddy. Holy hell, sign me up." Jenna holds her hand up to her face and repeatedly jabs her tongue to the side of her mouth. Sick.

"Ew! Stop!" Deanna pipes in. "You probably did that before you came to dinner."

Jenna shrugs. *Double ew.* "Maybe. Not the point. It's about Mel tonight."

Deanna extends her hand to cover mine, her eyes filled with sympathy. "Girl, I know this is out of your comfort zone, but I feel like you need this. Like a reboot."

"Reboot?" I laugh. "I'm not a computer. You can't just control, alt, delete, and make my life all rainbows and butterflies."

"We're not!" Jenna boasts. "We're going to control, alt, bang! So, let's drink up and find you a guy to bang!"

chapter three

Ctrl+Alt+Bang

Melanie

I CAN'T BELIEVE I'M DOING THIS.

Yes, I can. With my friends? Yes. I. Can.

My eyes start to burn after scrolling through so many profiles. And holy options! There were big ones and small ones. Some *for sure* fake ones. I couldn't believe this site was even legal! But talk about having to go through a lot of frogs to find a prince.

"How about that one?" Jenna points. "He's hot, and his tight pants show he's well endowed." She is about to fall out of her chair to get a better look at the current prospect. "I mean…come on, cop suit? Total swipe material."

"Are you kidding me, read his bio! *Have you ever said, 'Fuck the police'? Now's your chance.*" Jenna busts out laughing and falls over onto the ground.

"I mean, I've always fantasized about being tied up," Deanna chimes in, her cheeks overly flushed. Maybe we should consider cutting her off soon.

"Yeah, right, Dee." Jenna snorts. "You know you were more than tied up in Canc—"

"Don't say it!"

I shake my head and swipe left. Sorry, Mr. Officer, you're concealing more than just a large gun.

"Dude! You swiped the wrong way! He was perfect! Three miles away!"

"I need a starter dick! That guy might break me in two! I'm looking for someone more on the smaller side for practice."

Jenna huffs and throws herself back in her seat, waving down our waiter, who can't wait until we leave. I move on to the next guy. He's pretty cute. Nothing crazy, but he has a nice smile. His bio reads: *Will do anything for alcoholic shots. And I mean anything.* Swipe left.

Next: *Don't worry, it'll fit.*

Swipe left.

Next: *Girls who swallow only, please.*

Jesus! Swipe left.

Next: *I don't care at this point if you're a serial killer...*

SWIPE LEFT!

Next, next, next.

"This is hopeless. I have a better chance of finding a guy at a—"

"Don't say funeral." Jenna shakes her head, shoving an olive into her mouth.

"What! Why would I go to a funeral to find a guy?" Ew! "Jenna!" My nose scrunches.

"What? I was at a stoplight and saw this cute guy walk into a funeral home. I don't discriminate."

Jesus.

I sigh heavily. "Look, I know you guys are just trying to help me, but seriously, I'm good." I stand up and sway a bit to the right. Whoa, maybe I'm not in any better shape than Deanna.

"Whoa, where you going?" Jenna whines.

"I'm tired. Should probably call it a night." After a dramatic whine from Jenna, we pay our bill, and our waiter sighs in relief. Jenna, of course, can't help herself and squeezes his ass on the way out. We're probably being banned from ever eating there again as we speak.

As much as I have zero interest in finding a guy this way, I can't help my curiosity. I mean, these guys are ridiculous! I swipe another one, reading his bio. "You have got to be kidding me! This guy's profile pic is literally his di—*shit*!" I drop my phone as I run into a wall. I lift my hand to my nose because I may have broken it. When my eyes level out, I realize it wasn't a wall at all.

Well hello there...

Tall, dark, absolutely delightful, hopefully single. *Why are my eyes trailing down his tight shirt and not stopping until they check out his—*

"See something you like, baby?"

And nope.

Ew.

My gaze shoots up, ignoring his toned biceps, tanned skin, and Adam's apple I'd lick, given a chance. No—I'd actually start with those plump lips. Shit, I'd lick his nose. Damn, he is hot. How do I swipe right—

"Earth to stalker. You gonna keep staring at me or move out of my way?"

—I mean left. Asshole! "Yeah, I'm not checking you out."

"I didn't say you were. But since *you* just did, I agree, you were checking me out."

"I was not!" I was until he opened his mouth.

"Sweet cheeks, you look like you need a dessert, and I'm a walking ice cream cone." He laughs along with his buddies behind him, and it lights a fire inside me. His laugh is deep and lovely, and I have to remind myself he's being a total jerk. I don't have time for jerks.

"For starters, I prefer salt over sugar. Second, I don't pick up jerks in restaurants—especially not condescending ones. But feel free to pretend you're wanted. Make your tiny dick feel better about itself. Now, if you'll excuse me." I look down, mortified to see my phone landed screen up. A nice, big ol' dick staring back at me. I reach down to snag it, but he's faster.

Shit!

"Hey! Give me that back!"

He doesn't. Go figure because who wouldn't take an interest in a stranger's phone with a huge penis winking up at you. "Wow," he starts. I reach for my phone, but he pulls it away and begins to tap on my screen. "You don't pick up guys in restaurants, huh?" he laughs, continuing to inspect my profile.

"It's not what you think," I grumble, my cheeks close to melting from embarrassment.

"Really? 'Cause...*MagicMike25* gives you five stars—says you were a cheap dinner date and dessert was priceless."

I'm going to kill Jenna. "Yeah, not what you—"

"Greg—five stars. Swallowed like a champ." His brow raises in interest. Mine scrunches as I turn to Jenna.

"Sorry!" she shrugs.

"So, *MegaMouthMel*, it says to make you an offer you can't refuse. What are you willing to do for another five-star, sweetheart?" His friends burst out laughing. I've had enough. Hot or not, he's the kind of dick I'm most certainly not interested in.

"Tough luck, pal. I don't open these legs for tiny dicks. The way you seem to treat women, I'm guessing you're compensating for something. And the only thing a man has to prove is his dick size, which, let me guess..." I lift my fingers, measuring an inch, "This small?"

His friends break into another fit of laughter, but his smile falls. "You wish, babe. If you want me to prove you wrong, we can go into the alley right now. And since it says here you're a swallower, if you do a good job, I'll reward you with a *salty* treat."

He winks at me.

My girls hiss behind me.

I throw my hand up for them to back down. I got this. "Oh, good luck with that. You couldn't pay me to pretend to be interested in someone like you."

"And who's that?" His condescending smile is back.

"Oh, I don't know, men who probably still live with their mothers and jack off to their old high school photos because they've never amounted to anything but being bitter assholes."

His brows crinkle. His frown is a point for me. "Oh, wait, did I hit a sore spot? You hear that? It's your mom calling you home for meatloaf night." I snatch my phone out of his hand while he's caught off guard. "That's what I thought. Enjoy your dinner, boys. I'm gonna go enjoy myself some *dessert*." I make a popping sound with my lips, wink at the douche, then sashay away.

"Wow, that was the hottest thing I've ever witnessed!" Jenna exclaims.

Knowing we're out of eye range, I whip around to her. "Are you for real? That guy was a total jerk! And *seriously*, Jenna?"

"That dude was eye-fucking you even after you insulted him about living with his mom. I'm pretty sure he's still thinking about you."

Yeah, thinking about bitch slapping me. Man, why do the super-hot ones have to be the biggest jerks? I should have known right away no one who looks like that is a decent human being. More like a guy who's full of himself. I hug my friends goodbye and take an Uber home. The whole ride is consumed with that jerk's crude comments and his plump lips—

"Ugh, go away!"

I stare out the window, needing to reroute my thoughts. Maybe I should give this app a try. What's the worst that can happen? "Dick can happen. And it's clear I need dick."

"Excuse me?"

Shit. I lift my head to the driver. "Sorry, nothing. Never mind. Ducks—I saw a duck."

After getting to my building, I stumble into my apartment and toss my heels across the room.

"Honey, I'm home!" I laugh. No one is coming to greet me. My lips purse at the reminder of Tad. I search for the pain in my chest that I used to feel knowing we were done, but relief is the only emotion that surfaces. I walk over to my fridge, open it, and sigh. All the stuff I bought for myself is still there. The milk cap is on, and the cheese package isn't ripped open, collecting fridge mold. This is…great!

I shut my fridge, taking in and enjoying every single thing about having Tad gone. "Why the hell didn't I kick him out sooner?" I ask myself, changing into a soft pair of pajamas. As I snuggle into bed, my phone dings. Probably Deanna, letting me know she got home, or Jenna screenshotting me a photo of a bar she ended up at.

I gaze at my screen, and my eyes widen. It's a friend request—on my FitItIn app.

Dallas James would like to be friends

Intrigued, I pull up his profile. He's super attractive. Dark blond hair, green eyes, and a toned body. His interests are sports, cooking, and golf. His bio says *All Game*. Seems normal. Since I'm drunk and will end up deleting the app come morning anyhow, I accept.

The message comes through instantly.

DallasJames: Hey, MegaMouthMel, I'm in the mood to make you an offer you most definitely won't refuse.

Ew. That damn bio. I need to change that. If I'm keeping the app, that is…

I type back.

MegaMouthMel: No longer accepting offers. Sorry. I'm actually about to delete this app. Hope you find what or who you're looking for.

Three little dots pop up. I'm about to click off when his message appears.

DallasJames: Oh, man, sorry. I'm new to this. I'm not very aggressive, and my friends told me to be. I'm really just looking to chat with someone. I don't know how people can just meet and seconds later have sex.

"I totally agree, Dallas James." I snuggle into my bed.

MegaMouthMel: I totally agree! To be honest, my girlfriend set this app up for me. The reviews aren't even about me. Sorry to disappoint.

I wait for him to get offline now that the big secret is out, and I don't actually swallow, but he responds.

DallasJames: Oh, good! Your profile was intimidating. It is too much to assume your pic is real?

It's the only thing Jenna did tell the truth on. It's a picture of us all at an old college roommate's wedding. I'm smiling wide, super tipsy, but my hair and makeup are on point.

MegaMouthMel: That actually is me.

I wait for him to respond, but it takes him a bit longer. Thinking he's lost interest, I put my phone down on my nightstand, then snatch it back up when it dings.

DallasJames: Wow. I'm sure you know how gorgeous you are, so I won't scare you off with cheesy pickup lines. Humor me—why does someone as beautiful as you need to be on a site like this?

Well, my friends suck for starters.

MegaMouthMel: My friends thought it would be a good idea to get me back on the market. My boyfriend cheated on me, so to get over him, you know what they say…get under someone new. Gah! Why did I just admit that!? <insert crying emoji>

Why am I telling a complete stranger my business? And admitting I'm a loser who got cheated on? I need to get off this app.

DallasJames: What's his name? I'll go kick his ass. I hate cheaters. To be honest, that's why I'm on here too. I guess it's not too embarrassing now that we share the same reason.

MegamouthMel: LOL!

MegaMouthMel: I mean, not lol that you got cheated on! Shit, sorry. I meant funny how we both ended up on here. And yeah, cheaters suck. Can I ask how long you were with your girlfriend?

DallasJames: Two years. She cheated on me with a guy from her work. Swore they were just friends until I caught them red-handed.

Why do people cheat? It's such a cop-out. No one's perfect. And if they are, I probably wouldn't even want them. I'm drawn to flaws. Perfectly imperfect people. Take a look at Jenna! Tad wasn't the best candidate for a husband and partner, but we meshed. We never fought. *Never had sex.* Cohabitated well. *Never spent time together.* Enjoyed the same things. *Did not see eye to eye on me paying for him to become a male whore.*

Jesus, have I been in a coma for the last two years?

MegaMouthMel: Gross. Same with mine. He took all my money then cheated on me with more women than I can count on my fingers and toes. But I got revenge, so it's cool. My pride is slowly mending. <insert smile emoji>

I don't see the three dots and smack myself with my phone for word vomiting! This guy has to think I'm so pathetic.

DallasJames: I'm sorry that happened to you. You seem pretty cool. He obviously didn't deserve you.

Awww, thanks, Dallas James. He sure didn't.

Surprisingly, we fall into a comfortable conversation. I share more about myself, and he does the same. He avoids specific questions like what he does for a living and where he lives, but I'm sure it's just the whole being uneasy and letting a stranger know your personal info, so I let it go.

Before I know it, it's close to three in the morning.

MegaMouthMel: Shit, I need to get some sleep. I have to be up early to meet my friends. I had a great time chatting. Maybe… we can do it again sometime?

Yeah, I asked it. I asked a random guy on a hookup site on a second chat date. I blame it on the exhaustion. And when he turns me down, I'll never speak of it again.

DallasJames: I've been crossing my fingers you'd ask. I'd love to. Sweet dreams, Mel.

Then he signs off.

Shit…

Are those…butterflies? "Shit!" I smash my face into my pillow, laughing at how unconventional this is. Did I just make a connection with someone online? Based on a photo and text messages? My cheeky grin confirms it. I sure did.

"Sweet dreams to you too, Dallas James."

chapter four

Eating out of the palm of my hand for five-hundred, Alex

Lukas

I PUSH THROUGH THE DOORS OF THE CROWDED SPORTS BAR. LOUD voices and the smell of wings fills the air. Harry waves at me from across the room, and I beeline toward their table. Football and beer—exactly what the doctor ordered after last night.

It was supposed to be a crazy night: meet up with the guys, enjoy an overpriced steak, and get laid. That is until a hot little brunette put a damper on my mood. She thought she was all high and mighty, talking shit to me in front of her prissy friends. Shit, even my asshole friends laughed. But I sure as hell didn't. I met her match for match until she got one up on me and walked away before I could cauterize her.

As she walked away, I fought not to grab her back and wipe that smug smile off her face. Kiss it off, more like. Damn, she was hot. Almond eyes, plump lips, legs that went on for days. But that mouth… I wouldn't have had a problem silencing her. All women have mute buttons, but this one…I couldn't get her to shut up. She got under my skin. Insulting me in front of my friends. Thinking she one-upped me. She may have won the battle, but I plan on winning the war. No one crosses me like that.

She needed to be taught a lesson, and I was willing to take on the task. I sat at dinner and appreciated the scenery. New York's biggest hot spot for singles. Blondes, brunettes, redheads. It was a sea of available and willing women. Too bad I had my eyes and mind set on one mouthy brunette.

MegaMouthMel

That was all I needed to get my revenge started. I downloaded the silly hookup app, FitItIn. Okay, maybe it was already on my phone. I'm single and have no interest in being tied down. I don't do romance. I do sex. Physical, yes. Touchy-feely bullshit? Not a chance. Hence why, even after her little mouth pissed me off, I was still willing to take her around the side of the building and let her gag on my cock. A big cock, by the way. It pissed me off when Joe and Harry laughed at that shit. They've heard enough stories and enough one-night stands beg for a second round to know this dick is spectacular. Tiny, my ass.

A quick search—and voila! There she was. And how convenient. Only three miles from me. Her perfect smile. Her flushed cheeks. She looked happy. Too bad I'm about to change that. Her profile was impressive if I was looking for a quick, hot lay. Though, a bit of an overachiever if you asked me. Usually, I would steer clear of these types of chicks. On paper, they come off as the perfect hookup—hungry for cock, and that's about all. Her reviews pinged her as just that. But there was something fishy about her I couldn't put my finger on. If I had to guess, she's a money chaser. No one likes dick *that* much.

I friend requested her and set my plan in place: get in her good graces, ask her to meet, and humiliate her. Yeah, I'm an asshole. It's why people don't mess with me.

Who would have thought she was a fraud? Certainly not me. Those plump lips were a sure thing, and even though I had no actual intentions of touching her, I couldn't stop thinking about fucking that bratty little mouth of hers.

Her friend had set up the profile. *That* shit caught me off guard. Disappointed, it didn't deter me. She still had to pay for her actions.

After finding out she was fake, I changed routes. Getting straight to the point of "let's fuck" was off the table. Apparently, she wasn't a cock gobbler after all. She had a story. A wah-wah sob story. So, I played along. Switching gears, I did what all sappy girls want: I befriended her. I played the victim alongside her and had her eating out of the palm of my hand. She opened up like a blooming flower and practically told me her whole life story. Her cheating ex sounded like a douche, and part of me did want to find him and kick his face in. But mending her broken heart wasn't my problem. Getting revenge was. If she were mine, I wouldn't let her out of my sight. But my intentions aren't pure. I plan on doing worse than breaking her heart. Again, I'm an asshole. I'll never claim to be anything but.

What I didn't expect was to talk to her until the early hours of the morning. I told myself it was part of the plan, but she had pulled me under her spell, and I found myself ditching my friends and heading home. I laid in bed, imagining her doing the same, and made small talk. Fed her bullshit to keep her wanting more. I almost slipped and gave her real details of my life instead of Dallas James'. No one puts their real names and pictures on those apps. Dallas? Let's just say I'm a Cowboys fan.

By the time I got off the phone with her, I was conflicted. She wasn't the bratty little bitch I'd pinned her to be. She was nice and funny. And the more she sucked me in, the more I wanted to get to actually know her. Take her out.

Then I remembered what she'd done. All the weird shit she was making me feel was bullshit. I didn't do romance, and she wasn't going to change that. Plan back in place. Tomorrow, I get her to meet up with me and see how she likes to be humiliated.

"What's that smile for?" Joe asks, bringing me back to the present.

I claim my seat at the pub table and take a hefty sip of my beer, my smile ear to ear. "Oh, just a pet project I'm going to have fun with."

chapter five

Cowboys Suck

Melanie

I WALK INTO THE PACKED SPORTS BAR, A SPRING IN MY STEP, A SMILE ON my face, and a new buzzing in my belly. Dallas James. Handsome, funny, future possibilities. And what an unexpected surprise he turned out to be. We had so much in common that by the end of the night, I felt like we'd known each other for years. Which means....

My cheeks flush. I'm going to ask him out. Gah! Is that too eager? Will I send the wrong message? Once inside, I scan the place, searching for Jenna and Deanna. I spot Jenna instantly, glad she snagged a great spot and head toward the center of the bar. "Hey, ladies. Sorry I'm late. Long night. You're never going to guess—"

"Hey, look, it's the girl from last night!" My head whips to the table next to us and my eyes bulge as three familiar faces stare back at me. Two smiling like Cheshire cats, and one frowning. *Him.*

"You gotta be fuckin' kidding me," the asshole growls, slamming his beer on the table. We have a stare-off until one of us finally uses our voice. "You stalking me now, priss mouth? Really want my cock, huh?"

His friends laugh, and Jenna starts to get up, in attack mode. I stop her, shoving her back in her seat. "Don't bother. He's a waste of time—which I'm sure every girl says after five seconds in his presence." I climb onto my chair and mentally pat myself on the back when his friends bust out laughing. I win, jerk.

The waitress brings me a Bloody Mary, and I take a big sip. Too bad it's going to take more than just this cocktail to calm my now rattled nerves. Who the hell does this guy think he is? Macho. Arrogant. Just as good looking as he was last night. Not even that scowl hurts him on the sexy factor. But sexy or not, he's a jerk. Dallas springs to mind, reminding me there are good guys out there.

I brush him off and turn my attention to my friends. "So, how was the rest of your night? Mine was great. Met a guy."

Both girls gasp, spitting out question after question. "No way! How? Did you use the app? Holy shit! Tell us everything!"

I take another sip of my drink. "Sorry, ladies. I don't kiss and tell."

"Probably because you're full of shit," Hot Asshole grumbles next to me. My head jerks in his direction, and his scowl deepens.

"Excuse me?"

"You heard me, princess. No one as uptight as you got laid last night. Unless you're calling your hand a *new guy*." His friends laugh. Mine snicker?! Traitors! Point for him.

I match his scowl. "I think it's clear the only one who didn't get any is you by that snarl on your face. You look pretty tense. Why is that? Still waiting for tiny dicks to come back in style? Oh wait, they never were."

The scorching fire in his eyes heats my cheeks. I imagine those eyes burning into my flesh as his tongue drags down my body, taking out all that anger on my sex. The tiny dick thing is a ruse to get him fired up. I stole a peek at the bulge in his pants last night, and he definitely looks well-endowed.

"Jesus, you sure you two hate each other? Looks like you're about to fuck right here in the bar." One of his friends laughs and high-fives his other buddy. I pull my eyes back to my own table and reach for my phone. Pulling up FitItIn, I go into my messages.

<user updated profile name>

Melanie: Hey, really enjoyed our talk last night. Hope you were able to get some sleep.

It's showing he's offline, so I put my phone down and try to focus on my friends and some football. I can't help but shift my gaze to my right, catching Hot Asshole grinning like a jerk at his phone.

Probably just got the test results that he doesn't have chlamydia—this time around.

My phone dings and I grab it, my own smile spreading across my face when I see Dallas responded.

DallasJames: Same. And sorry, no sleep for me. I had this girl on my mind. Nice name change. What's my pretty girl up to today?

My cheeks flush. *My pretty girl.* Kind of fast, but I like it.

Melanie: Spending the day watching sports with my girlfriends. I have to suffer through this Cowboys game before the game I want to watch comes on. Not sure who you root for, but the Cowboys suck.

"Are you fucking kidding me?!"

Everyone, including me, turns at Hot Asshole's outburst.

"You cool, dude?" his friend asks.

He picks his head up. "Yeah. Just peachy." He doesn't waste an opportunity to set those steely eyes on me.

DallasJames: I'm not a huge sports fan. But I heard the Cowboys were good.

He's not lying when he says he's not a sports fan.

Melanie: They suck. If you want to root for a team, I suggest the Chiefs. They're a sure win.

The bar erupts when the quarterback for the Cowboys fumbles, costing them a touchdown.

Melanie: So, I was thinking…maybe we can hang out sometime…

His location is showing he's right on top of me… Wait, is he here? I look around the bar to see if I can spot him.

Melanie: Hey, strange. Your location is pinging right by me. You're not at Miller's Sports Bar, are you?

He immediately signs off. Huh. That was weird. Did I scare him by being so upfront? Did I ask him out too soon? He called me his pretty girl. Ugh, why is dating so hard!

"Aw, what's that pout for? Get denied a guzzle session?"

This guy is such a jerk! I twist on my stool to face him. "You know what, you have to be the vilest human I've ever had the pleasure of crossing."

"What a compliment. Sounds like you're asking me to go steady."

I gasp. "Far from it. More like asking you to play in traffic."

He leans forward, too close for my liking. "Would you be the one pushing me? Hmmm, having your hands on me before I meet my death doesn't sound so bad. Maybe a quick hand job would be nice or since you like it salty a quick blow—"

I toss my Bloody Mary in his face and hop off my chair. Not intimidated by his death glare, I get in his face. "You only wish you had these hands and lips around your junk, which I'm sure is less than mediocre. Which is why you're such an utter ass. And I'd love to touch you—if it led to you falling in front of a semi-truck and exploding all over Main Street—"

This time, he shuts *me* up.

His hand seizes the back of my neck, and he kisses me.

Kisses me!

My eyes threaten to pop out. My hand raises in preparation to slap him off me. But I don't. I kiss him back. His lips are plump and silky against mine, and like some looney toon, I welcome it. No, I *savor* it. *Push away, what?* Not a chance. His mouth has an agenda, and I'm falling down the rabbit hole of his kiss. The raw tension between us fuels us as we fight for control. Tremors travel up and down my spine, and I'm too ashamed to acknowledge the fireworks going off behind my eyelids. His tongue slides against mine, and I lose myself in his taste. His feel. The way his hand tightens against my nape. Goosebumps assault my flesh, and my heart begins to skip every other beat. The world around me fades, and I melt into him, relishing in our connection.

A small moan escapes me.

A low, sexy laugh falls from his lips as he abruptly pulls away, leaving me unsteady on my feet. Then he opens his big, fat, jerk mouth. "Hmmm…the way you just kissed me, you most definitely want those lips on more places than my mouth. Shame I'm not into shitty sports fans and even shittier kissers."

He stands, almost knocking me over, and storms off toward the bathroom.

chapter six

Nothing like jacking off to a football game

Lukas

I STORM RIGHT PAST THE BATHROOM AND CONTINUE WALKING STRAIGHT out the back exit. That fucking girl. My blood boils. I just fucking kissed her. And holy shit, I liked it. No, I *loved* it. Thank fuck we were in a public place because I would have stripped her bare and done more than taste her pretty lips.

I jump on my motorcycle and rev the engine, the growling sound similar to the rumbling inside my chest. I'm supposed to hate her. Humiliate her for humiliating me. An eye for an eye.

Instead, I kissed her.

I kick up my kickstand and peel out, needing to cool off. My phone vibrates in my pocket—no doubt the guys wanting answers. But I can't deal with them right now. Since the moment she bumped into me, my life has felt out of control. My anger spikes at how easily I've allowed her to affect me. So what she insulted me? She has no idea who I am. I know my guy down below is a stallion. So why do I care that she doesn't know that? Because for some sadistic reason, I do.

Fuck that.

No, I don't.

I've never cared about what a chick has thought about me, and I'm not starting now. I stop at the local liquor store to pick up a twelve-pack and head back to my apartment. I'm pissed I'm missing the second half of the Cowboys game…because of her. As soon as I get situated on my couch, the game ends on a touchdown. Cowboys lose.

This is all her fault.

My phone dings and I look down to see Melanie has sent me a message.

Melanie: My Chiefs aren't off to a good start. <photo attached>

Attached is a selfie of her staring away from the camera, her lips in a cute-as-fuck pout. I shouldn't respond to her. This plan is starting to backfire on me. I should delete her ass before it goes too far.

DallasJames: Your cute pouty face is worth it, though. What would you look like if they were winning?

Why?

Why am I egging this on? Tell her to fuck off and delete her. She's not even my type: blonde, compliant, no attachments. Shit, I can't even remember the last time I gave a girl more than twenty-four hours of my attention. But with her, I just want to steal it from her as if she owes it to me. As if it's mine to steal.

Melanie: <photo attached>

Fuck me.

I get offline and throw my phone to the floor. I watch the Chief's game like I give a shit and cheer when they do well, knowing she's probably happy. I stare at her photos like a jag-off and then actually jack off. Then I consume all twelve beers and pass out on my bathroom floor.

chapter seven

It all started with the kiss of death

Melanie
One week later...

WALKING INTO THE COFFEE SHOP, I GROAN AT THE LONG LINE. IF I don't get caffeine in me, I'm going to wither away and die. That or my pre-caffeine inner demon is going to take over and wreak havoc. Pulling out my phone, I check for new messages. My face lights up when I see one from Dallas. I swipe open my app.

DallasJames: Morning, beautiful. How's my girl doing today?

My cheeks are sore from always smiling—all due to him. We've been chatting nonstop since last Sunday. He's funny and caring and so attentive and responsive. He's like my very own Prince Charming—who I still haven't technically met.

At night, I imagine him lying next to me. His words have a voice, and his real hands skate down my belly. In my head, they're large and warm. Rough and not shy. He takes exactly what I offer and fills my sex with his thick, glorious fingers. He works me up until I'm on the verge of detonating, then gives me what I really ache for: his long, thick cock. Every night, I lose myself to this fantasy and explode into the most intense orgasms.

The problem is Dallas always morphs into the face of Hot Asshole.

It's all *his* fault.

I have this great guy who treats me amazingly…well, it's all virtual, but he makes me smile and laugh and not feel like shit. And instead of thinking about him, my mind goes to *him*.

I blame it on that kiss of death. If he hadn't kissed me, I would have been fine, and I wouldn't have given him a second thought. Those lips, though…

I huff, staring at my phone. I need to push Dallas to meet in person. We've done enough getting to know one another. I don't see why we shouldn't take this to the next level. I'm done with the constant masturbating. It's time to have real sex. I *need* real sex! Not fantasy sex using Hot Asshole's—

"You gonna move or not? Other people want coffee too."

That voice! My brows crease, and I cock my head and look behind me. "You."

"*You*," he mimics.

"Jeez, you're like a bug I can't kill. Are you stalking *me* now?" He looks great in his ripped jeans and worn dark t-shirt.

"Hardly," he utters and continues to stare at me as if waiting for something. *No way* is it an apology for throwing my drink at him. If anything, he can apologize to *me* for kissing me. Which hasn't stopped replaying in my mind. "Did you want to go another round, or do you normally stare at people like you want to devour them?"

Insert bubble popping sounds.

Asshole.

I whip around and focus on the menu board. "I'd rather saw my lips off," I hiss.

He's suddenly too close, his cologne threatening to strangle the sense out of me. His warm breath skates across my neck, and I fight the shudder of goosebumps gathering across my arms. "I'd hate for you to do that. Even though you're a bit much, I quite enjoyed kissing you."

I swear, if my knees choose now to buckle and I fall to the ground, I will die! His comment simmers in my head, the words having their intended effect. A tremor of heat blasts down my spine, right to my inner thighs. Shit. I squeeze my eyes shut, desperately needing to pull myself together. My rebuttal is on the tip of my tongue, but my throat is suddenly too dry.

His next words almost paralyze me. "Let's call a truce."

I swear, if I twitched, his lips would touch my flesh. *Just twitch, girl. Blame it on a sudden earthquake only you felt.*

"And what makes you think I want to call a truce with you?" The hoarseness of my voice clearly says, *Yes, let's call a truce and seal the deal with an old-fashioned bang back at your place.*

"Because I think in some sort of way you like me. And in some sort of way, I like you. And I think, if we got along, there are a lot of things we would like together."

I don't know whether to tell him to fuck off or ask him where to sign. I pivot around to face him. He truly is a sight. He's got that bad boy look—his dark hair a mess, eyes the color of the most luxurious emeralds, and his teeth, perfect, just like his smile. Shit…I'm in trouble.

He sticks his hand out. "Lukas."

Still suspicious, it takes me some time before I reach out and shake his hand. "Mel—" Dammit! A delicious shiver runs down my spine, like a bolt of electricity. He feels it too. I snatch my arm back, ignoring the spark between us. More like a livewire threatening to electrocute us.

"Damn, sorry. Must be the dryness in the air." He clears his throat. The hipster behind us whines for us to move up, so we do. But instead of staying behind me, he steps next to me. "So, what's your usual here?"

Oh, now we're buds? Gonna chat about sports teams and favorite coffee recipes? I'm still trying to gather my bearings when it's our turn to order.

"What can I get you two?" the barista asks, and I almost request my sanity back.

"I'll take a coffee, black. She'll have a vanilla latte—skim milk, no whipped cream."

How the…? "How—How did you know what I like?" He's an alien. That's the only reasonable answer.

"I just pinged you as a sweet drinker. Loves her sugar but still manages to watch her calories." His smile is infectious. I want to reply with how creepy that is, but I find it cute.

Did I just say *cute*?

Get it together. He's not cute. *Hot. Sexy. Bad boy material.*

Internally slaps self.

"My turn? Black coffee, I'm assuming to match your soul?"

I thought his smile did funny things to me, but his laughter is like an aphrodisiac to my soul. "Something like that." When our order is ready, he grabs both, and I follow him to a small table, leaving us to sit super close. His legs extend under the table, brushing against mine. There's no hiding this attraction. Whether we want to admit it or not, it's there. I wonder at the change in him. He seemed pretty set on being a jerk, and I was okay with hating him. But now, sitting across from him, I want nothing more than to see what his intentions are.

"Sorry I was an asshole."

"And?" He's not getting away that easily.

He grumbles, and it's obvious he's not one to apologize. "Sorry for being an asshole and…being an asshole. What do you want me to say? I sure as hell ain't apologizing for kissing you."

I *phew* internally.

Keeping my game face in place, I say, "How about for all the mean things you said to me?"

"How about calling my dick tiny?" he fights back.

"You called me a swallow—"

"Your profile said it! How was I supposed to know—know if it was true or not? Is it?"

I'm about to slap him! "No! Listen, this was a bad idea." I move to stand, but he grabs my hand.

"Sit down…please. I'm sorry. I don't think you're a swallower. Unless you are. But I wouldn't know unless…shit, I don't know how to do this shit."

I never expected him to be the nervous one. He seems so sure of himself, and right now, he's got his tail between his legs. I'm kind of loving it. I reclaim my seat. "It's fine. For what it's worth, that profile is fake. My friends made it up to help me get some action. Some shit happened in my life, and they thought doing that would fix all my problems. You caught me in a vulnerable situation, and maybe I was a bit harsh too."

I guess the apology is happening after all. My eyes travel down to our still joined hands. He catches my meaning and releases me.

Boo…

"So, what now?"

He shrugs, gaining back some of his composure. "We see if we can stand each other long enough to finish our drinks. If we survive, then we try lunch. Or dinner. I'm not hopeful. But I'm willing to give you a chance."

What an asshole. Cute. Sexy. Kind of funny. Asshole.

"Fine. I'll do my best to stomach you. If that happens, which is doubtful, then lunch."

We both nod and go for our coffees.

This is going to be interesting.

chapter eight

Fuck hookup apps

Lukas
One week later...

WHY WON'T SHE DITCH THAT FUCKING APP?

I made a bold move. I won't use the word stalk, but dammit, I had to do something. She sent Dallas... well, *me* a message, throwing down the gauntlet. She wants to meet. Which means sex. How does she want to have sex with that fucker! *That fucker is you.* I'm jealous of my damn self. She's so easy going with him, but she's rigid and cold whenever we come into contact—and it pisses me the fuck off. So, I did what I had to do: I showed up at the coffee café, knowing she goes there every morning and played the part.

I got her to accept my truce. We spent almost three hours talking. Not once in my entire existence have I spent so much time with a woman doing that. Sex? I show up for sex. That's on the agenda. No doubt. I will have her in my bed, fucking the life out of her, but I need her to stop thinking about me. Well...fake me.

We made it through coffee and lunch, which turned into dinner the next night and lunch the day after that. And like a big ol' pussy, I didn't want the dates to end. This thing we were starting? Yeah, it was a done deal. We exchanged numbers. It allowed me to chat with her freely, which I found myself doing a lot. The problem was she was still chatting with the other, fake me. I had to get rid of Dallas. He was killing my vibe. She was this sweet, quirky girl with Dallas and this cheeky spitfire with me. And I was struggling to remember who I was supposed to be.

We spent the week playing cat and mouse, flirting like teenagers with our back and forth banter. I got almost giggly and shit whenever my phone would ding, but when it was for *him*, it was like a kick to the balls.

There was only one solution: get rid of Dallas and claim her as my own. He had served his purpose. *Thanks, pal.* But I don't share. Even if it's with myself.

I look at the time. She's going to be here soon to watch football. I ignore the bullshit texts from the guys, pissed I'm blowing off our Sunday Funday, and silence my phone. A knock on the door has me checking the plethora of snacks I picked up before answering.

"Are those wings I smell?" She walks in looking fucking delicious—minus her tacky Chiefs jersey. I have to force myself not to throw her against the wall and maul her.

"My wings. I got you some stale chips." She takes a swing at me, nailing me in the gut with her purse, and walks farther into my place.

"Asshole," she snickers, dropping her bag on the table. "Nice place. Does your mom live with you?" That fucking smart mouth. I spank her ass, and she yips, jumping up and backing away, allowing me a second to adjust my hardening dick.

"Yeah, I told her you were into pussy, so she's waiting for you in the bedroom. Said you have a nasty tongue, so be gentle with her."

Like magic, she sticks her tongue out at me and makes herself comfortable on my couch. Damn, she looks good on it.

This is how it's been.

Our banter is nonstop. And I fucking love it. I don't have to sweet-talk her to make her laugh. She actually appreciates my asshole side. Probably because she gets her dose of sweet from Dallas. That prick.

I throw myself down on the couch next to her, close enough that our thighs touch. "Ready to watch your team choke?"

"Pfft…the Cowboys probably won't even score the first half. I'll be so bored watching my team slay yours, I may take your mom up on her offer."

I regret making the joke because jealousy swarms in my gut at any tongue but mine touching her. And why would I make a joke about my mom? Idiot. This is why I don't do this shit. Sex. I do sex.

Until her.

"All right, priss mouth. You're so sure about your team, let's make a bet. Every time your team scores, I'll take off a piece of clothing. Every time my team scores, you strip."

Her brows perk at my suggestion. She stares at me, debating. "You know what? Deal. I have faith in my team. Better hope the tiny dick tale isn't true because we're about to find out when you end up buck naked next to me."

I stick my hand out, and we shake on it. "Deal. But I wouldn't be too sure, princess. I'll be introduced to your granny panties by the second half."

We both grab a beer from the coffee table, twist the cap, and cheers.

It's on.

chapter nine

Definitely didn't see that score coming

Melanie

"GET THE FUCK OUT OF HERE! THROW A FLAG!"

I buckle over laughing while Lukas spits at the television. "Told you the Cowboys suck." I cover my smiling lips with my beer bottle.

"They don't suck. They have shitty refs. That was clearly pass interference."

"Sure, pal. Whatever you say." With his shitty team who can't catch the ball, my team made an interception for a touchdown. "You know what to do, pretty boy." I wave my index finger around, signaling it's time.

He stares back at me.

I've only lost my jeans, so I'm chilling in my cute cheekies and jersey. Normally I'd feel a little insecure hanging out in my underwear, but the six beers have made me quite comfortable.

On the other hand, Lukas has lost his pants and socks—which I thought was a total cop-out, but since we didn't lay down rules beforehand, I allowed it. And if it matters, he's a boxer briefs kind of guy.

"This is bullshit."

"Your game. Come on. We don't have all day."

I sip on my beer as he obliges. When his jersey is up and over his head, exposing a chest full of muscle and more muscle, I choke on my beer.

He pulls his jersey back down. "What's wrong? You okay?"

"Yeah, beer's stale. Keep going." Lord all mighty, if he stops again, I'm going to rip it off for him with my teeth. I knew he was stacked. His arms are made of stone, so I could only assume his chest would be too. But this is way better than I could have imagined. My fingers tighten around my beer so I don't reach out and touch him. Even though I want to *jump* him. God! I've been so horny all week. Lukas brings out this wild feline in me, and I just want to maul him. Lick him up and down like a warm glass of milk. And sitting here, buzzed and half-clothed, I'm not sure I'll make it through this game without attacking him.

Once the jersey goes flying across the room, I force myself to focus on the TV. My legs start this nervous tap, and I gnaw on the inside of my cheek. *Stay put. Do not engage.*

The TV suddenly switches to another channel, and a home cooking network starts teaching us how to make chicken pot pies. "Dude, the game!" I snap.

"Shit, where's the remote?"

"I don't know." We both search around.

"Oh, I know…I normally put it…" He reaches over me, pecs rubbing against my chest, and sticks his hand into the couch. My jersey is too thick for him to feel my hard nipples, right? "I normally jam it in here…" Please, oh please, do I want him to jam something else somewhere. "It's just…normally…"

His eyes catch mine, and that livewire? Yeah, it finally lashes out and zaps the crap out of us both. The remote and game become a distant memory as he suddenly crushes his mouth over mine.

I wouldn't argue if someone just told me it was the Fourth of July. Sparks burst all around us. His hand slips under my jersey, and I grab at his shoulders. A deep grunt resonates up his throat when I dig my nails into his flesh at the feel of his erection against my belly. We can't get close enough. A shiver ripples through me as his tongue slips into my mouth, colliding with mine in a savage dance.

"Shit, you feel good," he groans, taking my mouth deeper. I moan when his hand cups my breast. Suddenly, he repositions me on his lap. Our lips fuse back in place, and his hand reaches around to unsnap my bra.

Just as quickly, my jersey is pushed up my chest.

"Your team didn't score," I mumble through our kiss.

"Oh, I'm about to score all right." He rips away from my swollen lips only to tug my bra to the side and wrap his mouth around my nipple. He sucks to the brink of pain, and I throw my head back, letting out a pleasurable moan.

"This is cheating," I pant, gripping his hair.

"I've never been known to play fair." He lets go of my nipple, then moves to devour my other one. I'm just as guilty of cheating because I find myself grinding against his erection.

"Fuck, don't do that." He grabs for my hips, digging into my skin. Instead of stopping me, he thrusts my hips back and forth along his length.

"I thought you told me to stop."

"Yeah, because you feel too fucking good. When I come, it's going to be in your sweet pussy, not my fucking pants."

God, that sounds irresponsible, yet super freaking hot. Especially when I grind against his cock and can confirm he has to be a million inches long. Not to mention wide.

His hands slide down my hips to cup my ass, and no doubt, I'm in the same compromising situation. I'm going to orgasm. I'm about to suggest we slow down when he flips me around, laying down with my back against his couch. His luscious body covers mine before—

Oh God, he's going down!

It's been over a century since a guy ventured down there. Not that I don't keep it pristine, it's just what if…

"Lukas."

"I'm celebrating early. Team win bonus."

Jesus. "There's no way the Cowboys wi—*shit*."

He rips my panties off, and like a magician, he starts doing magical things with his magical tongue—*aaaand* that's a finger! I squeeze my eyes tight, enjoying the ride. Holy hell, why have I gone so long without this? *No willing applicants.* Oh, yeah. Tad probably couldn't figure out his way around a vagina with a map. *"Ohhh, fuck."* Two fingers.

"Oh, I plan on it, princess." He pumps into me, his tongue like a magical wand hitting all the right places. I want to play it cool, but I'm a lit firecracker ready to detonate. With every swipe of his tongue, my wick burns brighter, until, three, two—"Oh, *God!*"

God Bless America rings in my head as my hips shoot off the couch, practically knocking out Lukas. A deep rumble of laughter tickles the insides of my thighs. Lukas pulls off me, and I'm afraid to open my eyes. How obvious is it that it's been like forever since someone has gone downtown on me? Especially like *that.*

He sits up, and when I pop an eye open, his lips are blossoming into a huge grin. "For the record, it's Lukas. But if you wanna call me God, princess, I'll let ya." He climbs up to me, going straight for my lips. The taste of my arousal mingles on his tongue as he kisses me deep and hard. The heat between us is explosive. I suddenly feel like I'm suffocating in my jersey.

"Off," I moan, gripping a chunk of his hair.

"Love it when you get bossy." His fingers dig into the lining of my jersey, and *poof*! It's gone along with my bra. I should feel exposed with my breasts on full display, but the only thing coursing through my veins is lust, intense desire, need.

"Pants off," I growl, arching my head back when his teeth graze my nipple.

"As you wish, princess." He hurries out of his boxers, and I almost faint at the feel of his warm flesh against me. Holy shit, this is happening. Is it? *Should* it? I technically hate this guy. *No, you don't.* He's such an asshole. *One who creates this tornado of butterflies with every text, stolen glance, and simple touch.* He's moody and grumpy, he hardly ever has anything nice to say, and if I was honest, he's way too arrogant for my liking. But for some crazy reason, I think he's… perfect.

His lips break from mine, and for a second, I worry he has the same doubts and is jumping ship. "Condom." He winks and leans over the couch, retrieving one from his jeans. I try not to look so fascinated as he opens the packet with his teeth and rolls it down his monster dick. *Now*, I'm officially mortified I ever called him tiny.

Because he's… "Huge," Lukas says, reading my mind as I'm ogling his junk. Huge isn't even the right word.

"I was going to go with average, but huge works." I avoid saying massive. Colossal. Just may split me in two.

He adjusts himself between my quivering thighs, and I hold my breath, waiting to be destroyed by his cock. I'm not sure how this is even going to feel good. If it even fits.

"Mel."

"Yep?"

"Breathe."

"Got it—*ahhh*…" He slides into me, and I'm a goner. He pauses to make sure I do, in fact, start to breathe before moving. His lips drop from my mouth and begin feathering kisses across my cheek, then down the line of my jaw.

"Shit," he hisses, picking up the pace, thrusting in and out, inch by glorious inch. No matter how much I tell myself to breathe, I struggle to bring air into my lungs. At least he's no better. A hiss of breath falls from his lips, followed by a deep groan. My hands are back in his hair, tugging, gliding down his back, my nails scratching, grabbing his tight butt, squeezing. "Fuck, you're like a little minx." He powers into me like a man on a mission. I wrap my legs around his waist and hold on tight. He rides me hard and quick, and before I know it, my eyes are rolling into the back of my head, and I'm having an out of body experience. My orgasm blasts like a rocket up my spine, and I curl my toes as I blow the fuck up.

"Dammit, you're…so…tight, fuck!" Lukas howls. With one final drive, he loses his own battle, hissing out his release. He collapses against me, and it doesn't even matter if I can't breathe. I'm too concerned with the fact that I can't feel my legs. "Fucking devil pussy." He pops up and disappears into the bathroom.

Huh?

Not quite the first thing you want to hear after mind-blowing sex. At least for one of us. He returns, reclaiming his spot on top of me.

"Yeah, say again?" I'm going to need him to confirm what

exactly he meant because it *definitely* didn't sound like, *wow, you were amazing.*

God! Why did I fall for his luring seduction? An asshole is always an asshole.

"Marry me."

What!

"Shit. No…that's not what I meant to say. Fuck, that came out wrong." Yeah, it did. I think. "Date. Let's date."

"You wanna *date*?" Jesus, what's happening here? He went from calling my vagina the devil to proposing.

"Shit, I don't know how to do this shit. That was…you have me under this spell, and that was… We're gonna do that again. And again. 'Cause holy shit…" His expression goes from sated to pained. "I'm fuckin this up, aren't I?"

I mean…

"No, it's fine. I *think* what you're trying to say is I'm the best you've ever had." He opens his mouth to reply, but I beat him to it. "And! You'd sell your soul to the devil for another round." Again, he opens his mouth, but I cut him off. "And for another chance with me, you're willing to admit the Cowboys suck—"

"Never!"

"Oh, man. Too bad. I actually enjoyed your average—"

His mouth slams over mine, granting me the most devastating kiss. "I'm not average."

"Define not—"

Fuck! He bites my lower lip. "I'm not average, the Cowboys don't suck, and you're mine now." His lips graze down my chin. "You should be lucky I'm able to get past your love for your crappy football team—not to mention you're stubborn, have a mouth on you, and like pineapple on your pizza. But I'm a generous—ouch!" I dig my nails into his ass cheeks. "Dammit, devil woman."

He doesn't let up, no matter how hard I squeeze. "Keep it up. I like my women aggressive. You're just making yourself more enticing."

Jesus.

This guy.

If he insists.

"*Ouch*! You're about to jeopardize your five-star review." I slap his ass. "Four-star." Again. "Three-star!"

"I told you that profile was fake. I don't guzzle or skip dinner. You most definitely have to feed me to get in my pants."

He pulls away, his eyes lighting with humor. "Deal."

His lips find mine once again, and after pulling on another condom, he pushes back into me, inch by glorious inch. This round's even wilder. The one after that is even hotter. And the one after that one is…just wow.

We don't call it quits until he runs out of condoms, and I run out of energy. Sprawled out on his bed, taking a much-needed breather, he blurts out, "Delete the app."

Confusion registers across my face. "What app?"

"FitItIn. Delete it."

I have no problem deleting it, but I'm curious why he cares so much to ask that.

"I'll lose all my ratings if I do," I joke.

He rolls me onto my back and stares down at me. "I'll give you plenty of ratings. Delete it. You don't need that shit. It's fake anyway. What's the big deal?"

He's right. It's not. But a small tinge of guilt resonates when I think of Dallas. We've become friends. But maybe that's all it was ever meant to be. He's great, but there isn't that spark like with Lukas. This is real. And asshole or not, I want it.

"Sure, I'll delete it. But you better stick to your word. Stellar reviews. Or it's going back on." He grips my hips as his mouth covers mine.

"Whatever you say, swallower."

"Whatever, asshole."

"Priss."

"Average."

"Mine."

He wins.

I'm spent. I can barely hold my phone to my face without my arms shaking. Thank God Lukas passed out. I was going to have to lock myself in the bathroom if he tried for one more round. If my legs even worked, I would get up and find an ice pack for my poor vagina. She's not used to such an extensive workout. Or using such heavy-weights—if you get what I mean.

I turn my head, enjoying the gorgeous view beside me. Lukas is sleeping, his lips parted, breaths even. Yep. This is gonna be fun. Who would have thought a simple run-in would turn into something so insanely awesome? To think about how my life has shifted in the past month. I muster up a giggle. I couldn't be happier.

I bring my phone into view and open FitItIn. Navigating to the messages, I find my chat with Dallas.

Melanie: Hey, Dallas. Thanks for being such a great friend. I really did enjoy our conversations, and I'm sorry we never got to meet in person. In all honesty, I met someone. And I really like him. It's crazy to say, but I really see this working out. And with that, I'm deleting this app. I do hope you meet someone as funny and kind as you are. Good luck. I wish you the best.

I press Send, and then as Grumpy demanded, I delete the app.

Lukas's phone goes off on his nightstand, and I debate waking him up but decide I'm selfish and want him all to myself. Placing my phone on his nightstand, I snuggle up to him and close my eyes.

To be continued…

Will Lukas dodge the bullet of his online scam and keep the girl?
Add *Ctrl+Alt+Bang* to your TBR for all upcoming news!

about the author

Best-selling author, J.D. Hollyfield is a creative designer by day and superhero by night. When she's not cooking, event planning, or spending time with her family, she's relaxing with her nose stuck in a book. With her love for romance, and her head full of book boyfriends, she was inspired to test her creative abilities and bring her own stories to life. Living in the Midwest, she's currently at work on blowing the minds of readers, with the additions of her new books and series, along with her charm, humor and HEA's.

J.D. Hollyfield dabbles in all genres, from romantic comedy, contemporary romance, historical romance, paranormal romance, fantasy, taboo and erotica! Want to know more! Follow her on all platforms!

Keep up to date on all things J.D. Hollyfield
Twitter
Author Page
Fan Page
Instagram
Goodreads
Amazon
BookBub

acknowledgements

First off, a huge thank you to Willow Winters for allowing me this amazing opportunity to contribute to the Live a Thousand Lives anthology and be a part of such a worthy charity. I am forever grateful.

Thanks to all my eyes and ears. Having a squad who has your back is the utmost important when creating a masterpiece. From betas, to proofers, to PA's, to my dog, Jackson, who just gets me when I don't get myself, thank you. This success is not a solo mission. It comes with an entourage of awesome people who got my back. So, shout out to my assistant Gina Behrends and graphics designer at HEA Studios, Ashley Cestra, Jenny Hanson, Molly Wittman at Novel Mechanic, Monica Black at Word Nerd Editing, Melissa Shipe, Cindy Camp, Brandi Zelenka, Kristi Webster and everyone in my amazing reader group at Club JD I appreciate you all!

Want more from J.D. Hollyfield? Check out the books below!

Love Not Included Series

Life in a Rut, Love not Included

Life Next Door

My So Called Life

Life as We Know It

Standalones

Faking It

Love Broken

Sundays are for Hangovers

Conheartists

Lake Redstone

Junkie

Chicks, Man

Paranormal/Fantasy

Sinful Instincts

Unlocking Adeline

#HotCom Series

Passing Peter Parker

Creed's Expectations

Exquisite Taste

2 Lovers Series

Text 2 Lovers

Hate 2 Lovers

Thieves 2 Lovers

Four Father Series

Blackstone

Four Sons Series

Hayden

Dirty Little Secret Duet

Bad Daddy

Sweet Little Lies

A romantic-suspense short story

ALEATHA ROMIG

chapter one

My knuckles blanched on the steering wheel as I pumped the brakes of my rental car. Even though I'd been told—more than once—that automatic brakes didn't require pumping, I couldn't help myself. The action calmed my nerves, giving me the illusion that I had an ounce of control as the tires slid and scooted upon the ice-covered road and large snowflakes the size of oranges fell from the sky.

With the sheer quantity of snowflakes hitting the windshield, I knew any sense of control I thought I possessed was nothing more than a figment of my imagination. If circumstances were different, I could relax and see the beauty around me. If instead of driving by myself to an unknown future, I was sipping hot chocolate next to a roaring fire with loved ones, I might be able to appreciate that I had somehow managed to enter a giant snow globe, and that whole world had just been given a strong shake.

My attention went back and forth between what I believed was the road before me and my GPS. According to the screen, I was still on the pavement; thank God the GPS could differentiate because from my viewpoint, everything between the endless borders of tall pine trees was nothing more than a white ribbon.

Though I continued forward, my estimated time of arrival continued to grow later and later. That was in no doubt due to my decreased speed. Between the snow-and-ice-covered surface, the lack of defined road, and increased blizzard conditions, including gusty wind, it seemed as if instead of driving, the car was crawling forward. The speedometer varied between fifteen and a whopping twenty-five miles per hour.

When I'd left Chicago this morning, the forecast had been clear. The weathercaster said that snow wasn't supposed to arrive until late tomorrow. With only a seven-hour drive, my plan was to arrive at the hotel in Ashland, Wisconsin, before nightfall and get a feel for the city. With less than ten thousand people, it would be drastically different from what I was used to in Chicago.

That, in a nutshell, was exactly why I applied for this job.

"Good plan, Julia," I said aloud to myself.

Maybe after hours of driving north from Chicago, I was hungry to hear a human voice, one not singing or on a podcast. Or perhaps, I was too exasperated with my situation to keep quiet any longer.

"Did you ever wonder why this job was available? It's because whomever this client is could be a psycho and on top of that, it's located in the middle of nowhere."

Sadly, nowhere was exactly what I'd sought.

Going back to my analogy of a shaken snow globe, that was my life.

Shaken.

Hours of driving had given me a new perspective, one that benefited from a bit of distance. I knew there were many people who faced greater obstacles and more adversity. I also wasn't the princess in the ivory tower that many believed.

My eyes narrowed as I tried to make out the road before me. The headlights created a tunnel of illumination filled with glistening large snowflakes above a thick white blanket.

"Come on, you can make it. Just" —I looked again at the GPS— "another hour."

My stomach growled as I held tighter to the steering wheel, feeling the way the wind gusts pushed me sideways. I shook my head, wondering if I'd see any signs of civilization: a gas station or small town. The darker the sky became as my car plowed through the accumulating snow, the more I admitted if only to myself that I should have stopped in the last town.

As I crept onward, the phrase 'should have' seemed to repeat on a loop in my thoughts.

I should have stopped in the last town, filled the gas tank, gotten something to eat, and found a hotel.

I should have said no to Skylar Butler when he asked me to

marry him. I should have seen the writing on the wall. I should have discouraged my parents from planning the most lavish wedding of the century. I should have known his parents were more excited about our nuptials than he was. I should have questioned Skylar's schedule, his trips and the times he didn't answer his cell phone. I should have trusted what I'd known most of our lives.

In my defense, as the sayings went, hindsight was twenty-twenty and love was blind.

In my case, I think a more accurate assessment of our impending nuptials was that our love didn't have vision problems; it quite simply never existed, not in the way that made your heart beat faster or palms dampen. It wasn't that Skylar was bad on the eyes.

He was handsome and he knew it.

That has been an issue since we were young.

Skylar was also capable when it came to foreplay.

Further than that, and I was in the minority of women in Skylar's orbit. I didn't know if the rumors of his sexual prowess were accurate. We'd agreed to wait for that final consummation of our relationship. That's not to say we hadn't gotten close. The thing was, we'd been a couple since either of us could walk or talk. It was difficult to think of one another in romantic terms.

The agreement of remaining pure was implied.

Apparently, it was an agreement between Skylar and me, not him and...well, anyone else.

My grip intensified on the steering wheel. It wasn't the worsening conditions, but the memory of finding the text message from my best friend and maid of honor, Beth.

Let me backtrack.

A year ago, at a large holiday gathering surrounded by family and friends along with some of the most powerful people in both our families' world, Skylar took my hand and on bended knee proposed. Like everything else in his life, the entire scene was a performance. My smile and acceptance weren't as important as the hushed whispers, the pregnant pause waiting for my answer, and the cheers from the crowd when I said yes.

And then my fiancé was off for cigars and bourbon with our fathers and others in the industry to celebrate the uniting of our families. It wasn't as if I were forgotten. No, I now had an important role. I was immediately surrounded by our mothers and all the ladies in Chicago's high society who could welcome me into the married world of Chicago's finest.

Becoming Mrs. Skylar Butler was a destination I never questioned. The road map had been not only sketched but written in ink since the day of my birth, just three months after Skylar's.

Time moved on. My wedding showers were completed. Our newly constructed home was mostly complete, filled with gifts and all the luxuries money could buy. Our two-week overseas honeymoon trip was booked, and RSVPs to the big day were coming in by the hundreds.

Our wedding was set for New Year's Eve.

It will be—*was* to be—the event of the decade.

No expense had been spared for the union of Julia McGrath and Skylar Butler.

This was not only a love story—according to all the society pages—but the business deal of the century. My family lost majority interest in Wade Pharmaceuticals before 2000 when our hold went below fifty percent. The reasons could be cited as bad management, the economy, or a number of decisions that didn't pan out. Regardless, my family lost what we'd possessed since my great-grandfather founded the company.

My father's controlling interest existed by a paper-thin margin.

He blamed it all on my grandfather's decision to take Wade public, to allow investors. Over time, there had been buyouts, splits, and turnovers. As was spelled out in my grandfather's will, the shares of Wade Pharmaceutical would go to me upon my fulfillment of his criteria, the final step being marriage.

The Butlers held roughly twenty-five percent of Wade stock. By uniting the Butler and McGrath stock, the founding family could once again fend off attacks from Big Pharma. It was my father's constant belief that a coup was in the works. He believed that the giants in the industry were picking up shares here, with another there, to swoop in and swallow up Wade.

With my family's thirty-nine percent and the Butler's twenty-five, Wade would be secure.

The evening after my last bridal shower and a week before Christmas, Skylar and I were to attend a charity event at the Chicago Philharmonic. Before the performance, we drove out to our new estate, west of the city, on a sprawling twenty-acre plot of land—our future home.

Skylar had laid his phone on the kitchen counter before going out back to check on some last-minute construction changes. Our wedding was only two weeks away and the house needed to be ready upon our return from our honeymoon.

When I saw my best friend's name flash on the screen of his phone, I envisioned a planned pre-wedding surprise. I justified that she'd call Skylar; after all, she was also the maid of honor in our wedding.

Opening the text message, I was without a doubt surprised.

"Oh no." My scream echoed as the rental car lost its footing and began to spin, flinging me from the thoughts of the recent past to the here and now.

Still a ways from my destination, my life flashed before my eyes as the white ribbon appeared to be replaced by trees and then back to the ribbon. Like a child's top, I continued around and around.

In those visions, I saw Skylar and myself as we were growing children. I recalled my desire to pursue literature and journalism, an unacceptable major for the future owner of a pharmaceutical company. Double majoring in business and literature, I squeezed in a minor in journalism from Northwestern. The academic road took me an additional semester, allowing me to complete my degree in time for the grand engagement.

The car came to a stop, bringing me back to the present.

Letting out the breath, I laid my forehead on the steering wheel and closed my eyes. Opening them, I saw that I was no longer on the white ribbon of road. The hood of the car was mostly buried in a snowbank and from my vantage, it looked like the bumper must have stopped inches from a tall pine tree.

I reached for my cell phone. There was no signal.

Glancing into the rearview mirror, I saw my own blue eyes. "Happy holidays, Julia. You had a fiancé, a family, a company, and a brand-new home. Maybe you should have stayed."

Swallowing, I stared out at the white surrounding me.

With each passing minute, determination surged through my veins.

If I stayed where I was, I'd freeze.

If I began walking, I could freeze.

"You didn't get here by staying put."

It was a conversation with myself, but it was accurate.

After learning that my best friend was expecting my fiancé's baby, I bolted from our newly constructed home, leaving Skylar stranded. As I drove away, I recalled a job listing I'd seen nearly a month earlier.

Pulling over outside Chicago, I searched, only to find the listing still existed. It read:

Financier seeks writer to pen memoirs. No experience required. Must be willing to live on-site until the project is complete. Salary negotiable. Contact Fields and Smith Agency for more information.

It was a crazy idea—a crazy idea that would allow me to walk away from my life's planned trajectory, and in the process, utilize my degree in literature and journalism. From the side of the road, I sent a message to the Fields and Smith Agency, a legal firm in Ashland, Wisconsin.

Less than an hour later, I received a phone call. The gentleman sounded older. He asked all the appropriate questions. It was when I asked who the financier was that Mr. Fields informed me that his client wanted to remain anonymous until it was time to meet a candidate.

"Have I heard of this person?" I asked on the call.

"I'm not certain who you've heard of, Miss McGrath."

"Is he old? Or is he a she?"

"You will have your own quarters. My client's gender and age are irrelevant."

"Is there something wrong with your client?"

"No, miss. My client prefers his privacy, and this project is something he takes seriously. I assure you, if you are selected, you will be well compensated."

The only clue I'd managed to glean was that the client was male.

It wasn't compensation I wanted. It was the chance to get away from my commitments and obligations—my shares of Wade would remain in my father's hands, to take some time away from all the lies I'd accepted, and to find out what it was I truly wanted.

"I'd like to have an interview, Mr. Fields."

"How soon can you be to Ashland?"

"In a few days."

"There is the holiday."

"I am aware, Mr. Fields, but I'd like to move on to this or to something else."

My note to my parents simply said that the wedding was cancelled, and I would be in touch. Throwing clothes and cosmetics into two suitcases, I waited until morning and began to drive. Hell, I didn't even know who this client was who wanted privacy. I envisioned an old man on death's door with war stories to tell—stories he felt would be relevant to someone.

Before they'd passed, I'd been close with my grandparents. The idea of listening to some old man's stories in the middle of nowhere and writing them down wasn't unappealing. I wished I'd spent more time listening to my grandfather's stories.

Taking a deep breath, I secured my lined boots, added another layer of a down coat, and donned my gloves and hat. As I took one last look in the rearview mirror, determination continued to grow. I was here and by God, I wasn't going to freeze to death in a car on the side of the road.

Reaching for the door handle, I opened the latch. It took pushing with my full weight, but I wedged the door open into the snow bank.

After securing my belongings in the trunk, I climbed up onto what was the road. Ducking my head from the pelting snow, I continued to follow the white ribbon.

chapter two

THE MONOLOGUE IN MY HEAD LOST ITS FEROCITY. MY SELF-ABSORBED determination to leave my life behind became more morose as I contemplated the possibility that I had facilitated that very goal—leaving my life, not by choice but by death.

Despite my gloved hand protecting my face, my cheeks ached from the cold. My fingers and toes were no longer felt as I trudged forward. During the hours of my drive, I'd only seen a half dozen other vehicles, and yet as I moved forward, that was what I yearned to see.

The snow glistened as white light danced on the newly fallen accumulation.

Looking back, I hoped to see a car, a truck, or maybe a snow plow.

I'd read once about igloos. The thought came and went as I imagined digging into the growing drifts. It still seemed as if it would be cold, but at least I'd be out of the wind.

The howl of the blowing played tricks as I searched again for a vehicle.

Nothing.

Time lost meaning as my thoughts went to my parents. I couldn't imagine their disappointment at my behavior, at leaving the city before the holiday and two weeks before my wedding. And yet I loved them and I knew they loved me. We would work this out, unless I never returned.

I spun again at the sound of something over the howling wind.

Do mirages only appear in deserts?

Two headlights pierced the snow-filled darkness, growing bigger and brighter.

Is this real?

My heart beat faster, my circulation returning and delivering pain to my extremities.

Tears threatened to freeze on my cheeks as through the darkness, a black snow-covered truck appeared.

Waving my arms with what little energy remained, as the truck came to a stop, my knees gave out, and I fell to the snow. A face appeared before me. The air filled with small vapors as a man spoke.

"Jesus, lady, are you all right?"

Piercing green eyes stared down at me from below a bright orange hat and above a brown heavy coat.

"Cold." It was all I could articulate with my frozen lips.

"Fuck," the man muttered as he reached for my hand.

"Ouch," I called out as pain radiated from my fingers.

The man's head shook as he reached beneath me. "Can you lift your arms?" His deep voice rumbled through my freezing mind, cracking the ice, and infiltrating it with warmth.

I wasn't sure if I answered, nodded, or spoke. My concentration was on doing as he asked and lifting my arms around his neck. Strong arms lifted me from the snow and pulled me toward his coat-covered chest. I tucked my cheek against him. Inhaling against the warm material, the scent of a campfire such as those from real wood filled my senses.

"What are you doing out here?"

My teeth chattered as I tried to speak.

Holding me with one arm, he opened the door to his truck and placed me on the seat. "I'm going to get you someplace warm."

Strapping the seatbelt over me, he inclined the seat. Marvelous warmth blew from the vents as I closed my eyes. The scent of burning wood brought back a happier time. I remembered sitting by the fireplace in my grandparents' cottage. It was on a lake with a real wood burning fireplace.

Memories lulled me to sleep.

I snuggled against the softness of the warm blanket moments before my eyelids fluttered open.

Before me was a raging fire, flames jumped as damp logs snapped and crackled. The fireplace was made of sandstone, much like the one at my grandparents'.

Panic bubbled within me at the prospect that maybe this was heaven, a place of comfort in my memory. Maybe there weren't clouds, harps, streets of gold, and pearly gates. Instead, the afterlife was one of comfort. My stomach twisted in hunger.

I shouldn't be hungry in heaven.

Raking my fingers through my disheveled hair, I began to look around. The only illumination was from the fire and a small kerosene lamp sitting on a table. Sitting up, I wrapped the quilt tighter around me. Out of the corner of my eye, I noticed my clothes, lying over the footboard of the bed, stretched out to dry. Peeking under the quilt, I confirmed that I was only wearing my bra and panties.

Wiggling my fingers and toes, I could feel them ache. The skin was red. My cheeks felt sun burnt, and my hair was disheveled.

Quickly, I turned from side to side, wondering who I'd see, who was with me, and who took off my clothes.

The cabin where I found myself was rustic like my grandparents' place, but smaller.

"Hello?" I called.

The only answer came from the fire's sounds and the wind beyond the cabin walls. Beyond the windows the night sky was still filled with falling snow. It wasn't difficult to tell that I was alone. There was nowhere to hide in one room.

Faint memories of a man came to mind. Green eyes, an orange hat, and a deep voice.

With my feet bare, yet warmed, I stood, the aftereffects of the cold sent needles and pins to the soles. Tentatively, I walked around, admiring the quaintness of the furnishings. In the warm firelight, I ran my hand over each piece. Most appeared handmade, a table and two chairs, a bed with a wooden headboard and footboard, and a wooden sofa with long cushions.

Near the bed was a table with an old-fashioned pitcher and wash basin. Above the old china set was a cloudy oval mirror. The reflection wasn't of the heir to Wade Pharmaceuticals or the future Mrs. Butler.

My long brown hair was wavy from the snow and drying by the fire. Any makeup I'd applied was gone, yet Mother Nature had left her mark. My cheeks and lips were pink. I ran my tongue over the bottom lip and then the top, bringing a bit of moisture.

A quick check confirmed that my clothes were still too wet to be worn.

The kitchen area, separated by the small table, consisted of a sink with an old pump, the kind that needed priming, a counter, some shelves, cupboards, and a stove that also used wood as heat. Upon the two metal burners were an old coffee pot and a pan filled with water.

I turned off the burner under the water, as it was beginning to boil. Using a small towel, I held onto the coffee pot's handle and lifted, pleased to find it heavy. Dark drops percolated within the glass top on the lid as the aroma of coffee joined the scent of the fire.

While coffee would be good, my empty stomach hoped for more. I opened a cupboard to find a few cans of soup. By the way it looked beyond the windows, sending for Uber Eats was out of the question. That thought led me to thoughts of my phone. I found it on the table near the bed, without signal and with very little battery.

There was nothing to suggest this cabin had electricity. Charging my phone or anything else was out of the question.

The cool cement floor beneath my feet was covered with an array of rugs of all sizes. The wood walls gave the feel of a real log cabin. The farther I moved away from the fireplace, the cooler the air became.

It was as I settled back on the thick blanket where I'd awakened and wrapped the quilt around me that the door to my side opened wide. A gust of cold wind filled with snow preceded the man from my memory. His arms were filled with logs. After giving me a quick glance, he kicked the door closed with his long leg. When he stood erect, he was tall.

I obviously didn't know him or anything about him, other than he'd saved my life and apparently disrobed me, yet without a word, my pulse increased and my cheeks felt flush.

His green eyes came my way before setting the logs in a round holder near the fireplace. Wiping his gloved hands one over the other, he dusted the bark and dirt to the floor. One by one, he pulled the gloves away from his long fingers, and still his gaze stayed glued on me.

I tugged on the quilt, suddenly reminded that this had been the man who removed my clothes.

The ends of his lips twitched, perhaps humored by my unease.

Unzipping the front of his brown coat, he shrugged it off, shaking the snow to the floor. Next, he removed his stocking cap, revealing a crown of messy dark hair. Finally breaking his stare, he turned to hang the coat and his stocking cap upon a peg near the door. The shirt beneath was flannel and unbuttoned over a thermal shirt beneath.

Survival 101 came to mind with his layering.

Without glancing at my clothes, I knew I'd failed that test.

I worked my way to my feet and when he turned back, I spoke, "Thank you."

He lifted his chin. "Not exactly a good night for a walk." His gaze went to the window as white swirled in the darkness. "Of course, you're welcome to leave, if you want."

I shook my head. "I don't want that, not now."

Nodding, the man walked to the stove and pulled two metal mugs from a shelf. Without asking, he filled both with hot coffee and brought one to me.

His lips curled into a smile as he scanned the quilt and handed me the mug. "I usually try to introduce myself before I take off a lady's clothes."

"Usually?"

He nodded. "Usually, as with any rule. There are exceptions."

I placed the mug of coffee on the hearth, and extended my hand. "Thank you for saving me. I'm Julia."

The flames reflected in his eyes like glowing embers. As I

stepped closer, the aroma of the outdoors surrounded us, fresh and cool. Although he'd been outside, as his fingers encased my hand, his touch wasn't cold. It was the opposite, as if there was energy within him flowing from him to me. Our connection was a jolt like I had never experienced. It shot through me, electrifying my skin and sending sparks to my insides.

Pulling my hand away, I stared down at my hand, wondering if he'd felt the same thing.

What was it?

Maybe it was from the near frostbite.

As I lifted my chin, he began to speak. "Are you sure?"

"Am I sure?"

"Julia, perhaps you should reconsider your gratitude." He looked around. "You're in a blizzard in northern Wisconsin without a way to contact civilization. Does that sound like you were saved?" Small lines formed around his vibrant green eyes as he grinned. "Or are you perhaps captured?"

chapter three

MY MOUTH FELT SUDDENLY DRY AS COLOR DRAINED FROM MY cheeks. I feigned a laugh. "I believe saved. You see, I would have frozen to death without your help."

Amusement danced in his gaze along with the reflection of the fire. "Julia, I'm Van. I suppose now that we know one another's names, taking off our clothes is acceptable." He tugged on the sleeves of his flannel shirt and pulled it off, tossing it onto the sofa's cushions. Without the flannel, a light gray thermal shirt remained, nicely stretched across his wide shoulders and chest.

Sitting on the blanket, I said, "I believe I'm down to as few clothes as possible."

Van shook his head as he picked up his mug of coffee. "I know for a fact that's not true."

Technically, he was right. I was still wearing my bra and panties.

I reached for the mug I'd set on the hearth and wrapped my fingers around the warm metal. "How long do you think it will be until we can leave?"

"If that was your car I saw down the road, I think you may need to consider a tow truck after the spring thaw."

"What?"

"In all honesty, we'll need some melting to find it. It was mostly buried." He took a sip of his coffee. "I'm glad I saw it. That's why I started looking for the driver."

A deep sigh left my lips. "It's a rental car. I can't tell the rental company I lost their car in a snowbank."

Van scoffed. "You could tell them you ran it off the road, but the good news is you didn't hit a tree."

My mind went back to the car. "All of my things are in the

trunk. I even left my purse in there." I tilted my head toward the bed. "All I took with me was my phone."

He nodded. "That would be why I couldn't find anything to identify you." He tilted his chin toward the phone. "That's not going to do you much good here. Once the snow stops, you may be able to go up the hill and get a signal. I recommend you save whatever battery you have."

My shoulders slumped as I shook my head. "It figures."

"And what is that, Julia?"

"I finally decide to do something for myself and look." My lips came together.

The tips of his lips curled upward as his green gaze scanned me. "I'm looking."

Setting down the coffee mug, I stood again, pulling the quilt tightly around me and took a step toward the small table. A million things were swirling in my head, not unlike the snow beyond the window. I didn't know Van. That meant, I could keep quiet or maybe take the opportunity to vent. I decided on somewhere in between. "My whole life has been planned and the one time I decide to take charge, I mess that up." I pulled out one of the chairs from the table and sat. As I did, I ran my hand over the table's surface. "Do you live here?" I asked, hoping to change the subject.

"No."

My chin snapped up. "Who does?"

"No one, to my knowledge."

"Are we trespassing?"

"This cabin is used during hunting season. I believed it would be empty. With as cold as you were, I thought the risk of me driving off the road trying to get into town wasn't a good plan."

"Are you from around here?"

Van nodded. "But you're not."

"No," I said with a sigh. "I thought I could…" My head shook. "It doesn't matter."

Van reached for my coffee and brought it to me, placing it on the table. "Are you hungry?"

"Famished." I looked around. "Is there…food besides the old cans of soup?"

He scoffed. "I see you've searched."

"There isn't much to search."

"The good news is that I have a case of nectarines in my truck. And yes, there is always the soup." He nodded toward a cupboard under the counter. "I'm not sure how old the cans are. We could search for expiration dates. There is a pan to warm it if we want."

That reminded me of the pot of water on the stove. "I turned the water off, it was boiling."

Van nodded as he went to the pan and poured the water into a large jar. "This is to drink. I'm not sure about the water out of the pump. Boiling it first is best."

It felt as though I was secluded with one of those mountain men from the movies.

"Why do you have nectarines in your truck?" I asked.

"I like nectarines."

It was my turn to smile. "So you keep a case in your truck, just in case?"

"I order them by the case, and I'd recently picked up a shipment from the post office in town. At this moment, I'm glad I forgot to take them in my house."

"Me too."

Van headed toward the door, and stopped, picking up his flannel shirt from where he'd dropped it on the sofa. "You're welcome to keep wearing the quilt, but I would guess that this shirt would make a decent length dress." He brought it to me. "Your choice, but your clothes are still cold and wet."

I reached out and took the shirt. "Thank you."

"There isn't a lot of privacy here. If you want to put it on, I'll be outside for a minute getting our dinner."

Another thought came to me. "What about a bathroom?"

"There's an outhouse about twenty yards from the door."

For only a moment, my mouth dropped open. "You're not serious."

He grinned. "As a matter of fact, I am. I even shoveled a path out to it when I went for more wood. And the increased accumulation of snow works like insulation. Once you're inside, the wind won't freeze you."

"The wind doesn't need to, the cold will."

"Not if you hurry."

My head shook. "This is just unbelievable."

Van went to a skinny cupboard near the table with the old pitcher and basin. Opening it, he pulled out a pair of what appeared to be rubber pants, complete with boots and suspenders. "After you put my shirt on, you can wear these out to the outhouse."

My eyes narrowed. "What are those?"

"Waders," he replied, as if I should have known the answer.

"Waders? Aren't those for fishing?"

"Very good."

"You said the cabin is used for hunting."

"During the summer, it's used to hunt fish," Van said with a grin. "Instead of a gun, a fishing pole is used. There's a lake nearby."

"Nectarines." I reminded.

Leaving the waders on the bed, Van put his coat back on, his orange hat, and his gloves. When he turned my way, he winked. "I don't think I've ever looked forward to seeing that old shirt more."

His gaze lingered a bit longer than it should before he turned and disappeared beyond the door, leaving a powdering of snow on the floor in his wake.

Despite the gust of cold air, Van's comment warmed me, from my head to my toes. How was it that this man I barely knew could incite the visceral response with a relatively benign comment about clothing and the man I was engaged to couldn't or didn't make me feel that way even when he was kissing and touching me?

I refused to give that any more thought.

Besides, I wasn't engaged.

Not anymore.

Lifting my left hand, I stared at my bare ring finger.

The last time I saw the huge four-carat diamond, it was on the counter next to Skylar's phone and a note that read:

Beth needs you. Good-bye, Julia.

Of course, after I left, Skylar has tried to call and text. I haven't answered.

Taking one last look at the closed door, I dropped the quilt. As I reached for Van's flannel shirt, the tempered air sent goose bumps over my skin and caused my nipples to tightened beneath my bra. Without thinking, I brought the soft material to my nose, closed my eyes, and inhaled.

The fresh scent of soap, the aroma of fire, and the spice of cologne all created an enticing concoction that even in this short time had me thinking of Van. Slipping my arms into the sleeves, I realized that Van had been right; this could be a dress. As I began to button the front, the tails in the front and back came to just above my knees.

While I had dresses that were shorter, wearing this man's shirt—a man whom I barely knew—somehow felt more scandalous. I was in the process of rolling the sleeves when the door opened. As he'd done before, Van used his booted foot to kick the door closed. This time, instead of logs, his arms were filled with a wooden crate that he set down on the floor. Between the slats of wood, the orange spheres made my mouth water.

After shedding the hat, gloves, and coat, Van retrieved the crate from the floor and brought it to the kitchen counter. Once there, he turned in my direction and smiled. Without a word, his green stare scanned me from my messy hair to my bare toes.

With each passing second, I became more self-conscious, and yet he didn't speak. Van's lips formed a straight line, his cheeks rose, and his eyes sparkled with flakes of gold I was just now noticing.

"Thanks for the shirt," I said, slapping my thighs with the palms of my hands. "It's better than wearing that quilt."

"It definitely is."

His deeper tenor and slower cadence twisted my core and returned my nipples to their hardened state from the earlier cool air.

"You're making me self-conscious. What are you thinking?"

Van walked around me, all the way around, the entire time keeping his eyes on me. "I think it's better if I don't say."

"What?"

His smile grew. "I'm thinking that if I ever plan an abduction in the middle of a blizzard, I need to remember a flannel shirt because on you, it's sexy as hell."

I lifted my hands to my cheeks feeling the growing heat.

Van took a step toward me. "Come on, Julia, there has to be a man in your life who tells you how damn sexy you are."

Swallowing, I turned away, avoiding the subject, and began to open the crate of nectarines.

As I tugged on a plastic cord holding the lid in place, Van's hand came over mine.

The electricity from before returned.

When I looked up, Van held a pocket knife in his other hand. "Step back so you don't get cut."

Without speaking, I did as he said. The plastic snapped as the blade sliced through it. The muscles in his arms bulged as he lifted the lid and placed it under the counter. Turning, he held out a nectarine. "Dinner."

I took the orange fruit from him, careful that we didn't touch again. "Thank you."

Retrieving our mugs, I added more coffee to each one and took them to the hearth. Even with the roaring fire, the air farther away was chilled. Basking in the warmth, I settled on the blankets and rugs where I'd awakened. After taking off his boots and leaving them by the door, Van joined me on the blanket.

With our legs crossed, we both stared into the flames. Every once in a while, our knees would touch as we both ate our nectarines and drank our coffee. As the fire warmed my outside, coffee and his incidental touches warmed my insides.

chapter four

My teeth chattered as I opened the door to the outhouse and sheepishly smiled up at Van. The snow blew around us as he tucked me under his arm and we hurried back to the cabin. Once inside, I shivered as I shrugged off my down coat and looked down at the ridiculous waders.

"Thank you for going out there with me."

"What good is it to hold a beautiful woman captive if I let her freeze to death?"

"Or if she's eaten by wolves." I had been ready to venture out to the outhouse by myself until I heard the howl of a wolf. There weren't many literal wolves to deal with in the Chicago suburbs.

"Wolf attacks are rare," Van said with a grin.

"Rare implies that they do occur." Holding onto the wall, I pushed down the giant rubber waders until I could step out with one foot and then the other. When I turned, Van was looking in my direction. "If you say the waders looked sexy, I'll know you're lying."

He came toward me and grabbed the waders, taking them to the pegs on the wall to let them dry. "No, Julia, the waders aren't sexy."

I nodded. "Maybe you don't lie like other men."

My attention went to the one bed. I reached for a pillow. "I can sleep by the fire."

"There are plenty of blankets on the bed. You'll be warm."

"How do you know?" I asked, pulling back layer after layer of blanket. "You're right."

Van gestured out to the room. "I figured if all these blankets are out here, there would be plenty on the bed."

"Shit," I said, noticing my phone. Picking it up, I saw that not only was there no signal, the battery was down to less than ten percent. "I meant to turn this off." Once I did, I put it back on the bedside table. Slowly, I turned toward Van. His dark hair was messed from the hat and there was dark stubble on his cheeks. His coat and boots were again near the door. Starting at the floor, I scanned his wool socks, long legs in faded denim, the way his shirt stretched over his chest and arms, his five o'clock shadow, high cheekbones, emerald green eyes, and back to his messy dark hair.

It wasn't until my scan reached his stare that I realized Van had been doing the same to me. Nervously, I ran my fingers through my hair and laughed. Seeing the door, I asked, "Should we lock that?"

"If anyone finds their way out here, they deserve a warm shelter."

"But what if they're bad people?"

"What if I told you that I was a bad person?"

I reached again for the pillow and hugged it in front of me. "I wouldn't believe you."

Van took a step toward me. "Why?"

I stepped back as I hugged the pillow tighter. "Because you saved me. You gave me coffee and fed me." I grinned. "And saved me from the wolves."

He came even closer, his scent clouding my thoughts as he reached toward me and then…beyond me and pulled down the blankets on the bed. "Climb in, Julia. You'll be warm in no time, and I promise it's more comfortable than the floor." He lifted his chin toward the fireplace. "I'll sleep by the fire and keep it going so we don't freeze."

Bending my knee, I knelt on the soft mattress and wiggled my way under the blankets. Once I did, Van pulled them up over me. For a moment he hesitated. Shaking his head, he turned, but before he could go, I seized his large hand.

"Wait."

Turning his hand over, I ran my fingers over his palm. "Your hands, they're not callous."

"I have a great lotion regime."

A smile came to my lips. "I was beginning to think you lied about not living here. But if you lived out here and chopped wood, your hands would be rougher."

He shook his head. "Don't try to figure me out, Julia."

"Is that mutual? Are you not trying to figure me out?"

Sitting on the edge of the bed, he sucked in a breath. "I think I have you figured out."

"Am I that obvious?"

"Somewhere there's a man who did you wrong. You're searching for a life that isn't planned out, and in the process, you found yourself stranded in a snowstorm."

"I wasn't completely stranded," I said. "I followed the white ribbon."

Van's gaze narrowed. "The white ribbon."

"With all the snow, I couldn't see the road, so I told myself to follow the white ribbon."

He nodded. "What did he do?"

Pressing my lips together, I shook my head.

"I don't say this often, but I'm sorry he hurt you." Van's finger traced down my cheek in a display of familiarity that felt surprisingly right. "I hope you find what you're looking for."

"I'm not sure what I'm looking for. I think it was to get away."

His smile bloomed. "If that was it, I'd say you got it."

"I did." When he started to stand, I again reached for his hand. "I just ended a…relationship, and I'm not looking for a new one."

"That's good because I'm not the relationship kind."

"You're the good kind, though. You didn't need to rescue me or take care of me, but you did."

"Julia, I promise, I'm not good."

I fought the tears as I held tight to his hand. "I'm tired of pretending to be happy and pretending that everything is the way it should be. I thought maybe I could get away and find me." My gaze went to his eyes. Letting go of his hand, I reached up to palm his cheek. "I found you instead."

"I think technically, I found you."

I scooted over to the cold side of the bed. "You can sleep here. Maybe tomorrow the snow will have stopped."

Van shook his head. "Julia, you don't know what you're doing."

"I do."

"Listen, I'm not against a one-night stand. It's that you're not the kind of woman I would want a one-night stand with."

"Oh," I said, turning away.

"Shit." Van reached for my chin, and turned it back. "That was a fucking compliment. I'm the damn wolf you heard out there. It's who I am in my private life and in my career. You are Little Red Riding Hood and the last thing you should do is invite the wolf into your bed."

"Weeks before our wedding, I found out my best friend is pregnant and the man I was engaged to is the father."

"Fuck."

I nodded. "I'll sleep over here. I'm not asking you to make love to me. I'm offering half the bed."

"I don't work that way," Van said as he walked away.

My eyes closed as I tried to make sense of anything that had happened over the last forty-eight hours. The stress and cold had worn me down. I opened my eyes to see Van crouched near the fireplace, tending to the fire inside. His words made me wonder about him.

What kind of private life did he have?

What did he do in business that he considered himself a wolf?

I was almost asleep when I heard the wind as the door opened. When I looked up, the kerosene lamp on the table was extinguished and Van was gone.

He probably went to the outhouse, I told myself.

Time passed.

Uncertain of where he could have gone or if he'd leave me alone, I sat up against the hand-carved headboard and pulled the blankets over me. The fire snapped and crackled. The wind outside continued to blow. I reached for my phone to see the time, and then, remembering it was turned off, I set it back on the bedside stand. My eyelids grew heavy, but I refused to lie back.

Finally, to my relief, the door opened. Through the firelight, I watched as Van took off his hat, gloves, coat, and boots. My lip disappeared behind my teeth as he unbuckled his belt, unfastened his blue jeans, and allowed them to fall to his ankles. His silk boxer briefs weren't those of a mountain man. They showed each bulge and pulled tight over his muscular behind. Reaching over his head, he tugged on the back of his thermal shirt and pulled it over his head, revealing his wide chest with just the right amount of dark hair.

Inconspicuously, I moved lower under the blankets so as to not alert him that I was still awake.

The moving of the blankets and leaning of the mattress caused my eyes to open. "Van?"

"You'll regret this, Julia."

chapter five

VAN SLID UNDER THE BLANKETS UNTIL HE RADIATED WARMTH BESIDE me. The twisting in my core at watching him disrobe turned painful as he turned to me, our noses nearly touching. His large hand gently came to my cheek as he pulled me closer until our lips met.

Firm and strong, there was nothing tentative in his approach. Van tasted like coffee and nectarines as his tongue teased my lips, and I willingly allowed him entrance. Moans and whimpers echoed throughout the cabin as his touch skirted under the long flannel shirt freeing my breasts from my bra and taunting my nipples.

His green eyes blazed with the power of a raging forest fire as he stared down at me. "Take off my shirt."

It wasn't a request. It wasn't even disguised as a request. Van's tone left no room for argument as my fingers hurried with the buttons, one by one until the final one was freed.

Van pulled back the blankets as I freed my arms. With a quick move behind my back, he released the clasp on my bra, and without a word he removed it, sending it somewhere to the floor.

His breathing deepened as he stared. "It took every fucking ounce of restraint to not do that when I undressed you, and now, you're even more gorgeous than I imagined." He leaned down, sucking one nipple and then the other. As soon as his warm lips would disappear, the cool air would attack.

Blood rushed to my breasts making them heavy as his five o'clock shadow abraded my skin.

"Van." I couldn't articulate any further.

His finger came to my lips. "You invited me, Julia. The rest is up to me." Fire crackled in his stare. "That's my rule. Can you follow rules?"

The answer was that I could, I had all my life, but at this moment, it felt the opposite, as if I was breaking free.

"Julia."

I nodded against his finger. Opening my lips, I took it in my mouth and sucked.

"Fuck," he growled. His head dipped as he kissed lower, down my ribs, my stomach, and to the waistline of my panties.

No longer was I stranded in a blizzard. I was lost in a cloud of wanton lust, unlike any I'd experienced before. My mind was incapable of thinking beyond the bed, beyond Van, and beyond the assault on my sensory system. This must be what it was like to be with a man who knew how to please a woman and did so without fanfare. Van's touch was commanding, yet enticing.

I couldn't keep track of the ministrations of his lips or hands. Like a sculptor, he molded me to his liking, bringing more pleasure than I knew existed.

Whatever Van was doing, I wanted more.

If I was asked when my panties disappeared, I wouldn't be unable to answer. If I was questioned on when his boxer briefs vanished, I'd be at an equal loss.

My fingernails threatened the cotton sheets as he moved lower, nipping, licking, and lapping my core. My back arched and knees squeezed as Van brought me to orgasm unlike any I'd ever experienced.

As I worked to catch my breath, Van's green eyes appeared before me. "You said you didn't invite me to this bed to make love."

I nodded. "I didn't."

"I don't want to make love, Julia. I'm so fucking hard; I want to fuck you like you've never been fucked."

"I never have."

His entire body stiffened. "What did you say?"

"Please." I held tight to his shoulders. "I've done…this…up to… but we stopped." His eyes closed. "Van, I know I may never see you again. Hell, I don't even know your last name, but please, I saved myself for someone who didn't deserve me and look where it got me. Please, fuck me."

His head shook. "You really don't know what you're asking for."

I reached my hand lower, finding his hard cock. Wrapping my fingers around him as best as I could, I ran my hand up and down. "I do."

With his body between my bent legs, Van pushed up on his hands, on either side of me. My heart beat in triple time as he stared down at me. "I want to take you."

"Do it."

"I'll hurt you and that won't stop me."

I wiggled my hips. "I've been hurt, Van. This is physical and I promise I can take it."

There were things I'd built up in my head. I made them out to be better or worse than they were. The Eiffel Tower was smaller than I imagined. The British crown jewels were more spectacular than I anticipated. Sex was always right outside my reality. I'd heard other women talk and read books. As Van and I came together as one, the union was both worse and better.

I cried out, unable to stifle my scream as Van took what I'd saved for someone else.

Even though he said my pain wouldn't stop him, it did. He stilled and brought his nose to mine. "I promise it will get better."

Swallowing, I nodded. "I believe you."

The worst was over as the better grew.

Like a volcano, the heat within me increased. Van didn't only satisfy my core, filling me completely, he also tended to the rest of me, and his touch was everywhere. Synapses fired and nerve endings responded. Never had I been so alive, or so lavished with attention.

The ecstasy didn't end with my next orgasm or even his.

Throughout the night one of us would wake and it would begin again.

I wasn't certain when it occurred to me that we hadn't used protection. As soon as it did, I justified that I was on birth control—after all, I was to be on my honeymoon in two weeks. While I hoped Van was clean, I couldn't ignore the way he felt inside me, his skin against mine, and our bodies united.

Finally, sleep won.

When I awoke, light seeped through the windows and the bed at my side was cool. I sat up, feeling tenderness where I never before had been tender. As memories came back of everything we'd done the night before, a smile came to my lips.

Sitting up, I saw Van near the fireplace, teasing the embers. He was fully dressed as he'd been before coming to bed.

"Good morning," I said sheepishly.

"I let the fire go out. I should have it going soon." He turned my way. "Stay under the covers. It's probably forty degrees out here."

I wiggled my nose, realizing it was cold. "After you get the fire going, you could join me."

Van remained quiet, his concentration on his job as fire master.

I saw the glow radiate against his skin at the same time the logs began to snap.

Van stood tall and walked toward me. "Julia, if things were different. If *I* was different, I would want a woman like you in my life. I'm not different. I told you that you'd regret last night, and I am sure you do."

My head shook. "I don't." Keeping the blankets up to my shoulders, I sat. "Van, I'm not some damsel in distress." I giggled, thinking that was exactly who I was. "Not usually. I'm not looking for a man to save me. I don't regret last night. I'll carry it with me forever. You made me feel desired and…" I searched for the words. "Good. I felt good and real, the way it feels to not pretend. It felt amazing. I don't need to know your last name or you mine. I'm on the pill. This was two people stranded along the white ribbon."

Van took a deep breath. "The snow has stopped. I was going to walk out to the road. If it's plowed, I think we can get you into town. As for your car—"

I waved him off. "Town is good. Ashland, right?"

"Yes, that's the closest town." He came closer.

"Good. I have reservations at a hotel there. I'll deal with my car later. You, Van no last name, have done your part in rescuing this damsel." I reached for his hand. "I regret nothing. I hope you don't."

His Adam's apple bobbed. "I have regrets, but last night isn't one of them. My regret is that I'm not someone else."

My cheeks rose. "I like who you are."

"You don't know who I am." Walking to the end of the bed, he lifted my clothes from the footboard. "Your clothes are dry."

"Then I guess I'm done wearing your shirt."

"I'll never look at that shirt the same way."

"You don't owe me any promises," I said as I pulled back the covers. Turning to Van, I asked, "Have you seen my panties?"

chapter SIX

A day later

"MISS MCGRATH?" THE OLDER GENTLEMAN ASKED, STANDING to shake my hand.

I reached forward and shook Mr. Fields's hand. "Thank you for seeing me today."

"I was surprised you were able to get here so soon. We've had some difficult weather."

Warmth filled my cheeks as I recalled the difficult weather. "Yes, I had a problem with my rental car. Thankfully, Chase at the automotive shop was able to rescue it and all of my belongings."

I was currently dressed for success. With a silk blouse, high-waisted black slacks, and high-heeled black boots, I wasn't left to interview in a shirt owned by a man with only a first name. Yet as I stood in the office of Fields and Smith, I knew that the white ribbon had taken me to a place that not only rescued me from the cold, but showed me that I could survive without Skylar or life's well-laid plans.

"You're wrong, Van. I don't regret a thing." That was my thought as I waited for my interview.

I deleted the numerous text messages from Skylar and my parents on my now fully charged phone. I'd spoken to my mother. She was caught somewhere between supporting my decision and not. "There's more than love involved here," she told me more than once.

She was right. There was also fidelity and trust.

"Miss McGrath, Mr. Sherman will see you now."

"Is he your client?" I asked.

"Yes, ma'am, Donovan Sherman is a private man. He'll have the only voice in your hiring. Please don't take it personally if he decides against it. As I said, he's private and particular."

"He wanted to see me?"

"Yes. I can't promise you more than that."

As I walked down the hallway toward the conference room a step behind Mr. Fields, I decided private would be nice. If I got the job offer, I liked the idea of having time to myself.

Mr. Fields opened the door.

The man within was turned toward the window. His attire was what I'd expected, an expensive suit all the way to the cuff links and Italian loafers. His shoulders were broad and the suit was custom, accentuating his toned torso and trimmed waist. It was as he turned that I sucked in a breath, the blood drained from my face, and my knees felt weak.

"Mr. Fields," Van said, his green gaze fixed on me, "thank you. I'll let you know if we need you."

"Mr. Sherman, I'm willing to stay and—"

Van interrupted, "That won't be necessary."

As Van spoke, the fire from the cabin ignited in his eyes.

Once Mr. Fields was gone, Van came closer. "Am I to think this was all coincidental?"

"You said your name was Van."

"Donovan. Van is shortened."

So is Don, but I didn't say that. Honestly, Mr. Fields had never told me his client's name. Shaking my head, I turned to leave. "I'm sorry, Mr. Sherman, this isn't what I was…"

He reached for my hand. "When I saw the name Julia on the schedule and read your resume, I had to know if it was you."

My hand tingled in his with the electricity of our first touch.

"I-I…I'm not looking for anything except a job to take me away from my life."

"Write my story, Julia. Once you learn about the real me, you'll be able to see me for the wolf I warned you I am."

"You want me to stay?"

"You realize the job description includes living on my estate."

A smile crept across my lips. "Estate? It's one room."

"No. That was a cabin on the outskirts of my property. You'll have your own suite."

"Isn't that generous?"

His green eyes shimmered. "At first."

Van opened a briefcase on the table and removed something small, holding it in his hand. "I got this object on the farfetched chance that Julia McGrath was Julia no last name."

"What is it?"

"Will you take the job?"

"I don't need the money," I said. "I want you to know that."

Van's head tilted. "Before you answer, I have an even more enticing proposition."

My pulse increased. "I'm only looking for a job."

"I told you that I'm a wolf in business. I take opportunities when they present themselves."

I shook my head. "I just walked away from a relationship that involved business."

"And Skylar Butler fucked your best friend."

I sucked in a breath. "How do you know that?"

"You told me."

"I never told you his name."

Van's jaw clenched. "Do you want to fuck him back?"

I took a step away and walked toward the window, looking out on snow-blanketed Ashland. The snow globe had settled over a quaint community. "I told you, we never—"

Van was behind me, his warmth on my back, and his breath at my collarbone, sending chills over my skin. "Figuratively, Julia. Marry me."

I spun around until my breasts were against his strong solid chest. Tilting my chin upward, I asked, "What?"

"It can be in name only. You'll live with me. Sex will be...discussed. As of this morning, I own twenty-one percent of the shares of Wade. Marry me and send Skylar and Marlin Butler into bankruptcy or at least out of Wade Pharmaceuticals."

"I don't know how you know this. Did you save me for this reason?"

He laughed. "I had no idea who you were, just as you didn't

know who I was." He lifted my left hand as he pulled something from his suit coat pocket. "I'm well aware that you don't need money, but you do need controlling interest in your family's company. Your father's paranoia is justified, just not coming from the direction he believes. Marlin Butler has been in negotiations with two large pharmaceutical companies. He has plans for Wade. He's been biding his time, waiting for his son to marry you to make himself very wealthy at the expense of your family's company."

I couldn't believe what Van was saying and at the same time, I did. I imagined a grand scheme orchestrated by Marlin Butler. I knew deep down that he was capable of what Van suggested.

Did Skylar know? Was he part of the plan or an unknowing pawn like myself?

"Marry me, Julia. You don't need the money, but together, we'll secure controlling interest in Wade Pharmaceutical and as a bonus, I'll enjoy watching the Butlers squirm."

"Van, I…I don't know you."

"You know what it's like to have me inside you." His voice dropped an octave, twisting my core. "You yourself said you and Butler never went that far. You were going to marry a man you didn't really know, one who fucked your best friend. Marry one who you know can satisfy you."

Still holding my left hand, Van turned mine palm up and laid something light in my grasp. When his hand moved, I saw it. A white ribbon.

"Say yes. Say the white ribbon brought us together."

My heart beat against my breastbone as I stared down at the coiled ribbon in my hand. When I looked up, his emerald stare was on me.

"Come, Miss McGrath, I require an answer."

"If I say yes, is that my invitation to you?"

"Are you asking if the rest is up to me, if from now on I'm in control?"

I nodded, remembering what he'd said as he joined me in the bed.

"Do you regret following that rule in the cabin?"

"No, but even you said that rules have exceptions."

"Not that one. My rule hasn't changed. My control will reign in public and private." He grinned. "That doesn't mean I won't enjoy your plays for power. Let's see where this ribbon leads. Marry me."

"Will I regret it?" I asked, recalling Van's warning from before.

"Less than you'd regret marrying Butler." His eyebrows rose. "Your answer?"

It was the most insane thing I'd ever contemplated doing, and I'd contemplated more than a few less-than-sane things over my twenty-four years.

Seeing Van with my small hand in his, for the first time, I felt the flutter that was supposed to accompany this question. With his intense gaze shining down on me, it was only the two of us, as it had been in that cabin. There was no room full of people and no big presentation. My answer wouldn't incite cheers and applause. No one would hear it except the man who proposed.

There wasn't even a ring, only a white ribbon.

I closed my fingers around the ribbon. "Yes, Van, I'll marry you."

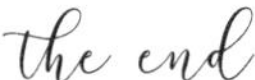

Would you like to learn where the white ribbon leads?
Check out WHITE RIBBON on Aleatha's website to learn more.

Are you looking for more stories with sexy, sometimes controlling, alphas and strong determined heroines? Be sure to browse Aleatha's series, complete and ready to binge.

SPARROW WEBS

Web of Sin (book one SECRETS is FREE on all platforms)

Tangled Web

Web of Desire

and still releasing: *Dangerous Web*

INFIDELITY SERIES (Not about cheating)

Betrayal (Free on all platforms)

Cunning

Deception

Entrapment

Fidelity

CONSEQUENCES SERIES

Consequences (Free on all platforms)

Truth

Convicted

Revealed

Beyond the Consequences

LIGHT DUET

Into the Light

Away From the Dark

STANDALONE MAFIA THRILLER

The Price of Honor

STANDALONE EROTIC THRILLER

Insidious

For more of Aleatha's works, go to her website.

about the author

New York Times, Wall Street Journal, and *USA Today* bestselling author of the Consequences, Infidelity, and Sparrow Web series.

once upon a snowstorm

JENNIFER BENE

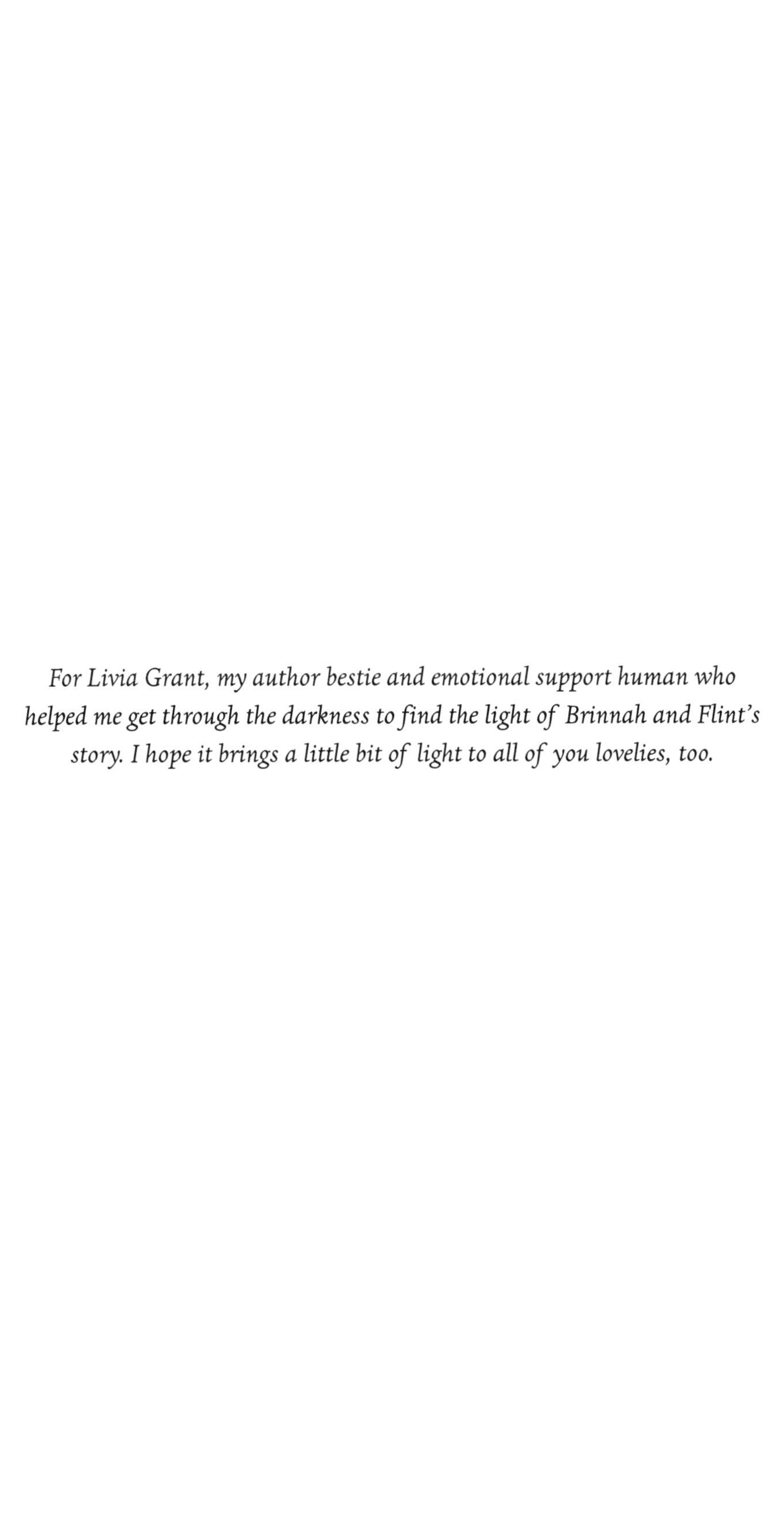

For Livia Grant, my author bestie and emotional support human who helped me get through the darkness to find the light of Brinnah and Flint's story. I hope it brings a little bit of light to all of you lovelies, too.

chapter one

Brinnah

THERE'S NOTHING ABOUT ME THAT MAKES ME STAND OUT FROM A crowd, but Flint Etheridge won't stop looking at me.

I'm sure it's because I'm not technically supposed to be here. Yes, it's my training concept, and *yes*, I did argue with my boss to be here for the pitch, but I didn't expect my childhood crush to be sitting at the other end of the table.

I should have done my research.

I should have *known*.

It's my own fault for walking into this meeting like a fucking idiot. If I'd taken five minutes to search ColdPoint Enterprises I would have seen his picture somewhere on their website, then I could have had some warning that the boy I used to know as 'Flintstone' was now just 'Flint,' or rather 'Mr. Etheridge,' the owner and CEO of the company that's supposed to be my breakout project.

This is all wrong.

This company was supposed to need my expertise. I was supposed to show up with a unique approach to leadership training that would right the ship of ColdPoint Enterprises and get them back on track—which, I have. I mean, I definitely have that. It's why I'm here.

But Flint Etheridge was lanky and awkward the last time I saw him, and he's… definitely not now. He's also *definitely* not supposed to be staring at me.

I casually glance in his direction, pretending to skim the faces of the other people present for the meeting before I look at him again and, *yep,* he's still staring. *Why*?

Does he remember me? There's no way. We were only friends for a couple of years before his parents moved to Massachusetts, and it's not like we were best friends. Our friend groups had just collided and stuck, like some kind of messy car crash that he had extradited himself from in seventh grade.

There's no way he remembers me. I've got boring brown hair that sometimes looks nice in the right kind of sunlight, at the right angle, or if I've recently got highlights, but it's nothing special. I don't have the complexion of a movie star, and I've definitely missed more than a few trips to the gym, but he's still looking at me. Wearing that little smirk that has me shifting in my seat and definitely not paying attention to my boss's lazy attempt at pitching *my* training concept that he obviously didn't even read completely.

Normally, I'd speak up about now to elaborate on his pathetic attempt at summarizing my plan, but how am I supposed to do anything at all when Flintstone has turned into 'Flint,' the incredibly hot —and apparently very successful —CEO who won't stop looking at me?

"Ms. Grosset, is there anything you'd like to add?" Luke Butler, my idea-stealing douchebag of a boss, looks at me and I manage a small smile as I push myself to my feet and nod.

"Yes, thank you." Clearing my throat, I walk to the end of the table and flip through several slides of the PowerPoint I put together that Luke didn't actually use. Settling on the slide reflecting their current trends, I face the table and try not to look Flint in the eye. "As you can see, when we were planning out a training program for your leadership team, we focused on the areas of opportunity your own data identified. Let's begin with turnover."

Back in my element, it's easier to block out Flint's intense gaze, and the delicious way his lips purse when he's thinking. It's hard, but I continue to discuss all of the data and details I reviewed about the company that somehow skipped completely over the CEO himself.

How did I miss this?

I can feel a blush spreading into my cheeks as I talk, bringing heat to my face, but I try to ignore it —which is working about as well as ignoring Flint Etheridge's thoughtful nods and thought-provoking smirks.

Just as I reach a stopping point, my boss interrupts. "Thank you,

Brinnah, for that detailed analysis of our training strategy. Let's see what questions everyone has."

"Of course." Swallowing, I hold the clicker in my hand with a death grip, trying to look as relaxed as possible while I force that polite, girl-in-a-meeting smile that I hope won't threaten the old white guys in the room, or make the only other female in the meeting feel like I've damaged all the progress we've made in corporate America. It's a tightrope walk of balance, but I feel like I've spent enough time in this particular circle of hell to do it well —and based on the vague smiles and nods around the table, it seems I've done okay.

Don't look at him. Don't look at him. Don't look—

I look. I can't help it. My gaze drifts over the random faces I don't know to return to those indulgent brown eyes that I thought of too often in middle school.

Flint 'Flintstone' Etheridge was my dream guy. Almost a year older than me, so well-spoken even then, he'd loved anime as much as me and been the kind of guy that I could chat with after any movie we saw with our group of friends. I'd dreamed of the day he might ask me out… but looking at him now I know he's squarely out of my league.

There's not even a competition.

He's the head of an extremely successful company, likely very rich, and definitely very handsome. I'm nobody in comparison to him. A peon. Plus, it's been twenty years, and he probably has no idea who I am —he probably doesn't even remember me —but why the hell is he still staring at me like that?

A few people around the table ask questions, which my boss answers, and I occasionally add on a robotic addendum to politely correct his bullshit. Eventually, it seems like we've nabbed the contract to provide leadership training services to ColdPoint, but I have to admit I haven't been paying close enough attention to tell for sure.

I blame Flint.

If he'd take his eyes off me for more than a few seconds I'd be able to breathe, collect myself, but he hasn't even allowed me that much.

Did I spill something on my shirt this morning?

It's tempting to check, but since I'm still awkwardly standing at the front of the table, it would be too obvious to look. Instead, I flip through my PowerPoint until the screen goes dark and then set the clicker down to return to my seat. I laugh along with everyone else at whatever joke I missed while spiraling in my own personal pit of self-loathing and manage a passing glimpse at my blouse as I take my seat.

No obvious stains, but Flint *fucking* Etheridge is still smiling at me like he knows something I don't.

What the hell is it? Is there something in my teeth?

"Thank you so much for coming in today, Mr. Butler," Flint says, and his voice reminds me of the one I remember… except it's better. Deeper, more resonant, and I hate myself for the flicker of arousal that rushes down my spine at the sound of it. Standing up, he nods at my boss who looks like he'd lick Flint's shoes for a chance at this contract, and then he stares right at me again. "We have a few more things to decide on, but we'll get back to you soon with our decision."

"Thank you, Mr. Etheridge, and everyone. Higher Thought would love to partner with you in your training plans," Luke replies, and I nod politely in agreement as everyone stands. As we all gather our things and move toward the exit, and the coffee and pastries waiting outside in the hall, I watch as Luke shakes hands with the others around the table. He's wearing that smarmy grin that I hate so much, the one that screams 'salesman' instead of 'training partner' —which is what we're *supposed* to be —but he's never understood the difference, and why should I expect him to? He got to walk into this job without a single question, or the experience any of us needed to get our jobs, and I'm used to his utter ignorance by now.

Nepotism at its fucking worst. That's Luke Butler to a T.

Just as I'm about to grab a danish, mostly just to keep myself from correcting him in public again, I feel a hand on my arm, and I turn right into those deep brown eyes that steal my breath away.

"Hey, Brinnah."

"Hey, Flintstone," I reply, and immediately regret it. It wasn't conscious, it was some kind of reflexive word vomit that makes me want to sink through the floor, but Flint just laughs and grins at me.

"Wow, it's been forever since I've heard that." He shakes his head, sending his dirty blond hair fluttering over his forehead before he corrals it with a casual brush from his fingers. For a moment I can't think straight because I would have bet anything that he didn't remember me at all, but he confirms it in the next few words. "This is crazy, I can't believe it's you."

"Yeah, it's wild," I mumble, still in awe that he's this gorgeous and remembers me and is actually talking to me.

"You know, I really hate these formal meetings. How about you and I have a real brunch and catch up while we talk over this training concept together?"

"Um, okay. Sure," I reply, unsure if my voice was even audible, but then his fingers are firmly on my elbow, leading me past the others, and all I can do is shrug at Luke when he stares at me in shock. If I had a moment to explain myself, I'd tell my boss I was feeling just as surprised to have run into my middle school crush, but there's no opportunity.

It seems like between one breath and the next I'm in the elevator, taking a deep breath of Flint's intoxicating cologne and trying to figure out what tree it reminds me of when he presses the down button.

What have I got myself into?

chapter two

Flint

It's hard to believe that Brinnah is standing next to me in my company's building, but she is. In black tights, a charcoal skirt, and a white blouse that leaves more to the imagination than most of the women that show up to meetings with me.

But I've always had a great fucking imagination and I love using it.

She's got soft curves, barely hinted at by her choice of clothes, and it has my mind spinning at the possibilities of what's underneath —not that there's any guarantee I'll get to find out. But I've always been driven when I see something I want, and I've wanted Brinnah Grosset since I was eleven. Back then all I wanted was the chance to kiss her, but now I'd be interested in a lot more if the lack of a wedding ring and her agreement to lunch means she's single.

Fuck, my head is moving way too fast. Ideas and plans rotating as I glance down at my phone to open up a text to my assistant before tucking my phone back in my pocket to text unseen —a handy skill when I'm stuck in meetings most of the time, and right now it's paying off because it's letting me get a better look at her. When we were younger, we were about the same height, but now she just comes up to my shoulder and it makes me want to throw an arm around her and pull her close. I want to bury my nose in that auburn hair that used to distract me when we were all hanging out at the park and memorize what kind of shampoo she uses. Probably something soft, like her.

Shit.

I'm definitely staring again, which is probably starting to freak her out. Hell, I basically just stole her from her boss and walked out with her without even telling my team where I was going, and with the plan unfurling in my mind it's trending a lot closer to a straight-up abduction, but how can I pass up this opportunity?

I need to say something. *Talk, Flint. Now.*

"That was your training plan, wasn't it," I say, framing it like a question even though it absolutely isn't one. When those blue-gray eyes flick up to meet my gaze, I can't help but smile when a blush fills her cheeks. Just like during the meeting. "It's just you and me, Grossy. You can tell me the truth."

Her nose wrinkles at the old nickname and I chuckle which brings that fiery temper to the surface in a flash. "You know how much I hated that name, right?"

"Oh, I remember, but you were being so quiet I figured it was the best way to get you talking." Winking at her, I lean back against the wall of the elevator to avoid the urge to touch her again. "Plus, you called me Flintstone, so… fair is fair, right?"

"Fine, but I still hate it." Brinnah rolls her eyes and I laugh as the elevator slows at one of the lower floors. When the doors open a few people get in, and I'm actually glad they did because it forces her to move closer to me.

"Good morning, Mr. Etheridge," one of the guys in a suit says, and that instantly silences whatever conversation the trio had in-progress when they stepped on. All three of my employees stare at me and I offer a polite smile.

"Good morning. Having a good day so far?"

"Yes, sir," the man answers, followed quickly by similar affirmations from the other man and the woman. I have no idea who they are, but everyone in the building makes the company run and I try to be nice and seem approachable. Still, they always look like panicked deer when they see me.

If they knew I used to be short and awkwardly skinny and called 'Flintstone' they'd probably be a lot less awestruck.

When I glance over at Brinnah she's clearly trying to suppress a grin, and that makes mine resurface. I nudge her a bit and when she looks up, I mouth the word 'sorry' and she shrugs. It's such a small thing, but it makes me feel more normal than I have in a decade.

The elevator finally dings for the lobby, and as the doors open my employees wave me out first, which I'm not going to argue. I want to get Brinnah alone so we can catch up. I touch her elbow again to lead her across the lobby, finishing the text to my assistant with my hand hidden in my pocket as I pull her to a stop near the front doors.

"Let me help you with your coat," I offer. It's the right thing to do, even though it's really just another excuse to touch her.

"Oh, thanks," she says, looking a little stunned when I take her purse on my arm so she can slip her coat on. "Where are we going for brunch?"

"It's a surprise."

"I don't like surprises." The way her brows pull together creates the cutest wrinkle in her forehead, and all I want to do is kiss it and smooth it away, but she might smack me for that, and it would be a really bad idea in the front lobby of my company's building.

"Here's your coat, Mr. Etheridge, and Joel is bringing the car around," Stacy, my assistant, announces as she walks swiftly toward me, heels clicking on the tile. She must have hopped in the other elevator the instant I sent the first text, because she made it down in record time.

"You're the best, Stacy," I tell her, and she gives me that 'you owe me' look that I receive so often from her, but it's true. Based on that glance alone, I know she's already planning just how I'll return the favor for all the trouble it's going to cause as she reschedules the afternoon for me.

"That's true," she agrees, turning to Brinnah with a smile before she waves and heads back upstairs to clean up whatever mess my spontaneous change of plans has caused.

"Wow, that was smooth, Flintstone."

When I glance down at her, she's biting back a laugh and I let out a chuckle as I shrug. "It wasn't meant to be. Stacy just works magic, and she keeps me sane. She's the best damn assistant I've ever had, and I think the company would go down in flames if she ever tried to leave."

"I doubt that," Brinnah says, and her laugh is so warm and comfortable and relaxed. Not forced or fake like the crap I'm surrounded by every day.

"It's the truth, I'll explain in a second." Pulling my coat on, I double-check that my wallet is in the pocket and then lead Brinnah to the doors as soon as I see Joel pull up out front. "Come on, the car is here."

We're settled into the back of the town car a moment later, and as soon as Joel gets back in the driver's seat, I catch his eyes in the rearview mirror. "Where to, Mr. Etheridge?"

"Roy's please," I answer, keeping my voice as even as possible. I know this plan is a gamble but going with my instincts has got me this far in life and I've learned to trust them.

Turning to Brinnah again, I'm still in shock that she's here, and I'm tempted to pinch myself just to make sure it's not some kind of boredom-fueled daydream and I'm still trapped in a meeting somewhere upstairs.

Keep talking, Flint. That's what you're good at.

"So, you want to know about Stacy?" I ask, smiling when Brinnah meets my gaze.

"Sure. Tell me how she's holding ColdPoint Enterprises together, Mr. Etheridge."

It's my turn to roll my eyes and groan. "Please don't call me that."

"You plan on calling me Grossy again?" she challenges, and it sends a zing rushing over my skin. All that fire in her auburn hair has always just been a warning about that fiery temper she has under the surface.

"No, I promise. It's never made sense anyway, you've always been the furthest thing from 'gross' I can imagine, Brinnah." The words came out faster than I could process them, and as her cheeks turn red, I know I need to change the subject before I send her running for the hills. "Stacy does hold the company together though. She was the best hire I think I've ever made. Over twenty years of experience, most of the time she knows what I need before I do. I think it's because she's got three kids."

"And that helps her handle a CEO?" Brinnah teases, and I laugh.

"Yep, I think it does." I take a deep breath and feel myself relax a little. "She always says she has to 'mom' me, and I honestly don't mind it. I'm always in my head, thinking about too many things, and she keeps the day-to-day stuff running. Makes sure I eat, don't miss appointments or events, all that stuff."

"She sounds great."

"She is," I reply, remembering how grateful I was to find an experienced assistant that didn't rub me the wrong way. "It's hard to find someone you mesh with, you know?"

"Yeah, I do." Brinnah crosses her legs, and my eyes follow the line down to her heels. Not those crazy four-inch spikes I see on some women, but simple black heels that look nice with her monochromatic outfit. "It's important to mesh with someone, especially if you're going to work closely with them all the time."

"Exactly. A lot of executives treat their assistants like trophies, and I hate that. I wanted someone who would actually help me stay on track, and Stacy does that with zero office drama. She's been married for almost thirty years, and two of her kids are grown, the youngest is still in college, and she just had a granddaughter earlier this year. Family is important to her, and as she always tells me she just sees me as an extension of her family."

"She sounds pretty amazing. I'm glad you have her," Brinnah replies, and my first instinct is to feel defensive, to listen for some kind of sarcasm or unnecessary jealousy, but after a few seconds I realize that she really means it.

I'm such an asshole.

Brinnah isn't like that. She never has been.

"I'm glad, too," I eventually reply, and we fall into an easy silence.

She turns and glances out the window at the passing traffic, her breath fogging the glass as it keeps out the winter Boston air, and I find myself staring at her lips. I can't tell if that pink is natural or lipstick, but I've never been good at guessing stuff like that —either way, it looks good on her.

Hell, *she* looks good, so damn good, and I can't stop thinking about what it would be like to kiss her. The only time our group of friends ever got brave enough to play a game of spin the bottle, we got interrupted by some younger kids before either of us even got to go. It seems stupid now since I know we've both kissed someone, and done a lot more than that, but I can't forget how much I wanted Brinnah Grosset to be my first kiss.

"So, what kind of food is at Roy's?" she asks, and her voice yanks me out of that afternoon in the park after school and back to the present.

"Nice try, but I'm not telling you anything."

"Come on, Flint. Give me a hint," she pleads, and the flirty smile she gives me *almost* breaks my willpower.

"A hint?"

"Just one," Brinnah urges, leaning closer to me, and I catch a soft, citrusy scent that could be her perfume or her shampoo, and I want to know which it is.

"Hmm…" I stall for time, thinking over the hints I could offer without giving away the plan I have before the first surprise reveals itself. "Okay, here is your *one* hint."

"Yeah?" She sits up straight, that beautiful, excited grin on her face, and I can't help but chuckle because the hint I've come up with could either be creepy or impressive —but Brinnah is worth the gamble.

"It has to do with your school supplies in seventh grade."

chapter three

Brinnah

"My *what*?" I ask, confused as hell, but Flint just gives me that stupid, sexy grin of his as he pushes his fingers back through his hair and leans against the door.

"Your school supplies," he repeats.

"In seventh grade."

"Yep." His grin is cocky, and there's a playful light dancing in his brown eyes that reminds me of all his daredevil antics when we were kids. When Flint was 'Flintstone' he used to jump off everything at the park where we all hung out, climbing trees or anything he could manage, and whenever he did something incredibly wild like that, he always had the same damn look.

This look.

And how the hell does he remember my school supplies from seventh grade?

Groaning, I rub at my forehead and adjust my purse on my lap. "You've got to be kidding. *I* don't even remember my school supplies from back then."

"Really?" He purses his lips slightly, that same thoughtful expression from the meeting appearing on his face as he drums a tempo on his thigh. "Well, then I guess you're just going to have to wait and see. That's the only hint you're going to get."

"Oh, come on, you do *not* remember my school supplies in seventh grade."

Flint shrugs, grinning at me again. "I'm surprised you don't remember them. You had quite the theme."

Theme?

I'm so busy wracking my brain about the bullshit hint he's given me —which may just be some kind of trick and not worth my time

—that I'm pretty much on autopilot as we play the catch-up game on our families and what happened after he moved away. Everyone's good, still alive and happy. After high school he went to the Ivy League while I went to a state school. He went straight into an MBA and then rose up the corporate ladder swiftly before getting head-hunted for ColdPoint Enterprises, while I dove into various jobs in corporate life until I eventually settled into the training field six years ago.

"So, do you like your job?" he asks, and I shake off trying to remember school supplies for a minute.

"I do, and I'm actually pretty good at it. A good training plan can change the course of a company, and it can really help people." Sitting up a bit more, I start talking with my hands as my passion for the job takes over. "See, so often we just try to shove information at employees and expect them to learn it without pausing to figure out the best way to give it to them. The *how* is infinitely more important than the *what* when it comes to training. Once you've figured out the right way to share different kinds of information, what you're actually teaching people becomes secondary."

"That's a really good point," Flint says quietly, and I can tell he's either thinking about what I've said… or completely bored out of his mind.

Dammit.

"Sorry, I just get really excited about this stuff."

"No, no, Brinnah. I'm impressed by how clearly you can see all that, and I wish I could get half my leadership team to feel even a fraction of that kind of passion over training their people."

Tucking my hair behind my ear, I shrug and laugh a little. "Does that mean we have the contract?"

"Maybe," he teases, and I groan. I'm about to say something smartass when I look out the window and realize we're not in the city anymore, we're in some kind of industrial area, and…

"What the fuck? Is this an airport?" I ask, twisting in my seat to look out the back window at a small airplane lining up to takeoff. Anxiety flurries in my stomach as I watch the plane accelerate down the runway. "Flint! Why are we at an airport?"

"Surprise?" he says, and I can hear that his chuckle is a little nervous. When I turn to look at him, his eyebrows are raised slightly, a half-smile lingering on his lips. "Don't freak out, it's just a quick hop to where I want to take you to brunch… or really more like lunch by the time we land."

"You want me to just get on a plane with you?" I ask, stunned, and he grins.

"Don't you want the contract with ColdPoint?"

A laugh bursts past my lips as the car swings around to an open hangar where I can see a plane inside that's about ten times smaller than anything I've ever been in. "You've got to be kidding me, Flint. Are you really blackmailing me into getting on a plane with you?"

"Come on, Brinnah, don't make it sound so sinister. I promise we'll be back by tonight, and just think of all the time you'll have to tell me about your plan without your idiot boss interrupting you."

"You think he's an idiot?" I can't stifle the smile plucking at my lips as Flint rolls his eyes and flashes that grin at me again.

"You don't?"

"Dammit, you are completely ridiculous." Shaking my head, I stare in awe as the car stops by a beautiful plane that has the ColdPoint Enterprises logo emblazoned on the side. "Do you normally take your training designers on plane trips for lunch meetings?"

"Only the ones I really like spending time around," he replies, looking too fucking gorgeous and tempting. If I didn't know better, I'd say this felt like a date, but I know it's not. We're just old friends and he wants to catch up and… take me on a plane ride for lunch.

That's normal. Probably totally normal for someone like him.

"What do you say, Brinnah? You in?" Flint holds out his hand, and I get a sudden flashback of the last time he offered me a hand when I fell trying to follow him on one of his stupid stunts. I'd slipped and fallen off the side of this wooden playground equipment he'd been scaling, landing hard on the woodchips below, and he'd jumped down after me to help me up.

When I'd taken his hand back then, I hadn't wanted him to let go. I'd had a ton of ideas about him being my boyfriend, about us holding hands at school, and as I slip my hand into his again… I can't deny that the same stupid ideas flutter around my head again.

"Good choice," he says with that cocky grin, opening the side door and sliding out, pulling me after him.

"Are you going to tell me where we're going now?" I ask, feeling the heat in my cheeks as he keeps hold of my hand to lead me to the stairs for the jet.

Flint pauses on the first step and glances back at me. "Have you figured out your hint yet?"

"No! Who remembers their school supplies from middle school?"

"I remember yours," he says with a shrug, and pulls me up the steps and into the plane. *His* plane.

"Good morning, Mr. Etheridge." The pilot leans out of the cockpit area and smiles at us both. "Mrs. Teague has informed me of your plan for the day and that you're bringing a guest. Please tell me if you need anything once we're in the air."

"Thanks, Roy, and for the last time would you just call me Flint?"

"No, sir," the pilot answers with a smile before nodding at us and returning to the cockpit.

Flint sighs and guides me to two of the plush seats that face the front of the plane. "You should take the window."

"I've, um, never been on a plane this small," I mumble, trying not to let my sudden anxiety ruin this opportunity, but all of my nerves melt when Flint takes my hand again and squeezes.

"Try not to think about it. This is one of the safest private jets on the market, and I've flown on it for business hundreds of times."

"Right, and your company is okay with you just taking a private jet for lunch with an old friend?" I ask, letting out a nervous laugh as I sit down and he takes the seat beside me.

"Well, first of all, this is a business trip because you're going to be telling me all about Higher Thought's training plan for our leadership team, and second of all, I'm the CEO." He grins at me and I just shake my head as we buckle in.

"If you get me in trouble I'm going to be so pissed."

"I think your boss will be happy at the end of the day," he says, winking at me before tightening his seatbelt. Then he offers his hand again, palm up in the space between our seats. "Give me your hand."

That bossy edge to his tone is all CEO and it has me obeying without thinking about it. His skin is so warm, which is nice since my fingers feel like ice and I'm pretty sure they'd be shaking if he didn't squeeze them firmly.

"Take off is going to feel different, so just crush my hand if you feel nervous, okay?"

Staring into Flint's eyes, with his hand holding mine, has me feeling infinitely safer than it should, but I don't care. There's an eleven-year-old girl inside me squealing with joy, dancing around her bedroom with the diary I wrote in so often about the very man now sitting beside me.

"I can't believe I'm doing this," I whisper.

"Don't think about it," he answers, turning to nod at his driver who takes one of the seats at the back of the plane, leaving us in relative solitude after the pilot secures the door. When the engines kick on a moment later I grip Flint's hand hard and he chuckles. "Focus on the hint I gave you. I really can't believe you don't remember all those school supplies you had. They were all on the same theme and—"

"Paris!" I shout, my eyes widening as I look at him. "No way, you are not taking me to Paris."

"No." Flint laughs, running his thumb soothingly over the back of my hand. "We'd need a very different plane to go overseas, and there's no way we'd be back home tonight, but I do know of a very nice French restaurant in Montreal. It's one of my favorites."

"You're taking me to Canada?" I ask, stunned because my mind is still reeling that Flint 'Flintstone' Etheridge remembered all my Eiffel Tower and Paris themed folders and binders and pencils.

"That is the plan, and see? I knew you'd remember all those supplies eventually." The plane starts moving and I turn to glance out the window as the hangar rolls past and we move toward the runway. Then Flint taps my hand and pulls my attention back to him. "Have you ever been to Paris?"

"No," I reply, shaking my head as I remember how obsessed I used to be with all things French. "I took French in high school, and a year of it in college, and I always planned on going but I just haven't had the chance yet. Not that I remember much of the language anyway," I add with a laugh.

"*Êtes-vous sûr de ne pas vous souvenir du français*?" Flint stuns me with the beautiful French flowing over his lips and I don't think I've ever wanted to kiss him more than I do right now, but that would be really over the line. I'm so surprised by it that it takes me an awkwardly long time to roughly translate what he even said.

"Did you ask me if I remember French?"

"I think that answers my question," he replies with a wink, and I roll my eyes.

"My French was never that good."

"It just takes practice. Being around native speakers helps a lot, and you'll get the chance to practice a bit at lunch today." His grip on my hand tightens slightly and that wild, playful glint is in his eyes once more. "Ready?"

"Oh God," I groan, looking out the window as we start accelerating down the runway. My stomach does a flip-flop as we take off, wobbling a little before the plane steadies and ascends more smoothly. "This is the kind of plane people die in all the time."

"Don't think about it, Brinnah. Why don't you tell me all about your training plan, because I know you were the one that really created it."

"How do you know that?" I ask, getting comfortable in my seat in a way where I can keep holding his hand.

"Your boss made several mistakes that you had to correct," Flint pauses, flashing me that bone-melting grin again while his thumb picks up a hypnotizing rhythm as he moves it back and forth on my hand. "You were very tactful, by the way. I'm sure you really wanted to tell him to shut up."

"True," I confirm with a laugh, imagining how shocked Luke would be if I actually did that in a meeting. It would *almost* be worth getting fired over. "He's the son-in-law of one of the big wigs at my company and so they just gave him the management job when it opened up. He doesn't have a fucking clue what we do, or why we do it."

"Sounds like an asshole."

"He is." Shaking my head a little, I bite down on my lip to stop the stupid smile that keeps trying to take over my face. "I really shouldn't be saying any of this to *you*, though."

"Why not? I'm just Flintstone today."

"I thought this was a business lunch?"

"I only said that to get you on the plane," he says with a grin, waggling his eyebrows, and we both burst out laughing. "Seriously though, break it down for me. I was a little distracted staring at you during the meeting and I'll admit I wasn't paying attention as well as I should have."

His words send heat rushing up my back, the blush burning my cheeks, leaving me flustered.

"You—What? I had a… a freaking PowerPoint and everything!" I stumble over my words while that cocky grin on his perfectly handsome face seems to taunt me.

"I know, and it was a lovely presentation, but I want to hear it from you. Come on, Brinnah," he encourages, still rubbing the back of my hand, and I have to pull it free just so I can focus enough to think. "Please?"

"Fine, as long as you promise to pay attention."

"I swear." He actually drags his finger in an X over his heart, and I roll my eyes, trying to laugh off the swell of nervous energy that his words brought up because *that* definitely sounded like flirting. It really did, and I don't think I was imagining it, but I've never been great at flirting, so I have no idea what to say in response.

Just talk about your plan and all the research you did.

chapter four

Flint

WATCHING BRINNAH TALK ABOUT ALL OF THE TRAINING PLANS she has for my company is intoxicating. Her blue eyes are vibrant, absolute alight with energy as her hands move around the air in front of her while she describes different ideas, and all of the in-depth research she did with the data ColdPoint provided her company. It's impressive, and when I can manage to not get distracted by the perfect swelling curve of her lips, or the way the light from the window sets fire to her hair, I agree with everything she's saying.

The training plan is perfect, and if we implement it in the right way, I think we'll see massive reductions in turnover and a much better first quarter next year. But I made that decision about ten minutes into her talking… now I'm just listening because I love how damn passionate she is.

It reminds me of when we used to get together to talk about anime with our friends. Brinnah was never afraid to speak her mind, to stand up for what she believed about characters or storylines, and I remember how we used to go to Greg Bolton's house after school sometimes to watch anime and how much I wanted to have the guts to sit next to her on the floor.

I never did though.

I was awkward and gangly back then, had no idea how to talk to girls, and definitely didn't have the balls to even hold her hand, much less kiss her —which is all I wanted to do whenever she laughed.

Hell, it's all I want to do right now.

It would just be incredibly stupid to make a move when she's trapped on a plane thousands of feet in the air with me, especially since I *technically* did blackmail her to get her on board. Not that I meant it,

I was always planning on going with her plan because it was the best one we've seen and she's so damn invested in it… which is clear by the way she's still talking about the five steps to engaging in conflict conversations, even though I haven't said a word in a while now.

"Mr. Etheridge," Roy calls from the front of the plane, and I give Brinnah an apologetic smile for him interrupting her.

"What's up, Roy?" I call back.

"There's bad weather near the border and they're saying we won't be able to land. Storm system moved in from the North and it's dumping a ton of snow, looks like we'll have to turn around."

I curse internally, frustrated that my plans are fucked up by something as mercurial as weather, but flexibility is the key to success in any situation, and I've always been good at dealing with adversity. Raising my voice, I try to keep the irritation out of it as I answer. "Thanks for telling us, Roy. Do what you need to do."

"Are we okay?" Brinnah whispers, and I reach over to take her hand without asking this time, squeezing it tight.

"Roy is the best, okay? We'll be just fine. I'm just sorry I won't be able to take you to *Le Cygne Ascendant*. It really is the best French restaurant on this side of the Atlantic."

"I'm more worried about the plane than the food right now," she says as she leans over to stare out the window at the dense, gray clouds.

"Just take a deep breath," I say and it's definitely a nice distraction for me to watch her chest rise and fall.

Not the time.

"We'll be back home in no time," I add, giving her an encouraging smile when she looks at me again. Unfortunately, all of the lively energy in her beautiful blue eyes has been replaced by worry, and they look almost as dark as the clouds out the window.

"What's going on, Roy?" I shout, holding tight to Brinnah's hand as another rumble of turbulence shakes the plane. In the past twenty minutes things have gone from smooth sailing with my plan to an utter clusterfuck, but I'm trying to stay as in control of the situation as I can.

"Weather is moving in too fast. We're going to have to land early."

"What?" Brinnah squeaks, and I know she's panicking, which just means I need to be calm and confident for the both of us.

"Where are we landing, Roy?" I call toward the front, but I can hear Roy talking into his headset and it's a few minutes before he's able to reply.

"Looks like it's going to be Burlington, Vermont. Just got clearance from the tower to put down there. Everyone stay buckled up." He's got that I'm-The-Pilot voice on, and since I don't know how to fly a damn plane, I have to put my trust in him and bothering him with more questions isn't going to help the situation.

"Looks like I lied," I say, chuckling as I turn back to Brinnah who looks a little too pale.

"Lied?" she repeats.

"I don't think we'll be back home tonight."

"Right." Brinnah nods, glancing out the window again, and even I have to admit that the sleet crackling against the windows is more than a little disconcerting.

"Hey." I tug at her hand, trying to think of something to distract her. "Do you remember when we all binge-watched Sailor Moon, before binging shows was even a thing?"

"Yeah. Greg downloaded them. Pretty sure that was illegal," she adds with a nervous huff that could have been a laugh if she weren't so tense.

"Definitely illegal, but I think the government was more concerned with cracking down on US movies and music than subtitled anime from Japan."

"Probably," she replies, but I can tell she's still focusing on the way the plane keeps jolting and shuddering.

"Well, do you still think Sailor Neptune and Sailor Uranus were 'together' together? Or were they just cousins?" I ask and she finally looks at me.

"Of course they were together!" Brinnah snaps, taking a deep breath, which is good even though her inhale and exhale are both shaky. "The US companies were just so concerned about being politically correct that they screwed with the show and tried to make them 'cousins' instead, which was bullshit."

"Hmm… I'm not so sure," I tease, baiting her into an argument, and by the way the color is returning to her cheeks I think it's working.

"You've got to be kidding me! Didn't you agree with me back then?"

"I just haven't seen it in so long, and it's not like either of us knew Japanese. What if the subtitles were wrong too?" I manage to keep myself from grinning when she launches into a speech with all the reasons the two characters were actually in a lesbian relationship, which I've always believed. Shit, it was one of my favorite fantasies as a pre-teen boy, along with all of the very revealing transformation scenes in that show, but whatever keeps Brinnah calm until we're on the ground again is worth it.

I continue to tease her with doubting comments while I text Stacy to update her, keeping the phone hidden at my side. I can feel the buzz of her responding, but I keep my eyes on Brinnah so she stays focused on me. I know that Stacy will get it handled so we have somewhere to go when we land, and a way to get there, that's her job and she does it well.

My job right now is to keep this beautiful woman in front of me from having a full-blown panic attack, because the plane is bouncing hard, and if either of us pay too much attention to it… that won't be good at all.

I'm not sure how long it's been when I hear the landing gear grinding underneath us, and I glance toward the cockpit.

"We're landing, Mr. Etheridge, and with the wind it's going to be a little rough, but it's fine. We beat the snowstorm," Roy shouts from the front, and his announcement interrupts our walk down memory lane with Sailor Moon.

"See? We're fine," I tell Brinnah with a confident smile that I don't one-hundred-percent feel at the moment but *fake it 'til you make it* works just about anywhere.

"I'll believe it when we're on the ground," Brinnah mumbles, and I chuckle a little, squeezing her hand again. If eleven-year-old Flint could see me now, he'd be bouncing off the walls and pumping his fist in the air with excitement.

"Won't be long now." I point out the window at the approaching ground, and while I can see snow on the ground, and based on the clatter against the plane there's more falling, we definitely beat the storm like Roy said.

Brinnah goes completely stiff as we get closer and closer to the ground, and I keep my mouth shut, rubbing the back of her hand with my thumb as I check my phone. Stacy has sent a flurry of texts with confirmation numbers, weather updates, and links to some AirBNB she managed to book.

I say a silent prayer of thanks to the universe that I found her, and then send her an actual text of thanks before tucking my phone in my pocket and focusing on Brinnah again. The landing is as rough as Roy estimated, but after a few bounces we're down and I manage a deep breath.

"Safe and sound on the ground, and Stacy already has stuff booked for us," I say, waiting for Brinnah to relax. This definitely isn't how I imagined the spontaneous lunch date going, but in all of our conversations she's never mentioned a boyfriend —or a girlfriend for that matter —and now I'll have even more time with her to see if she's as interested as I am.

And I'm definitely interested.

She's the most honest, real person I've been around in so long. Hell, she makes *me* feel more real. She reminds me of the person I used to be before my days revolved around endless meetings and financials and industry surveys. I don't have to pretend at all around her, and that's the kind of comfortable feeling money just can't buy.

"I know what you did up there, and… thanks," Brinnah says softly, pulling my gaze back to her.

"What do you mean?"

"The whole Sailor Moon argument," she adds with a small laugh. "I haven't talked about anime in years, and I know you just brought it up to distract me from the possibility of dying in a fiery plane crash, but I appreciate it. Thank you."

"You're welcome, but it was the least I could do. After all, I got you onto the plane with less than ethical methods, and now you're my responsibility." I give her a wink as we taxi toward a grouping of other small planes forced to land by the weather.

"Your responsibility?" she repeats, looking a little offended.

"Oh yes, and I'm very diligent with my responsibilities." *Time to gamble.* "Especially when it comes to a beautiful woman that I never realized how much I missed."

"You…" Brinnah starts, her eyes wide with surprise, but before she can finish, the plane stops and Joel is out of his seat and at my side a second later.

"Stacy sent me everything. Just stay on the plane and I'll go check on the car, then we'll get indoors as soon as possible." Joel checks his phone again, tapping at something before he looks up. "Says it's about a thirty-minute drive into the city where she has the reservations."

"Into the city?" Brinnah says, sitting up, and I'm surprised by how disappointed I am when she lets go of my hand. "Why don't we just stay here at the airport? I'm sure they've got a hotel here, and they usually have decent food and a continental breakfast in the morning."

Joel's lips press together like he's hiding a smile, and I give him a nod to cut off whatever he might say. "Thanks, Joel. Just stay warm out there."

"Sure, thing," Joel answers, and I definitely see a grin on his face when he turns away from us to meet Roy at the front of the plane.

"Flint, why don't we just stay here at the airport so we can fly out in the morning?" Brinnah asks, and I sigh.

"Okay, don't freak out, but the weather might keep us here a couple of days. It's a snowstorm coming down from Canada and it looks like it's going to drop quite a bit of snow. But, look, Stacy got some AirBNBs booked close to each other in the city," I explain, pulling up the information on my phone.

The first link is preceded by a short note that reads 'for you and guest,' and I try to click that one before Brinnah can see it, but I wasn't fast enough.

"I'm staying with you?" she asks as the AirBNB info pulls up, and I scroll down to see two beds with relief, because that's the last thing I need to try and explain right now —no matter how much I'd like to share a bed with her.

"Two beds, one bath. The views look nice though, and there's a fireplace." When I hold out the phone toward her, she takes it and starts flipping through the photos. It's such a casual act, something good friends would do with each other.

Or lovers.

Clenching my teeth, I try to push that idea out of my head. Sure, I'd jumped at the opportunity to take her out on a date and spend some time with her. Halfway to catch up with her, and halfway to see if all of those middle school crush feelings were still hanging around.

Unfortunately, the answer to that is a resounding *yes*. If anything, I think I like grown-up Brinnah even more, but getting her stranded in a strange city with me wasn't exactly the kind of dating opener I was looking for.

This is creepy, not romantic.

Fuck, fuck, fuck.

"Where are Joel and the pilot going to stay?" she asks, and I'm surprised by her concern for them for a moment, but I don't know why I keep underestimating her. She's not like the gold-digging women who flock around our corporate events like piranha. She's never been that kind of person. She's genuinely concerned, and that just makes me like her more.

"Stacy got them a place too," I answer, clearing my throat as I slip my phone from her hands again.

"Oh, sorry. I didn't mean to just take your phone, I'm just kind of in shock right now," she says, waving a hand toward my phone. "That's a really nice place, please tell Stacy thank you."

"I will." Tapping out the thanks from both of us, I scroll back up to the other AirBNB that's on the same street as the one Stacy got for me and Brinnah. When I get to it, I offer her the phone again and she blushes, waving it away.

"It's okay, I believe you. I'm just glad they'll have a place to stay too."

"You think I'd just abandon them here at the airport?" I ask, only half-playing.

"Oh, God, no! That's not what I meant, I just—"

"You were worried about them," I finish for her and she nods, that pink flush back in her cheeks, and before I can stop myself, I lean forward to kiss her and at the last second manage to divert it into a kiss on one of her rosy cheeks. "You've always been a good person, Brinn. They're good guys, thanks for caring about them."

She looks stunned when I sit back, and I don't blame her, but she doesn't slap me so I'm counting that as a win.

"Um, here. Check out the BNBs, I need to use the restroom." Awkwardly fumbling the phone into her hands, I try to get up before unbuckling my seatbelt and end up cursing under my breath as I toss it away and escape to the bathroom at the back of the plane.

As soon as I'm inside I lean back against the door and take a deep breath. That was probably too forward, too fast. After all, we just narrowly avoided a plane crash, but at least I managed to not kiss her on the lips… even though I really wanted to.

Dammit.

Her lips look so soft and based on how long we've been in the air I'm pretty confident that pink tint to them is natural, not lipstick. I can't help but think about what kissing her would feel like and standing in the bathroom of my company's private jet I somehow feel as awkward and nervous as I did when I was eleven.

It's not like I thought about Brinnah every day for the last twenty something years, but she's always been there in the back of my mind. Whenever I saw a woman with auburn hair like hers I'd always look twice just to see if I recognized her, but I never went so far as to hunt her down online. Even though I could have found her, because apparently her name never changed.

She's never been married, and neither have I, but that doesn't mean anything. Not really.

Yet… somehow this all feels like it was meant to be. I may not believe in destiny or fate or any of that stuff most of the time, but I can't deny the strange set of events that brought my middle school crush into my company to give me a second-chance at connecting with her.

It would have been better if my plan had gone the way I wanted. A lighter, less pressure-filled situation to test the waters and see if we still mesh the way we used to… but that's not even the question for me anymore. Talking with her for the last couple of hours has been as easy as breathing. Everything about her makes me feel *good*, and I can't think of the last time anyone made me feel like this.

I don't know if anyone ever has.

Which means I absolutely, unequivocally cannot fuck this up by thinking with the wrong head.

chapter five

Brinnah

I THINK I'M DREAMING, OR HALLUCINATING, OR... SOMETHING.

Nothing about today feels real, and I'm still trying to process all of it because it just doesn't feel possible. I mean, what are the chances that the company I get assigned is the one where Flint 'Flintstone' Etheridge is the CEO?

My company deals with hundreds of other companies, and I've never been great at math but I'm pretty sure the probability of me ending up in that meeting today is somewhere around a million to one.

And then he invites me to lunch? Takes me on a private jet?

That would have been a day for the record books even before a freaking snowstorm tried to kill us and forced us to land. And... he said he missed me. Well, more accurately he called me beautiful and then said he missed me, which would have taken the day to epic before the kiss. But Flint Etheridge actually kissed me. On the cheek, but it still counts, and I can still feel it, and now we're somehow going to spend the night together.

Holy shit, I'm going to spend the night in the same place as Flintstone.

I have to remind myself to breathe, but it comes out as more of a gasp, and Flint turns to look at me in the backseat of the car.

"You okay?" he asks, offering me his hand again, and I take it because I'm greedy, and while I'm doing everything I can to get my wild fantasies under control, I can't stop thinking about what *could* happen tonight. "Brinn?"

"I forgot that you used to call me that," I reply, clearing my throat before I sit up a little more in my seat. "I mean, yeah, I'm good, I promise."

"Good, we'll be there soon. Brinn fits you, by the way. For the record, I never liked that the guys called you 'Grossy,'" he says, a grin spreading over his lips. "But I think the only reason they did was because they all had a crush on you."

"No way, Greg was obsessed with Felicia," I retort, and he laughs.

"Holy shit, you're right. Okay, not Greg, but everyone else."

"Including you?" I ask, and I'm ninety percent sure my face is actually on fire and my palm is sweating against his and he probably thinks *that's* gross, but I can't help it when I feel like I just bet my 401k in Vegas.

Flint is way too quiet for way too long, but I'm trying not to panic because he's looking at our hands and his thumb is doing that rhythmic rubbing thing along the back of mine, but I'd really, really like him to talk.

Oh shit, what have I done?

"Sorry, I shouldn't have—"

"Yeah, that includes me, Brinn," he replies quietly, and it's another too-long moment before his deep brown eyes meet mine. "But I want you to know that I didn't plan this, and if you want me to have Stacy find you another place then I can do that because I don't want you to think, I mean I don't want you to feel like you have to respond, or do anything, or *shit*..." Flint shakes his head and drops his gaze again. "This isn't how I planned for any of this to go, Brinnah, I swear. I just knew when I saw you this morning that I couldn't let you slip away again without at least seeing if..."

"Seeing if...?" I press, and my heart is pounding so hard I can hear it in my ears over the droning weather report on the radio. I have no idea if the two men in the front seat can hear us, but at the moment I don't care, I need Flint to finish his sentence more than I care about privacy.

"If we still meshed." Flint flashes that smile at me and it definitely has a flirty edge now.

I nod, mouth too dry. "Meshing is important."

"Yes, it is," he confirms, and glances out the window behind me. "Ready to go inside?"

That's when I realize we've been stopped outside of a building for some time and I don't know how long, but my head is spinning so fast that I don't know if I should be embarrassed or excited or if I'm reading way too much into all of this. All I manage is a nod as I clumsily open the door beside me before Roy, the pilot, is able to get to it.

"You have the info you need, sir?" Joel asks, and Flint lifts his phone in the air as he joins me on the sidewalk, pulling his coat tight against the light snow.

"Got it right here," he answers. "You guys get indoors and be safe tonight, okay? We'll figure out what's going on with the weather in the morning."

"Yes, sir. Have a good evening." Joel waves at us, and Flint rests a hand on the small of my back as I try to wrap my coat harder around me.

"I shouldn't have worn a skirt today," I grumble, because the wind is cutting through my legs like icy knives, but Flint just chuckles.

"I think you look fantastic, albeit cold." He grins at me as he punches in the door code for the building and the blast of heat has me rushing inside ahead of him, rubbing my hands together to try and warm them back up.

"You said there's a fireplace, right?"

"I'll get it going as soon as we're inside, I promise," he says, leading the way upstairs. Outside of the apartment, Flint punches in a code on a lockbox and gets the key. When he opens the door, it's even more beautiful than the pictures made it look. Tall ceilings, a wide-open floor plan that flows from kitchen to living room where floor to ceiling windows let the light pour in, giving a fantastic view of the snow falling outside.

"Wow." I'm barely aware of saying it out loud as I wander toward the windows to soak in the view. There's a chill in the apartment, but it's nowhere near as cold as outside, so I don't mind it. "I can't believe you just rented this place. I mean, it's only been an hour or two."

"Stacy always works magic," he answers, joining me by the windows. "She definitely has good taste though."

"The hotel at the airport would have been fine," I say, glancing up at him. "But thank you, this is nice."

"I'm glad you like it. Let me get the fire going, and then we can make something to eat."

"Make something?" I ask, turning to watch him as he fiddles with the gas fireplace.

"Yeah, just go look in the kitchen to see if there's anything you like."

I'm giving him a 'what the fuck' look, but he can't see it because he's leaning into the fireplace to make sure the flue is open. "Um, Flint? This is an AirBNB, they don't leave food here."

"Trust me. Just go check the kitchen, Brinn," he says, and I roll my eyes as I march into the kitchen and throw open the pantry door. I'm about to point out how empty it is when I realize it's… not.

The pantry definitely isn't full, but there's brand new boxes of different things, and when I open the fridge I find more food. There's even a wine rack with four bottles of wine on the counter, a loaf of bakery bread, and a bundle of bananas.

"Told you so," Flint says right behind me and I jump before I turn around and smack his arm while he laughs.

"Don't scare me like that." Rolling my eyes, I wave a hand at the stocked kitchen. "So, how much did this cost?"

"What do you mean?" He's peeking in the fridge now, and grabs a bottled water from the door, turning to offer me another. "Here. I love this brand because it doesn't have a weird taste and the bottles are made from recycled plastic."

"I've stayed in AirBNBs before, Flint, and none of them were stocked with anything more than the occasional condiment and salt and pepper if you're lucky." Taking the bottle from him, I hold it up as an example. "And they definitely don't have your favorite bottle of water in the fridge."

"I guess Stacy did it?" he suggests, and I laugh, leaning back against the counter as I take a drink.

"She really does take care of everything for you." I raise a hand when he looks defensive, shaking my head. "Not that it's a bad thing,

I just think you should know this isn't how it is when most people show up at a rental."

"Well, I guess you're lucky to be here with me and my long-distance magic worker, aren't you?" he teases, and I'm about to say something smartass when he's suddenly right in front of me.

In my personal space. In my *very* personal space.

There's maybe six inches between us, and he's got one hand braced on the counter beside me, which means there's nowhere for me to go since I'm in a corner —not that I want to go anywhere. If anything, looking up at him has me wanting him to kiss me for real this time, and judging by the way he's staring at my mouth and not my eyes, I think he's got the same idea.

It would be our first kiss.

Something that should have happened over twenty years ago in the park during that damn game of spin the bottle that got ruined.

"Brinn?" The way he says my name has my skin buzzing. There's a slight growl to it, and his voice is just a little deeper, and I really wish I didn't have this damn bottle of water in my hand so I could pull him closer without it being awkward.

"Yeah?"

He reaches up to trace his thumb just under my lips, following the line of my jaw until he rests his hand against the side of my neck, and even though I just drank water my mouth is already dry again.

"Flint?" I whisper, summoning the courage to move my free hand to his button-down shirt, tugging on it lightly.

"Dammit," he curses under his breath, and pulls back suddenly, plucking his shirt from my grip with the movement, and I'm left holding a water bottle with my heart tattooing the inside of my ribs while he faces away from me. He lets out a long breath and braces his hands on his hips, staring up at the ceiling, and I have no idea what to do.

That felt like a moment.

The way he touched my cheek, how close he was… I should have just made a move.

Stupid, stupid, stupid.

"I promised you lunch, and I'm sure you're starving by now. Why don't you go warm up by the fire and I'll get something going." He's still facing away from me as he speaks, and I tighten my grip on the water bottle because I know I did something wrong.

I just can't figure out what I did.

Embarrassed and a little nauseous, probably from a mix of the hunger and the humiliation, I manage to blink back the sting of tears as I brush past him and head into the living room. I choose the chair that faces the windows and the falling snow instead of the gorgeous man in the kitchen, because I'm pretty sure if I look at him again, I'll either leave to find my own place to stay, or start crying, or both.

chapter six

Flint

IDIOT.

I'm a goddamn idiot.

I just told her in the car outside that I wasn't going to expect anything from her, that she didn't need to say anything back, and then I corner her in the fucking kitchen like some creepy asshole with a hard-on jutting against the front of my slacks.

Groaning, I glance down at the slowly fading erection and I hope that the cold from the fridge is chilling it out enough to stay down so I can try and pretend I'm more of a gentleman than I just was. All I can hope is that she didn't notice.

Please give me that today.

I'm so caught up in feeling like an imbecile that I'm barely paying attention to the actual items in the fridge. I always wondered if Stacy did it, after all finding my particular brand of water in a fridge is odd, but I never wanted to ask about it and look like a fool.

Of course, right now I'd gladly look like a jackass in front of Stacy instead of Brinnah. Especially since I think she wanted me to kiss her.

Did she?

At the moment I don't even trust my judgment. I was definitely thinking with the wrong head, and although everything about her seemed like she wanted me to, it wasn't fair. She's trapped in this damn city because of me, and I was so excited to have more time with her that I didn't even think about how fucking creepy it would come across that I assumed she'd want to share an AirBNB with me.

Not to mention, there are supposed to be two bedrooms here, but I only see one, which is going to look even worse.

Plucking my phone out of my pocket, I send a quick text to Stacy asking about it before grabbing the chicken breasts from the fridge and some pasta from the pantry. I'm not an expert in the kitchen, but even I can pull off baked chicken and spaghetti.

I do search for a baked chicken recipe just to double check myself on the baking time and then I get to work. Once everything is cooking, I check out the wine and decide that it's either exactly what we need, or a terrible idea, but I know that I want a glass for sure.

"Hey Brinn, do you prefer red or white wine?" I call out. "I've got chicken and spaghetti going."

"Either is fine," she calls back, but her voice is way quieter and she's facing away from me without even a glance around the edge of the chair she's buried herself in.

I fucked up.

Gripping the edge of the counter, I resist the urge to punch it or the fridge because while I had no idea when I woke up this morning that I'd want anyone in my life, I know for a fact that I want at least a chance with Brinnah.

And I had a good plan.

Spontaneous plane ride, French restaurant to show her that I really do remember her, delicious food in a romantic atmosphere, evening flight back under the stars. No pressure, no creepy guy moves… just a solid start to a possible relationship.

Now I've probably ruined it.

Grabbing the bakery bread, I yank the bread knife out of the block and start cutting slices off to make some quick cheese toast as a side, then my phone buzzes with another text from Stacy.

It's short, but it confirms what I expected: 'The couch in the living room is a fold-out. Not a lot of options, boss. Sorry.'

Not two bedrooms then, two *beds*.

Somehow that's worse, but at least Brinnah can shut the bedroom door. Lock it to keep out the creepy dude from her childhood. Dammit, dammit, dammit.

"Need help?" Brinnah's voice makes me spin around with the bread knife still in my hand, and I instantly turn back to set it on the counter.

"Um, sure. Want to cut a few more slices of bread?" I offer, stepping away from the knife to be less creepy, but it's not like there's a lot of room in this little kitchen.

"Okay. Thanks for getting dinner started," she says, taking up the bread slicing job, which leaves me without anything to do since the pasta isn't quite done, and the chicken still needs about five minutes.

Wine. I should open the wine.

I have to check a couple of cabinets to find the wine glasses, but I'm lucky they're on my 'side' of the kitchen so I don't have to creep her out anymore, which shouldn't even be an issue except I can't control my dick.

Now everything feels so damn weird and I hate it, but it's my fault.

All of this is my fault.

Pouring two glasses, I take a deep breath and slide one onto the counter beside her before taking a sip of mine. "Here, you should try it. It's actually pretty good."

"Thanks," she answers, but in the brief glimpse I get, I'm pretty sure her eyes look red, and her face is a little flushed —which could be from the fire, or she's been crying, and I have a feeling which one it is.

Just back off.

Eating in silence is horrible. Especially since we've been having such great conversations all day. Well, until I creeped her out. Now I can barely get a word out of her while she eats tiny bites of my mediocre lunch.

I've tried anime, her training plan, her favorite food, color, etc. Hell, I even tried to talk about the weather, and Brinnah has barely given me a sentence in response to each of them.

Swallowing another mouthful of wine, I clear my throat and try a new tactic —my specialty this afternoon, the blunt idiot tactic. "Listen, Brinnah… I'm sorry if I creeped you out earlier, I didn't mean to, and if you want me to leave, I will."

When she looks up at me, I don't see relief, or disgust, or anything I expected. Instead, her brows are pulled together in a look of utter confusion. "What?"

"When I cornered you in the kitchen, with the... you know," I say, gesturing at my idiot stick. "I swear I'm not a creep, I just thought you felt something too and—"

"You had a hard-on?" she asks, still looking confused, and now I feel even worse.

Hello, mouth —insert foot.

"Yeah, I thought you'd noticed and that's why you were... upset."

"You didn't change your mind?" she asks, her forehead creasing as her brows draw tighter.

"Change my mind about what?"

"You dumbass," Brinnah groans, rubbing at her face before she grabs a napkin to wipe her mouth. "Actually, I don't know who's more of a dumbass right now. You, or me."

Now it's my turn to be confused as she finally takes a drink of her wine because I'm not sure why she's calling herself a dumbass. "This is my fault, Brinnah. Not yours. I had no right to—"

"Just shut up for a second, Flint." She laughs under her breath, taking another sip of wine before she sets it down and rests her hands on the edge of the table. "Are you telling me that the reason you didn't kiss me earlier in the kitchen is because you got a hard-on and you panicked?"

"Brinnah—"

"Answer me. Is that the reason, and not because you changed your mind and decided that you didn't want to kiss me?" she asks, and I'm flooded with relief as things click into place.

"That's why you were sulking in the living room? You thought that I *didn't* want to kiss you?"

"Well, hard to think of anything else when you turn away at the last second and tell me to go sit down," she quips, finally sounding like her fiery self again, and I'm out of my chair in a second and moving around the table to stand over her.

"If that's what you thought then I have to agree with you," I say, bracing a hand on the back of her chair as I lean down, my gaze glued to the sassy smile on her lips.

"Agree with me about what?"

"We're both dumbasses." Moving my hand into her hair, I cradle the back of her head just before I lean down to kiss her. Within seconds her arms are around my neck and I pull her out of the chair, teasing the seam of her lips with my tongue until she parts them to let me in.

It's better than any pre-teen fantasy I ever had about kissing Brinnah, and I'm almost relieved this is our first kiss because I'm a hell of a lot better at it now than I would have been back then. Her lips are soft, and she tastes like wine and the pepper in the sauce, and the little noises she's making are just a tease.

I want more.

Tightening my hold on her hair, I move her back to the wall, but I'm still having to lean down too far to kiss her. It's pure instinct when I wrap my hands under her thighs and pick her up, bracing her against the wall. It's not until I can feel the heat of her body through my slacks that I realize what I've done. Breaking the kiss, I lean my forehead against hers, our eyes meeting, and although I only see excitement in those vibrant blues, I still have to ask. "You okay with this?"

"Very okay," she confirms, squeezing me closer with her legs wrapped around my hips, which does dangerous things below my belt.

"Keep that up and this isn't going to be a PG-13 make-out session," I warn, and she grins at me, trailing her devious little tongue along her bottom lip.

"You're the one that put the brakes on earlier, Flintstone," she teases before leaning forward to take my lip between her teeth gently, pulling back until it pops free, and then she flicks her tongue over the spot.

Fuck.

I don't bother stifling the groan this time or hiding the hard-on that I know for a fact she can feel because she's grinding on it, setting my skin on fire with need. "You're going to have to tell me if you want to stop, Brinn."

"Stop thinking and kiss me, Flint," she says with a sigh.

"Say it again," I urge, mostly because I just want to hear it from her lips.

"Kiss me, Flint," she purrs. Then she grins, and it's that same bright smile from all those anime binges, but now it was a much more wicked side, and I like it even more. I want her, and I'm definitely not thinking like eleven-year-old 'Flintstone' right now.

Keeping one hand under her thigh, I slide the other one up her side, brushing my thumb across the outside of her breast before I slip it into her hair and crane her head back to expose her neck. I start out slow, nipping and licking, figuring out every little noise I can draw out of her while we grind against each other on the wall like a couple of teenagers.

"Flint," she whines, dragging her nails down my back, but with my shirt in the way it's dulled, and I wish we were naked already, but I'm not going to fuck this up for real.

Take your damn time.

"Tell me what you want," I whisper right against her ear, loving the way she shivers against me before pulling me tighter into her. All I get in response is a soft moan, and I chuckle before I nip her earlobe. "That wasn't an answer, beautiful."

"I want you." Her hands come up to cup my face, and this time she's on the offensive, controlling the kiss for a moment before I take it back, pressing her harder into the wall until the way she's grinding has my dick threatening to pop-off way too soon.

"Hold on to me." That's all the warning I give her before I pull her away from the wall, wrapping one arm around her waist as I scan the small apartment, debating the options. "Your choice. Fireplace or bed."

"Fireplace," she answers right against my ear, returning the favor of nipping it and then running her tongue down my neck, and all I can do is bite down on a moan as I figure out how the fuck to make that work.

Got it.

Carrying her to the couch, I set her down and unwind her legs from my hips, pushing her knees apart slowly, giving her time to stop me as I drop a knee to the floor. When she doesn't hesitate, I push them farther apart, forcing her skirt to slide up her thighs. Dipping my head down, I run my lips along the thick fabric of her tights, then nip the inside of one knee, followed by the other, reveling in the way she twitches and whines.

"I'm going to get us something to lay on, and when I get back out here, I want the tights off."

"Now I can see why you're the CEO," she says, drawing her skirt up higher, which momentarily distracts me from my plan.

"Why?"

"Because you're so bossy," she continues, trailing her fingers over her thighs. "But I like it."

Fuck me. She's better than a wet dream.

"Then listen to me and take those tights off before I get back." Winking at her, I force myself to turn away and walk into the bedroom. I sit down on the bed and take off my shoes, then my socks, shoving them out of the way underneath before I rip the comforter off. I debate for a second but decide it's better to be over-prepared and grab the top sheet too, along with a couple of pillows, before heading back into the living room.

And then I almost drop all of it.

Brinnah is in the same spot on the couch where I left her and she's got her knees spread apart again, only now there's no tights, giving me a perfect peek between her thighs at the scrap of black fabric hidden there.

It takes me a moment longer for my brain to function well enough to notice that both of our wine glasses are on the side table, along with the bottle, but that's definitely secondary.

"See something you like?" she teases, grinning at me, and I'm pretty sure I'm in love with her. Obviously not say-it-out-loud love, but I can't think of anything more I could want from a woman, and I've wanted Brinnah for too damn long already.

"Everything about you," I answer. Tossing the pile of bed stuff in front of the chair, I cover the distance between us in another heartbeat, bracing my knee on the cushion between her thighs so that I can kiss her again. She moans against my lips, and it takes every ounce of my self-control not to just skip ahead, because I want to be inside her more than anything, and my dick definitely agrees… but I want this to be memorable.

Every single thing with Brinnah is a first. Not a true first for either of us, I know that. But if my family hadn't moved away, she *could* have been my first in everything, and that's not something I want to rush through.

Shifting her sideways on the couch, I lay her out and find enough space between her thighs to prop myself above her. Her hands go for my pants, and I catch one and move it above her head, *tsk*'ing her. "I thought you liked it when I'm in charge."

"I want you," she whispers, tugging at the button of my slacks, and I grin.

"And I want to taste every inch of you first."

Her eyes widen a little, her pink tongue flicking out over her lip again before she whispers a soft, "Okay."

Capturing her mouth in another kiss, I run my hand up her side, cupping her breast through her shirt, teasing the button of her nipple with my thumb until she returns the favor and lets her hands start to explore. I can't help but grin as I move up and pop the first button on her blouse, kissing every bit of newly exposed skin, the swell of each breast, moving down to her ribs until the last button is free and I can see the gentle curves she was hiding.

My imagination didn't do her justice.

Brinnah is beautiful, peppered with the occasional freckle, and I want to memorize them, to kiss each one, but she's already slid two of the buttons on my shirt free. When I catch her hand this time, she gives me the sexiest pout. "Fair is fair."

"Are you trying to get me naked, Ms. Grosset?" I ask, feigning surprise, and that earns me a wicked grin as her hands make quick work of the other buttons.

"Yes, Mr. Etheridge," she says, sitting up to plant teasing kisses on my neck. "I am absolutely trying to get you naked."

"So naughty," I tease, but the way she suddenly kisses me tells me just how much she liked that, and I'm more than happy to talk dirty. Breaking the kiss, I sit up to toss the shirt aside, and go ahead and take my undershirt off as well before I lean over her again. "You like being a naughty girl?" I ask, loving the soft moan she lets out in reply. Running my hand up her side to squeeze her breast, I nip the swell of it and then lean down to whisper in her ear, "Or do you like being a good girl?"

"Which one will get you into bed faster?" she asks, and I sit up in time to catch the wicked grin on her face.

"Definitely a naughty girl then." Tilting my chin toward the other end of the couch, I add, "Hands above your head then."

"Why?" she asks, but she does it anyway, and I just wink at her before I dip my head down to kiss along the edge of her bra, teasing her. "Come on, why?"

"Because naughty girls can't be trusted with their hands," I answer, popping the cup of her bra down to take her nipple into my mouth. She arches under me, grinding uselessly against my stomach, and I love how vocal she is. Every little whine and moan and muttered curse is fucking music to my ears, showing me just what she likes and how she likes it. When I nip her skin, she gasps but it turns into a sweet moan and so I repeat it, teasing her until she's got a hand around the back of my neck, encouraging me to bite a little harder.

Definitely a naughty girl, and she's so fucking perfect.

Reaching under her, I unhook her bra, and she tosses it and the shirt away in another second. This time when I kiss her, we're skin to skin. All of her soft curves pressed into my hard edges, and we're grinding like high school kids. It's the most wonderful kind of ache, because my dick is still trapped behind my zipper, but every roll of her hips is a tease and a promise of what's to come.

When I can't handle it anymore, I shift my hips back to make room for my hand, slipping it under her skirt until I find her underwear soaked, which makes it that much easier to find the hard nub of her clit and focus my fingers there in quick circles.

"Oh God, oh God, Flint…" Brinnah whines, arching in the most perfect way, and I can't resist drawing one of those pert nipples into my mouth, biting gently as I push her closer to the edge, listening to each sound she makes to figure out exactly what she likes. "Yes, yes, please!"

"Let go, I'm nowhere near done with you yet," I whisper against her ear, picking up the pace until her babbling pleas turn into a shout and her hips jerk away from me, forcing me to cup her through her underwear to keep up the friction as she whines.

"Shit, shit, Flint, wait!" she begs, and I slow down, but I don't stop yet.

"You sure you want me to stop, Brinn?" I ask, flicking a tongue over her nipple which sends another shiver through her muscles as she soaks the thin scrap of cloth between her legs. Her scent is everywhere, mixing with the citrus of her perfume, and the way she's squirming underneath me is testing my limits.

Fuck, I want to taste her.

"Skirt off," I command, barely able to put the words together as I force myself back to the chair to fumble with the wadded mess of bedding. It takes a minute, but I push the chair out of the way and get it laid out in front of the fireplace. Before I can even beckon her over, Brinnah is off the couch and crawling toward me on her knees like she slipped straight out of one of my fantasies. "God you're beautiful."

"You look pretty hot yourself," she says as she stops at my feet, kneeling and looking up at me with those knock-out blues. I'm speechless when she pops the button of my slacks free, dragging the zipper down. "And I think it's my turn."

"Who says you get a turn?" I tease, but when I reach for her hand, she shakes me off too easily. Although I'm not exactly trying to stop her. The idea of those soft pink lips wrapped around my shaft is pure sin, and I've never been much of a saint.

"Tell me if you want me to stop." The naughty little smirk on her lips as she lets my slacks fall around my ankles is so damn naughty, but before I can come up with a response she's rubbing me through my boxer-briefs and all language has officially disappeared along with the blood leaving my brain to head south.

I know that I wanted to taste her first, but I've been an idiot all night and there's no reason to stop now. Especially when she seems so intent on—*Jesus fucking Christ.* All I manage to get out is something that is half-groan, half-growl as Brinnah drags her tongue along the underside of my shaft before sliding me into her mouth. Warm, wet heat wraps around my dick and shuts off all higher brain function, but I know for sure that her tongue is devious and a hell of a lot of other words I can't think of as I weave my fingers into her hair.

"Fuck, Brinn…" I groan as she draws me to the back of her tongue, teasing me with the thought of her throat as she swallows around me, forcing me to ball my other hand into a fist to resist the urge to thrust. "Yessss…"

When she starts to move with shallow teases, her wicked tongue dancing over the head of my cock, followed by sucking me in to swallow around me, I'm lost. There's just an insistent nudging at the back of my mind that won't go away, growing more urgent when she cups my balls in her hands and squeezes lightly just as she pulls me deep into her mouth again. Powerful waves of electric energy rolls through my nerves, tightening at the base of my spine, and I jerk my hips away just in time.

"Come back," she whines, but I try to step back and almost trip over the clothes tangled around my ankles.

"Naughty girl. Naughty, naughty girl," I say through a rough chuckle as I desperately push away the urge to come.

"Was that naughty? It seemed like you enjoyed it." Her lips are reddened, shiny with saliva, and my hand in her hair turned that auburn hair into a mussy halo that has me pausing to memorize her just like this.

Come on, brain, back online.

"That was naughty, *and* you were a very good girl." Kicking my pants and boxers free, I point at the bedding. "Now it's my turn."

"Ooo, if that's my reward I can be a good girl." Brinnah lays back, knees bent and together, but I fix that as soon as I get down on the floor. Pushing them apart gently, I kiss my way down the inside of her thighs, alternating between left and right until I can only place one more kiss just at the top of her mound.

"Going to be a good girl for me?"

chapter seven

Brinnah

Every inch of my skin is lit up with buzzy tension as Flint kisses his way down my thighs. He's moving so painstakingly slow, but I already know how good he is with his hands and it's the anticipation more than anything else that has me panting and needier than I've ever felt.

"Going to be a good girl for me?" he asks me in that low, thrumming baritone that I can practically feel against my skin, and if I wasn't already soaking wet *that* would have done it.

"Yes, I will, just please don't tease me," I beg, arching my back and lifting my hips, but he just wraps his arms around my thighs and holds me exactly where he wants me for that first torturously slow lick through my folds. All I can do is whimper as he flicks the tip of his tongue against my clit. "Flint, please!"

"You taste incredible," he growls, and then he dives between my thighs, dipping his tongue inside me only to drag it up and latch onto my clit, sucking until I can feel my muscles trembling, fists clutching at the sheet underneath us —only for him to start all over.

"Flint… oh God, Flint, come on." Those are the words I keep repeating as he teases me with oblivion again and again, and I'm starting to wonder if he plans on keeping this going until I explode, but then he finds my clit again and stays there. Focusing on it until I'm trembling once more, babbling something that would probably be words if I could think past the rising wave of pleasure.

It's perfect, or at least I thought that was perfection until he slides one finger inside, quickly followed by another, and finds my g-spot like he's got a fucking homing beacon on it. The merciless focus on my clit combined with the tapping on that bundle of nerves inside me sends me over the edge in a cacophonous rush of bliss that erases the world temporarily, blitzing it out of existence until I realize that he hasn't stopped.

"No, no, no, no, Flint!" I shout and he sits up instantly, looking concerned for a second until I start laughing. "Oh my God, no. I want you now. *You.*"

Sucking his bottom lip between his teeth, he bites down for a second and it's quite possibly the hottest expression I've ever seen on a man. Especially since he just devoured me like the big bad wolf and looks like he isn't done.

"Please," I beg, and I don't feel an ounce of shame in it. If he gives me another orgasm like that, I'm not even going to be functioning, and I want to experience every moment of sex with Flint Etheridge.

"You are so fucking perfect," he growls, moving up my body, and I can't pretend I'm not impressed by his body. He's that perfect blend of fit but real, not ridiculously muscled, just a gorgeous guy with a whole lot of skill with his hands… and his tongue… and with the way he kisses… and talks… and, *fuck*.

He's perfect, not me.

I don't get the chance to argue though because he captures my lips in a kiss, and I'm suddenly filled with anxious excitement as I feel him move between my thighs. It's not my first time. Hell, it's not even close, but for some reason it feels like it is. We're crossing a line we can never uncross, going from crushes and childhood friends, to a whole lot more than that, and I've never been more excited to take that step with someone.

When he hesitates, I lift my hips to meet him, feeling his shaft slide through my wetness, and the low growl that earns me paints a grin over my lips that he erases with the first inch he pushes inside me. We both moan in unison, and hearing him right against my ear, breathing and making those hungry sounds, only makes me want him more.

This time when I lift my hips, I pull him deeper, and then he pins me back to the floor and finishes the thrust, stretching me and filling me in the most incredible way. All I can do is gasp, letting out a little moan of bliss before I manage a hushed, "Oh God."

"You okay?" he whispers, lifting up to look into my eyes, and I nod, wrapping my arms around his back.

"Don't stop," I answer, and he kisses me. Gently at first, playful nips and long, slow kisses that match the rhythm of his thrusts. He's bigger than I estimated when I had him in my mouth. I knew I couldn't fit him all the way in but having him inside me is a completely different experience. Every slow, powerful shift of his hips seems to reach a new place, stoking a fire that he feeds with every kiss, every touch.

"You feel amazing, Brinn," he groans, low and soft. The words buzz against my lips, and I can't even manage a response, so I just kiss him again, our bodies rocking together in perfect tandem, stretching out this slow, methodical friction that is somehow too much and not enough at the same time.

Wrapping my leg around his waist, I push his shoulder, and he gets the hint, holding onto my hips as we roll, leaving me on top. When I sit up, he takes advantage, trailing his fingers over my ribs, my stomach, and my breasts as I rock. I manage to keep the slow pace for a few minutes, grinding my clit against him with every swirl of my hips, but then he thrusts up, driving just a little deeper and I know I want more of that. "God, yes. Again, Flint."

He repeats it, bracing one hand on my hip as we both pick up speed until we're breathing hard, and I love how he curses under his breath, pressing his fingers tighter into my skin as the friction builds, turning the steady burn into an inferno.

"Fuck, I need you under me," Flint growls, and I nod, rolling with him again, and with the next thrust I feel just how much power he's been holding back.

"Yes!" I shout, dragging my nails down his back as he bends one of my knees toward my shoulder and somehow hits even deeper, giving the slightest twinge of pain with the whirl of ecstasy from the next hard thrust. "Fuck, yes, Flint! Harder, make me yours, please…"

"You like it?" he asks, slamming hard enough to move me on the floor, and I answer him with a moan, encouraging him without words because I can't focus as he drives deep again. "God, I've wanted you so long, Brinnah," he growls. "And now you're mine."

"Yes, yes, yes, yours," I babble, holding on and trying to meet his thrusts as he fucks me hard, claiming me, owning me in the most intense, intimate way I've ever felt. Our kisses are harried, rushed, broken over and over by the next hard thrust or gasp for air as we lay claim to each other, the unforgiving floor making every rough slam of his hips into mine a gloriously powerful ache that has me walking a brilliant tightrope toward orgasm. The heat of the fire seems to make everything more extreme, our skin quickly turning slick with sweat, but it's like both of us are holding on to make it last just a little longer.

That's not possible though, and I know it, I can feel my nerves buzzing with electric bliss, my skin tingling with the promise of release, and as every muscle in my body draws tight, I hold my breath for one more perfect moment of Flint driving deep, filling me, and then everything crashes. A chaotic whirlwind of heat and ecstasy as the orgasm rips through me like a wildfire, leaving me barely enough air to shout his name before the world shatters into a million prismatic shards of pleasure.

"Brinnah, *fuck*, yessss," Flint growls, thrusting a few more times before he slams deep and I feel him come, spilling heat inside me as his weight settles over me, sealing us together.

For a while everything feels hazy, blurred by the chemical cocktail still alive and burning in my veins, but I know my arms are wrapped tight around his back, and we're still connected.

That's all I need for the moment. I need to breathe, I need my heart to beat, and I need Flint Etheridge to stay right where he is as the pieces of my world settle back into place in a new pattern, which definitely has him in it.

When Flint lifts his head again, his warm brown eyes look as dazed as I feel, but the way he kisses me is gentle and sweet and everything I could want. Pushing himself up on one elbow, he looks down at me, smiling slightly as he traces his thumb under my lip, gliding it along my jaw until he can rest his hand alongside my neck. "You're incredible, Brinnah."

"You are," I retort, overlaying his hand with my own.

"I think I lo—" Flint cuts himself off, just staring into my eyes, and I'm breathless for a moment. There's a warm flood in my chest accompanied by the rapid beat of my heart, and I know what he wants to say.

"I think I do too," I whisper, and his eyes widen a little before that cocky grin spreads.

"Yeah?"

"Yeah," I confirm, and he rocks his hips, making us both moan softly before we laugh.

"Sure it's not because of this?" he asks, and I lift my hips and squeeze around him, reveling in the way his eyes flutter closed for a second. "Damn."

"I think *this* might be part of it, but it's not all of it. I think I've felt it since the moment I saw you in the meeting this morning." *Holy shit, was that really this morning?*

"Yeah," he whispers, running his thumb back and forth over my cheek. "I felt the same way. I couldn't keep my eyes off you."

"I noticed."

He chuckles, leaning down to press a light kiss to my lips. "I figured it was hard to ignore, but all of this just seems…"

"Like it was meant to be?" I finish and he meets my gaze, nodding.

"Exactly," he says, sliding from me to lay down at my side, and although I miss that connection, I love the way he pulls me into his chest, letting me rest my head on his shoulder. "You know, I never believed in the idea of destiny or fate before today, but I can't think of any other explanation."

"I don't know either… but I feel it."

"A connection," he adds, and I tilt my head back to smile at him.

"Exactly," I answer, and he grins, leaning down to kiss me before tossing his arm under his head to lay back down. Turning on my side, I rest my hand on his chest, intertwining our legs, and he just pulls me closer. "A connection… I think that's the perfect word." *For now.*

A word like love gets thrown around a lot, and I'm pretty sure we both feel that too, but what's between us is something more. Something deeper.

We were always connected. Across distance and time.

It just took a strange, miraculous set of events to get us back together, to give us this second-chance to get it right, and it could be the post-orgasmic bliss I'm still riding, but I can't imagine ever walking away from this. It's more than just the incredible sex, it's *him*. It's *this*.

It's *us*.

And our story is like something straight out of a fairy tale, miraculous and magical, once upon a snowstorm…

the end

about the author

Jennifer Bene is a *USA Today* bestselling author of dangerously sexy and deviously dark romance. From BDSM, to Suspense, Dark Romance, and Thrillers—she writes it all. Always delivering a twisty, spine-tingling journey with the promise of a happily-ever-after.

Don't miss a release! Sign up for the newsletter to get new book alerts (and a free welcome book) at: jenniferbene.com/newsletter

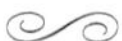

You can find her online throughout social media with username @jbeneauthor and on her website: www.jenniferbene.com

also by
JENNIFER BENE

The Thalia Series (Dark Romance)

Security Binds Her (Thalia Book 1)

Striking a Balance (Thalia Book 2)

Salvaged by Love (Thalia Book 3)

Tying the Knot (Thalia Book 4)

The Thalia Series: The Complete Collection

The Beth Series (Dark Romance)

Breaking Beth (Beth Book 1)

Fragile Ties Series (Dark Romance)

Destruction (Fragile Ties Book 1)

Inheritance (Fragile Ties Book 2)

Redemption (Fragile Ties Book 3)

Dangerous Games Series (Dark Mafia Romance)

Early Sins (A Dangerous Games Prequel)

Lethal Sin (Dangerous Games Book 1)

Standalone Dark Romance

Imperfect Monster

Corrupt Desires

Deviant Attraction: A Dark and Dirty Collection

Reign of Ruin

Mesmer

Jasmine

Crazy Broken Love

Standalone BDSM Ménage Romance

The Invitation

Reunited

Dark Suspense / Horror

Burned: An Inferno World Novella

Scorched: A New Beginning

Noxious (Anathema Book 1)

Mephitic (Anathema Book 2)

Viperous (Anathema Book 3)

Appearances in the Black Light Series (BDSM Romance)

Black Light: Exposed (Black Light Series Book 2)

Black Light: Valentine Roulette (Black Light Series Book 3)

Black Light: Roulette Redux (Black Light Series Book 7)

Black Light: Celebrity Roulette (Black Light Series Book 12)

Black Light: Charmed (Black Light Series Book 15)

Black Light: Roulette War (Black Light Series Book 16)

Black Light: The Beginning (Black Light Series Book 17.5)

Black Light: Unbound (Black Light Series Book 18)

BOOKS RELEASED AS CASSANDRA FAYE

Daughters of Eltera Series (Dark Fantasy Romance)

Fae (Daughters of Eltera Book 1)

Tara (Daughters of Eltera Book 2)

Standalone Paranormal Romance

Hunted (The Dirty Heroes Collection Book 13)

One Crazy Bite

Dangerous Magic

the devil's chessboard

SKYE WARREN &
AMELIA WILDE

chapter one

Gabriel

A MAN IN A DARK SUIT SITS DOWN NEXT TO ME.

We've never met in person, but I know who it is before he speaks. "Thanks for meeting me," I say, raising a glass of aged whiskey. "Do you want one?"

He sits down, graceful despite his large frame. "Thank you for the invitation. I've heard about the Den but never had the pleasure."

A cocktail waitress steps close. "Can I get you anything?"

"Coffee," he says.

When we're alone again, I lean forward. "I'm building a chess set. The board will be made of African Blackwood and White Oak. Interlocking parts, immovable, no hardware. The pieces will have marble bases and intricate mixed metal sculptures on top."

"And what do you need the diamonds for?"

I name the artist I've commissioned for this project. She's made a splash in the post-modern art world. She's also a third generation jeweler, which is why Luther Hades will know her.

He raises an eyebrow above his black, bottomless eyes. No—almost black. My sources were incorrect about this detail. A thin ring of blue surrounds huge pupils. "Impressive. I know rich people tend to throw their money around, but is there a reason you're building a chess set instead of buying an island or taking a man to the moon?"

That pulls a wry smile from me. "My wife."

"Ah."

"She loves chess, and I love her. We're expecting our second child soon, and this will be my gift to her. Of course it can't compare to the children she brings me, but it will have to suffice."

"So the designer wants diamonds."

"Two large stones. Smaller ones to form eternity bands. For the queens."

"Only the queens?"

"The kings will have to content themselves with copper."

"I suppose that's what they get for being so fucking useless."

We share a low chuckle at that, and pause as he receives a steaming mug. Both of us are kings of industry, authorities in business, billionaires on paper, but I know from my sources that he's recently married. Society may look to us as leaders, but we both bow to our queens.

He meets my direct gaze. "You could have called my Director of Operations. We have a very capable team for direct high-dollar sales."

I smile. "Those are for the diamonds you sell. I want the ones you don't."

A look of surprise passes over his granite features. I get the impression he isn't surprised very often. His personal collection isn't exactly public knowledge, but people whisper. Massive geodes, museum quality tapestries.

And of course, the best diamonds from his mine.

"What makes you think I'm willing to part with them?"

"Everything has a price."

"Don't you mean everyone has a price?"

"Precisely."

"Your reputation precedes you. I know what you're worth. Even so I'm not sure you can tempt me. When a man makes enough money, he starts to want other things."

He wouldn't have taken this meeting if he weren't willing to make a bargain. "I think we can come to an agreement. Perhaps you would like to join my wife and I for dinner tomorrow night?"

Hades pauses. "So that's your game."

"You can ask my wife what she loves so much about chess."

He laughs abruptly. "You're used to getting what you want, aren't you?"

"Yes, I'm an arrogant bastard. So are you. Let's work together."

The empty coffee mug meets the table. "There are some other things I hope to take care of during our visit to Tanglewood. And yes, I'm willing to meet you. Persephone will appreciate having new friends. But I make no promises on the diamonds."

I shake his hand before he leaves, then I sit back to finish the rest of my drink. The whiskey here really is the best in the world. *When a man makes enough money, he starts to want other things.* Yes, Avery taught me that. Love. Family. She's brought me a peace I've never thought possible. I'm determined to spoil her with the very best this earth has to offer.

When I'm done with my drink, I head outside. The waiting limo takes me home.

I walk in to a house full of quiet.

The black cat curled up on the large wooden chess set peeks one eye open but doesn't move as I walk through the living room. The Christmas tree twinkles against the balcony.

A large curving staircase takes me to the bedroom, where I find my family asleep. Avery curls around our little girl while Helen naps with her mouth open, arm flung over her mother's pregnant tummy in peaceful little girl slumber.

Part of me wants to wake Avery. Helen doesn't nap every day anymore, and we have precious few moments alone during the day. But moreso, I know that my wife needs her sleep. Her second pregnancy is rougher than her first.

More morning sickness, though that part has passed. More discomfort at night.

So I'm silent as I slip off my shoes and take off my jacket. I curl around my girls—all three of them, still and safe in my arms, and fall into a peaceful sleep.

When I wake up both of them are coming drowsily alert. Helen's already slipping off the edge of the bed with a cheeky grin and running off, most likely to get into trouble.

Avery leans back against me and rests her head under my chin. I pull her close. "Do you want to keep sleeping?" I murmur against her hair. "I can keep the little imp away."

Her hand captures my arm, pulling me tighter around her. "Don't go."

Her breasts warm and heavy against my arm, her ass tight against my abs, both of them have the predictable effect. I become hard, and she wriggles when she feels me.

A low moan escapes her, and I shudder at the sensual sound.

"Naughty," I mutter.

I can hear the smile in her voice. "Are you going to punish me?"

Behind us the door is open, but I know that our child is already in her room playing. She's usually good by herself after a nap, playing on her own, as if she's afraid that if she comes to us she'll be trapped in another afternoon nap.

I pull the blanket over us to be safe, covering my hands as they pull up her dress and slip beneath her underwear. She's always so welcoming. Her legs spread for me, giving me access, and I slide my fingers deep inside her.

"How can I punish you, darling?" I find the special place inside her and rub the pads of my fingers over it, making her squirm and gasp. "When you feel so damn good?"

I thrust in and out of her, fucking her with my hand as I grow hard and desperate against her ass. She comes in urgent little mewls and tiny thrusts of her hips. I continue stroking her softly, softly, letting her sink gently back to earth.

"Thank you," she whispers, voice heavy with satisfaction.

When I press my lips to the curve of her ear, she's already asleep again.

Ruefully I remove my hand. I lean down to breathe in deep from her hair, her skin, her musky sexual scent. My hard cock will have to go on throbbing, because she needs her sleep.

chapter two

Hades

I DON'T TRAVEL, AS A RULE.

Not to meetings in places I don't own. Not to shadowy street corners in a nondescript car I've driven here myself. And not to stakeouts on jewelry stores.

Rules, of course, always have exceptions. They come up against conflicting parameters.

For instance:

I do not deny my wife anything, as a rule.

There are exceptions to that, too. Persephone likes to be denied some things, in some ways.

Not this.

Many of my rules are coming under fire today. Interesting how that happens the moment you're outside your own kingdom. Fortunately for me, I won't be here long enough to bend this whole city to my will. Unfortunately for others, I'll be here long enough to bring parts of it to heel.

One part in particular.

When Oliver, my head of security, told me about this scheme I brushed him off. It's absurd on its face. No one sells my diamonds but me. Everyone knows this. They have their suspicions and rumors about the things that go on in the mines I own, but they never question the integrity of the diamonds. It makes no difference to me if some cretin from Tanglewood is running a con.

Oliver is an intelligent man. He knew better than to press me on bullshit. But Persephone insisted.

"Tell him the rest."

Oliver sighed. Persephone raised her eyebrows. A battle fought and lost in the space of an instant.

"Children," she said, before he could get a word out. "They're using *children*. For labor." She didn't have to say the rest: and what else?

"We've gotten word that they're sending another shipment in two weeks," Oliver said.

"Of diamonds?"

"Of children."

A straight line travels from those words to me, sitting behind the wheel and watching the lazy fall of snowflakes from sky to street.

The jewelry store across the pavement has no distinguishing features. It looks like all the other buildings around it. A glassed-in front entrance. A slim alleyway off to one side.

No lights. The shop is closed.

Nothing happens.

Nothing happens for so long that I start to fantasize about firing Oliver for this waste of time and resources.

I could be in the hotel suite with Persephone right now, doing any number of things to her. With her. I don't lie to her, as a rule. Tonight is yet another exception. A lie of omission is still a lie.

And now it's for nothing.

It would be a pleasure to respond to the anger heating my palms, but I won't. Not until later. Not until it's convenient. Persephone has a way of turning that sensation into something else entirely.

I'm reaching for the key to the ignition when something moves in the alley.

It's almost imperceptible, a shadow inside a shadow. The permanent state of my eyes means I have no choice but to see it.

Well, fuck.

The shadow resolves into a shape—a small, red coat.

Perhaps I'll let Oliver keep his job.

The red coat is only the first in a line of jackets. Six, seven, eight.

I don't regret leaving my dog, Conor, with Persephone. Not

until this moment, anyway. Because five men are following the children.

The number doesn't concern me so much as the possibility of collateral damage. Disgust burns the back of my throat. These useless pieces of shit.

A flash of white at the far corner of the street illuminates the whole setup. The van is huge and white and could be from any delivery company in the city. Only this one is going to deliver children from one hell to another.

This will never be my daughter. But if it were…

Well.

Nothing on this street would be left standing.

I send a single text to a prearranged number and get out of the car. Adrenaline swan dives into my veins. Down to my toes. Down to my fingertips. I cannot fucking believe how cavalier and obvious they're being. It's as if they were sure I wouldn't care.

One of the men moves first. He's big and weighed down with a bulletproof vest. His nose cracks under my fist, no thanks to the vest. He falls into the brick corner of the alley.

I can feel the rest of them weighing their options. The van is coming. The children are scattering, three of them sprinting across the street.

I've already chosen my next move.

The closest one is a scrawny thing and I get one hand around his throat before he's made the decision to run. His nearby friend is loyal to someone, at least, because he tries to stop the strangling in process. I end it early out of convenience. It leaves just enough of an opening for the last one to try and tackle me from behind.

To *tackle* me.

Like a fucking fool.

He succeeds in scratching me across one eye—or is it a knife? The cut catches on my cheekbone. Fuck that. My eyes are what they are. That doesn't mean I'd be better off with one missing. I throw him over me and onto the concrete and plant one shoe on his neck.

Oh, look. The van has arrived.

There are no children left to climb in, but there are three remaining men who scramble for it, fumbling for the handle on the door, pounding on the windows.

Fucking cowards.

And late cowards, too. Because the cavalry have arrived.

Red and blue lights pierce the dark at the end of the street and drive knives into my pupils. They're alternating with sun-bright flashes and a single flicker of concern for myself blinks its way into being. There's no time to indulge it. Not in the immediate scramble of other people arriving to make arrests and search out the children. I offer an anonymous statement and leave.

The drive back to the hotel hurts. So do the lights in the lobby, and the ones in the elevator.

At the entrance to the penthouse suite the door opens before I can reach for the handle. Persephone is adorably disheveled, one cheek pink from sleep. I have my hands on her even before the door closes behind us. My mouth on the side of her neck. She's so warm, so soft, and I'm going to wreck her. Just the way she likes. I get a hand between her legs and she gasps, slinging one arm around my neck.

"You're bleeding."

"I don't care."

I take her to bed without caring. I don't think about it again until much later, when she's curled dreamily around a pillow, her breathing even and deep. Conor rustles in the corner, turns around, goes back to sleep. He hasn't noticed my return. So much for man's best friend.

The cut is shallow, but it still stings.

And the fight was too easy.

chapter three

Gabriel

THE NEXT DAY, UNCLE CHRISTOPHER AND AUNT HARPER AGREE TO be our last minute babysitters. Helen greets them at the door already in her Peppa Pig pajamas, eager to eat popcorn and watch Christmas movies. I welcome Christopher with a handshake.

Harper tries to convince Helen to watch It's a Wonderful Life with Jimmy Stewart. "There's an angel that comes down from heaven, a run on a bank, and a romance for the ages."

My little girl frowns. "How the Grinch Stole Christmas has a cute puppy."

"She knows her own mind," I warn Harper. "A cute puppy is hard to beat."

"I think they have a dog, the family." She looks at Christopher. "Don't they have a dog?"

I don't hear his response because my wife steps out onto the landing. I'm at least eighteen feet away, a full story below her, but I feel like she whacked me with a two by four. A silver dress hugs her baby bump. When she takes a step down the stairs, a high slit shows off her gorgeous legs.

"Jesus, Mary, and Joseph," I mutter.

"What does that mean?" Helen asks behind me.

Harper answers, "It means your father respect your mother's mind above all else, that he considers her an equal, and he doesn't only look at her as a symbol of sex and fertility."

"Cool," Helen says.

I'm halfway up the stairs to greet her so I can growl against her neck. "What the fuck are you wearing? Do you want me to rip your dress off in front of everyone?"

Avery lets out a giggle. She doesn't always giggle. Only when she's pregnant, I've found. She pats me on the chest and she passes me on the stairs. "Come on. We'll be late."

My growl of frustration makes Christopher snort. "Have fun, kids."

When we get into the back of the limo, Avery snuggles up against me, her wool winter coat exterior a contrast to her warm, pliable body. I press my face into her curls and breathe deep. Snowflakes and cold air and the sweet scent of her.

I shift in the warm leather seats, trying to ease the ache. But there's no way this club is going to fit into my slacks comfortably. "This is going to be the longest drive in eternity."

"We could do something to pass the time," she says, her voice hopeful.

"Not if you want that dress to be in one piece during dinner."

She does that giggle again, a sweet, breathless sound. It's almost childlike in its wonder, but that doesn't stop me from holding her body close—all woman—and panting after her on our way into the city. Snow pelts the darkened window and creates a blanket around us. We exist in our own universe for the space of forty three minutes, safe from the cold.

Tanglewood is flush with restaurants appropriate to a high-end business double date, from the established steakhouses to the sleek farm-to-table upstarts. Tonight we're at Nigiri, an upscale Japanese restaurant with fresh sushi, incredible hot pots, and some of the best Wagyu beef in the country. Avery's cravings range from milk tea ice cream to warm sesame buns. When I told her we were going here this morning, she started moaning over the umami in their brown butter mushroom nigiri. Our second child definitely has a preference for Asian food.

Luther Hades and his young wife are already seated when we arrive. They stand as the waitress shows us to the table.

She gives us a shy smile and holds out her hand. "It's so nice to meet you."

Avery embraces her in a warm hug. "Sorry," she says, laughing, breathless. "Sorry. It's a pregnant woman's prerogative. I have to hug everyone now."

Persephone doesn't seem to mind. "I love it. When are you due?"

Normally I'm happy to listen to Avery gush about Helen and our yet-to-be-named second child, but I notice something interesting. There's a bruise on the side of Hades' face that wasn't there yesterday afternoon. We pull out chairs for the women, but before we sit down I take him aside.

A raise of my eyebrows is the only question required.

"Business," he says, clearly reluctant to say more.

I cock my head. Everything I've heard about Luther Hades says he's fierce but fair. I haven't heard any whispers about him being a crime lord, but I won't have my wife's chess board tainted with blood diamonds. I also won't have her sitting down with a man who's dangerous to her. "You have anything more to share?"

He sighs. "There were children, being put to work. Abused. Now they're not."

My eyes narrow. "In Tanglewood?"

He gives me a cold smile. "Things like that happen in every large city. Abuse. Neglect. Exploitation. Did you think yours was exempt?"

"No, but I'm surprised you handled it yourself. You could have told me."

"They were passing off the diamonds as coming from my mine."

"Ah."

"And…." He glances toward his wife. "She convinced me to care."

I give a curt nod. "Wives have a way of doing that."

We take our seats beside the women as a waitress comes around to take drink orders. Avery orders a sparkling water, and the rest of us choose non-alcoholic out of respect for her. We choose avocado sushi and grilled edamame as the appetizers.

There's a pleasant hum of conversation in the restaurant. Low drum-like panels hang from the ceiling create a cozy atmosphere.

There's more action near the bar where chefs create elaborate sushi displays, but we're nestled toward the back, with a screen separating us from most of the diners. The women chatter about the sights that Persephone wants to see while she's in Tanglewood. The Tanglewood Library, for one thing. The Grand Theater.

She glances at Hades. "I've heard about this incredible mural artist who has work on the sides of buildings throughout the west side. There's a walking tour tomorrow, but Hades says it's not a safe area of town."

"He's right, unfortunately," Avery says with a sympathetic smile. "That's partly why Harper focuses her work there. So that the children who grow up in those city blocks will see her work and know that someone cared about them."

"Wait, do you know her?"

Avery's cheeks turn pink. "She's my best friend. Oh my god, how long are you going to be in town? There's a private showing of her new work at the Den on Saturday night."

The crash of a wine glass comes first. It might have meant nothing—a drunk customer or a tired waitress. Every hair on the back of my neck rises. It might mean nothing, but it doesn't. Something is happening. My instincts go on high alert.

Hades is already half out of his seat when the blast happens. I throw myself on top of Avery, crushing her against the concrete floor, trying to shield every inch of her body. The shots come through too fast to count. A glass splinters into pieces on the table. A plate falls to the floor. The paper screen rips down the middle.

Silence falls over the restaurant. There's a beat of stillness before everything erupts into frenzy. People scramble toward the door, screaming. Waitresses are crying. Cooks are shouting. There's a distant wail of a police siren.

Hades' dark gaze meets mine. There is no blue left in his eyes. His expression is furious.

I'm still covering Avery, not letting her up in case the shooters come back around. "Were they after you? Who the fuck did you piss off?"

"Maybe," he says with a hard shake of his head. "I thought I finished them, but maybe someone got away. I need Persephone somewhere safe. The hotel won't be enough."

"My house. It's got the best alarm system that money can't buy." As if to prove my point, my driver comes running through the melee. He's more than a driver. He's a bodyguard. I don't take any chances with my family. "We can escort the women home."

"Good," he says with a curt nod. His nostrils flare. "And then we hunt."

Hades

"It was the Russians." Gabriel Miller slips his phone back into his pocket and returns his hand to the steering wheel. He swings a hard right turn, then a left.

"And you have that on good authority?" I don't like relying on other people for anything, but this isn't my city. I don't have the best information.

"I have it on Damon Scott's authority."

"A friend of yours?"

"You could call him that. If something happens in the dark side of Tanglewood, he knows about it. And he found out who shot up the restaurant within minutes of it happening."

Fine. I'll take his word for it. It's completely unsurprising that agents from Russia would have been involved. My brother Zeus, who usually works the hardest to fuck with me, has finally been usurped by foreign operatives. He won't be pleased about losing his title.

"Do you always bring your dog on hunting expeditions?" Gabriel's tone is light but his hands are tense on the wheel. He didn't protest when we stopped to pick up Conor from the hotel. Just as well for him.

"All of them." Of course I do.

Conor goes with me everywhere, unless he's guarding Persephone. The pain in my head is still dull, but insistent enough that convincing Conor to stay behind would be a near-impossible task.

I won't be telling any of this to Gabriel.

"We're here," he says.

Here turns out to be a warehouse on the edge of the city. A single lightbulb casts a yellow glow down the side of the building. "Are they desperate for cash?"

"They must be, if they came after you."

Now I'm the one coming after them. What an incredible twist of fate.

We find a side entrance to the warehouse. The lock is flimsy enough to break with my hands, so I do. My teeth are on edge. All of me is on edge. Conor knows it, too.

He swallows growl after growl and hangs close.

There could be any number of people inside. They'll all pay. My anger has cooled to a frozen thirst for revenge. They endangered Persephone.

Inside the building it's dark. Gloomy.

Empty.

Conor tenses by my side. Empty except for the back office. Light leaks around the doorframe. Gabriel looks at me, a question in his eyes.

The answer is to finish this. That's the only answer.

I expect them to be ready.

They're not ready.

The back room explodes in shouts and panic and the trained Russians aren't so very trained after all. They don't know what to do when faced with someone like me, and someone like Gabriel. They haven't left themselves with an exit. They haven't left themselves with anything except guns, and they're not fast enough for those.

One goes down with the butt of his pistol imprinted on his forehead.

Another crumples under a broken arm. I can't see what Gabriel is doing until he's finished, two men in a heap in the corner. He rubs his hands together, the movement as perfunctory as a head chef finishing dinner service.

There's only one left.

He's the ringleader—that much is clear from his glare. He sent the rest of his buddies out to meet us and backed up into a corner. Conor has him trapped, hackles raised, teeth bared. One word from me and the man's throat will be a memory.

"Conor," I say.

My dog backs up, eyes still tracking our prey. A wary relief skates across the creature's gaze. I haven't spared him. He doesn't know that yet.

Gabriel and I do not have to speak to finalize our plan.

He goes in first. The last Russian waits as long as he can, then tries to bolt. It's useless. Gabriel has his arms pinned. The man is larger than Gabriel, but clearly less skilled. His thick legs flail uselessly. He howls in Russian, but he's pinned by Gabriel's knee.

And I have a waiting fist.

The blow snaps his head back and he drops.

"Nice," says Gabriel.

"Yes, well." I straighten my jacket. "It's fucking rude to interrupt dinner."

chapter four

Hades

I CAN FEEL PERSEPHONE WAITING FOR ME.

The house is quiet.

Gabriel points me toward a guest room and starts to head toward another wing of the house.

"Those diamonds," I say, halting his step. "I'm going to charge you an arm and a leg."

He turns back with a small smile. "Perfect."

It's definitely the most unconventional deal I've ever made. I never planned to sell the diamonds in my private collection. They're too perfect, but at least I know Gabriel Miller will appreciate them. And he helped protect Persephone. That's worth its weight in diamonds.

I give him a nod and head toward the room where my wife waits. My heart is still beating fast from the confrontation. I'm surprised she doesn't follow the sound out into the hall. Conor pads along beside me until I pat his head and tell him to wait. Not all night. Just for now.

This time, I'm the one who opens the door.

Persephone is sitting on the side of the bed.

She lifts her head. How many times does she watch me enter a room every day? It still stops my heart dead to see it. Her eyebrows rise, lips parting, color rushing to her cheeks. She is possibly the only person on earth who has never tired of me.

I stop her before she can scramble off the bed, lay her back, and kiss her. She tastes fresh and clean, like springtime.

And Persephone, my little queen, is distracted.

I take her chin in my hand and tip her face toward mine. She doesn't stop moving her hands. Over the buttons of my jacket, my shirt collar—everywhere. "What are you doing?"

"Trying to take your clothes off."

Her voice is edged in fear. Not the delicious kind. I catch both of her wrists in one hand and pin them over her head. "No need to beg."

"There is a need." She twists and fights in my grasp, which only makes me want her more. It only makes my entire body bend toward the arc of fucking her. "I was worried. I was so worried. You could have been hurt. You could have been stabbed. You've been stabbed before. I saw it. And, you know, knives can kill people. They—"

I close and kiss her cheek. It's the matching place to my own bruised face. "Why are you still worried about me? You of all people know I'm practically a god."

The worry melts from her eyes. A small nod. "I know."

Now we're both equally motivated to get rid of my clothes, and hers. Hers come first, then mine, and Persephone stops me at the side of the bed, her fingertips on my chest.

She looks at me for a long time.

"Are you calling me a liar?"

Her huge, silver eyes meet mine. "I just wanted to be sure."

A hand on her throat silences her. No pressure. Just a reminder of the consequences of falling for a man like me. Persephone shivers, her pink nipples peaking. She lifts two hands to circle my wrist while I work us both onto the bed. Her hips have already started rocking when she tips her face up to mine for a kiss that burns us both.

A more patient man would take his time with her.

I'm on fire with impatience. With the closeness of her. The heat of her. Even that silver fear in her eyes. I want to fuck it right out of her, and then some.

I don't feel fear, as a rule. Persephone is one of a very few exceptions.

But not right now.

Now she spreads her legs for me and welcomes me in, every thick, vicious inch of me. She makes a noise in the back of her throat that makes me brace one hand against the headboard and take her harder. The flutters and clenches of her muscles tell me this is a struggle, at least at first, and there's nothing Persephone likes so much a struggle.

She likes it with such intensity that it borders on obsession, my filthy queen. Persephone moves my hand over her own mouth to quiet her whimpers and moans, but I don't give it to her right away. No, no. I give myself room to put my fingers between her legs—all sweet and wet—then gag her with those same fingers. The slick heat of her tongue alternates with pressure from sharp teeth.

"It must be hard to be such a good girl," I say, low into her ear. "You love when other people listen in."

She shakes her head to deny it, but the rest of her body exposes her for the liar she is. One of her favorite games.

I slow my pace enough to play one of mine.

It's nothing to move her into the perfect position for more contact on her clit. She'll have to focus if she wants to come this way, because I can't stop. I can't slow down again. She's too tight, too wet, too made for me. There's no resisting the pull of her.

She squeezes her eyes shut tight and I feel it starting—the rhythmic grip and release of her imminent orgasm. At the very last second she wrestles my hand away from her mouth and bucks her body against mine, fighting it even while she goes down.

All the way down.

And then all the way up, sucking in a breath and coming so hard that it takes me over with her.

She shudders out the last of her release, hands still pushing at me so that I'll push back. It's as if she can only be convinced through pleasure and pain that I've lived to see another day.

Persephone curls against me when it's finished, one hand reaching blindly for the light.

It's only when we're in darkness that the last of the pain ebbs away from my head. I let out a long breath without meaning to.

Her fingertips on my forehead trace the outline of where it hurt before. Now there's nothing but pleasure.

Persephone's voice in the darkness is already heavy with sleep. "You're okay?"

"Now I am."

An indignant little noise. I think she might argue with me, but instead she inches closer, body languid.

Quiet comes in. My mind wanders. I prefer to sleep only in places I own, as a rule. But I would stay anywhere for Persephone.

Wives will do that to you.

I get up to let Conor in. He'll sleep next to the bed, the way he usually does. Alert for anything.

Persephone catches my wrist before I can take a step. "Are you coming back?" she murmurs, half-awake.

"Always," I tell her. It's the rule.

THANK YOU for reading *The Devil's Chessboard*, a short story that celebrates two of our favorite couples. If you'd like to read more about Gabriel and Avery, you can download THE PAWN from book retailers now: www.skyewarren.com/books/the-pawn

And you can read more about Hades and Persephone in the myth retelling with KING OF SHADOWS by Amelia Wilde here: www.awilderomance.com/books/king-of-shadows

delicious

DYLAN ALLEN

chapter one

Max

"I GOT YOUR NOTE," I GRIN AT THE BOMBSHELL SOPHIA LOREN look alike who just answered the door in a pale pink robe that's just short enough to be sexy but long enough that it's clear she doesn't mean for it to be.

She squints up at me, brushes her long chestnut colored hair out her eyes and frowns. "Then why are you knocking on my door at seven thirty in the morning?"

Her lips, wide and full even as they frown up at me, are the same color as the peonies blooming in huge pale pink clusters in the bushes framing the grey bricked path that leads to her house. But prettier.

"Hello?" she waves a hand front of my face and pulls me out of my very enjoyable study of her mouth.

I take my time moving from her lips and linger on the small beauty mark on the left side of her mouth. Her skin is flushed with sleep, and her cheeks have a glow to them I have a feeling is always present. She's got a long straight nose that, like her mouth, is on the verge of being too big for her face.

"I came to apologize and introduce myself. You know, be neighborly," I say when I finally reach her eyes. They are the color of the sea. Dark green, clear and, right now, just as turbulent.

"I'm Maximillian Edwards, but you can call me Max. It's what my friends do," I mention as I extend my hand.

She eyes it for a second and then puts hers in it.

When our hands touch, the warmth of her palm pressed to mine, I feel a tingle all the way up my arm. Judging by her surprised gasp and the way her eyes fly between our joined hands and my face, she does, too.

I say a silent *thank you* to whatever good luck brought this goddess to the long vacant beach house next door to mine.

"I'm Franchesca Parisi," she says, her lips turning up in a smile that's subtle, but still reaches all the way to her gorgeous wide eyes. "You can call me Franchesca, Maximillian." She pulls her hand out of my grasp and fusses with her hair again. Her eyes

"Ouch," I flatten hand on my chest in a wounded gesture that's only half feigned. "Are you rejecting my offer of friendship?"

"Yes," she says even though her smile grows wider. "I'm not friends with morning people. I don't trust them," she deadpans.

"I'm not a morning person. I'm an *all-day* person," I retort.

"Even worse," she chuckles. It's husky, effortless, and I think it's my new favorite sound.

She tightens the belt of her robe, and the motion draws my eye to her waist. It's small, and the ample curve of her hips and the generous breasts that strain the fabric of her robe accentuate it even more.

"Ahem..." She clears her throat pointedly.

I force my eyes back to her face and offer her a contrite smile. "I'm sorry. I don't usually ogle women, I swear."

She quirks that sexy mouth into a disbelieving smirk.

"Really," I protest.

She just raises one of her sable colored eyebrows and taps her chin with one of her dark red finger nails. Against the pink, brown and green tableau that makes up the rest of her, they hint at tendency to buck conformity.

"Let me guess... you're just so overwhelmed by me in particular that you've suddenly started behaving out of character," she says in a dry tone that says she thinks that it's more likely that aliens live among us.

I cock my head at her in surprise. "Yes. You're traffic stopping beautiful," I tell her honestly.

She flushes, but her smile disappears. I know by the look on her face I've said the wrong thing. "Flattery won't get you anywhere. At least not with me," she says tightly.

"I'm sorry," I apologize immediately. I'm not the type of guy to press unwanted advances on women. I realize how my presence, coupled with my ogling and my blatant flirting, must seem.

"I came to apologize for all the noise. Now, I'll add being a creepy neighbor to the list of my transgressions," I say sheepishly.

She relaxes and smiles through a moan that is erotic in a way she can't possibly mean, and it immediately replaces her laugh as my favorite sound. I want to pull that sound from her again.

"I'm sorry, Max," and hearing her use my name loosens something in my chest. It sounds nice rolling off her tongue, and I love that she's dropped my full name. "We've gotten off on the wrong foot, haven't we?" she says graciously.

"We? No, just me. I haven't had neighbors for a long time. I'm used to playing my music as loud as I want and laying flooring at midnight because it's convenient. I'll keep it down. I won't knock so early. And I won't stare at you inappropriately," I say hoping that even though I'm being lighthearted, she can tell my apology is sincere. Her eyes soften.

"I didn't find your regard inappropriate," she says softly looking up at me through her lashes.

That look, coupled with the very faint blush that blooms on her cheeks, is so utterly sexy and charming I find myself saying words I haven't even thought to say in months. "I'd love to make it up to you. Can I cook you lunch?"

chapter two

Franchesca

My new neighbor is ridiculously hot. Hotter than he looks on television… and that's saying a lot. He's an inch or so shy of six feet, but with my five foot one and three quarter inch frame, he's more than tall enough. His baby blue eyes twinkle in a way that reflects his good humor, but the way he's looking at me now reminds me of the blue center of a flame. The way he's worrying his lip as he waits for me to answer his question is charming. He's not known for being charming. He's known for eviscerating the hopes of the young chefs who fail to produce anything less than perfect. I can't imagine any woman saying no to his invitation. I've seen him every morning since I got here. He runs on the beach, comes home and does all sorts of horror inducing things like jumping rope, lunges, push-ups, pull ups, crunches on the deck. With his headphones in, singing or rapping along to whatever's blasting in his ears.

It woke me up my first morning here, and I watched with fascination as his sweat drenched upper body flexed and rippled.

I wasn't being dishonest when I said I'm not a morning person. Every morning I've gotten up and enjoyed my coffee while I've watched him. However, last night, a couple hours after I'd gone to bed, I was awoken by the sound of blaring music and the very distinct thwack of a nails plunging into wood. Rapidly and repeatedly.

I dragged myself out of bed, stuffed my feet into my flip flops, and marched down my walkway. I rounded the fence that separated our porches and stumped up his. I knocked loudly, but I could hear the music from outside and knew I was wasting my time.

I went back to my house, wrote a note that was as scathing as I could manage on my sleep fogged brain and stuck it on his front door.

I didn't expect him to show up here. I hadn't wanted him to. Hot guys with no regard for others were a breed of man I knew very well.

So, his appearance here, his clearly sincere apology, and his invitation to cook me dinner were all unexpected.

"You're going to cook? For me?" I ask, unable to hide my smile. Of course, I along with the rest of the world knew about his spectacular fall from grace. I remember the interview where he swore he'd never cook for "the undeserving public" again.

"Yes, for you," he says in that deep rambling voice that still carries the lilt of his native Colombia. His gaze grows even more penetrating. Even if I wanted to, I'd be helpless to say no, but I most definitely did not want to say no to him.

"I'd love that," I respond. My inner foodie pops champagne as I imagine what he's going to whip up for dinner. I've been living on frozen wonton soup, grapes, pita chips, coffee, wine and sparkling water since I got here. I haven't found the energy to venture to the grocery store and the thought of eating the same old same is so unappealing.

"Wonderful. What are you doing for lunch?" he asks, and I double take.

"Lunch?" I ask surprised.

"Yeah, lunch. Today." He reiterates.

"Uh, well… I usually skip lunch," and dinner I omit.

"You miss the most important meal of the day?"

"I never miss breakfast."

"Oh, that's just a great big propaganda message by the orange juice, dairy, egg and bread lobbyists. Lunch is meal of champions. Breakfast is nothing but something to tide you over until lunch." He says with a straight face and the laughter that bubbles out of me, for the second time this morning feels so… good.

"Well, it's been a very effective messaging campaign because it's the only meal I don't skip."

"I can't wait to convert you. Let's say one thirty? I can cook here if it would make you more comfortable," he offers.

I think about my bare cabinets, the paper plates, and plastic forks and shake my head.

"No, I'll come around to yours, if that's okay?"

"Sure, any hard limits?" he asks, and I don't miss the innuendo in his tone or the way his eyes linger on my mouth.

My nipples tighten as his blue eyes darken when he meets my eyes again.

"No. I'm easy," I say and slap my hand over my mouth when I realize what I've said, and he bursts out laughing.

"I mean, about food. I'm not a picky eater," I stammer.

He puts one of his big hands on my shoulder, and I can feel his heat through the flimsy fabric of my robe; it sends a wave of warmth through my entire body.

"I know what you meant," he says with a smile that has more than a hint of mischief in it. He lets go of my shoulder and leans against the frame of my door, his broad shoulders nearly filling it, his legs crossed at the ankles. Even in his running clothes, he looks like the poster boy for a high fashion campaign. He's the walking definition of sexy.

"Now, I'm going to work extra hard to impress you. People who say they're not picky eaters are my favorite because I want them to leave my table pickier than they were before they sat down. I want to give you something that will make everything that comes after me feel inadequate. That'll make you crave seconds." The way he speaks to me makes my toes curl.

Good Lord.

He talks about food the way most people talk about sex. Now, I'm wishing that's what he was talking about. It's been a long time since I've had sex worth the trouble of coming back for seconds.

"I can't wait," I say honestly, and he winks at me.

"Neither can I, Franchesca," he says my name with a smile and then he walks backward down the walk.

"One thirty and come hungry," he winks and then turns and jogs away.

I close my door and lean back against it. Who would have thought the man who struck terror in the hearts of the audience who watched him, as well as the chefs who vied to impress him every night, would be… nice?

This is going to be interesting.

chapter three

Max

"THIS LOOKS AMAZING," FRANCHESCA BEAMS UP AT ME AND somehow, those three words make me feel a deeper sense of pride than years of cooking for heads of State, celebrities and some of the most critical palettes ever have.

"I hope it tastes as good as it looks," I say.

"I hope so, too. Nothing worse than a dish that looks better than it tastes," she says and takes the napkin I'm hold out to her. She drapes it over her lap and looks up at me expectantly.

"Where's your plate?"

"Oh," I shake my head and walk back to the stove and prepare myself a plate. "Old habits die hard," I apologize as I walk back with my plate of ginger and teriyaki glazed salmon, grilled endive and fingerling potatoes drenched in an herb butter I churned by hand.

"I have a feeling my no lunch habit will be very easy to break. I could get used to this," she responds and picks up her fork and knife.

I find myself unable to look away as she puts a little bit of everything onto her fork and then puts the food into her mouth. She's wearing a light pink lipstick that makes her lips glisten and as she chews, I forget about the food and wonder what it would feel like to kiss her.

When her lips part and that moan that I jerked off to in the shower floats out from between them, I feel my cock stir again. Her eyes drift closed as she chews and she sways a little like she's listening to music instead of eating. I can't take my eyes off her.

God, it's such a turn on to watch someone eating just for the joy of it. Not to critique the meal, not snapping a picture they'll put up on Instagram —just because they're enjoying it. This is what was missing from my career, real people who were eating for the joy of it. This is why after the rest of my life imploded, I walked away from my television show, my restaurant and the very lucrative contract I had with the world's largest cookware manufacturer.

This is the first meal I've been inspired to make in over a year, and now, I'm itching to get back to it.

I watch her chew and only when she's done does she open her eyes. Their dark green depths are hazy with a pleasure that's contagious.

"It's amazing. How do you make the salmon so…" she searches the air as if the word is floating above her head.

"Perfect?" I offer with a shrug.

"Yes. It's perfect. It's cooked, but so moist," she says drawls happily, and I lean back with a smile. If it means she'll look at me like that, I'll cook for her every day. "I meant it when I said I didn't have any hard limits. I'm not picky about how my salmon is cooked, but I clearly had no clue what I was missing," she says and puts another forkful into that sexy as fuck mouth.

"Five hundred degrees, five minutes a pound," I tell her.

"Can I tell you a secret?" she asks between forkfuls, her eyes dancing as she watches me. I nod and then dig into my own meal. The salmon is amazing. I've made it several times in the last year, exactly like this. Just for myself. But it's never tasted better. The ginger zings, the teriyaki smoothes out its bite, and the fish melts in my mouth.

"I can't cook," she says and then pauses with her eyes wide, waiting for my reaction. I'm not surprised at all. I hear this all the time, and I'm glad for it. Restaurants depend on people just like her. They like to eat, don't have the desire or time to cook, and have enough disposable income to eat out regularly. I'm making assumptions about her income, but these beach houses are some of the most expensive real estate in on the Gulf of Mexico, so she's gotta have some money.

"That's okay. I can," I tell her in between my own bites.

"I wish I could, but when I was in medical school, there was no time. When I started my residency it was even worse. I sometimes wouldn't go home for days."

"You're a doctor?" I ask unable to hide my surprise.

"Yes," she says and takes another bite of food.

"What kind?" I ask when she doesn't say anything else.

"A neonatologist," she says with a shrug as if it's no big deal. I didn't even finish college. I can't imagine all of that school. I didn't know women like her really existed. Beauty, brains and she loves to eat.

This is the woman of my dreams.

I stand up and walk to my fridge and pull out one of the many bottles of Veuve Cliquot I keep chilled out of habit.

"Are we celebrating?" she asks, her eyes wide and her smile full of merriment.

"Yes, we are," I say vaguely as I pull two champagne flutes down from my cabinet and walk back to the table.

"I'm always down for that," she says gamely, and I like her even more.

"So, are you going to be working at the hospital?" I ask as I place a glass in front of her. I pull the foil from the cork and then slowly work it loose.

"No, I'm on sort of a hiatus," she says, her gaze drifts to her lap, and I know there's more to the story, but I can also tell that she doesn't want to talk about it. I totally understand. I've spent the last year avoiding my friends, family and basically everyone but my twin sister, Kingsley. Suddenly, I find I want to talk about it because I want to know what drove her to this remote part of the Gulf Shores by herself.

"Well, I'm figuring you know that I'm on one, too," I say.

"Uh, yeah. I mean, I wasn't going to mention it. Eat TV was my favorite channel. I watched you every night," she tells me and then she blushes. Yes. This woman. I am really feeling her.

"Did you?" I ask and fill her glass.

"Mmm-hmm," she affirms through a mouth full of food.

I fill my glass and hold it up.

She wiggles her shoulders excitedly. "This is fancy." She picks up her glass and holds it next to mine. "So, what are we toasting to?"

"New neighbors, good food, and even better company," I say, and she nods.

"Oh yeah, I'm all about that. What luck. I'm glad I left that note now." she says, and we clink glasses.

I take a sip and promptly choke on the cold bubbles as I watch her throw back the entire glass in one gulp.

"Can I have more?" she asks, picking up the bottle before I can nod. She pours another glass and throws that back, too.

"You know, it's meant to be savored?" I say after I recover my voice.

"Yeah, I am savoring it. Quickly. Life is short," she says and snaps her fingers for emphasis.

"I bet you know that better than most," I say with an assessing glance.

"Yup. I do." She pours herself another glass but only takes small sip before she puts it down on the table. She sits back in her chair, crosses her arms over her chest, forcing her ample breasts up and out over the already low neckline of her white tank top. I force my eyes back to her face ready to apologize for being a perv. She's looking at me, but her eyes are unfocused and distant.

"I wanted to be a doctor so badly," she says quietly. "So badly. Since I was six years old. It's all I wanted. After a rotation in the NICU at an amazing hospital in Boston, I decided I wanted to be part of a team that made miracles happen every day," she smiles wistfully. Her eyes cloud over with sadness as she focuses them on me.

"How naive I was," she says and takes another huge gulp of her champagne.

I finish mine and pour myself another.

"What do you mean?"

"I went to work for a county hospital where the preemies weren't born to parents who sat with them in the nursery. Most of the babies were delivered to women who were drug dependent. Some of them were even in jail. There weren't enough nurses to give them the attention they so desperately needed. There wasn't a day last year that I didn't lose at least one patient. I know it's part of the job…" she stares off again and the bleakness in her eyes makes me want to put her in my lap and hug her. She sighs, deep and long, and shakes her head. "Two months ago, we had a woman back in with her second preemie. She had been clean when her pregnancy started, but at her twenty-week appointment, she tested positive for narcotics. When that happens, in Maryland, anyway, they immediately refer to CPS and in her case, when the baby was born three months early, the state took custody,"

"Wow, that's so awful," I say feeling like more inadequate words had never been spoken. But it's all I could offer.

"Yeah, for everyone, " she says. "Mom got out of rehab a month later and came back to the hospital. Armed." She says grimly.

My stomach drops.

"What happened?"

"She shot me, then herself," she murmurs, and my eyes nearly bug out of my head.

"She shot you?" I gawk at her.

"Yes," she says simply before she stands up. She pulls up her top and shows me a jagged, pink scar that mars the otherwise flawless skin across her ribs.

"Holy shit." All I can do is stare at the scar.

"Yeah," she runs her fingers over the scar absently. "It wasn't a serious injury. I was lucky she didn't have better aim," she says and then sits back down. "But after that, I couldn't go back into the hospital. I took a month off. I knew I couldn't ever go back. I want to practice medicine, but it felt more like trying to stem a gushing artery. I felt like a failure, a quitter. But I needed to leave. I resigned. I started looking for a place where I could clear my head and hide from the world." She glances around my kitchen. "So, here I am."

"Where's your family?" I ask her in awe of how calm she is.

"My parents live in Newport News, Virginia. They were thrilled when I quit. They never wanted me to practice medicine. It's not what the daughter of socialites does. I couldn't go home. No one understood. My boyfriend said I was being dramatic," she says and a wave of disappointment rushes over me.

"Where's he?" I ask even though I don't really want to know.

"In Maryland. We broke up. Or at least I broke up with him. He thinks I'm going to come to my senses and come home."

"Are you?" I ask a little kernel of hope lodges itself into my chest.

"Nope. We were together for six years and walking away from him was easier than walking away from my job. I suppose I'll always love him, but…"

"But…" I prompt, desperate to know what she's going to add.

"He's not the one. At least not for me." Relief replaces my worry, and I nod in very false sympathy.

"That's too bad," I say.

"No. He cheated on me constantly," she shrugs.

"Well, he's a fool," I state the obvious.

"I guess," she says as if she's not sure. "I didn't find out until a few months before the…incident. He asked me to work it out. He told me the women didn't mean anything to him. It meant something to me. I don't know why I stayed as long as I did, but after everything happened and he called me dramatic, walking away wasn't hard at all."

"I'm sure he's kicking himself," I say.

"Maybe. But it doesn't matter. It shouldn't take losing someone to know you want to be with them. I think he'd do it all over again. He didn't want to be my man. He just wanted me to be his girl."

"I know a lot of men like that. Want to possess a woman, but don't want to give her as good as they get," I say thinking about all of the guys I'd met since I started being a celebrity chef.

"What about you?" she asks, her eyes narrowing slightly in suspicion.

"What about me?" I ask purposely, evading her question. My dating record was nothing to write home about.

"You single?"

"Yeah, I was kind of married to my job. I worked a lot. I didn't have more than the casual fling. At least not since culinary school. I just…" I try to think of how to be honest without sounding like a total douche. "I was holding out for something special. Someone who loves life. Someone who wants more than just money and fame. I'm not saying there's anything wrong with that. But it's not why I became a chef. I didn't handle things the right way when I left, but I felt like I was drowning. I hated the way I made those young chefs feel," I admit. I've never said this to anyone, but every time I think about the show, I cringe.

"Why? Were you harder on them than they deserved?" she asks with genuine interest.

"No. Culinary school was brutal, but it wasn't televised. No one saw me get reamed for my mistakes. One of the guys I kicked out of the kitchen gave up cooking. I was sick to my stomach when I heard. I just couldn't do it anymore. I hated cooking. The people who ate my food only seemed interested in finding fault with it or bragging about eating at my restaurant. I've enjoyed this meal more than any other I've cooked in over three years. I loved watching you eat it."

She flushes.

"Really? Well I loved that you watched me eat it. In fact, I'm loving this whole afternoon," she says with a smile that is just bordering on seductive.

"Me, too. I think we should make this a standing date. Lunch, with champagne. Every day."

"I like the sound of that," she says and leans forward.

I lean across the table and grab her hand. Her eyes fly to mine wide with surprise and then.

"I want to kiss you, Franchesca. In the worst way. Like I've never wanted to kiss anyone. I know this sounds totally insane seeing how we met this morning."

She squeezes my hand back. "I've been watching you for a week," she confesses. My mouth goes dry, and it takes herculean effort not to hurdle across the table and kiss her right then. Her eyes are locked on mine. There's no blushing, no coy glances. I fucking love it. "My attraction might be a little more advanced than yours. I didn't expect you to be so damn nice. And easy to talk to. I want you..."

"I want you, too. But...are you sure this isn't the champagne talking?" I ask and glance pointedly at the nearly empty bottle.

"Maybe," she says her gaze never leaving mine, the heat in her eyes never dimming."But it's only saying what I've been thinking since the first time I saw your running up your walk way."

"Fuck," I groan. "Really?"

"Yes, really." She nods and then she lifts out of her chair, leans over the table so that we're nearly nose to nose.

And then she says, "Let's add fucking to our list of lunch time activities, shall we?"

Franchesca

I can't believe I just said that, but as soon as the words are out of my mouth, I'm glad I did. His eyes go from heated to blazing. Before I can wonder if maybe I've been overzealous, he growls and cups the back of my neck and kisses me. His mouth is like nothing I've ever felt before. Yet, at the same time, I know his touch. The sigh that leaves me is one of relief and happiness. My lips have dreamed of a kiss like this. *I* have dreamed of a kiss like this. I thought it was the stuff of fairy tales and romance novels.

Now, it's happening to me, and all I can think is that I'll never be the same. Nothing could compare to this. I run my hands up his broad, strong shoulders and hold on for dear life. His tongue sweeps my bottom lip and open for him. As soon as our tongues touch, the kiss changes.

It becomes hungry and desperate. In the periphery of my awareness, I hear the crash of glass and the thud of silverware hitting the floor. Then he's lifting me off my feet and laying me on the table.

"Franchesca, your lips. They're the most delicious thing I've ever tasted," he murmurs as his mouth leaves trails across my cheek.

"Oh, Max…" I sigh when his lips close over my ear lobe and then fasten to my neck. My thighs spread, and he nestles between them. Our bodies fit like they are two halves of the same whole and when I feel the hot, hardness of his erection pressing into the throbbing core of my body, I groan. His lips hover over mine; the champagne on his breath makes me giddy and sends a streak of excitement through my entire body.

"Say my name again, Franchesca," he commands with a short, sharp thrust of his hips that presses the head of his cock into my clit.

"Max," I half sob, and suddenly I feel a desperate need to feel his skin on mine.

I start o tear at his shirt, "Baby, please…" I moan mindlessly.

"You don't have to ask for anything, Franchesca," He lifts off and pulls it all of the way off with one hand and yanks my tank top down in one swift tug that takes my bra with it. His blazing blue eyes burn a path over my body. I'm normally so self conscious about my double Ds but right now, I hope he never stops looking at them.

"You're so fucking sexy," he says and for emphasis, he bites his fist. Any other time I might have laughed, but watching his teeth sink into his fingers makes my entire body jealous.

"Bite me like that," I whisper, and his eyes drop to half mast. He leans over me, brushes my hair out of the way and nips my shoulder. I shudder, and my core feels like it's made up of nothing but molten liquid.

He bites and kisses his way down my body until he gets to my breasts. He cups them both and stares.

"These are going to be my after lunch snack. In between the salmon and dessert…" He says and swipes my already rigid nipples with his thumbs.

My body is quivering, my chest is heaving and yet, I find the presence of mind to ask, "There's dessert?"

"Yes, for me, anyway," he says and flicks the tip of tongue over my right nipple.

"Hmmm?" I ask not even sure what he's talking about.

"After I'm done with my snack, I'm going to fuck you. Then, I'm going to eat your pussy for dessert," his voice full of sinful promises and nearly palpable need.

"Oh my God. Yes, all of that. I want all of that…" I croon into the crown of his head while his hot mouth covers my nipple and starts to suck and bite until it feels like he's pulling a string between it and my pussy. Every suck draws the tension tighter and tighter. I let go of his head and reach between us to unbutton my shorts.

"Do you have a condom?" I ask him.

"Do I need one?" he says after releasing my swollen, pulsing nipple from his mouth.

"Don't you?" I say, surprised and turned on by his question.

"Fuck no," he murmurs, and I look down to find his very serious eyes on my face. "I want to fuck you bare so badly. I want to feel you creaming on my cock. Are you on birth control?"

"Yes, I am. I've never had sex without a condom," I tell him.

"Me neither," he says and leans up to kiss me. His lips are swollen and warm from the attention he paid my nipples.

He hooks his fingers on either side of my shorts and yanks them down.

"Fuck me, Franchesca. Your panties are so fucking sexy. I might need to skip straight to dessert."

He drops to his knees in front of my perch on the table and puts his face between my legs and breathes in.

"Fucking ambrosia," he whispers before he covers me with his mouth. My back arches, and he grabs my thighs and drapes them over his shoulders. He sucks me through my panties before he pulls them aside. "So fucking pretty and wet," he says before he runs his tongue from my clit to the puckered entrance between my ass cheeks

I cry out and then scream when he moves his mouth to my clit and sucks it gently between his lips. He puts two of his thick fingers inside me and starts to fuck me while his mouth devastates me from the inside out. My orgasm is cresting, and I'm calling his name when surges to his feet and presses into me. There's a delicious burn as I spread to accommodate the thick head of his cock, but my soaking wet pussy makes slide feel like heaven.

"Oh, my fucking God," I hiss when he pulls out after only entering me half way. "Please don't tease me. Fuck me."

"If I fuck you like I want, I might hurt you. Let me take my time."

"Hurt me. I want to feel you every time I stand up or sit down for the next week," I demand.

He groans and grips my hips in a punishing grasp. Then he slams into me so hard the entire table moves.

"Ah. Ohhhhh, Oh...." is all I can manage. His face is a fierce mask of determination, and I'm so turned on by it I feel a surge of moisture between my thighs.

"Fuck, Franchesca, this pussy. I thought eating it was heaven, but being inside you feels like being born again," he grunts before he drops his head to my shoulder wraps his arms around my waist and starts pounding me in earnest.

The orgasm that was building breaks with a blinding intensity that forces my eyes shut.

"Max," I wail his name and press my face to the side of his and hold on while his hips starts to move even more erratically, and I feel the spurts of his release as it fills me, spills out of me, runs down the crack of my ass coating me in the delicious essence of us.

I fall back onto the table, taking him with me. We lie in a heap of shallow, quick, deliciously exhausted breaths for a few minutes before we fall apart.

I stare at the ceiling and try to reconcile what I just did with who I've been my whole life. I've never had sex on a first date, much less fucked a man I met hours earlier without a condom on his dining room table.

But, I've never been so wildly attracted to a man as I am to Max. I slide my gaze over to him and find him watching me.

We stare at each other or a few seconds. Our gazes are searching. I wonder for a split second if he's feeling regret or he's worried I'll read more into what we just did than was there. But I push that away. He's looking at me like he never wants to stop. I know what passed between us, what's lying between us now, is mutual and rare. "What are you thinking?" I ask him softly.

"When's your birthday?" he responds, and I snort a surprised laugh before we both dissolve into laughter.

I wipe tears from my eyes and go willingly when he pulls me by the waist to him. I snuggle my head into his shoulder and marvel at how easy it is to be with him. There is no awkwardness. I feel happy, in a way I haven't in so long. He trails his fingers up my bare arms and says, "Tell me all the stuff I can only know from you telling me," he says.

"As opposed to?" I ask and press a kiss to bare chest and snuggle even deeper into the crook of his shoulder.

"As opposed to the things I can tell just from looking at you and talking to you." He presses a kiss to my forehead, and I think I've found paradise in this man's arms.

"Like what?" I drawl while I trace circles on the hard planes of his chest.

"You're smart and passionate. Idealistic yet grounded.. You're unwilling to settle for anything less than being happy. You're sexy as fuck but not the slightest bit vain, and you take pleasure things just for the sake of enjoying them. No motives, no pretense." He says all of this without pausing to think.

My heart swells to hear him describe me exactly as I view myself. I was with Tad for six years, and he didn't know half of those things about me.

"And when I'm inside of you, it feels as good as cooking used to," he adds, and I throw my arm around his waist and squeeze him.

"I was born June fifth nineteen eighty-six to Valentina Falisetti and Gerardo Parisi. Both of them are from Naples and came here to expand my father's family's soft drink distribution business. I'm an only child."

"I wear a size ten dress and a seven and a half shoe but only because my right foot is bigger than my left foot. I love all food except for liver and sometimes eggs make me queasy," I tell him.

He laughs and turns us so we're lying on our sides, facing each other.

"That's all good to know," he says before he leans in to kiss me.

"Okay, you tell me."

"I was born January sixth nineteen eighty-eight," I gasp and my eyes widen.

"What?" he asks completely befuddled.

"I'm older than you," I press.

"And?"

"The man is supposed to be older!" I tell him, shocked that he doesn't know this.

"Well, I'm supposed to be living in Los Angeles. You're supposed to be living in Maryland. How about we agree that what's supposed to be, is. That we're right where we should be. This feels too right for anything else." He says and brushes my hair off my forehead.

"Well, I was just kidding, but now, I can add something to the list of things I already know about you."

He huffs out a laugh. "This should be good."

"It's been than good. You're a romantic… compassionate. You've got a great sense of humor and you're not too proud to apologize. You're observant, a great cook and you make me feel beautiful."

His eyes soften. "I hope it's not just me that makes you feel that way. I hope you've always known it. Beauty comes from within, and it just makes what's visible to the naked eye even more stunning."

My heart races at his words. Excitement, nerves, glee all infuse my being, and I am so happy I could scream.

"I can't believe this is happening," I tell him.

"Believe it," he says.

"I was born to Jane and Allen Edwards in a small town in outside Medellin. I have three brothers and a baby sister. I expect her to show up here any day. I haven't been home in months, and we're very close. I love food, but I love music even more I think. If I could have played an instrument or carried a tune, music would have been what I did with my life."

"I'm five feet and eleven inches tall and like my clothes tailored to fit so I don't wear a standard size. My feet are size twelve, and I sleep on the left side. I love the water, and I love the sun."

"You're perfect," I say before I can even stop to think.

"Nope, but I'm glad you think so cause I plan on spending a lot of time with you, and it would suck if you thought I was an ass."

I smile at him, and it's so big and broad that my cheeks start to hurt right away,

"So, this lunch thing is going to be a regular thing?"

"Until you tell me you don't want it to be."

"Well, then let's go to the store because I have a feeling we're going to need *a lot* of food."

chapter four

Three Months Later

Max

I STAND ON THE DECK AND WATCH MY GIRL MOVE THROUGH HER TAI CHI poses. In the last three months I've learned a lot more about her. She snores. She's an overzealous flosser. She farts when she's nervous. She's brave, generous, and honest to a fault. I love her. So damn much.

And I have plans for her…For us.

I stuff the letter from the restaurant in Houston into my pocket next to the ring I'll be give her when I ask her to share forever with me.

Life has never been more delicious. But I have a feeling our next chapter will be even sweeter.

the end

shaken submission

LIVIA GRANT

chapter one

LANIE WATCHED THE DIGITAL CLOCK ON HER DESK FLIP TO 4:00PM. What a complete waste of an afternoon, waiting… worrying. As each hour crept by, she'd switched to regret. She should have just kept her head down and her mouth shut.

Then the sharp buzz of the office phone in her workspace made her jump. As tempting as it was not to answer, she lifted the receiver, attempting to sound more confident than she felt.

"Good afternoon. This is Alaina. How may I help you?"

"Ms. Bennett." It was a statement, not a question. Based on the internal extension information flashing on the LED readout of her phone, it was coming from a conference room extension instead of an assigned office. "I'd like you to please join me for a short meeting on the 44th floor."

"Em… Okay. What time would you…"

"Immediately," the gravelly voice on the other end interrupted.

Unable to contain her nerves, she asked, "Is this about the meeting I had with my boss, Peter, earlier this morning?"

"All will be explained when you arrive. The executive receptionist will direct you when you get off the elevator. Please leave now."

The line went dead.

She tried not to read too much into the abrupt tone of the call, reminding herself it was the nature of working in an engineering firm. The engineers and architects working at Rossi, Anderson, & Hart weren't exactly a hotbed of social engagement, but then again, she hadn't become a CPA for excitement either.

Grabbing her cell phone, she locked her computer screen before pushing to her feet. She was tempted to detour to the ladies' room to pee and apply fresh lip-gloss but knowing the owner of the gruff voice was waiting, Lanie went straight to the bank of elevators instead. She intentionally bypassed the door to the staircase she normally used to move between floors, not wanting to arrive at this most important meeting out of breath. Taking the stairs a floor or two was healthy. Schlepping up the eleven stories to the executive level was closer to torture.

Determined to remain calm, she reminded herself that she wasn't the one who'd done something wrong. She'd merely done her job as a staff accountant, ferreting out the irregularities in the company's books and then bringing them to the attention of her supervisor. While she hoped the errors she'd found were honest mistakes, it would take help, or at least additional security clearance, to truly get to the bottom of the issue. All she knew for sure was there was a lot of revenue missing that, so far, no one above her seemed interested in investigating.

She may only have a few years of work experience under her belt, but her sixth sense had alarm bells blaring as she exited the elevators and approached the reception desk. "Hi, I'm Alaina…"

"Mr. Graves is waiting for you in the office at the end of the hall," the severe-looking woman said, motioning with her arm to the left. The diamonds in her expensive tennis bracelet glittered in the afternoon sunshine.

Momentarily distracted by wondering how a PA working in one of the most expensive cities in the country could afford such an expensive piece of jewelry, it wasn't until she was almost to the closed door that Lanie realized she'd only been on this particular floor one other time in her six months working at RAH, and that had been the day she'd come for her final interview. The plaque on the wall next to the dark wooden door confirmed her realization that she was about to meet with the Vice President of Human Resources.

Taking a calming breath, Alaina forced herself to knock, looking forward to relaying the details of her investigation again in hopes of getting the help she'd need to get to the bottom of the discrepancies. Of course, Peter would have gotten Human Resources would be involved as the investigation may require sanctions for any wrong doers.

Expecting to hear a man's voice bellowing to advise her to come in, she jumped when the heavy door swung open and a tall man she recognized from security opened the door.

"Oh, hello. I'm Alaina Bennett."

"Come in. We've been expecting you," the man in the black suit replied, motioning for her to enter. She was almost to the center of the office when she realized there were two others present.

The portly man behind the huge desk, she assumed, was Mr. Graves from HR. Sitting in one of the two chairs facing their host was her boss's boss's boss, CFO of Rossi, Anderson, and Hart, Jack Leahy.

"Have a seat, young lady," the guy from security ordered, motioning to move deeper into the room. She startled as he was much closer than office etiquette dictated.

Intimidated by the three older men in the room, Alaina moved slowly to take the final seat, leaving the man standing ominously behind her. The western sun pouring through the wall of windows cast a shadow across Lanie, reminding her how close he was standing.

Several long seconds passed before Mr. Graves finally spoke. "I assume you know why you've been invited here."

Clearing her throat, Lanie focused on keeping her voice steady and calm. "I believe it's to discuss the accounting irregularities I reported to my boss, Peter Blankenship." When no one confirmed her observation, she added, "I'm happy to go through my findings again with anyone you need me to in order to get to the bottom of things."

It was the CFO on her right that cut her off. "Oh, that won't be necessary, Ms. Bennett. Believe it or not, we actually have many professionals here at RAH that do know what they're doing."

Okay, she hadn't expected the employee of the year award, especially since to her knowledge, no such award existed at Rossi, Anderson, & Hart, but she had at least expected a tiny bit of appreciation for digging deep enough to be able to sound the alarm.

She felt the heat of Mr. Leahy's glare from the few feet separating them but kept her focus on the man behind the desk, after all, they were in his office.

"At no time did I indicate that my peers didn't know what they were doing. I merely wanted to point out that in my role of staff accountant, I have the opportunity to see a bigger picture of the company's financial footprint and as such, the discrepancies sort of just jumped out at me. My hope is there are very reasonable explanations, but in my position, I'm not able to..."

Jack Leahy cut her off. "Don't you mean in your position you were able to pilfer funds from your employer and when your manager indicated that he'd found the paper trail of missing funds that led directly to you, that you then came up with this insane story to cast doubt on your innocent co-workers in an attempt to deflect blame?"

Lanie felt like someone had gut-punched her. Spinning to her right to take in the angry glare of the CFO, she opened her mouth to defend herself, but no words came out. Her heart raced as she tried to make sense of what was happening. She'd come prepared to explain her findings, to even have someone convince her that she must have made a mistake, but never had she expected to have the accusations fly back in her direction; particularly not from a man she'd only passed in the hall.

"Perhaps Peter didn't share all of the details I provided to him when I turned over my findings," she answered, wishing her voice sounded more forceful.

The CFO interjected, "Mr. Blankenship has done a very thorough review of every spec of the so-called proof you provided, and it was that inspection that led us to conclude we do indeed have a serious problem in our accounting team. I came to discuss these concerns with our Human Resources team, and we have come to the conclusion we must terminate your employment, Ms. Bennet, effective immediately."

"My employment? But why in the world would I get fired?" Her timidness had fled, quickly replaced with righteous anger. "I'm the one who pointed the problem out in the first place! What kind of an idiot do you think I am that you think I'd raise red flags on myself?"

"I'm confident you would have remained silent, had Peter not uncovered your scheme and confronted you."

"Wait, he said he approached me? It's the other way around! I took my findings to him! Maybe he's the one responsible for the missing money, did you ever think of that?" Lanie accused, wishing she'd just kept her big mouth shut longer until she'd been able to discover who was behind the deception.

"Mr. Blakenship has been a trusted member of this accounting team for over five years now. He's the hardest working manager we have, working late, weekends, and even through holidays. He is the most dedicated accounting employee we have, and I will not have you trying to sully his reputation with your accusations," the CFO barked, his face getting ruddy as he shouted.

"Well, I sure as hell am not going to sit here and allow you to sully *my* reputation with your accusations. Let me go to my desk and get my laptop. I'll walk you through the same proof I showed him this morning and then you can make your own determination."

The VP of HR spoke. "Interesting, he warned us that you'd try to deflect things when we confronted you with proof."

"What proof? You haven't confronted me with jack shit!" she shouted.

It was the guy from security that stepped in front of her, posing an intimidating figure as he groused, "He also warned you could become verbally abusive."

Lanie scoffed, trying her best to remain calm so she could reason with these men who obviously had been lied to by her boss—the boss she had trusted.

"I'm sorry I cursed, but I'm understandably upset. I demand to see exactly what proof you have that I've done anything wrong."

"Oh, you'd like that, wouldn't you? Then you could try to take it with you so you could doctor it." It was then that Mr. Leahy patted a tall stack of papers sticking out of a briefcase next to his chair.

"Why would I need to do that? All the proof we need that Peter is behind this is on the server. Start with auditing the Accounts Payable disbursements. They're out of balance with the P&L statement by over a quarter of a million dollars, and that's just within the last six months. Who knows what we'd find if we go back farther!"

It was Mr. Graves that put an end to her defense. "Enough! Peter has already provided a detailed paper trail that dates back to the very week after you started here at RAH, Ms. Bennett. You wasted no time at all getting to work with your deception. I'll be honest, if it were up to me, I'd have called the police and turned you in. There is no place for this kind of illegal behavior in the business world. You should be thanking Mr. Leahy here for advising that it would be best for Rossi, Anderson, & Hart if we just quietly cut ties with the root of the problem rather than having to take the proof of your deception to the police as that would require notification to the board of directors."

Alaina's heart was racing. She'd never so much as been reprimanded, let alone fired. It was hard to concentrate when faced with three angry men. Still, a sliver of something niggled in her brain, fighting to be heard.

But before she could come up with a new way of reasoning with them, Mr. Graves pushed a big packet of papers across the desk at her. "I've prepared your termination papers. I need you to sign them now, indicating that you are leaving our employ of your own volition."

"But I'm not. More importantly, I *won't*. You want me out, you're gonna have to fire me," Lanie gritted out, trying to hold back her panicked tears gathering.

"So you can try to claim unemployment? I don't think so," the HR guy countered.

She couldn't sit there and take their insane accusations a minute longer. Determined to leave and regroup, she shot to her feet and brushed past the security dude. Yanking open the door to the office, she was blocked by yet another burly guy dressed in the same black suit of the rest of the building's security team, only this guy was holding a huge box full of things. There was the frame sticking out at the top, her State of California CPA certificate behind glass.

Spinning to address the men still in the room, Lanie unleashed the anger that had been growing. "You had someone pack my things while I was away from my desk? Are you fucking kidding me?"

"That is quite enough, Ms. Bennett," Mr. Graves sanctioned.

The maniacal laugh she heard was her own. "Oh, believe me, it's not even close to enough. How dare you have someone go through my things. I assume you are going to try to prevent me from stopping down on my floor to even say goodbye to my co-workers, or to even check to make sure you've packed all of my things?"

Reaching into his top desk drawer, Mr. Graves came out with his business card, holding it out to her from across the room. "Take my card. If you find you are missing anything, email me. In fact, I am to be your only contact at Rossi, Anderson, & Hart after you leave here today. You are not to contact your previous co-workers." He couldn't even get his fat ass out of the chair to walk it to her. Well screw that.

"Keep your damn business card. I don't need it. I also won't be contacting my co-workers, since any one of them could be in on the clearly illegal activities that you are all so very fast to cover up. No, the only people I plan on contacting will be a lawyer and each and every one of the members of the board of directors!"

She'd gritted out her parting shot, using up all of the adrenaline spiking through her system. But her righteous anger was morphing to less productive emotions. As furious as she was, she was a realist. There would be no changing of minds with the men in the room, and that meant she needed to retreat and regroup.

Lanie grabbed the box, yanking it from the guy who had so far stood in the doorway silently. She tried to brush past him, but he was blocking her. Only when she used enough force to crash the box against his chest did he stumble out of the way. As she took the first few steps into the hall, she saw another whole pile of her belongings leaning up against the wall under that damn plaque.

She only had a few seconds to look through the items, deciding to walk away from several framed inspirational posters, the fern she'd been keeping alive since her Grandma's funeral the year before, and the smaller box with a desk lamp, calculators, and other office supply items. It was nothing important.

She was halfway down the long hallway when the first tear fell, but she'd be damned if she was going to let anyone see her cry. But when regret for leaving her grandma's plant hit her, she stopped to turn and grab it, only to crash into the security dude who had the nerve to be following her as if he didn't trust her to leave the premises.

"Get out of my way. I need to go back and get my plant."

She wasn't expecting any kindness so when he softly instructed her to, "Stay here, I'll get it for you," another tear fell.

Balancing the heavy load of her box against the wall, she quickly lifted her fingers up to swish away the trace of wetness.

The next few minutes were a blur as she struggled to carry her heavy box back towards the bank of elevators, one of which would take her to the lobby for the last time. She took the train into work each day. How was she supposed to get all this crap home? Her hands were too full to press the call button, but the guy helping to carry her plant moved in to press it for her.

She couldn't see over the strewn pile of her belongings but heard the ding of the arriving elevator. She stepped into the enclosed space, but when the security guy moved to follow her, she'd had enough. She needed to be alone.

"Just put the plant on the floor and leave. I don't need your help."

She couldn't see his reaction, only the movement in her peripheral as he stepped in just far enough to place the basket holding the dying plant near her feet before retreating.

Her first sob escaped one second after the elevator doors closed. She'd somehow held it together when she'd had an audience, but now that she was alone, the built-up anger and humiliation of the last hour popped as surely as a balloon encountering a pin. How the hell had this day blown up so spectacularly?

Only when the elevator moved into motion a minute later did she realize she'd been standing in an unmoving elevator, which usually happened when you don't press any buttons. Worse, she was going up, not down, and since the only floors higher than HR in the building were the executive-level suites, God only knew who might get on when she stopped next.

More importantly, she may not know exactly what time it was, but it had to be getting close to five, which meant there would be people waiting, trying to grab an elevator to leave for the day, all the way down to the first floor.

Too soon, Lanie felt the lift stopping and heard the swoosh of the doors opening behind her. Trying her best to avoid making eye contact with anyone, she pressed deeper into the corner of the elevator, keeping her back to the door and setting the corner of the heavy box on the handrail that circled the space at waist-level, helping to steady her load.

"Em… do you need help with that?" a low voice asked.

"No. I got it," she spat, keeping her voice strong.

"Okay… what floor?"

She was tempted to call the unseen rider an idiot but bit her tongue. He wasn't who she was mad at.

"Lobby, please."

Seconds later the doors snapped closed and they were thankfully going down. She was grateful for each floor they passed without stopping. She wasn't sure how she would hold it together if someone she knew got onto the elevator with her.

"So, you quit?" the stranger asked too cheerily to suit her.

His jovial tone irked her. Shifting the load that was getting heavier by the minute, Lanie bit back. "More like fired."

The lame instrumental 80's music piped into the small space was the only reply for the next few floors of downward motion.

"Sure you don't need help? That looks heavy."

She felt no need to repeat her answer. Instead, she hoped the elevator music was loud enough to camouflage her racing heart. The thought of getting all of this stuff not only down to the lobby, but then somehow crammed into an Uber and then up to her apartment felt like a mission impossible in that moment.

Lost in replaying the disastrous last hour on auto-loop in her brain, she was slow to recognize the shimmy under her feet. Her first reaction was that she had to be more upset than she'd realized as it felt like she was going to topple over. It was only when the lights overhead started to flicker, and the walls of the elevator began to vibrate, that it dawned on her what was happening.

Her elevator partner was the one who put the verbal label on it. "Earthquake!"

And she didn't think her day could get any worse.

She was wrong.

chapter
two

THE SHIMMYING VIBRATIONS ESCALATED TO ERRATIC LURCHES AS Lanie lost her balance. Forced to take a step back to keep from falling, the weight of the box slid off the handrail, crashing to the floor at her feet with a thud.

Loud shudders surrounded them as the building swayed, suddenly at the mercy of Mother Nature. For several seconds she thought it might be over, but then the strongest shake yet tossed her backwards, crashing her back against hard muscle.

Strong arms hugged her from behind, helping her to remain on her feet, as he shouted over the racket. "Get into the corner… just in case the ceiling collapses in on us!"

Lanie scrambled back towards where the shaking walls met, latching onto the handrail to try to stabilize herself. Her fellow elevator passenger pressed in behind her as the metal box screeched and shuddered as it continued a slow earthward slide. The overhead light flickered out, throwing them into darkness just as the abrupt halt of their downward fall crashed her forehead against the wall with a loud *thwack*.

Around them a light coat of what felt like dust rained down from the ceiling until the chunks started to get bigger. She couldn't see, but felt her companion maneuvering his suit jacket up and over their heads, sheltering them from the shower of falling ceiling particles.

Being thrust from one crisis into another had Lanie's heart racing, yet even as she saw her life flashing before her eyes, the faint scent of woodsy masculinity surrounded her, calming her unexpectedly, tamping down some of her fear.

The dim emergency lighting flickered on just as the last shudder of the earthquake rocked the box they were dangling inside of. If she had to guess, they were maybe around the twentieth floor—far from the lobby.

Both occupants huddled frozen in the corner for a few long seconds, unsure if the quake was over or if they were about to be bounced around again like snow in a snow globe. Only when they heard alarms sounding in the distance did the man pressing against her take a step backwards, shaking the debris off his suit jacket.

In shock, Lanie remained silent. She wasn't sure what the right words were for this particular social crisis. Thankfully, her temporary partner-in-transport moved into motion, pulling the emergency alarm button, dousing them with the piercing siren.

Lanie threw her hands over her ears just as a voice spoke through the still-functioning intercom.

"This is Tom from security. Is everyone okay in your elevator? Any injuries?"

Unsure why her companion wasn't answering, Lanie turned and looked up to take her first good look at the man standing just a few feet away. This time, she found herself short of breath, but for a completely different reason. Even in the dim lighting, his dark persona was larger than life. That he was staring at her expectantly scrambled her thoughts until he finally prompted her. "Are you okay or do you need medical attention?"

Lanie shook her head, gritting out a simple, "I'll be okay."

"We're uninjured. Not exactly sure what floor we stopped at. Did the entire building lose power?"

"I'm afraid so. Looks like we're on backup emergency systems only at the moment. It's gonna take us a bit to do a full safety check and then execute our evacuation plan."

It was difficult to hear over the alarm, so she was grateful when her companion turned it off, reporting to security, "Well, you've got us recorded as stuck in this elevator, right? Any chance you can get enough power to us to open the door so we can get off and walk down the stairwell?"

"I'm afraid not. The error code is indicating you are between floors eighteen and nineteen. The building engineers and the fire department will have to evaluate the best way to extricate you. How many of you are there?"

"Two."

"Okay, well, sit tight. It could be a while."

She heard a click sound as if Tom had severed the emergency connection. A new awkward silence filled the confined space.

If she had to guess, she'd say he was around thirty-five years old, tops. Lanie tried not to get caught watching him as he took his suit coat off before leaning back against the wall of the elevator, sliding down until he was sitting on the floor, his legs bent, feet flat on the floor where he reached into his coat pocket, coming out with his cell phone.

He didn't bother looking up at her as he suggested, "You should get comfortable too. Like the security guy said, we're probably gonna be stuck in here for a while."

Wishing she'd worn slacks instead of her favorite narrow pencil skirt, Lanie gingerly lowered herself next to the plant and box of belongings she'd dropped earlier, reaching to throw a few random items back into the container that had flown out on the way to the floor.

"Shit…" he muttered, finally looking up at her. "My phone is almost dead. I was gonna try to get some information on what's going on outside of the building… to see how bad things are out there."

She hadn't even got that far yet. There were enough things falling apart in her sphere of control, she didn't need to worry about the rest of the world just yet. Still, she felt around, coming out with her own cell phone, adding her own, "Damn… mine's at only ten percent. But it won't matter much. I have no bars or Wi-Fi either."

They each set their phones aside, useless at the moment.

After a full minute of awkward silence, he broke the quiet by asking, "You aren't one of those people who are claustrophobic, are you?"

"Claustrophobic, no. I can't say I'm too excited about dangling eighteen stories above the ground in an earthquake, though."

"You might be in good company in that club," he assured her.

Unsure what one discusses in situations like this, Lanie focused on taking long, calming breaths to fend off her growing anxiety.

Her companion didn't seem as comfortable with their silence, asking, "So were you really just fired?"

Determined to stay strong and not cry, she snapped back, "No, I just like to drag all of my belongings back and forth between the office and my place every day."

To his credit, he raised his hands up, the universal sign of surrender. "Okay, sorry I asked." He let his superficial apology last for only two seconds before he added, "So what did you do that got you fired?"

"Seriously? Don't we have enough problems right now without making me relive the last disastrous hour of my life?"

"Fair enough… I just thought it might help you to talk about it."

"Well, it won't. It's a bunch of bullshit." This time she was the one who grew uncomfortable with the silence and went on offense with her first question. "I've never seen you here before. What were you doing here today?"

"I just finished an interview before I caught the elevator," he answered, loosening his tie at his neck before unbuttoning the top button.

"Well, take it from me, you don't want to work here," she replied, trying not to get distracted by the glimpse of tan skin and dark hair peeking out at the neck of his expensive looking dress shirt.

"That's not what I've heard. I thought Rossi, Anderson, & Hart was one of the best engineering firms on the West Coast."

"Yeah, well they may build strong buildings and bridges, but they don't know shit about running a professional organization that I'd want to work in."

His low whistle bounced around the confined space. "Wow, someone really pissed you off. Why don't you tell me what happened?"

"I don't think so."

"Ah come on, what else do we have to do?" He waved a hand in the air as if to remind her their entertainment options were limited.

Sighing, she realized it might help to talk through what had happened with an innocent bystander. Even if he didn't help her, she could at least keep him from making the mistake of agreeing to work at RAH.

"You won't believe me. No one does."

"Try me."

She took a deep breath before plunging forward with the ugly truth. "I was accused of embezzling from the very company I'm working to protect. Like I said, if they call you back for a second interview, I'd think twice about accepting. And if you do, be sure to watch your back."

"Okay, I'll bite. How the hell does one go about embezzling from an engineering firm? You selling construction supplies on the black market?" he chuckled, having entirely too much fun at her expense.

"Seriously? I am… I mean… I *was* the chief staff accountant." When he didn't add another smart-ass retort, she added, "I started here six months ago and almost from day one I started to find irregularities in the books. At first, I just thought the company was still using out of date processes and that I'd eventually get everything to balance, but the deeper I dug, the more concerned I became."

The guy shot her a dubious glance before challenging her. "I'm sorry, but this sounds a bit unbelievable. While RAH may not be a publicly held company, they do have a board of directors and regularly go through rigorous audits."

Lanie gave him the side-eye. "How would you know? I thought you were just interviewing here?"

His retort was immediate. "I did tons of research, that's how. It's one of the reasons I knew I wanted to work here instead of any of the competitors who have tried to woo me away."

"Well, your research missed this, because I'm certain."

"Okay, say I believe you, why is it you're the one that got fired, then?"

"That's the million-dollar question, isn't it? All I know is I took my findings to my boss this morning, asking for his help in gaining access to some of the confidential reports I didn't seem to have access to so we could take the investigation deeper. The next thing I know, I'm called up to HR and accused of embezzlement myself."

"But you must have some proof, right?"

"Of course, but they wanted no part of hearing about my findings. They refused to let me get my laptop and walk them through what I'd shown my boss earlier. Not only was I not allowed near my computer before I left, they didn't even let me pack up my own office. When I opened the door to leave the HR office, I was met with a guy from security holding all my stuff. I even had to leave some of it behind because I couldn't carry it all. Oh crap…" Her voice trailed off as she leaned over the box next to her. "They better have put my purse in here or I won't have my wallet or keys." Her rummaging was successful as she found her bag at the bottom of the box, pulling it through the other items until she extricated it, glancing through quickly to make sure all was there.

Her companion was determined to keep up the small talk. "I really regret skipping lunch, now. You wouldn't happen to have a steak in there, would you?"

"Fresh out. And I'm regretting not stopping at the ladies' room before my meeting with HR." Refusing to worry about the fact that she really needed to pee, she pressed him, "How long do you think we'll be stuck in here?"

"Sorry, I forgot to bring my crystal ball with me today." Even though she knew he was making fun of her, she forgave his teasing since it was accompanied by a broad smile that made her breath hitch.

They fell into another long silence until he once again became uncomfortable enough that he broke the quiet. "Since it looks like we're gonna be here a while, don't you think we should introduce ourselves?" When she remained still, he added, "My friends call me JR."

Interesting. "What do your enemies call you?" she teased, realizing she was smiling, something she'd have thought impossible today.

He had a rich chuckle that had a way of putting her at ease, not exactly the easiest thing to do considering the last hour of her life. "I guess they just call me Jacob, like everyone else."

"Jacob," she acknowledged, before asking, "Is it JR as in junior, after your dad?"

"Thankfully, no. My older brother got that dubious honor. How about you?"

What harm could telling the guy her name do? Sticking her right hand out, she introduced herself. "Alaina Bennett, but my friends call me Lanie."

His handshake was firm—steady—unlike the aftershock that chose that moment to literally rock their world. She allowed the contact to go on longer than etiquette called for, drawing comfort from his grip until thankfully, the aftershock ended.

Pulling her hand back, she added, "I've lived on the West Coast my entire life, but I never get used to the weird sensation of quakes."

"Well, you should take comfort that we're in one of the safest buildings in the city. The Tower was built to withstand much stronger quakes than today's."

"How would you know that?" she probed.

His smile was back as he used his finger to point above his head, gesturing as he reminded her. "Engineer, remember? I do my homework," he added before starting to unbutton the cuffs of his long-sleeved dress shirt, taking a moment to roll up his sleeves.

"Making yourself at home?" she questioned, trying not to admit she was enjoying the flash of a tattoo on his right forearm.

"It's getting freaking hot in here thanks to the air conditioning being cut off. This had to happen on one of the hottest days of the year so far."

Jacob wasn't wrong, but unfortunately, despite getting warm she didn't have as many layers she could take off.

"We've established you don't have a steak in there, but you have anything else to eat or drink in that box of yours?"

Pulling the box closer, she pulled her purse out, reaching in to grab the breath mints she carried with her. Lanie tossed the small box to him, grinning. "Have a Tic-Tac."

She'd half expected him to give her shit, so when he popped a few in his mouth and teased her with a smart-ass, "Ah… so filling, thanks," she couldn't help but chuckle.

Because he was being a good sport, she pulled the box even closer, rummaging around in the strewn items the security guy had obviously just dumped together with no regard to organization. The lighting sucked, so she had to rely on her sense of touch to find what she was looking for.

Waving her spoils above her head like a trophy, Lanie celebrated, "I found them! We're saved!" When she tossed one of the two protein bars she'd had stuffed into the back of her desk drawer, he almost missed catching it.

Despite his hunger, Jacob delayed opening the bar, while she dove in, taking a big bite.

"Don't you think we should ration this since it might be the only food we have for a while?" he questioned.

"It better not be. I'm counting on security getting us out of here and pronto." She stopped short of saying it was because she couldn't wait to get home and cry in the privacy of her own home over her lost job.

"I'm more worried about beverages. Mind if I go shopping?" he asked, lifting a few picture frames, as he asked.

"By all means," she deadpanned, not really upset but thinking the guy was pretty bold.

"Bingo!" he declared, pulling a bottle of the world's worst wine out of the box.

"Trust me, that's no bingo, it's a booby prize. Wait until you taste it. And anyway, we don't have an opener."

"Ah, you didn't know you got trapped with MacGyver, did you?" Leaning to the side, he took a ring of keys out of his pants pocket, holding them up and daring her to, "Watch, and learn."

She finished eating her protein bar in the almost five minutes it took him to get the cork out of the horrible wine, but it was entertaining watching him trying to avoid letting the small specs of cork he'd broken off fall into the red wine.

Finally, declaring victory, he held out the bottle, offering her the first swig. "Oh no, I insist, you go first," she urged.

The horrified face he made as he forced himself to swallow the swill made her laugh.

"I warned you!" she teased.

"What did you do to piss off the person that gave this to you?" he asked after he'd swallowed, sputtering slightly.

Having received it in the company gift exchange at Christmas, she corrected him. "I don't think they were pissed. More like cheap."

Jacob was clearly thirsty because he stole another swig before handing the bottle to her. "You should still drink. We don't want to get dehydrated."

The way her bladder felt, she knew there was no chance of that. "I'll pass. I already have to pee. I don't want to make it worse."

As if he were on a treasure hunt, Jacob dived back into the box, looking for any small trinket he could turn into nourishment. When he pulled out the Rossi, Anderson, & Hart company water bottle all employeees were issued when they were hired, he again looked like he'd found a treasure.

"Um... in case you missed it, the bottle is empty," she pointed out the obvious.

"That's why it's going to make a great toilet."

"Are you nuts?" she squeaked, sure he'd lost his mind.

"What? Just think how satisfying it will be to piss all over the company logo after they fired you."

"Well forget it. I couldn't. It's too weird."

Setting the bottle aside, he resumed his treasure hunt, adding, "Suit yourself, but fair warning. If they don't have us out of here in an hour, I'll be putting the damn thing to use."

"That's different. You're a guy."

He stopped to look up and smile. His "Thanks for noticing," was a bit too charming.

"Yeah, well, it was a bit hard to miss."

"What gave me away?" he added, giving most of his attention to her odd collection of belongings in the box.

"I don't know… the five o'clock shadow… your forearms… the tattoo on your arm," she listed, avoiding the more personal observation of how yummy he smelled and how she'd enjoyed the feel of his muscular chest pressing her against the wall of the elevator. Considering he'd only been gallant while trying to protect her, it was irrelevant.

"What, you don't have a tattoo?" he asked.

"I didn't say that…" she hesitated, unsure if she wanted to share.

"Aw, come on. I'll show you mine if you show me yours," he encouraged her.

"Let's just say, if I get desperate enough to use the bottle, you might get a peek at it."

"Interesting. Let me guess. A butterfly?"

She shook her head.

"You a dog or cat person? Is it paw prints?" he asked again.

"Nothing so predictable," she teased, picking up her phone to check if the service had been restored.

It didn't look like it would work, but since her power was now down to seven percent left, Lanie took a chance at sending her roommate a text. She wasn't surprised when it flashed, *undelivered*, when she tried to send it.

"Dammit."

"Still no service? It's not a great sign of what's going on out there if there is still no cell service."

She'd been thinking the same thing.

"You trying to check up on your boyfriend?" he asked, taking another swig of the horrible wine.

Surprised at his question, she glanced up. "You fishing for personal information?"

"Maybe. Like I said, what else do we have to do?"

Lanie chuckled. "So glad to know I can be of some use in a crisis."

His good-natured grin lit up the enclosed space, putting her at ease.

"If you must know, I was trying to text my roommate, who yes, is a boy… and he is also a friend… but I can assure you, Raúl is not, nor ever will be, my boyfriend."

"Raúl, eh? Let me guess. He bats for the other team?"

"Boy does he," she laughed. "He not only bats for them, but…" she paused, unsure how crude she should get. "Let's just say, he likes being part of *team sports*."

"That's kind of an odd choice for a roommate, then."

"Not at all. He's a hoot, but more importantly, he keeps things picked up, and is a great cook."

"I wish he could whip us up a steak dinner about now."

"You're obsessed with steak," she retorted, shifting the way she was sitting in an attempt to relieve more pressure on her ready-to-burst bladder.

"Yeah, well it's helping to keep my mind off needing to pee," he added.

The crackling sound of the building intercom system filled the elevator just before a voice spoke to them. "Hello, this is building security, giving you a status update. As you can imagine, city resources are spread thin, responding to emergencies. The fire department has been here to do a preliminary check, and everyone in the building has been evacuated, with the exception of those of you detained in the elevators.

"I'm sorry to inform you that the decision was made to wait for the elevator company's repair team to arrive to assist us with getting you out safely. If the city gets the power turned back on first, we'll be able to restart the elevators, but if not, it looks like you'll have a few more hours to wait for your rescue."

Jacob summed up her sentiment exactly with his quiet, "Fuck."

Security dude continued on, unaware of the curse. "We are monitoring things carefully and if anything changes, we'll let you know. If you have an emergency, please pull the alarm button again and we'll answer."

The static of the system silenced, just as Lanie called out, "What do you mean, if we have an emergency? We're stuck in the elevator, you idiot! This *IS* an emergency."

Jacob wisely didn't make fun of her outburst.

What a nightmare. They could be stuck there for hours more, and that could only mean one thing.

Reaching out with her left hand, she groused, "Hand me the damn empty bottle."

chapter three

JACOB HANDED OVER THE RAH WATER BOTTLE WHILE KINDLY OFFERING, "You need my help to hold it for you?"

Snatching it from him, Lanie pushed up to her feet and spat back, "Not only do I not want your help, you need to turn around… face the wall."

"You do realize I'll still be right here, right?" he said, turning his head slightly.

Recognizing how much she did not want to do this, she instructed him, "Put your hands over your ears."

"What are you, fifteen? It's not like I'm going to see anything new."

Despite his barb, he did at least keep facing the opposite wall as she struggled on her heels, working to just slip out of her panties and tossing them into the box with the hodgepodge of items already collected there.

After twisting off the lid to the bottle, she tried to decide what would be her best option. Holding the bottle up was awkward, but when she put the bottle on the floor and tried to squat over it, her narrow skirt made it impossible to get into the right position.

Taking a last look to make sure Jacob wasn't watching her ungraceful balancing act, she finally hiked her skirt up to her waist, trying her best to line up over the bottle. And then…

Nothing.

She tried to tell her brain to let go, but it was just too weird. The longer she squatted, trying, the more unstable she got, finally resorting to holding onto the wall to keep steady over the bottle.

"I'm guessing you don't camp, do you?" he teased.

"Be quiet. You're making me nervous," she argued.

Ever helpful, Jacob offered, "I might have a bit of power left on my phone. Want me to play one of those babbling brook or ocean wave apps to help you go?"

Another minute went by and she was about to take him up on the ridiculous offer when she finally got things moving. When finished, she was thankful that the security dude had just emptied her drawers into the box haphazardly as she grabbed one of the many napkins from the bottom of the box.

"Boy, you weren't kidding you really did need to go." She had started to pull her skirt back into place when he added, "So I'm guessing you were in a sorority?"

"Eh?" she asked, tucking the wet napkin away and digging to see if she could find a package of wet wipes to wipe her hands.

"Pi Mu Epsilon. Never heard of them."

Lanie reached out to punch him on his shoulder. "You peeked!"

"Of course, I did. I had to see your tattoo since you wouldn't tell me about it."

"Yeah, well Pi Mu Epsilon is a Mathematics fraternity."

"Wow, I bet that was a hotbed of social excitement."

"It was a professional organization, if you must know. Some of us went to college to do more than party," she replied, happily wiping her hands on the wet wipes she'd found.

Holding up his hands in the universal sign of surrender, Jacob tried to smooth things over. "I didn't mean anything by it. I'm just afraid I might not have been quite as dedicated of a student as you is all."

Lanie bit her tongue to keep from confessing she'd spent more Saturday nights studying than any co-ed ever should have, but not only did that sound pathetic, it just made getting fired that much worse. She'd worked her ass off, just to have it all get thrown away by Peter and whoever else he was in cahoots with.

She'd been lost in her own pity party long enough that she must have missed something Jacob had said since he was looking at her expectantly.

"Sorry, can you repeat that?"

"I asked for you to please pass the bottle. I might as well get this over with, too."

Not for the first time, Lanie was grateful for the dim lighting in the enclosed space. She tried not to think about it too much, reminding herself that she'd leave here after they were rescued from the elevator and not only would she not return to The Tower where RAH was the main tenant, but she would certainly never see Jacob again.

When he finished, she tossed him the packet of wet wipes. It was Jacob who eventually broke the long silence. "So, now what? You want to play a game to pass the time and help keep my mind off how hungry I am?"

"Sure, although I'm not sure what kind of game you think we can play with no phones or computers," she countered, finally untucking her blouse from her skirt and waving the fabric in an attempt to get some air movement to cool down a few degrees.

Jacob countered by unbuttoning his dress shirt as he laid out the rules to the entertainment trivia game he suggested they play.

"This sounds kinda hokey. Did you just make this up?" she teased.

"Maybe… But, like you said, we're short on resources. In fact, I just want to take this opportunity to officially thank you for getting fired today. Can you imagine how much worse things would be without your box of weird supplies? They've really come in surprisingly handy."

The grin on his face told her he was joking, and she wanted to laugh with him. Hell, maybe one day she would, but today, just remembering about how she was being railroaded by the company just gave her anxiety.

"I'm so glad that the total demise of my professional career was able to provide you with a tiny measure of comfort…"

"I think someone is being a bit mellow-dramatic, don't you? Who says your whole career is going to go down the tubes? I'll bet money that the truth is going to come out after you get out of the elevator, and then the people who really deserve to be fired will get the axe, and you'll be the hero."

Lanie scoffed, knowing that no matter how much she loved the sound of that scenario, it just wasn't going to happen like that.

"Okay, I don't want to get all depressed again thinking about it. This is your game, you go first," she prompted.

She had absolutely no idea how long they spent quizzing each other about some of their favorite TV shows, movies, and even books. By the time they moved on to talking about their favorite musical artists and songs, both of their phones had died, and they had no idea what time it was. Not only had they learned they had a lot in common, she had also learned that despite all of the depressing things that were happening to her, Jacob had somehow managed to make her laugh more times than she could count.

Unfortunately, one other thing they had in common was Lanie knew was she was now as hungry as her elevator partner.

Jacob's stomach growling loudly finally forced her to lean over the box she'd moved out of the way the hour before.

"Now what are you looking for?" he asked, peering over the edge of the box with her.

"I have to have something else in here to eat. Hand me my purse from over there. Maybe I have another granola bar, or maybe even a bag of peanuts from my last flight."

Without a flashlight, she relied on touch, caressing all of the items in her purse until she hit the jackpot, coming out with not one, but three Hershey chocolates.

"We're saved! I found chocolate!"

"You've been holding out on me? You know how hungry I've been?" Jacob said, leaning closer and stealing one of the chocolates from her palm like a tease.

"Hey! You stole my Kiss!"

While her statement was wholly accurate—it was a Hershey Kiss—Jacob stopped unwrapping the silver foil from the drop of chocolate, gazing back up into her eyes instead. Lanie's breath hitched at the heated look in his brown eyes. At least she thought they were brown. It was hard to tell in the emergency lighting and shadows.

She wasn't sure why he was frozen. She'd expected him to eat the treat quickly, more than happy to share with him. As each second ticked by, she sensed he was leaning closer… and closer…

"Fair warning, Lanie. I'm about to steal a real kiss, and not the chocolate kind. If you don't want that to happen, you'd better speak now or forever hold your peace."

The first brush of their lips was light, hesitant. When she didn't press him away, Jacob grew bolder, wrapping those muscular arms she'd been admiring around her waist, pulling her closer to him until she tipped into his lap.

For the briefest of seconds, she felt like she was falling, but the press of his tongue demanding entrance at the seam of her lips grounded her in the most unexpected way. It had been months since she'd gone on a real date—even longer since she'd liked a guy enough to be intimate. So, it was unnerving to recognize exactly how right it felt to be sitting in the lap of a man she'd never set eyes on until just a few hours before.

As her body melted under his touch, falling deeper under his spell, her brain tried to reason with her. Her reaction to his magnetic attraction was just part of the crisis response. It was a proven fact that people who went through traumatic experiences together formed temporary bonds to help them fend off stress. She couldn't read too much into this. Stress relief, that's all this was.

Probably.

Maybe.

Damn, she hoped not.

His hand moved to lightly cup her breast as he hugged her against him with his other arm, igniting a flame of need deep in her core. If the growing shaft under her ass was any indication, Jacob had a flame or two burning of his own. That she could make his body react with desire got her heart racing even faster until he finally pulled out of their kiss, staying close enough that she could feel his heavy panting as he tried to catch his breath.

"Shit, that was amazing," he said softly.

"Yep… even better than chocolate," she countered, glad they had leaned their foreheads against each other.

The hand that had been roaming before, moved up to cup her cheek. Leaning back a few inches, Jacob softly asked, "Open your eyes for me? Please."

A girl could get used to having a man look at her like Jacob did in that moment. Those gorgeous brown eyes had her melting into a puddle of need, but her brain fought for control. This was not like her. She didn't like to play around, yet what was happening between them didn't feel at all like a game.

She suspected he was trying to decide if he was going to be a gentleman and try to keep things from escalating between them. This realization only helped solidify her decision.

"You know..." It had been several long seconds since she'd spoken, so her voice sounded shaky as she tried to put the right words together. "When I get out of this elevator and my girlfriends ask me where I was when the earthquake hit, I'm going to tell the story about how my day had gone to shit. How I'd gotten called to HR where I was accused of embezzlement and then fired. How my belongings had been thrown into a box and I'd been sent on my own walk of shame just before the elevator I was riding in screeched to a halt, stranding me stories above the lobby.

"But instead of ending with just the bad, I'll also get to tell them about this really cute guy who'd been trapped in the elevator with me. I'll tell them how grateful I was that he made me laugh and took my mind off of not only the danger we were in due to the earthquake, but how horrible it felt to lose my job so unjustly."

Lanie paused there. She should stop talking.

But she didn't.

"Don't you think it will make for a much better story if we could add how we... well... you know...?"

That sexy grin of his lit up his whole face. "Hmmm. I'm not sure I'm following you. What is it exactly you're suggesting we do to beef up our already exciting earthquake survival story?"

Grateful for the dim lighting, she could feel her face blushing. "Well, we're technically still in a lot of danger. There have been so many aftershocks," she added, upping the ante of the game.

Jacob took her bet and raised. "All I know is you've totally rocked my world, and I'm not talking about the earthquake."

Their lips found each other again, this time with a new urgency. As his hands caressed her body, she let her own palms rest on that muscular chest she'd first felt as he'd protected her in the initial quake. As their tongues danced, their hands explored, pulling off pieces of clothing one by one until her breasts were free of her bra and captured first by his palm just before he broke their kiss to latch onto her left nipple instead.

Lanie threw her head back with a groan, loving every sensation he brought out in her. His dark hair was thick between her fingers as she subconsciously humped against the hard rod poking her through their remaining clothes.

Jacob somehow managed to pay homage to her ample breasts with his warm mouth while moving his hands down to unbuckle his own belt without so much as missing a beat.

"Lift your skirt up to your waist and straddle me. I want to take you for a little ride."

She didn't need to be told twice. She'd never bothered to put her panties back on after taking them off hours before. When she pushed up long enough to move into the new position, Jacob used the opportunity to push his own pants down to his knees. His cock sprang out, thick and long.

It wasn't until she felt the head of his shaft sliding through her wet and ready folds that he froze, a look of regret on his face.

"Shit, I don't have a condom. Any chance you have one in that magical box of tricks of yours?"

"Oh sure, I kept boxes of condoms in my desk in the off-chance I'd need them when I got stuck in the elevator." She could have left it there, but as he started to pull away from her, the thought of stopping seemed inconceivable. "But... well... I'm on the pill. As long as we're both clean, that should take care of..."

She didn't get to finish her sentence. Jacob pulled her the final inches until she impaled herself on his erection in one lusty thrust. His tongue was back in her mouth, dueling with her own just as his cock filled her again and again. She was grateful for the help he gave her, cupping her bare ass and lifting her with the muscular forearms she'd admired before letting gravity crash her down onto his rod, deeper with each thrust.

The sexy sounds of their fucking bounced off the walls of their temporary prison, adding to the excitement of the moment. She hadn't thought the masculine scent of his could get any better, but she'd been wrong. The smell of their joint arousal surrounded them, permeating the enclosed space.

Her lover read her body language perfectly, recognizing her legs were getting tired from her position on-top. Without missing a single beat, Jacob lifted her, keeping their bodies connected like perfect fitting puzzle pieces as he lay her on her back on the floor of the elevator. His hands grasped her own, moving them above her head so he could lay atop her, unfettered as he plunged his hips forward, burying his cock again and again.

She felt his breath on her cheek as he spoke near her ear. "Damn, Lanie, you feel perfect beneath me."

Despite the odd location, or maybe because of it, her orgasm built quickly. A niggling guilt tried to break into her euphoria, but she pushed it down. There would be plenty of time to wonder if she was making a mistake later, but one thing was certain as Jacob's lips nibbled behind her ear and into the crook of her neck—sex had never been better. Ever.

"Jacob! Fuck, that feels good. So good," she repeated as she leveraged her hips up to take him as deep as possible while squeezing their linked hands in hopes of never letting go.

She wasn't prepared for the intensity of his gaze when he lifted up, high enough to look into her eyes as he ordered her, "Come with me, baby."

After all she'd gone through that crazy day, his intimate use of the term of endearment brought tears to her eyes. She was a career woman. Independent. She'd never felt the need to get entangled in messy relationships that would distract her from pursuing her grander goals. Yet, as they each shouted out their pleasure in perfect unison, the first drop of sadness that this was more than likely just a one-time encounter closed in.

His weight blanketed her as they each came down from their high. Their hitched breathing returned to normal, and the hardness that had brought her such pleasure slipped out of her body. As warm as the enclosed space was, Lanie felt the brush of a chill as Jacob pushed off her, stopping just long enough to place a tender kiss on her forehead before kneeling up between her legs.

"Let's see if I can find us a few napkins in this box of tricks of yours to clean up a bit," he teased, reaching to his right to rummage through her belongings, holding up a handful of fast-food napkins victoriously. His smile was contagious.

Like the gentleman he appeared to be, he helped clean up their spilled wetness before putting some of his clothing back together. She should try to find her bra… and her blouse, but when she sat up, Jacob pulled her back into his lap instead, wrapping his arms around her in a comforting hug.

Like a light switch, a wave of fatigue fell over her. It had been such a long and eventful day, and adrenaline had kept her going strong. But between the combo of her sexual release and JR's protective arms wrapped around her, figuratively holding back the wave of bullshit waiting to wash over her again when they got out of the elevator, all Lanie wanted to do was lay her head on his shoulder and close her eyes.

"It's late. Why don't you take a little nap," he murmured.

One minute she was trying to talk herself into getting redressed—the next, Jacob was gently shaking her awake. It took several long seconds to remember where she was and whose arms she was snuggled in, regretting that she couldn't stay there longer.

It was the blaring light when she opened her eyes that jolted her fully awake. She had to squint against the sudden brightness.

"Looks like the city got electricity restored to the building. We'd better get redressed before we give the security guys a surprise if they get the elevator moving again."

His words got her moving faster, scrambling off his lap, heading in the direction she'd last seen her bra and blouse. She managed to pull her skirt back down her legs, covering her bare ass that had spent some untold amount of time in Jacob's lap.

She hated that the same awkwardness they had started their

journey with had started to seep back into the elevator along with the electricity. As she hooked her bra in place and buttoned up her corporate-looking blouse, Lanie mourned the intimacy they'd shared and now lost.

Jacob's arms encircled her in a hug from behind, pulling her against his chest in the same way he had when protecting her during the initial quake. How could so much change in just a few short hours?

"Hey, it's gonna be okay," he said, rocking them gently just as the crackling sound of the intercom could be heard.

"This is building security. As you noticed, we have been able to restore electricity to the building, and the elevator inspector is already on the premises and in the process of running a safety check on the system. Assuming no damage was done, we should have your elevator moving and you freed within the next few minutes. Please stand by."

As soon as the announcement completed, Jacob added, "See, just like I told you. It's all going to be okay now."

Hugging his arms to her, enjoying their last minutes together before she'd probably never see him again, Lanie couldn't hold back her truth. "Easy for you to say. I'm still unemployed. I still have to figure out how to get all this crap back to my apartment. And I'll still have to try to find another job with an accusation of embezzlement hanging over my head. It's not like anyone here at Rossi, Anderson, & Hart are going to give me a glowing recommendation."

Jacob's "You don't need to worry about any of those things," felt dismissive. Maybe he didn't need to worry about them, but she sure as hell did.

The elevator sounding a quick alarm tone just before slowly moving into motion towards the ground forced her to stop wallowing in her self-pity. She wiggled in his arms until he released her. Together, they silently bent to pick up the debris of items they'd strewn about in their hours of captivity, throwing everything into that same box carrying her belongings.

With each floor they passed, Alaina's pulse sped up. She'd spent hours wishing their ordeal would end, and now, when she was seconds from freedom… she wanted nothing more than to sink to the floor and take shelter in Jacob's arms all over again.

It was the definition of insanity.

Just as the elevator slid to a soft landing on the ground floor, Jacob reached out, grabbing her hand and linking their fingers together. As the doors finally opened to the controlled chaos of the lobby level, they were greeted by a contingent of security guards, fire fighters, and building engineers busy trying to put things right. She'd expected all of them.

Who she hadn't expected was Jack Leahy, the CFO who'd fired her just before she'd gotten in the elevator. He was about twenty feet away from the elevator bank, talking on his cell phone. He was the absolutely last person she was prepared to see. Desperate to escape the building before he turned and saw her, Lanie struggled to pull her hand out of Jacob's grip, but the harder she pulled, the tighter he squeezed until she finally had to turn to confront him.

Her breath hitched at the sight of Jacob. Even with all they'd gone through, in the light of the lobby, he looked like he could be a magazine cover model. But it was the unreadable glare in his eyes that drew all her attention.

"Lanie… I need you to stick with me here for a few minutes. I promise you, I'll explain everything."

What the hell was he talking about?

It was one of the building security guards in his uniform black suit that approached them first. "I'm so sorry, sir. You should have identified yourself at the start of the event. We've just recently identified those of you stuck in the elevators."

Typical. True, RAH had just fired her, but seriously could they be any more sexist? Was she invisible? The asshole had completely ignored Lanie while tripping over himself to apologize to Jacob for his inconvenience.

"It's fine," Jacob assured the man.

"No, it's definitely not. Mr. Rossi is on his way in. He is not happy."

"Shit," Jacob cursed. Turning her direction, he quickly said, "I want to give you a ride home. We should go."

"What? What time is it anyway? How long were we stuck in there?" she asked.

The security guard glanced at his watch before answering, "It's almost one in the morning. You were in there about eight hours."

"Lanie, come on. I want to get you home and fed, and then I have a few things we need to talk about."

The part of her who had been dreading saying goodbye cheered at his invitation, wanting nothing more than to grab up her beleaguered belongings and leave the building, never to return again. But a tiny nugget of something she couldn't quite put her finger on kept her feet grounded next to the elevator door.

"JR, thank goodness you've been extricated. What an unfortunate mishap."

Lanie turned to face the man who'd spoke. The voice was familiar.

She felt her knees give way. She would have stumbled to the ground if Jacob hadn't wrapped his arms around her, holding her up. Anxiety gripped her hard.

Jack Leahy—her boss's boss's boss—the same man who had fired her eight hours before—stood just feet away, and had addressed Jacob, not her.

"How?" She had to fight to get the rest of her question out. "How do you know Jacob?"

The CFO glanced behind her, confused, before finally speaking to her.

"Ms. Bennett, you're trespassing. You are no longer employed here. I'll have security call you a cab."

"That won't be necessary. I'm taking her home."

Darkness flashed in Jack Leahy's eyes as he turned on JR. "That would not be appropriate. There's a good chance we may end up in litigation with this little embezzler. You should distance yourself from her immediately."

He wasn't making any sense. Why would a guy they hadn't even hired yet need to distance himself from her?

But if they hadn't hired him, how did Jack Leahy even know who he was?

The niggling doubt she'd felt minutes before exploded into a shower of uncertainty.

She didn't have time to figure it out before a balding, older man shouted, "Jacob!" from across the lobby, rushing towards them.

She'd only met the man a few times at corporate social events, but there was no mistaking the President and CEO of the company, James Rossi. That the company patriarch was there was bad enough. That he knew Jacob, was worse. That he rushed to her side and pulled JR away from her and into his arms, giving him a hug, was the worst.

That was until he exclaimed, "We've looked all over for you. Why the hell didn't you have your cell phone on? I thought something bad had happened to you during the quake. Thank God we had security check the camera footage to confirm you'd been here in one of the elevators all along." The man then added the death blow to Lanie. "Let's get you to my house, son. Your mother is a nervous wreck. You need to call her right away."

Guilt doused Jacob's face as he pulled out of the man-hug, making eye contact with her. "Lanie…"

Her mind raced, flitting through every minute of their time together, piecing it all together.

"You said your friends call you JR." She paused, hating to say it out loud, but knowing she had to. "You're Jacob Rossi."

chapter four

"LANIE, PLEASE. I CAN EXPLAIN."

Her ears were ringing as unwanted tears threatened to fall.

Luckily, her anger won. Taking a step around the elder Rossi, Lanie pressed her palms to Jacob's chest and shoved as hard as she could yelling, "You jerk, you lied to me!" She took great satisfaction in watching him fall back against the wall, struggling to stay upright.

Like a predatory animal, he pounced back at her, grabbing both her biceps and not letting go.

"I never lied to you. Not once." Her venomous glare must have made him rethink his position because he added, "I just didn't tell you the whole truth, is all."

"I can't believe you! I pour my whole sordid story out and you pretend you were just here for an interview."

"I wasn't pretending. I did have an interview right before I took the elevator. It's just, well, I was the interview*er*, not the interview*ee*."

"You knew what I thought."

"Yeah, but at first I didn't want you to know I already worked here."

"Why, so you could trick me?"

"No! At first because I selfishly didn't want to get involved with the drama of you having been fired. But then, as you told me what had happened, I wanted you to just tell me the truth of everything you'd found. I worried if you knew who I was, you'd either hold something back or worse… that you might lie to sway me to your side."

She hated that he was making sense. She was furious. She didn't want him to make any sense.

"We haven't talked about RAH for hours. Don't you think at

some point during all of our… *discussions*… that you might have been able to bring up the truth?"

"I promise you, if it had been important, I would have told you. But…" Jacob's voice trailed off as he ran his hand through his hair nervously. He finally finished his thought. "Maybe I wanted to see if you liked me for just me… Jacob. Not my last name."

"Why the hell would I like you for your last name?" she spat.

"Because my last name, and all that comes with it, is what almost all women want first from me."

Lanie hated the sadness in his eyes as he admitted what she suspected was a hard truth for him.

It was Jack Leahy who saved her from having to reply. He had the gall to step next to them, unbelievably attempting to pull Lanie out of Jacob's grasp.

"I'm sorry you were trapped in the elevator at all, JR, but even more sorry you got stuck with this criminal. I made a grave error in not calling the police when I had the chance. Had I done that, she would have been in the back of a squad car when the quake hit instead of trapped with you."

A dark shadow passed across Jacob's face just before he released her biceps, spinning to the side, and grabbing Jack Leahy by the shirt collar. The CFO was forced to release Lanie when Jacob half-lifted, half-shoved the executive hard enough that he fell back against the security guard standing nearby.

"JR! What's gotten into you?" James Rossi shouted, trying to pull his son off the CFO.

"I hate to tell you this, but someone has been embezzling money from Rossi, Anderson, & Hart, Dad. And when Alaina Bennett, a member of our accounting team, discovered the missing money and reported it to her supervisor, she was immediately fired and thrown out without notice. I find it curious that our Chief Financial Officer didn't bother to do any investigation before jumping to conclusions and firing the very team member that reported the problem. I think he's hiding something."

James Rossi shook his head in doubt. "You're not making any

sense. Jack Leahy has been a member of the executive committee of RAH for over eight years now. Your brother hired him long before you joined the business. They went to Harvard together."

"I'm telling you, Dad, something's wrong and I trust Ms. Bennett's investigation. Now, you convinced me to finally come and join the family business. Are you going to trust me, or do I need to pack up and head back to Denver?"

"What? You're that sure?" Mr. Rossi questioned his son. "I find this very difficult to believe."

Jack Leahy was less patient. "This is ridiculous. I told you Jacob didn't have what it took to step into leadership of RAH after you retire. He's thinking with his johnson instead of his brain. Anyone can look at these two, cooped up in the elevator together for eight hours—she's got him wrapped around her finger, believing all her lies."

Jacob didn't back down one bit. He barked an order to the security team waiting nearby. "You, there!" he shouted, pointing at the closest guard. "Go into the elevator and get Ms. Bennett's purse and cell phone from the box on the floor. Bring them here. Then take the rest of the items on the floor back upstairs and lock them all in my office on forty-five."

"Yes, sir," the guard answered, speeding off to the elevator to do what he'd been asked to do.

Jacob wasn't done. Pointing at another guard standing behind the computer bank, he called out, motioning for the guard to join them. When he had, Jacob barked his next order. "Effective immediately, I want you to turn off building and computer server access for both Peter Blankenship and Jack Leahy. Tomorrow morning, we will begin a full forensic audit of the RAH books and we'll get to the bottom of exactly what is and isn't happening around here. Until then, Peter and Jack are on a paid leave of absence, which is considerably more generous than how they treated Ms. Bennett by throwing her out without even the most basic investigation."

"You can't do this. Tell him, James. I'm the CFO!"

Lanie wanted to shout with joy watching the asshole who'd

treated her so badly be put into his place. Even if Mr. Rossi didn't believe her, Jacob did, and that was all that mattered to Lanie.

The group stood, awkwardly waiting until James Rossi weighed in. "You heard my son. Do as he instructed," he told the guard.

For the first time since his arrival, the elder Rossi turned her direction. Taking a step closer, he extended his hand. "I take it you're the little lady that started all this hubbub." As soon as Lanie shook his hand, he smiled, adding, "James Rossi."

"Alaina Bennett, sir. And I'm pretty sure the earthquake had a bit to do with how we all got here at one in the morning."

"Indeed. Well, it's nice to meet you, Alaina Bennett. I was planning on stealing my son to help put his mother's worries about his safety to rest, but I'm pretty sure she'll understand if I tell her he was too busy safely escorting a beautiful young woman home, instead."

"Thank you, sir. I appreciate it, but your son has been promising me a steak dinner for hours now. Since I'm not sure we'll be able to find a steak place open, I'm gonna talk him into taking me for a burger instead."

Both Rossi men broke into laughter as Lanie accepted her purse and cell phone from the waiting security guard.

Jacob reached out his hand to her. "You ready?"

With a little wave at James Rossi, she took Jacob's hand, letting him lead her towards the garage. Only when they were far enough away that his father wouldn't hear him, Jacob put his arm around her, pulling her close.

"Consider yourself warned. I'm definitely picking up food for us, but we're taking it to go. I can't wait to get you behind closed doors with me again."

The End

about the author

USA Today Bestselling Author Livia Grant lives in Chicago with her husband and furry rescue dog named Max. She is fortunate to have been able to travel extensively and as much as she loves to visit places around the globe, the Midwest and its changing seasons will always be home. Livia's readers appreciate her riveting stories filled with deep, character driven plots, often spiced with elements of BDSM.

Connect with Livia!

•Sign up for her Newsletter and never miss a new release.

•Join Livia's Facebook Group: The Passion Vault

•Follow Livia on Facebook

•Follow Livia on Goodreads

•Follow Livia on BookBub

•Follow Livia on Instagram

also by
LIVIA GRANT

Black Light Series

Infamous Love, A Black Light Prequel
Black Light: Rocked
Black Light: Valentine Roulette
Black Light: Rescued
Black Light: Roulette Redux
Complicated Love
Black Light: Celebrity Roulette
Black Light: Purged
Black Light: Scandalized
Black Light: Roulette War
Black Light: The Beginning
Black Light: Roulette Rematch—coming February, 2021
Black Light: Rolled—coming 2021

Punishment Pit Series

Wanting it All
Securing it All
Having it All
Balancing it All
Defending it All
Protecting it All
Expecting it All
Celebrating it All—Coming 2021
Deceiving it All—Coming 2021

Stand Alone Books

Blessed Betrayal

Royalty, American Style

Alpha's Capture (as Livia Bourne)

Blinding Salvation (as Livia Bourne)

Out of Print Books

Psychology of Submission, Corbin's Bend Series

Life's Unexpected Gifts, Corbin's Bend Series

Melting Silver, Red Petticoat Series

Call Sign Thunder

Bite Me—Vampire Anthology

Just Breathe—Anthology

Royally Mine—Anthology

Heroes to Obey—Anthology

A Lovely Meal—RWA Anthology

i'm calling dibs

HARLOE RAE

I'm Calling Dibs

"I slept with someone else."

No girl ever wants to hear those words, especially from their boyfriend.
Well, sucks to be me. But it's going to suck worse for Josh.
That cheater will realize his mistake soon enough.
By then, I'll be far out of reach.

I'm not going to mope around campus, crying over his unfaithful ways.
Nope. I'm moving on to better and hotter.

My sights are set on Seth McHue.
The good guy with a body that drives all the girls wild—me definitely included.
He never dates.
Doesn't party past midnight.
Has a panty-vaporizing smirk.
Did I mention he gets perfect grades?
It's safe to say he's dedicated and driven.
I want to be his top priority.

Seth doesn't know it yet, but I'm calling dibs.

chapter one

Rayne

I SWAY MY HIPS TO THE ELECTRIC BEAT PUMPING THROUGH THE SPEAKERS. Fingers dig into my waist, the large palms spanning my torso with practiced finesse. This guy is no amateur. I'd shrug him off, but no lines have been crossed. Not yet, at least.

It's nice to feel wanted. Even in a shallow, superficial sense. At any rate, this faceless dude is harmless. He isn't getting more from me than a dead end in my current spiral. Maybe a few more wandering touches, if he's lucky.

A fluid ease relaxes my limbs and I allow the music to take control. The shots I slammed earlier are thrumming through my veins, heating me from the inside with a comfortable numb. If I treat myself to a few more, the pain threatening to shred my insides might dull to a muted roar. But the reality of me forgetting what he did is slim to none.

Josh fucking Loyte is dead to me. Even in this inebriated state, his name is a spike through my crumbling heart. All that he represents is splattered with tainted ink.

He's the beloved captain of our college football team.

Fraternity president.

Classically handsome.

Reigning beer pong champion.

My first serious boyfriend.

Oh, and an unfaithful piece of moldy trash.

There had been whispered rumors of him cheating on me before. Josh is often on the road and surrounded by temptation. But he never gave me reason to doubt his commitment. The calls and texts never hit a lull. He made sure the gossip didn't hold an ounce of credibility. I'd been reinforced to put my trust in him, and our relationship.

Until today.

A twitch attacks my eyelid just recalling the sordid scene depicted for me this afternoon. Several of Josh's teammates witnessed the flirting, kissing, dry-humping…every detail leading to the actual deed. Three years are tossed out the window for a quick piece of ass. Everything we shared—all of the highs, lows, and standstills—are proven worthless. He didn't bother denying the claims of his infidelity when I confronted him. All that bastard had for me were hollow words that severed what little remained of my hope.

Rayne, baby. You didn't really think we'd stay together after graduation, right?

I had, stupidly. Turns out I was the only one. Fool me once and all that. He's responsible for giving me a whopping dose of jaded medicine. I won't be so easily duped in the future.

But here I am, drowning my sorrows in a river of denial. Maybe if I drink enough, this horrible nightmare will turn out to be just that. I'll wake up and everything will return to normal. That thought gives me pause. Is that what I really want? Suddenly I'm not so sure. It could be the cloud of booze talking.

I thought Josh would propose after graduation. We'd get married and buy an adorable little house. Spend our lives beside one another, growing old, and building endless memories. What a damn pipe dream. My love is shriveling faster than his reputation around campus. That's one positive about this ordeal. Josh's name is being dragged through the mud. Score for the underdogs.

The song changes to something slower and the man behind me disappears. Probably scouring the crowd for a more interactive partner. Good riddance.

"Rayne?"

I squint at the gravelly voice through one eye. This newcomer sounds better than chocolate wrapped in peanut butter. When my vision clears, I suck in a sharp breath.

Oh, shit.

It's the hottie from my organic chemistry class. Pretty sure he's been enrolled in several of the same courses. Not that I've been staring longingly or anything. The dim lighting conceals his green eyes that are the perfect shade of emerald. He always smells like fresh laundry and naughty fantasies. I jerk out of those unhelpful musings. They'll only make my mouth water faster. He's already so out of my league and here I am, three sheets to the wind.

"Hey, you." I give him a wave of my fingers. It probably looks more like a sloppy flop.

"Seth," he reminds.

"I know your name," I grumble.

His smirk puts a wobble in my knees. "That'll make this easier."

A furrow squishes my brows. "Huh?"

"I heard about Josh," he deflects.

"Good for you."

"Well," Seth drawls. "For what it's worth, he's a total wanker. I can't believe he'd do that to you."

"Salt in the wound," I mutter. The floor tilts sideways beneath my unstable heels and I nearly topple over. I manage to straighten before going horizontal.

He squints at my tipping movements. "Are you drunk?"

Can he really blame me? I hold up a pinch between my thumb and forefinger. "I might've overindulged."

"You think?" A dry chuckle escapes him.

I rub at the sudden ache spreading across my temples. "Isn't that what I just said?"

"Are you staying much longer?"

"Uh," I mumble. The muck in my brain struggles to keep up with his change in subject. With clumsy hands, I whip out my phone. The screen is way too bright and I hiss at the sting. "I dunno. It's not even eleven. We have an hour to wait before the third happy hour kicks in."

Seth mutters something unintelligible under his breath. I don't bother trying to comprehend the string of nonsense. His gaze returns to mine. "Where are your friends?"

"Over there." I blindly gesture to their usual booth against the wall.

"Can I walk you home?"

"Now?"

"Preferably."

"Is that all you want to do?" The slur in my tone detracts from my accusation. Or is it meant as a suggestion?

"Yes, Rayne. Believe it or not, my intentions are decent."

A pout threatens to push out my bottom lip. But that's most definitely the alcohol's influence. "I wasn't accusing you."

"Yet," he adds.

"Are you going to give me reason to change my mind?"

"Never."

"Most guys would take advantage."

Seth combs through his blond hair. "Well, I'm not one of the masses."

I give him a slow once-over. He's everything Josh will never be. "No, you certainly aren't."

"Will you leave with me? You can sleep this off and wake refreshed. Alone, of course."

My eyelids grow heavier the more he talks about leaving. Snuggling under my covers has never sounded so good. I find myself nodding while turning toward the exit. "Uh-huh, let's go."

chapter two

Rayne

"THAT LYING PIECE OF SHIT." I HURL ANOTHER PICTURE FRAME AT the brick wall and get a sliver of satisfaction as the glass shatters. A sick sense of revenge shortly follows.

What's not so delightful is the pounding that's rattling my skull intensifying from the impact. This damn hangover is trying to ruin my closure. A headache is the least of my worries and won't stop me. I palm another meaningless gift from my box of mementos from that asshole and prepare to take aim.

"That's right, let it all out." Audria's soothing tone does little to cool the fire under my skin. My best friend has been watching my destruction for the better part of an hour. She deserves an award for her unwavering encouragement.

"Oh, I am. Josh will curse the moment his cock slid into someone else. And you know what else?"

She hums while tapping her chin. "There are so many—"

I don't give her a chance to finish before continuing my tirade. "He has a teeny weenie."

Audria cackles at that crude confession. "I love this spiteful side of you."

If I'm being honest, this toxic headspace is draining as hell. "I just need a solid ten minutes to freak out. Then I'll be done."

"Well, I'm here for it. Whatever you need."

"Just a couple more hunks of junk." I pitch the cheesy heart figurine still in my palm, smiling as it smashes into a cascade of red and pink smithereens.

"You're ruthless," she crows. "This is a gravesite of love gone wrong."

I stare at the broken pieces that once held so much value. In the light of morning, reality sinks in heavier than a lead balloon. Josh cheated on me. It's official. Nothing is changing that. I have to accept the truth and move on. No more denial or mourning the loss of my naive innocence.

Yesterday was spent moping around and licking my wounds. Now I'm letting anger slip behind the wheel. Tomorrow marks the beginning of a fresh outlook where Josh is a blip in the rearview. Hell, he won't even exist in my future paradise.

"Love should never hurt like this. I'm thinking Josh didn't care about anything except having a reliable lay."

She frowns at me. "Don't sell yourself short. Ever."

I hold out my arms. "He already did that for me."

"He deserves a kick in the crotch," she spits.

"And then some. I should've known. Half the football team has tried telling me for months, but I brushed them off."

Her smile is kind, even in the face of this dank topic. "You chose to trust him."

"Yeah, and look where that landed me. Does loyalty mean nothing?"

"It does to those that matter. Don't let him get you down."

"No, I'm not sad. Not anymore, at least. There's a yuck factor that isn't easy to scrub off. But I won't give him reason to believe he's missed. Come Monday, I'll be better than ever."

"That's my girl," Audria cheers. No wonder she's becoming a teacher. She can root with the best of them.

I point at her, my chest growing tight with pressure. "This is why he lost interest in having sex. The last time we did was…I don't even remember when. How sad is that? We're supposed to be in our prime and I'm not getting laid."

One of her shoulders bobs to a silent beat. "Maybe that's a good thing. He was protecting you from potential STDs."

Acid burns in my belly. "I don't want to think of him being considerate for that reason. Lord knows he could use a few extra lessons in respect. I should've broken up with him last summer. What a manwhore."

"Better to find out now," she reasons.

I just…" My words trail off in a pitiful whine. "How could he do this to me?"

Audria pulls me in for a hug, rubbing my back. "He's a dumb boy. Too busy playing with balls to grow up. He's very immature and doesn't deserve you."

"That's the standard response friends have to vibe in situations like this." Defeat clings heavy in my voice.

"Not true. If you were full of it, I'd tell you so."

I squint at her. "Yeah, you're too honest."

She shrugs again. "Almost to a fault."

"If only that trait applied to those who truly need it."

"What goes around," she sings.

"He should be the one suffering," I fume. "I want to punish that pile of worthless scum. He cheats on me? The one who's been dutifully by his side for years? What the fuck, Auds?"

"He's lost his marbles, obviously. We know this."

I'm nodding along with her. "Yep, and he does it with that skanky whore everyone with a jersey bangs? She's not even pretty!"

Audria grips my shoulder, offering all the moral support with that one touch. "Nothing but a homewrecker."

A hitch warbles my exhale. This is getting too dark. If I don't tread carefully, I'll hit a point of no return. I'm making shit up based on this random girl's social media uploads. Petty much? She deserves my wrath. Glaring at her pictures gives me a false outlet since she's nothing but a stranger. For all I know, the girl thinks Josh is single and available for all the celebratory shenanigans. That fucker is a sweet talker. He can weasel his way into exclusive events without a word. I wouldn't put it past him to lie smoother than a bearskin rug.

"No more cyber stalking," she scolds. "That will only infect the site of injury."

She's right, as always. "I just wanted a little peek. Brent shouldn't have told me her name to begin with."

"We know he's been hit in the head one too many times." Audria mimics bouncing off the siding.

I laugh at her reenactment. "He probably meant well. That's what I'm telling myself at least."

"Always thinking the best of people. You're such a good soul."

"Yeah, well, hopefully karma is fighting in my corner."

Her brown eyes sparkle. "I have a brilliant idea."

"Glitter bomb? Yeah, I was thinking the same thing."

She giggles. "I was going to say fire ants in Josh's underwear drawer, but glitter might be worse."

I rub my palms together. "Why not both?"

"That's the spirit, lady boss. You show him who's coming out on top."

"No more taking shit lying down." I slap a palm to my chest.

"You're going to find someone so much better. He'll treat you like a queen."

I almost admit that a certain fellow snagged my attention last night. Seth is everything I'd be lucky to have in a boyfriend. But it's far too premature for those ideas to be sprouting. For all I know, Seth was just being a decent guy and didn't want to see me get into the wrong hands. There are more complications, too.

"The dirty laundry of my breakup is still hanging out to dry. I shouldn't be thinking of other guys."

Audria waves me off. "Oh, please. Rules of etiquette don't apply when cheating is involved. Don't let your happily ever after pass you by."

When she puts it that way, it's hard for me to resist. Or argue. "We'll see."

"Just be open to options."

"I will, promise."

"Yes, girl. Get your redemption."

"Starting now," I vow.

"And what about this?" She points to the mess scattering across our garage floor.

"I'll get the broom. But creating all that wreckage has left me parched."

Audria bounces on her toes. "Mimosas?"

"Always."

I'm practically skipping inside at the promise of bubbles and citrus. Maybe I should pop in some toast, too. A loud knock interrupts my trek to the fridge. I stomp over to the foyer and fling open the door. That innocent knob of metal is next in line for taking the brunt of my frustration. If I was stronger, it might even creak under my efforts.

Familiar green eyes meet mine. I feel my lips part with a sputtering breath. Seth is at my house. Blurry snippets of last night filter in through the fog. He found me on the dance floor. I was a hot mess. We talked for a bit. He escorted me home while acting more regal than any version of a gentleman I've met. Before I could even consider inviting him in, Seth was saying goodnight with promises of seeing me soon. And now he's back.

"Um, hi."

"Breakfast?" He holds up two grease-stained bags.

My empty stomach grumbles. "Oh, my hero. It's like you read my mind."

"That's quite a pleasant reception."

"It's been a rough morning," I mutter.

His smile droops at the corners. "Is this a bad time?"

I shake my head, wincing at the dull ache. "No, no. Couldn't be better. You're a saint, swooping in at the right moment."

"This is nothing."

"Not to me."

Seth's signature smirk tilts his lips. "Well, it's a good thing I'm just getting started."

chapter three

Seth

RAYNE SWALLOWS THE LAST BITE OF CROISSANT WITH A GROAN. "AND once again, that really hit the spot. You seem to have a hidden talent for delivering what I'm craving."

The smile that slides onto my lips is natural. "Happy to oblige."

"And provide," she adds.

"Is that all right with you?"

"Do you hear me complaining?" She pats her stomach. "This habit of yours is becoming addictive."

My grin tips higher. It's been almost two weeks since my trial run at pursuing her. Since that first Sunday morning, I've found countless excuses to stop by her place or conveniently cross our paths. She's been receptive to my advances, which only encourages me. "I'll continue delivering breakfast so long as you keep opening the door, and make noises like that."

Rayne lets another moan loose. Purely for my benefit, I assume. "Be careful or I might get used to this."

"That's the plan." I begin gathering the trash in front of us.

A rosy hue stains her cheeks. "You're spoiling me."

"On purpose," I murmur.

She drops her gaze from mine. "Why?"

The loss of her stare hits me harder than it should. "Isn't it obvious?"

"Not to me. I've never been the type who jumps to conclusions." Rayne shakes her head, biting her bottom lip.

No, she's not. That's one of the many things I appreciate about her. I've been playing the long game--far longer than intended. But this girl is worth the wait.

Since Rayne broke up with Josh, I've been watching him strut across campus as if he's King fucking Arthur. What a douche. Doesn't he realize who's free from his clutches? Of course not because he's holding his head so damn high that he can't see what's no longer in front of him. His major fuck up is absolutely my gain. It's almost humorous how efficiently he fucked himself over. I couldn't have plotted a better ploy myself.

After catching sight of Rayne Trent freshman year, I've been not-so-patiently biding my time for her to be single. If only I had made a move before Josh butted in and got his meaty paws all over her. That guy never deserved her. He's a total fool, and I've never been more grateful for another person's demise. Rayne's connection to him has officially been axed.

I've been keeping tabs from afar, but now I'm stepping up to the plate. No more sidelines. This is the chance I need to prove she's meant to be mine.

"Will you go somewhere with me today?" I hold up my palms. "Still no ulterior motives."

Well, that's not entirely true. But they're genuine.

She relaxes further into her chair. "Oh, the fun isn't stopping with food?"

"There's more I'd like to offer, if you're okay with that." And hopefully this starts the beginning of something new.

Her nails tap on the table. "What did you have in mind?"

"The Rose Gardens," I murmur.

Her gasp is the reaction I was going for. "Really?"

"Yeah, I wouldn't joke about that. It's a favorite of yours, right?" I've heard her talking about the latest designs in class. And she typically goes alone.

"Uh-huh, I would love that. Mallory is the only person I can convince to stroll the blooming displays with me. I don't get it. Who doesn't love flowers?"

"I'd be honored to take you." That truth pulses through my tone with heavy beats.

"You're a really great guy, Seth."

I cringe, pausing for the inevitable. It doesn't come. "But?"

Rayne shrugs. "But nothing. You make me happy."

Air whispers out of me on a whoosh. "Thank Christ for that. I was preparing for the ultimate letdown."

"Nope. I like you. A lot." Her tongue peeks out, licking a trail along her bottom lip.

The fire that I'm sure is reflecting in my gaze rushes through me hotter than lava. How often have I imagined biting that plump flesh? Too many, and this isn't the moment to push that boundary. Kissing Rayne will seal this deal I've been near desperate to make. I didn't hold off on seeking more just to ruin it by being impulsive. Going too fast, taking what she's not ready to offer, isn't the strategy to win her over for the long haul. The last thing I want is for her to categorize me under friend-zone.

I scrub over my mouth, wiping the hasty decisions away. "I really like you, too. Have for a while. I'm hoping we can get to know each other better."

She nods. "I suppose these quickie visits aren't granting us ample opportunity."

"Hence going somewhere else. Together," I suggest.

"Like a real date?"

"Very much so."

When Ryane stands from her seat and moves to straddle me, the pounding in my chest is deafening. My hands automatically lift to her hips, holding our bodies together in an intimate embrace that makes a frequent appearance in my fantasies.

"What're you doing?" The slight croak in my voice doesn't go unnoticed.

"The next step," she murmurs. Her breath ghosts across my cheek from our close proximity.

I clench my teeth against the raging arousal hardening in my lap. "It isn't my intention to rush you. There's no pressure from me, Rayne."

Her hips rock into mine, that tiny flicker of friction is enough to set an inferno in my blood. "Do you want me to stop?"

Fuck that. Is she serious? "No," I state simply.

"You've made all the moves, Seth. It's my turn. I'm calling dibs."

And with that, she presses her lips onto mine.

chapter four

Seth

RAYNE GIGGLES BESIDE ME, SQUEEZING MY HAND IN HERS AS WE approach the next budding sculpture. "No way. Your brother sounds like he truly wanted to cause irrefutable harm."

"Eh, maybe he took his role as the older and wiser too far. The pranks were fairly extreme." I stop beside her when she pauses to inspect the complex design.

She snorts. "You think? The worst my sister ever did was put temporary dye in my shampoo. She did technically try to wrench out one of my baby teeth in elementary school. But that didn't pan out. We were trying to earn an early payday from the tooth fairy."

"That sounds painful."

"Marie is a weakling. She can't hurt a fly."

"Well, that makes me feel better about your childhood."

Rayne shakes her head. "Don't let her size fool you. She'll take you out at the kneecaps."

That gets a laugh out of me. "Solid strategy. Pretty sure it's their jobs to torture the younger siblings?"

"I suppose," she muses while we move along the last row of colorful plots.

"Are you two close?"

"Very. She lives in St. Paul so we see each other plenty."

"Family is important," I murmur.

"Are yours nearby?"

"Up near Duluth so not that far."

"Well, if you ever need a dose of sibling fun, Marie fits the bill. Maybe you'll meet her soon."

She's dropped a few hints about future dates. That sort of talk gets me wrapped a little tighter around her pinky. "That'd be great."

Rayne bumps me with her hip. "Okay, new topic. Are you actually enjoying this flower tour?"

I stumble to an abrupt halt. "Yeah, of course. Why wouldn't I?"

"Because it's not a typical choice for college-age guys. I don't believe many would pick this unless forced." She gestures to the sparse spectators, most of them female.

I grunt at that assumption. "They don't know what they're missing. And a more important question is are you having fun?"

Her head bumps up and down. "I love it here. So peaceful and beautiful."

Just like her. Can she blame me for wanting to experience this? "I'm exactly where I want to be." Honesty rings through my words.

There's a hitch in Rayne's exhale as she stares at me. "Okay then."

The look she's pinning on me is intense, a shock of electricity straight to an unknown source buried deep. I'm getting fucking sappy, which has never been an issue for me. Hell, I rarely date to begin with. There's something about this girl that makes me want to be different.

Better.

Softer.

And why wouldn't she? I've always known Rayne would strike hard when given the chance. The pedestal I built for her isn't nearly high enough.

I cough into a fist, mentally swerving onto smoother ground. "What're your plans after graduation?"

She wrinkles her nose. "I haven't given it too much consideration since that's over a year away."

That drags another chuckle out of me. "Not much of a planner?"

Her palm tilts side to side. "That depends. In this case, not at all. I prefer to live my youth to the fullest until adulthood comes knocking."

"That's fair. What's your major?"

Rayne quirks a brow my way. "You don't know?"

"Should I?" I squint at her. Is that a dig?

"You just seem to have a wide base of common knowledge where I'm concerned."

Something dark twists in my gut. "That makes me sound like a stalker."

She huffs. "I'm well aware you're not, trust me. Any girl on campus would be drooling at the chance of you asking them out on a date. Chasing me isn't necessary for a guy like you."

Little does she know. "Those other girls can keep dreaming. I'm only interested in one."

Her eyes twinkle under the afternoon sun. "You say the sweetest things."

"It's easy with the right inspiration." A frozen yogurt cart was conveniently parked just beyond the garden exit. "Want to get a cup?"

"Or we could share a bowl."

"You're taking things to an entirely new level."

"Is that weird for you?"

"That depends. What're your favorite flavors?"

Her laugh is becoming my latest addiction. "Strawberry, chocolate, and blueberry. In that order."

My taste buds sing at the tease. "Okay, we can take the next step."

"Speaking of, what do you wanna do after dessert?" The suggestion in her voice is impossible to miss.

I blink at the clear invitation searing into me. "Really?"

Rayne releases some wicked noise low in her throat. "Oh, yeah. I want you. Really bad."

"Shit, and here I am acting like a slow burn is more appropriate." I almost hang my head in shame.

She gives my shoulder a light pat. "We've taken the scenic route, which I appreciate. I just got out of a serious relationship and didn't think dating would be on my radar again for months. So, thanks for using the gentleman card up until this point."

"You're welcome," I mumble. There seems to be a catch clinging to the end of her statement.

A piece of her red hair gets twirled around a slender finger. "Let's get our ice cream and go rattle my headboard."

I choke on my tongue as it attempts to loll out of my mouth. "What?"

"You heard me, Seth. Let's make this official."

"Jesus, you're the perfect woman."

She walks her fingers up my chest. "You haven't seen anything yet."

chapter five

Seth

I race up the stairs two at a time while Rayne trails kisses up my neck. She purrs and adds her tongue into the mix. The delicate touch blending with those seductive noises almost makes me falter. The throbbing behind my zipper is nearly blinding, which doesn't bode well for what's to come. I grunt at the damn irony. And that pun isn't helping.

Taking the edge off earlier would have ensured a bit more confidence. I'm strung too fucking tight. Skipping the chance to relieve some of the strain will certainly bite me in the ass. Now it's too late. Holding off on getting laid for months on end is a great idea and all. Not being properly prepared is a rookie mistake that I'll deal with while facing my ultimate fantasy. I'll bust a nut before sinking into her welcome depths.

As if sensing my impending demise, Rayne grinds into me. "Hurry."

"Trying, baby." I barely reach the landing when her thighs grip tighter to my waist.

In a sorry attempt to regain some semblance of control, I crash my mouth onto hers. She groans against my lips, opening for me to delve in. Her tongue slides against mine in the most sensual of pairings. A hint of fruit and chocolate still lingers with a slight chill. The fire roaring in my blood rushes to extinguish any sense of cold. I'm instantly hooked on the combination, this woman becoming my favorite flavor from a few surface swipes. The need to burrow deep propels me forward.

"Which way?" I suck her bottom lip between my teeth.

She's panting against my cheek, the heat of her exhales fueling me. "Last door on the left."

I'm rushing that direction before she finishes speaking. Her ass is cradled in my palms and I take advantage, rocking into the bouncing gait of my haste. She throws her head back and joins in the choppy movements. I swing the door open, which Rayne immediately slams behind us.

"Get inside of me."

"That's the plan," I murmur while blindly searching the dark room. When my knees hit the mattress, I toss Rayne into the center. She giggles and sits up, immediately whipping off her shirt. A skirt and what I assume are panties hit my chest as she lets another tinkling laugh loose.

"You're falling behind," she teases.

"Didn't know this was a race." I shuck my pants and boxers, ripping the tee off my head with a single tug. Before lust can completely clog my brain, I grab the foil packet from my pocket and take a precious second to wrap up.

I crawl onto the bed and cover her body with mine. My lips seal over hers, passing a cascade of desire through that brief connection. She spreads her legs in invitation, rolling against me. I press at her opening with a gentle nudge. With a fluid motion, I enter her and connect us as one.

Rayne cries out, the staccato a blast into our silence. "Holy shit."

"Yeah, baby. I feel it, too." I'm not going to last more than a few shallow pumps. She's my kryptonite. The end game. Hopefully embarrassing myself won't cause her to kick me out immediately afterwards.

I glide forward and back, picking up a rhythm that has her clenching around me. Her nails spear into my biceps, clutching me closer. I'm buried to the hilt, slamming my length into her mound, but it's still not enough. A bolt of all-consuming need spears into me and I'm a slave to the onslaught. I'm plunging in and out without care of anything else. Nothing will top this moment, until I'm lost inside of her again. My body reacts to the molten desire driving me by doubling the already punishing pace. The way she's wriggling on the sheets suggests she's just as desperate.

"Please, please," Rayne begs. She bucks her hips into mine, chasing the pleasure that hovers so near.

"Almost there," I respond between punctuating strokes. At this point, I'm uncertain if it's meant to be a question or alert. I'm dizzy with the effects of her essence coupling with mine.

My motions turn more frantic. I'm certain we're barely more than a blur of wanton pleasure. She follows my lead, guiding my wild drives with precisely timed upward pitches. The way she swivels into me drains every last ounce of control. I do my best to tamp down the climax bearing down on me. Hot tingles race up my spine in a final notice. She bows against me, accepting me that much further into her silken warmth.

"I'm there. Harder. Faster. Now."

Her demands make me lightheaded until stars dance in my vision. I let go of the edge with a shout and she tumbles after me. My body jerks along hers, losing all sense of finesse. We're tunneling down a spiral of flooding release, quivering and shaking with the aftershocks.

"Wow," Rayne breaths. Her chest rises and falls to the same rapid beat as mine.

"Yeah," I agree.

"We're totally doing that again."

I grunt at the sheer possibility of the opposite being true. "Nothing could stop me."

She slaps my ass, the clap of contact echoing around the room. "Ready when you are, Dibs."

Barely recovered and sticky in sweat, that's the moment I fall even harder. "It's on, baby."

"I always had a feeling about you. It's very gratifying to discover I'm right." And that's the instant I know she's mine.

chapter six

Rayne

I SLIDE INTO THE BOOTH WITH MY BESTIES. THE LIBRARY--OUR FREQUENT watering hole, not the dusty stacks--is filling faster than the bartenders can pour drinks. Saturday night is continuing to be a real bang. That reminder sends a tingle of straight heat through my core.

My body is still buzzing from the numerous orgasms Seth granted me earlier. He works over my most intimate parts better than I do. I feel like a finely tuned instrument under his talented ministrations. Even our first time felt like a well orchestrated masterpiece. I bite my lip as a rush of need washes over me. Revisiting that burst of combustible endorphins can't happen soon enough.

"Our girl is high on love," Vannah coos.

I pop out of my blissful unawareness at her voice. My friend earns a glare from me for that comment. "Oh, whatever."

She lifts a slim brow. "Just good sex then?"

"No," I mutter. There's no chance of me selling what we share short.

"That's what I thought." Her expression glistens with a gloating shine.

"I just broke up with Josh. Isn't it a tad early to be hopping in the sack with a different guy?" Considering the alternative leaves an empty sensation swirling in my belly. I instantly hate that hollow gap.

Clea flicks some hair behind her shoulder. "Why are you even thinking about that pencil dick?"

A giggle escapes me. I have no regrets sharing that very miniscule detail. "I'm not taking his feelings into account at all. Trust me. I couldn't care less what he thinks. I'm more worried about--"

"People judging you?" Audria interrupts.

"Not necessarily," I murmur. But I'm a liar.

Vannah leans across the table and grips my hand. "Please, girl. You're the one who got scorned. They're all cheering you on."

"And if they're not, screw them." Mallory's grin is usually sweet, but this one is full of payback.

"But for real, are you feeling guilty or something?" Audria doesn't hide her wince.

"Nope. Not even a little bit."

"Good. The only reason I would suggest holding off on someone better is if your gut is telling you so. That sorry excuse of a limp noodle did you wrong. There's no reason you need to put a pause on a good thing, especially not for Josh's sake."

"Not sure why we're bothering with this discussion." Clea hums while pursing her lips.

A crease pinches my forehead. "What's that supposed to mean?"

"It's a bit late for pumping the brakes, Ray. That guy is smitten."

I glance over to where Seth is standing with his friends. Heat infuses my cheeks when he winks at me. My fingers lift automatically in what I hope is a flirty wave.

"Oh, damn. He's not the only one." Vannah snorts into her beer glass.

"Shut up," I mutter.

"Young love. It's so cute," she coos with a whistle.

"I'm seriously so happy you're moving on," Audria agrees. My other two friends bob their heads.

"You're all very wise," I state with a slight wobble.

Vannah points at me. "Don't start."

I sniff regardless of her warning. "But you guys are seniors. I'm a junior. In the fall, I'll still be stuck on campus while you're building careers and financial stability. Your credit scores will be so much better than mine."

Mallory huffs, sending her bangs flying. "Don't forget debt. I have to start paying off my loans soon. The horror."

Clea nods while taking a sip of her cocktail. "To be honest, I wouldn't mind staying in college for another year."

"I highly recommend you do." And secretly cross my fingers under the booth.

"That won't help with my debt problem," Mallory pouts. "Sorry, babe."

Vannah clucks her tongue at our antics. "Seems you have someone who's more than interested in keeping you company."

"Exactly. You don't need us," Audria assures. "We're leaving you in very capable hands."

A sigh escapes me as I look over at Seth again, finding his gaze already locked on me. "Yes, you certainly are."

As if the tether between us pulls taut and reels him in, Seth makes his way over to us. "Ladies," he greets.

They all provide a welcome in return, wearing matching grins.

His focus narrows onto me. "Hey, baby."

"Hi," I murmur.

"Mind if I steal your girl away?" He's addressing my friends, but his eyes don't leave mine.

Audria hums and I imagine she's mentally shoving me from the booth. "By all means. I believe she's yours now."

"Yeah." That panty-melting smirk makes an appearance as he offers me his hand. "She is."

That's all for Rayne and Seth. I hope you enjoyed their short little tale.

I'm Calling Dibs is a peek at a new set of characters that are all getting full-length standalone novels from me.

Up first is Audria in LHL (full title to be revealed soon). This small-town romance is expected to release February 2021. You can add this book on Goodreads here https://shor.by/LHLTBR

also by
HARLOE RAE

Reclusive Standalones

Redefining Us

Forget You Not

#BitterSweetHeat Standalones

Gent

Miss

Lass

Silo Springs Standalones

Breaker

Keeper

Loner

Total Standalones

Watch Me Follow

Ask Me Why

Left for Wild

about the author

Harloe Rae is a *USA Today* & Amazon Top 10 best-selling author. Her passion for writing and reading has taken on a whole new meaning. Each day is an unforgettable adventure.

She's a Minnesota gal with a serious addiction to romance. There's nothing quite like an epic happily ever after. When she's not buried in the writing cave, Harloe can be found hanging with her hubby and son. If the weather permits, she loves being lakeside or out in the country with her horses.

Harloe is the author of the Reclusive series, Watch Me Follow, the #BitterSweetHeat series, Ask Me Why, the Silo Springs series, and *Left For Wild*. These titles are available on Amazon.

Stay in the know by subscribing to her newsletter at
bit.ly/HarloesList

Join her reader group, Harloe's Hotties, at
www.facebook.com/groups/harloehotties

Check out her site at www.harloe-rae.blog

Follow her on:
BookBub: http://bit.ly/HarloeBB
Amazon: http://bit.ly/HarloeOnAmazon
Goodreads: http://bit.ly/HarloeOnGR
Facebook Page: Facebook.com/authorharloerae
Instagram: www.instagram.com/harloerae

you walked in

TIA LOUISE

chapter one

"Mims Watson is a two-faced, backstabbing bitch." My cousin Joslyn steps over a discarded tire making her way to a pile of twisted scrap metal.

"Wow. Harsh words."

"Trust me, Daisy Sales." She balances on the fat rubber tire. "She'll smile and act like she's so nice, but don't turn your back on her."

I walk over to a shed with a stack of old wooden signs leaning against it. "I'm pretty sure Mims Watson doesn't even know I'm alive."

Last month, I came to live with my aunt Regina in Fireside and her only daughter Joselyn, who we all call "Sly." Aunt Regina is my dad's younger sister, which makes Sly my first cousin, and it's the second Sunday in a row she's dragged me to the junk pile behind Owen Pepper's taxidermy shop.

She's searching for metal objects she can use to form the base of a giant flower sculpture she's building for the homecoming dance on Friday. My cousin wants to be a superstar florist and live in Manhattan or Las Vegas… or New Orleans.

I didn't even know you could make a career out of something like that.

"She knows. She's like one of those creepy androids, and Stephanie is her spy drone."

"I can't think of a reason she'd ever be interested in me." I slowly pull the signs towards me, one by one.

My dad said as long as we're sifting through old junk, I might as well see if I could find anything he might be able to sell in his antiques store in Greenville.

"Either way, it's important to know the mean girls." Sly tries to lift one of the pieces of cast iron before letting it drop with a grunt, then she straightens, scanning the driveway with a frown. "Where is he?"

"Where's who?" I snap a photo of a sign with gold lettering that reads, *Please Wash Your Hands Before Returning to Work*, and text it to my dad.

"Finally." Her hands drop from her hips as an old, red Chevy step-side pickup truck pulls into the driveway. "Oh, yay!"

She takes off in the direction of the truck, and I when I see who she's waiting for, my stomach jumps to my throat. I tug on the strap of my denim overalls and try to smooth the flyaway hairs around my face.

"Hey, girl. I brought a surprise." Scout Dunne hops out of the passenger's side of the car, leaning down to return my cousin's hug.

My hands get sweaty, and my fingers tremble on the phone—which is *so dumb*. I'm not looking for a boyfriend in Fireside. I'm especially not looking for the quarterback for the high school football team—as if he'd even be looking at me. Guys like Scout Dunne only date head cheerleaders. Or supermodels.

"I didn't know you were in town!" Sly bounces on her toes, holding the arm of another guy, who looks college-aged. "We'll get this done in no time. Daisy, have you met Scout's brother John?"

"John?" Scout's nose wrinkles, and when he grins, a deep dimple in his cheek appears. "Try JR."

That grin is still on his lips when his blue eyes land on mine, sending a bolt of lightning through my stomach.

"How do you do?" My voice breaks awkwardly as I nod at JR, doing my best to smile and not seem like a weirdo.

JR's ice blue eyes study me, and he gives me a brief smile. He's a little darker than Scout, but there's no denying they're brothers. They're just about the hottest guys I've ever seen in my life.

"I'm alright," he says. "What are we doing?"

"Just… Looking for hidden gems." I push the oversized, horn-rimmed glasses higher on my nose and shove a lock of stick straight blonde hair behind my ear. "One man's trash is another man's treasure."

"Okay." He shrugs and turns to my cousin. "What are you doing?"

"Come on." She catches his arm and drags him off towards the pile of scrap.

Scout looks after them, hesitating before walking over to where I'm digging through junk. His hands are in the pockets of his faded jeans, and my heart beats faster with every step he takes.

What is wrong with me? I'm not "boy crazy," as my dad would say. Nor am I looking to form any attachments to this Podunk little town.

I'm only here because after twenty years of marriage, my mother decided she'd had enough of the antiques-dealing life and walked out on my dad and me.

I tried to believe she'd come back for me like she said she would, but as one month turned into two, it became clearer she was done with both of us.

First, she said her apartment wasn't big enough, then she lost her waitressing job. Six months ago, we stopped hearing from her altogether.

Dad said I should move in with Aunt Regina and finish my senior year here with Sly. We'd played together as kids, and we used to text each other all the time. Aunt Regina told my dad I'd get the love and support I need here with her and her daughter.

Pushing the glasses up on my head, I go to the next pile of junk, thumbing through it on the chance I might find something of value.

"Daisy, right?" Scout's sunny voice is at my side.

He puts his hands on his hips, and the maroon tee he's wearing stretches tight across his chest. Lines of muscle run down his arms, and my throat goes dry. I can't help wondering how it's possible for him to look like that—like he stepped out of a superhero comic.

"That's my name. Don't wear it out." I try for casual, but I sound like a dork.

He grins, looking down at me. His blond hair hangs around his face a little too long, and his blue eyes remind me of the ocean. He's also ridiculously tall, at least six foot two, and the sun shines behind his head, creating a glow.

I should take a photo of him, because it might be valuable one day.

"You probably don't remember this, but we met when you visited Sly ten years ago."

"Ten years ago." I frown, like I'm doing math in my head. "When I was seven?"

"Yeah." He laughs, like he can do math, too.

This guy.

My eyebrow arches. "What were we doing ten years ago?"

"Sly had a birthday party with Shetland ponies. Remember? You were scared because that brown one tried to bite you?"

"Oh yes! I do remember that." My brows rise. "Shetland ponies are known for being headstrong and temperamental, especially if they aren't used to children."

He chuckles, and his blue eyes twinkle. I look away, refusing to be pulled in by his charm. I have a plan—I'm getting my high school diploma, and I'm getting out of here.

"You were scared. It's okay."

"I wasn't scared." I'm totally lying. I've never been a fan of horses. I always feel like they're too big and unpredictable, and Shetland ponies are ornery little assholes. "Horses have brains the size of walnuts."

I return to my quest for hidden gems, doing my best to discourage any more of this conversation. It's no use.

"Whistle Britches." Scout scratches his eyebrow with his thumb. "That little shit. I'm pretty sure he bit me the week before. Left a bruise on my shoulder the size of a quarter."

"So the Shetland pony is smarter than you?" I cut my eyes up at him.

A sly grin curls his lips, and he gives me a hot look, as if *I'm* the hidden gem in this junkyard. It makes me super uncomfortable.

"Oh, you're funny." He points a finger at me.

"I'm not so funny."

"Yeah, you are. You're cute, too. You know that?"

"I am not."

I'm very clear-eyed about my looks. I'm skinny with stick straight blonde hair. I use the oversized glasses to be interesting, but a teacher once told me I had an insolent nose. I'm still not sure what that means, but it's *not* cute.

"Hey," JR's sharp voice cuts through our conversation. "I said I'd help, not do all the work."

He stomps past carrying several pieces of cast iron, his biceps bulging nicely.

"I'm coming." Scout winks at me, and heat flushes through my midsection. "I'll see you around, Daisy Sales."

With that he jogs off to where Sly stands holding a crowbar in the middle of a pile of empty paint cans in front of the broken fence. I've made it to the pile of junk that was here the last time my cousin dragged me to this place, and I'm ready to go home.

Shielding my eyes with my hand, I call to her. "Do you need my help with anything?"

Her shoulders drop, and she shakes her head. "None of this is light enough for you to carry. It's okay."

"I'm heading on back. I've got homework."

She waves and returns to separating the cast iron components. "I'll catch a ride with the guys."

Nodding, I walk with purpose to Sly's waiting Kia. Scout glances at me from where he's helping his brother collect the heavy pieces of iron. I pretend not to notice, but I pause in the driver's seat to watch the lines in his stomach when he lifts the metal onto his shoulder.

His tee rises, and those two lines drop into his jeans, forming that V that makes me forget what I'm doing.

I'm driving away is what I'm doing.

Fireside is not my home, and I have plans that do not involve befriending the senior class heartthrob, captain of the football team, starting quarterback.

I have never been that girl, and I'm not about to start now.

That's a recipe for trouble, and I don't do trouble.

I do work.

chapter two

Kansas state quarters...
Green glass hen dishes...
Pokemon cards...
Reclaimed iron roosters...

THE MASSIVE, HARDCOVER *MILLER'S ANTIQUES ENCYCLOPEDIA* IS OPEN on the table in front of me, and I'm taking photos with my phone of the items my dad listed. They all seem like things I should be able to find in Fireside.

It's Wednesday, and I retreated to the library as soon as school let out, partly to do the research for my dad and partly to hide. Nobody comes to the library anymore.

Scout Dunne has been saying hello to me in the halls, and it's turned me into some kind of curiosity... Which everyone knows *nobody* wants to be.

God, I wish he'd just leave me alone. It's like he knows my eyes have been rebelliously drawn to him every day since our exchange on Sunday. Sitting in the lunchroom, I'm thinking about my plans, leaving this shitty little town, opening my own antiques store, and next thing I realize, I'm staring at him sitting across the room at a tableful of jocks.

And it's like he's got radar or something. He instantly meets my eyes and gives me that cocky grin that almost makes me drop my tray.

Blinking away fast, I spear a tater tot with my fork and shove it in my mouth. I'm not hungry, and I can't eat with my insides all tight and tingly. Still, I force it down.

Glancing to my right, then my left, I catch Mims and Stephanie glaring at me like I'm a black cockroach on the porcelain throne of their celebrity at Fireside High.

"Bradley Scout, what in the world?" Ms. Alice, the ancient librarian, makes my heart stop.

Tell me he's not...

"Hey, Gran! How's it hanging?" Scout enters the library like a rockstar, and Ms. Alice holds out her arms for a hug.

He rushes forward and grabs her around the waist, lifting her off her feet and shaking her side to side, which makes her shriek and fuss.

"Put me down this instant! You'll break my back!" She slaps him on his broad shoulders, but he only laughs and hugs her more.

They're totally breaking the *silence in the library* rule, and I slide lower in my chair, hoping he doesn't notice me.

Too late. His eyes hit mine and he puts his grandmother down, walking to me. "Whatcha reading, Einstein?"

"Einstein was a physicist." I close the book.

"Antiques encyclopedia. Seriously?"

"He also had ADD. Are you saying I'm hyper-focused?"

"Absolutely." Blue eyes laser on mine, and it's like a small fish is flipping around in my stomach.

"I have never been diagnosed with a cognitive disorder."

He blinks at me, fighting a grin, then shakes his head.

"What?"

"Nothing."

"You're shaking your head. Why?"

"You don't care."

My lips tighten. I'm annoyed I really *do* care what he thinks. "If you have something to say, you'd better say it."

"You are too damn cute."

Ugh. Blowing air through my lips, I collect my things, shoving my phone in my backpack and flipping it onto my shoulder.

"Why does that make you mad?" He jogs alongside me, and just when we reach the door, Mims and Stephanie burst through.

They're like twins dressed in shredded jeans and crop tops that show off their midriffs.

"Scout!" Mims does a little shriek, flipping her glossy brown hair over her shoulder. "We were just coming to find you!"

He pulls up short. "Hey, sorry, Mims, I was just—"

She doesn't stop. "Stephanie said you still don't have a date to homecoming. That's impossible!"

I walk faster, leaving them inside the door and doing my best not to care about their topic of conversation.

Who cares if he has a date or not. I have no intention of getting involved in school social events. I am only passing through.

I'm halfway down the block when he catches up to me. "Damn, girl, you sure walk fast."

"Why are you following me?" I look back to where Mims and Stephanie are standing outside the library with their arms crossed, slaughtering me with their eyes. "Don't you have things to do?"

"What's that supposed to mean?"

"You're the captain of the football team, starting quarterback. Aren't you supposed to add Homecoming King to the list?"

"Oh, that." He grimaces, shoving his hands in his pockets as he walks beside me.

Several moments pass, and he doesn't say more.

Fireside is so small, there's only one traffic light in town, and my aunt's bed and breakfast-slash-home is one block past it. We're almost there when I stop, turning to face him.

"Yeah, that." My arms are crossed over my chest.

By contrast to the VSCO girls we left behind, I'm in an oversized sweatshirt and black leggings. My glasses are in place, and my backpack is on my shoulder. My straight blonde hair is twisted into a messy bun on top of my head.

"We haven't won a game this season." He grins, not seeming damaged by this confession. "My brother was always the quarterback. I can just catch whatever he throws."

My lips twist, and I think about this. "I don't know much about football. Still… it seems like you'd put players where they're best."

"After JR graduated, we didn't have a quarterback. Coach figured the guys listen to me, and I've been playing the longest."

"But you don't want to do it?"

He shrugs, looking up the street. "I don't know. I mean, I love to play, but football's not my life."

"It's not?" My chin pulls back. "You could've fooled me."

The muscle in his square jaw moves, and he thinks a minute before exhaling a laugh. "You really don't beat around the bush."

"I'm just saying how it looks. You sit with the players at lunch, you wear your jersey to school…"

I don't mention how I saw him sleeping on a school bench with a football under his head once. Hell, I'm surprised he's not carrying a ball with him now.

"All that's expected if you're on the team. Like how the cheerleaders wear their uniforms on Fridays."

"I thought they did that to show off their butts."

He exhales a laugh again, shaking his head. He does that a lot when we're together. It makes me wonder if anybody's ever really talked to him before.

"Anyway, I was thinking… We're friends, right?"

"Are we?"

"I mean, sure. We see each other all the time. We've known each other since we were kids."

I'm not sure attending a birthday party ten years ago counts, but I decide to let it go. My curiosity is at an all-time high. It doesn't hurt he's pretty to look at.

"Okay." We start walking slowly towards the BnB. "What's on your mind?"

"I feel like if I ask one of those girls to the dance, the old ladies will have us married and start knitting baby blankets before we graduate."

"Ugh, small towns and old ladies." I shake my head. I'm familiar with the phenomenon.

"Old church ladies."

"The worst of all."

He gives me a real smile, and that flippy little fish is back. It makes me smile.

"I don't believe it." He winks at me. "Is that a smile from frowny Daisy?"

"I am not frowny!"

"You have not smiled at me once since you moved here. When I see you in school, you don't say hello. I was beginning to think you didn't like me."

"You just said we were friends!"

"I was friends. You were on the fence. Admit it."

He elbows my ribs, and I want to argue. He has no idea why I've been keeping him at arm's-length. We're at the house, and I stop at the front porch steps.

Aunt Regina's house is massive, red brick with dark wood accents and a wrap-around front porch decorated with rocking chairs and tables holding checker boards. It's a natural wind tunnel that catches the breezes.

The house is far too big for a widow and her teenage daughter—even with me here. It's why she rents rooms.

Turning to face him, I look up at where the sun is shining through his hair, making him look like a god. *Again*.

"I wasn't on the fence. I don't want to get too... *attached*." Chewing my lip, I glance to the side. "I'm not planning to stay in Fireside. I want to work in antiques, be a buyer. Anything that lets me travel, really."

"You should be on one of those TV shows."

"TV shows?" I can't get over this guy. "Have you seen me? Maybe I could do a podcast, but this is not a face you put on camera."

"You've got to stop that." His brow lowers.

A light breeze pushes past us, and my hair flies across my cheek. As if on cue, he reaches out and slides it off my face, tucking it behind my ear.

Clearing my throat, I take a step back, scratching my nails over the place he just touched as if to erase the sparkles he left behind.

"So what's this all about?"

"Go with me to the homecoming dance."

"No."

"What?" He huffs a laugh. "Why not?"

"I can't think of a worse idea."

"What's so bad about it? I think it's perfect. You don't want to be tied down, neither do I. We should have each other's backs this year. Whenever an event arises, we can sort-of… you know, protect each other."

"I don't have any events." Shaking my head, I walk up the first step towards Aunt Regina's front door. "I wasn't even planning to go to homecoming!"

Reaching out, he catches my arm. It puts us eye to eye. His are earnest, and I struggle to hold his gaze.

"You're right. You don't need a wingman, but I do." He exhales, glancing down. "Will you help me, Daisy? As my friend?"

Blinking fast, I look away. It's too much, and in that moment, it hits me. I'll never say no to him. I'm not sure what that means.

"Why don't you just go with Mims or Stephanie and don't worry about what everybody says. Do what you want to do."

"That's not how it works around here, and you know it. Look at JR and Becky. I know for a fact he expected they'd break up after they started college, but she's still hanging on."

My nose wrinkles, and I think about this. "Sounds like you both need to get some backbone."

"Come on, Daisy. What's it going to hurt?" He smiles, and the squeeze in my chest tells me exactly what it'll hurt.

Me.

I will get attached.

"I don't have anything to wear." Thank God for small mercies. "And I don't have any money to buy anything. I can't ask Aunt Regina for a dress for a fake date…"

"Hey, guys!" Sly skips up beside us. "What's up?"

"Nothing—" I answer too fast, but Scout speaks on top of me.

"I just invited Daisy to homecoming—"

"What?" My cousin's shriek makes me wince. "You're shitting me. You're taking Daisy to Homecoming?"

Her eyes are so wide, and the smile on her face grows bigger by the second. "That's incredible… My cousin and Scout Dunne!"

"I said no." My voice is flat, and she glares at me like my head just spun around 360 degrees.

"She doesn't have a dress..." He supplies.

"Oh, hell, we'll get you a dress." Sly catches my arm in hers.

"I don't have any money, and I can't ask your mom—"

"I've got tons of dresses. We'll fix you up." Turning to Scout, she smiles and nods. "Daisy would be happy to go with you to the dance. We can double."

"Sounds great!" Scout backs away, pointing at me. "You're a pal. I won't ever forget it."

I won't ever forget it.

It's like the world has gone to a low hum. I feel trapped, and as Sly leads me into the house, bouncing up the steps, I exhale a slow breath. This feels like the start of something incredibly dangerous. It's incredibly terrifying.

We're in Sly's room, and she's deep in her walk-in closet, dragging out garment bags of dresses as she goes on about how she wants to do my hair and makeup.

I stand in front of her mirror studying my black leggings. The oversized sweatshirt two sizes too big, and my straight hair piled on top of my head.

"Let me cut your hair."

"My hair!" I hold the sides of my head as she whips my bun off my head.

"Nothing crazy. Just a cute little bob. Trust me, it'll be so adorable. And I'll do your makeup. Very natural with a glossy pink lip."

"It's too much, Sly."

"Are you kidding me?" She steps beside me squeezing my shoulders with both of her hands and pressing her cheeks to mine. "You're going to homecoming with Scout Dunne."

My heart beats faster...

I know exactly what she means. My entire life is about to change.

chapter three

"JUST ONE MORE..." SLY THREADS THE LAST, OVERSIZED DAISY INTO a tiny clip at the top of my head. She steps back, exhaling happily. "You're perfect."

I turn to the mirror, and my stomach twists when I see my reflection.

The strapless, butter-yellow satin dress she loaned me stops mid-thigh, and the way it cinches at the waist and then flares to the hem actually makes me appear to have a waist.

"I can't believe it." Reaching up, I touch the pin curls around my ears.

She cut my hair and styled it so it hangs at the nape of my neck, and she's threaded white daisies around the top of my head so it looks like I'm wearing a flowered headband. Leave it to my florist cousin to decorate me with my namesake flower.

"You are so adorable!" She's practically bouncing on her toes, and I feel like I'm going to be sick.

Still, I can't argue with her. I look like something out of a teen magazine. *Fresh and Flirty!* I can imagine the headline would say.

"You look great, too." I'm quiet, nervous.

Sly is far more confident in her sage blue dress with the hemline of cute little ruffles. Her auburn hair is woven in a super-loose, fat braid over her shoulder with corn flowers threaded in the rippling strands. Going to her vanity, she lifts two plastic containers with small boutonnieres in them. Scout's has daisies wrapped around a single bud, and her date Henry's is one blue rose that matches her dress perfectly.

"You're so good at this." I take the bud hoping I don't stab my date while pinning it on his coat.

"I watched a show once where they made entire couture gowns

out of nothing but flowers." She runs her fingers along the front of her hair. "Can you imagine?"

"No."

"Sly? The boys are here." Aunt Regina's voice echoes up the stairs, and my cousin's eyes light.

"Scout is going to die when he sees you."

My stomach twists, and my heart beats faster. I've never liked being the center of attention, and I know I'm not ready for it now.

"I hope his response is not *that* extreme." I wonder if she can hear the waver in my voice.

She exhales a squeal and hops over to give me a hug. "You're Cinderella. It's going to be a night you'll never forget."

Clasping my hand, she drags me to the door, but I hang back as she trots expertly down the stairs in heels. I watch as she puts her hand on Henry's chest and kisses his cheek.

A night I'll never forget?

My heels click as I slowly descend the stairs, gripping the bannister so I don't get hooked and fall. I don't see Scout, and anticipation rises with every step.

Ever since he trapped me into this arrangement, he's been carrying my books around, waiting for me after classes… basically acting like he's my boyfriend, which is so not true.

Mims has been cutting death glares at me every time we pass in the hall, but I ignore her. It's not like this is real, no matter how excited my cousin is.

It's all pretend.

I'm *not* Cinderella.

Reciting these words in my head calms my breathing. It puts distance between me and this force pushing against my chest. It helps me focus on the future and not this very night.

Until I reach the second to last step and Scout steps into my sight.

He's wearing a classic black tux, and one hand is in his pocket. His hair has been trimmed so it's shorter in the back, longer on top, and it's styled in a messy way. When he cuts his gaze at me from under his brow, his blue eyes flare, and all my nerves rush to the surface.

He's straight out of a movie or one of those posters in the Abercrombie store.

He's so sexy.

Fake or not, my entire body lights.

"You're beautiful." His voice is uncharacteristically serious, and he lifts my hand, slipping a wrist corsage made up of a cluster of white daisies to match my hair.

A high-pitched squeal from across the room reminds me Sly and Henry are waiting. Aunt Regina has her phone on us, and she's shooting pictures of me and her daughter and our dates. My eyes return to Scout's, and I hold up the flower for his tux.

"I'm not sure I can do this." My fingers tremble, and I can barely remove the pin.

"Let me see." He takes it out and tucks it in the buttonhole of his jacket then pins it from behind. "There."

"One more photo..." Aunt Regina lines us all up and takes three more pictures until my cousin drags us out the door.

"I can't wait for everyone to see you." Sly looks back at me from the front seat of Henry's SUV.

Scout and I are on the second row, and I smile, feeling super self-conscious. Then he reaches over to take my hand, lacing our fingers.

"I like what you did with your hair. It's cute."

"Sly did it."

He grins, and the little fish flipping in my stomach moves lower as his finger slides lightly across my knuckles.

It's two right turns and a left to the high school, and it feels like the time moves too fast. I'm not ready for everyone to see me in this dress with my hair in flowers holding the hand of the sexiest guy I've ever seen.

"See you inside!" Sly grins mischievously, pulling Henry's arm. "I'm beating you two through the door. This entrance is going to be bigger than my palmetto sculpture."

Sly's floral arrangement is an oversized palmetto with palm flowers, hibiscus, and other tropical flowers to represent our state, and *The palm is sacred*, which Fireside's town motto, which is weird AF. Regardless, *it* is breathtaking... Unlike me and Scout at this dance together.

Scout helps me out of the backseat, lifting me by the waist and lowering me as if I weigh nothing. My feet touch the asphalt drive, and my heels wobble.

I grasp his arm, inhaling sharply. "Whoa."

"You okay?" His voice is a warm breath across my shoulders, which are completely exposed by my short hair.

It's tingling electricity, and I nod, blinking fast. "Not used to these heels."

His expression is not his usual megawatt grin. It's darker, more focused. I can't tell, but it seems like he's picking up on this new thing between us, this vibration that is decidedly not fake.

With an *Ugh!* exhalation, I push past him and start towards the gym.

Smart, focused, intentional—these are adjectives that describe me. Not boy crazy, ditzy, or infatuated. Sly put these ideas in my head... and the whole school acting like we're the hottest gossip since that lunch lady got caught in the janitor's closet with the lacrosse coach.

Now *that* was juicy.

It was also last spring.

"Hey, what's wrong?" Scout catches up with me, running his fingers down the inside of my arm gently.

He pulls me to a stop, and I look up at him, painfully gorgeous. "This is supposed to be fake, right?"

His brow tightens, and he hesitates. "Why are you saying that? I told you this was just friends."

"I don't know." Shaking my head, I look down. "Everybody's just so... invested. I wasn't ready for it."

"So you get it now." He steps back, crossing his arms. "You're feeling the pressure. No more 'you need to grow a backbone' or whatever bullshit."

He seems really pissed by that, and I feel guilty. "I shouldn't have said that. I'm sorry."

This force feels like the time I swam in the ocean and got caught in a current. The water swirled around me, and no matter how hard I fought, it pulled me where it wanted.

But is this feeling my fellow classmates, or is it him?

I can't think that way.

Slipping my hand into the crook of his arm, I force a smile. I'm strong. I'm not letting them get me down.

"We can do this. Let's go."

chapter four

His hands are on my waist, and we're swaying side to side on the dance floor.

Scout smells like soap and shave cream and something deeper, spicier, and I do my best to fight getting lost in his scent. I do my best not to close my eyes and rest my cheek against his broad shoulder and dream of what it would be like if this were real, if we left the dance and took his truck down to the beach. If we climbed in the back and made out, tongues sliding together, his knee moving between my legs, parting my thighs…

The band is playing something slow, instrumental, but it feels like a sex song. It feels like what I imagine his fingers would do if they slid under my dress, rising higher, raising sparkles of sensation as they reached my center, slipping beneath my panties, lightly touching my clit.

"Want something to drink?" His lips graze my ear, and I involuntarily shiver. It makes him grin. "Sorry."

I step back quickly, banishing those hot, sexy thoughts from my mind. Still, I'm flushed all over. At least in the party lights, I can hope he doesn't notice.

Clearing my throat, I shake my head. "Ticklish."

"Want something to drink?" He's watching me.

"Yeah, I'll meet you back here." Nodding towards the bleachers, I do my best to act like his friend, the smart, bookish antiques scout. "Bathroom."

He gives me that signature wink and heads towards the concessions stand. I hurry to the bathroom.

Standing in front of the mirror, I wash my hands, waiting for the water to get super cold. As soon as it's icy, I take my cold fingers and press them to the back of my neck. I do it again, waiting for the heat to subside. I'm not losing my way in all of this.

I took care of the dampness between my thighs, and I'm determined to keep my thoughts focused. This is a game. We're guarding each other's backs. "We're like those levees along the Mississippi River," I say to myself softly. "We're holding back the water."

"What water are you talking about?" Mims steps around the corner, narrowing her brown eyes at me.

Paradoxically, her snakelike appearance flips a switch inside me. This girl thinks she's going to intimidate me. She's got another thing coming.

"We're in the bathroom, Mims. What do you think?"

"The toilet? You talking about toilet water?" Mims narrows her eyes and steps closer. "What about it?"

"I wasn't talking about toilet water, I was talking about the ocean." A devilish thought occurs to me. "Scout and I love the ocean… all salty and slippery."

Her eyes flare, but she quickly grabs the reins. "You listen to me, Daisy Sales."

"I'm all ears, *Jemima*." I happen to remember from visiting here at seven, Mims was Sticky Syrup Panties to all the kids.

I don't know the story, since I wasn't a part of it, but I can tell she does by the way blue fire sparks in her eyes.

"How *dare* you?" she hisses. "You're messing with the wrong girl, Daisy Sales."

"What do you want?" My voice is calm, icy even. "Tell me and get out of my face."

Her brown eyes run up and down my body, lingering on the curls at my ears and the daisies around my head. "He's only into you because you're new."

For a moment, I consider correcting her. I'm not new. If I were, I wouldn't know about Jemima, and Scout and I wouldn't have been friends "for ten years," as he likes to say.

Instead, I decide to hit the devil head-on. "Or…" I step closer, looking down my nose at my nemesis, and feeling equally devilish. "He's into me because I'm a *bad* girl. Haven't you heard?"

Stephanie's eyes widen, and she clutches her Queen Bee's arm. "Let's go."

Mims knows she's lost this one, but I can see she's not happy about it. "We should get back to our dates." Then she steps to me once more. "This isn't over."

I don't blink. I don't move a muscle. I'm a stone-cold bitch staring down the meanest girl at school. Finally, she steps back and walks out the bathroom door, not looking back.

Letting out the breath I've been holding, I collapse against the wall with a sigh. Nobody knows. Nobody saw. Still, I know this is the start of a shitty year. Even if I have Scout watching my back, there's no escaping those two.

chapter five

MY BROTHER SAID IF YOU WANT SOMETHING, YOU HAVE TO GO FOR it. No holding back, no second guessing. Second-guessing is the killer of dreams, he'd say.

Daisy Sales is the thing that makes me second-guess everything, and I don't know what to do about it.

Swaying side to side with her small body in my arms, I lower my nose to inhale her scent of coconut and gardenia. She smells like a warm fire mixed with a day at the beach. *Perfect.*

"What do you want to do that takes you so far from home?" She tilts her pixie head and blinks those round blue eyes up at me.

With the daisies in her hair and the golden curls around her cheeks, she's like some kind of fairy. She's a sexy Tinkerbell taunting me.

That is not why I asked her to be my wingman... Wing woman?

Daisy is not supposed to show interest in me. She's smart and focused and nothing like the girls at our school, or the girls who chase me. Daisy will keep me focused on my dreams—like she's focused on hers.

At least, that's what I thought.

"Oh, you know." Clearing my throat, I look away from her, not wanting to tell her the pie in the sky dream I have.

Guidance counselors said kids who dreamed of starting rock bands or becoming movie stars or famous novelists didn't have a clear sense of reality. She gave us this whole long speech about how those kids had self-inflated notions of importance. Those kids thought they were somchow better than everybody else. *Special.*

We were encouraged to find sensible careers like auto mechanics or welding.

She never even considered the possibility that acting made me happy. That when I'd be in those school plays, I felt like I was ten miles high. I felt like I was taking the best adventure of all time.

I was getting to live another life, be another person. Not in a weird, creepy way, but in a fun way, like wearing a costume. And when the audience laughed at my lines or cried or cheered... Hell, it just didn't get any better than that.

Did that make me a disillusioned dreamer?

It actually makes me really insecure.

I'm pretty much guaranteed a win if I stick with football. Hell, I really like football—when I'm playing with my brother, catching his passes and running them into the end zone for a touchdown.

Otherwise, it's just a game.

Acting is next level.

"Have you decided?" Daisy watches me, that smart smile curling her pouty pink lips.

Her lips really make me want to kiss her.

Which would be a huge mistake.

"Decided what?"

"If you're going to tell me what makes you want to leave Fireside, when everybody here treats you like you hung the moon."

Lifting my chin, I look out across the gym. Can I tell her? I've never told anybody. I've been too afraid people would laugh at me... or worse, tell me I couldn't do it. Tell me I was selfish. Tell me I was stupid.

My eyes lower to hers, and I know the truth. Daisy Sales is special.

"I want to be an actor." My voice is just louder than the music.

We sway a few beats, and her eyebrows lift. She doesn't immediately laugh or tell me to shut up, which is encouraging.

"An actor." She pushes out her bottom lip and nods.

I really like how she's thinking about it as if it could actually happen.

"When you say actor, do you mean like Broadway or—"

"Hollywood. I want to move to LA after graduation and see what happens."

"Wow." She lifts her chin, then nods slowly. "You've definitely got the looks."

"You think so?"

Her eyes narrow, and it's the first time since the start of our conversation she's given me a look like I'm a dumbass.

"Don't act like you don't know how you look."

"Okay," I exhale a laugh. "I know I'm good enough for girls in Fireside. That doesn't mean I've got what it takes for Hollywood."

"You've got what it takes."

We keep swaying, and a warm sense of satisfaction moves across my chest. She believes in me. She's the first person I've told the truth, and she didn't laugh in my face.

She pretty much did the exact opposite.

My shoulders straighten, and I stand a little taller. Tightening my embrace, I look down into her violet blue eyes. "And you want to be an antiques dealer?"

"A buyer. Dealers have stores. I want to be the one out there scouting, finding the unexpected, priceless items hidden in the junk yard."

"Have you got a good eye?"

She grins at me. "The best." Then she gives me a wink, something I've never seen her do with any guy as long as she's been in Fireside.

Trust me, I've been watching.

"I know a winner when I see one." Her voice is so calm, so confident.

I believe her.

Henry drops Sly and Daisy at Ms. Regina's bed and breakfast by midnight, which Sly said is their curfew. We danced most of the night. I was named Homecoming King, no surprise there, and even less surprising, Mims Watson was Homecoming Queen.

We had to do one dance together, which thankfully was short. Mims is like one of those remoras you see hanging off the side of sharks. She latches on, and you can't get her off.

She kept going on about how perfect we were together, and wouldn't our parents be proud if we hooked up or whatever. I didn't even bother to remind her my mom's dead, and Dad hasn't seemed to care about JR or me since.

Henry walks Sly to the door, and I know he's dying to kiss her. She still thinks of him as a friend, but Henry is head over ass for her.

The hazards of living in a small town. We've all known each other since preschool. It's hard to forget Henry used to eat playdough.

Daisy's hand is in mine, and she hangs back, watching her cousin with wide eyes before turning to me and whispering at my chest. "How far are we taking this?"

Shit, I want to take it all the way. Still…

"As far as you're comfortable."

Lifting her chin, she blinks up at me and smiles. "You're not what I expected, Scout Dunne. You're really not."

"You're exactly what I expected." I grin, and she pushes my arm.

"Rude!"

Laughing, I catch her by the waist, pulling her body against mine again. "I meant it in a good way. You're just as smart and thoughtful as I knew."

Her lips twist and she looks down. "Sorry. That's really nice."

"I said before you were cute, but that wasn't right." Her head snaps up, and I huff a laugh. "I was going to say you're really pretty. You're beautiful."

She shoves my chest then, shaking her head and stepping back. "You don't have to flirt with me. We've already agreed to this."

I stand back, watching her go to the porch steps. What have I agreed to, exactly? And how do I change it? Do I want to change it?

Shit. My head's getting all mixed up.

"I'd better go."

She nods, but I can't let it end this way. Closing the space between us, I catch her arms. She stops, but her eyes don't meet mine. Little bumps of gooseflesh cover her skin, and her cheeks fill with color. She does that a lot, I've noticed.

"Goodnight, then." Her voice is soft.

Glancing over at Sims, I know it's now or never. "They're probably expecting us to kiss."

Daisy's eyes go wide. "We're supposed to be friends."

"They don't know that." My eyes are on her full, dewy lips, and I step closer. My body is so close to hers, I can feel the heat of her skin. I can feel the brush of her breasts at my chest as she breathes fast.

We're on dangerous ground, and I can't seem to stop. "We can be friends." I lean down, getting closer. "Friends who do this."

Capturing her lips with mine, I spread them apart. I pull her tongue into my mouth, stroking it with mine, curling and tasting her sweetness like I want to do between her legs.

I wonder what Daisy Sales would sound like when she comes, and my dick hardens.

Her fingers tighten on my coat. Her body in my arms is pliant. She's like a coconut-vanilla, soft and juicy treat, and I want more.

I want all of her.

Lifting my head, I look into her eyes. They blink open slowly, and she's breathing so fast, she puts a hand on her chest.

"Oh." It's all she says before shaking her head. "I don't think we should do that… or we might not be friends anymore."

That makes me grin. "No?"

Her eyes finally meet mine, and instead of girlish and flustered, the smart-girl is back. Daisy arches an eyebrow at me and shakes her head.

"I don't know, Scout Dunne. But I think you're going to be bad at being friends with me."

Clasping her chin between my thumb and my forefinger, I lean down to kiss that insolent nose. "I think you're going to be bad for all my plans, and it's going to rock."

Her lips press into a smile, and she turns, walking slowly up the stairs to her aunt's front porch. That dress sways over her ass, and I'm pretty sure she adds a little extra hip-shake for my benefit.

I'm tempted to catcall, but I don't want to wake the neighborhood.

When she gets to the door, she does a little finger wave before disappearing inside, and I know. This year is going to be way more than I ever bargained for….

Thanks so much for reading Scout and Daisy's introductory short story!
Their full-length romance**,** ***TWIST OF FATE***, is coming **Feb. 15** to Kindle Unlimited.

Read JR's romance ***THIS MUCH IS TRUE (link)***, Out Now…
JR is a grumpy single dad on a mission of revenge, until he meets a girl he can't leave behind.
Available now in Kindle Unlimited and on Audiobook!

Never Miss a New Release by me!
Sign up for my newsletter or get a text alert when it's live by texting TIALOUISE to 64600 now!*
(*Text service is U.S. only.)

bridge of love

NANA MALONE

chapter one

Bridge

"MATE, WOULD YOU HOLD UP?"

I knew what was coming. I'd taken steps to avoid it, but I hadn't been quick enough.

One of my best mates was going to ask for the one favor I couldn't give. To look out for his little sister over the holiday. Sadly I was the only choice. I was the only one going home for the holiday. Our other mates were off on family holidays.

I loved Toby. Best mate a bloke could ask for. But this favor…just no. It couldn't be done. For starters, Emma was a giant pain in the arse. And everyone knew it. She was just on the cusp of wild child and I knew for a fact she was a handful. Secondly, she had daddy issues, which meant she wanted to take them out on every bloke who dared look at her cross-eyed. And third…perhaps the most pressing issue of all…

I wanted her.

More than I'd probably ever wanted anything in my life. Henceforth why me anywhere near her was a terrible idea. Toby was looking for someone upstanding to look out for her…that wasn't me.

"Sorry mate, I've got to catch the train home."

Unlike the rest of my classmates, I didn't have a parent who was here to pick me up at Eaton. Toby was staying for the holiday, because he had a project going that he needed to keep an eye on.

He'd tried to explain it to me but once the science nerd part of him came out, I stopped listening.

Toby was the kind of mate that everyone needed. Affable, kind at the core, I'd never met anyone like him. "Tobs, you have that look on your face. I've got to go, I'll miss my train. Ben's car is giving me a lift to the station."

He frowned then. "You're not going home with Ben?"

"They offered to drive me, but for them to go all the way East, with traffic, you know how it is. Besides they have a late flight to catch to St. something or other."

Toby frowned. He did know how it was. Neither one of us particularly liked taking charity from our mates. It was almost better to be left to it than to be driven all the way back to London in a Rolls Royce, knowing full well that our fathers could provide but chose not to.

"Yeah mate, I get it. Okay look, it's just a small favor. Why do you have that look on your face?"

All around us in the cobblestones and stone parapets of Eton, stood hundreds of years of tradition and power, all contained in these walls. A sea of gray and navy blue floated around as students hustled to head home for the holiday. There were a few students who changed into their street clothes before going home. But even those were versions of the Eton uniform.

Suit. Trousers. A watch that would have fed my family for months.

I rolled my eyes. *Money.*

I hadn't changed, simply because it would have required more time. I just wanted out of the prison. I just was in a hurry to put distance between the place that promised me a future with strings and my past.

Also, I wasn't too eager to stick around on the off chance my father *did* show, which was extremely unlikely. But still he'd come before. And it hadn't been pleasant. I knew Toby was going to stand there until I gave in, so I sped up the process. "What do you need mate?"

His grin flashed, warming up his dark eyes. "It's not so bad. Will you chill? I only need you to keep an eye on Ems for one night."

She was possibly the hottest girl I had ever seen in my life. All dark hair, honey brown skin, melting topaz eyes that looked like a banked fire. The kind of things that give you months of dreams that you shouldn't have about your best mate's sister.

He continued pushing me into agreeing. "Look, I wouldn't ask, but I'm not going home. She's supposed to go to some concert. Some hip-hopper, pop star or whatever. I have a ticket. Would you just go keep an eye on her and keep her out of trouble? She's got some new friends, and I don't know what they're like. She's been looking forward to this. And I was supposed to go with her. If you could just do me this favor, I'd be a mate for life."

I shook my head. "Toby, no. Your sister, she's trouble. Pure fucking mischief. Do you remember that last time, the one where I stayed with you? She'd gotten into her mum's knickers with that friend of hers, what was her name again?"

Toby sighed. "Katy. You see why I'm worried? She's heading off to this concert with Katy. Come on, mate. I wouldn't ask. I was supposed to go and keep an eye on them. And now that I'm staying here, I can't. So please be a mate."

What else could I say? I couldn't say, 'Mate, every time I'm near your sister, I keep picturing sliding my tongue into her mouth, and feeling her far-too-big-tits-for-such-a-skinny-little thing and making her purr my name.'

Nope, those were not things you said to your best mate.

Behind us, I could hear Ben's low mumble. "What's the hold up princess?"

I rolled my eyes. "Me and you, who's the princess?"

Ben grinned then. *Ben Covington*, the fair-haired Viking, except more English than the lot of us. He was all bleached blond waves, broad smile, big shoulders. I was as tall as he was, but I was leaner. And I was the dark-haired devil to his sun-licked Viking. But he was another one of my best mates. And off the rear, came East Hale. Broad smile, laptop bag strapped over his shoulder, clutching on to it like it was his passport to the good life. "What the fuck is the hold up mate?"

I rolled my eyes. "Nothing's the hold up. Time to go."

But Toby wasn't letting me go that easily. "I'm just trying to get Bridge here to agree to do me a favor when he's at home."

East rolled his eyes, ribbing him gently. "Mate, I'm not sure why you like the dirty magazines, there's porn on the internet. It's free. You don't have to make Bridge buy them for you."

A flush crept over Toby's face even as he flipped East off. East, the twat, just grinned. He may have been all geeked out, but somehow he managed to give a lad's lad vibe to him. And he was actually all right. I'd never really expected to like him that much. But these three, and Drew Wilcox, they were my best mates.

The one that stuck around when the shit went haywire. Drew had already left for home. He had also offered to drive me, but again, I didn't like handouts. And his father had actually come to pick him up. So the last thing I needed was all sorts of questions on where my father was and what our family was doing for the holiday and if I was going to be at a ball or a gala or a society function. Questions that he already knew the answers to. My father was a friend of his. Why doesn't he just ask the old man?

Nope, better to avoid questions. Better to avoid too many entanglements.

Unfortunately, no one told Toby this.

"I'm just taking a shot at Bridge here to agree to look out for Emma at the concert."

East perked up. "I could go to the concert."

Toby shook his head. "No, you are not to touch my fucking sister."

East held his hands up. "Mate, I'm wounded. I wouldn't touch your sister."

This was a lie of course. Toby rolled his eyes. "Not with your hands. You'd use your mouth. No fucking way."

East just smirked, because as nerdy as he was, he'd research a hundred ways to make a girl come with nothing more than his mouth. It was worrisome to think about if you have a sister.

Ben shrugged. "I'll do it."

All three of us laughed then.

Toby rolled his eyes. "What, you? Pretty boy? No. When Emma was here last time, all she was talking about was how insanely pretty you are. Nope, you're not going anywhere near my sister."

Ben frowned. "I wouldn't touch her."

Toby's laugh was a low chuckle. "I'm not worried about *you* touching her. Emma would eat you alive. You're not ready for that. You're still a virgin."

Ben scowled at him.

"It's all right mate, it's true. But Bridge. Bridge can handle himself. And he is the least affected by anything out of all of us. Just do it." Toby begged.

"Why the fuck won't you just do it so we can just get on the road? I don't want to stay at school any longer than necessary." Ben growled.

The way they were watching me expectantly, I knew what I was going to have to say, and none of it was going to be appropriate. And whatever I'd say was going to piss Toby the fuck off. Normally, I didn't care about pissing people off, but this was Tobs. He never asks for anything as a general rule. So I was in no kind of mood.

"Fuck me. Fine. Text me the ticket info, but honest to fucking God, I'm not partying, I'm just getting her out of there and making sure she gets home all right, yeah?"

Toby nodded.

chapter two

Bridge

"YOU KNOW, SOONER OR LATER, HE'S GOING TO FIGURE IT OUT."

I slid my gaze over to Ben as we rolled toward the train station. "Figure what out?"

His chuckle was low, even as he rolled his eyes. "That you have the hots for Emma."

How the fuck did he know? My brow furrowed. "I don't have the hots for Emma. She's Toby's little sister. Nothing is going to happen there."

"Oh come on, you know Toby wouldn't be like that. You're his mate. He'd be happy if you're the one that goes out with Emma."

"Something tells me that that isn't true."

His grin flashed. "What, you would rather East date her?"

"If East puts his fucking hands on her, mate or no mate, I will kill him."

"Oh right, and you don't feel anything for her at all."

He has a point there, you wanker.

"It doesn't matter what I feel. Nothing's going to happen."

"Ugh, look. I saw it the last time we all went home when Toby was on holiday. It's only a matter of time till he sees it. All I'm saying is, it will be better if you tell him, than if he sees it for himself. Which, he will."

I was in no mood for rationality as the car lulled us back and forth. "Nah mate, I got it."

"If you say so, but it's written all over your face. Do you know what you're going to do when you see her?"

"Nothing. She's annoying. A total pain in the arse. Plus she's spoiled. A total princess who thinks the world revolves around her, or that it should, and sorry, but I don't deal with princesses."

"Right. You don't deal with princesses. Mate, this whole taking to the train station thing, it's ridiculous. Let me drive you home. I know that you get sensitive about this, but really mate be reasonable. Besides, your mum won't like it if you take the train. I honestly don't like it that you're on your own."

"Have you already talked to her?"

Ben shrugged. "I might have reached out and extended an invitation for you to come home with me on holiday."

I was going to kill him. "What the fuck mate? Didn't I tell you already?"

"Yeah, yeah. You told me that you need to go look in on her. But I happen to know that she doesn't need looking in on. She'll be working anyway, so what are you going to do?"

Ben's car smelled of new polished leather, and the heat in the back sunk into my bones, making me loosen up a little bit. It was so tempting to let him just drive me home, to accept the olive branch, to accept the help, to accept the friendship, but while I was going home, and while I didn't have to look in on my mum, there were other things I had to do. I was with people that needed to be looked in on. I didn't want Ben seeing any of that. So I held fast. "Mate, I appreciate it, but you know how it is. Sometimes I just need to tend to myself."

Ben's ice-blue gaze met mine. And there was a wisdom about them that I didn't always pay attention to. While Ben seemed on occasion, like the impulsive one among us, like the one most likely to say the wrong thing, or to fuck up, he was also, next to Toby, the heart of the group. He somehow understood things way beyond his years, because he just nodded at me. "All right, I'll do what you want, but one of these days, you'll realize you don't have to do everything by yourself."

Yeah, I knew he believed that. I knew that deep down, Ben believed the words he said, but while he was the son of a Lord, and he had grown up around all the wealth and trappings that that came with it, I was only the bastard's son.

I grew up on the wrong side of town, worked hard to shed my East London accent when I started going at Eaton whose crowd mostly think I didn't belong there. God knew my fucking father didn't think I belonged anywhere. Especially not anywhere where he might run in to me, or see me, or have to deal with me. The way it was, Ben and I had completely different upbringings. Toby wouldn't want someone like me for his sister. Emma Valma smelled clean and fresh like linens off the line. Her eyes always held a glint of mischief, as if she knew what I was thinking, what I was so desperate to have from her. And she wanted to tease me with it. But she was forever out of reach. And she would remain that way, because while my mates knew what friendships meant, they didn't know that they were how you survived. At least where I was from.

"I appreciate it mate. How about this, we'll compromise. You can drive me all the way back to Eaton. I'll ring you, and you could pick me up."

I was always surprised at the simple joy Ben got in doing something to help. As much as he seemed like the-devil-may-care one, if it came down to one of us that needed something, he was the first one to call. Because if he said he was going to do something, you'd get a damn well guarantee he was going to make it happen.

"Mate, that's good news. Fine, then I won't take it so personally that you won't let me drive you home. Whatever you do, take care. You do that, then I'll pick you up and we'll go back to school together. Besides, you know what we're waiting on."

The pit of my stomach balled.

Oh yes, the summons from the Elite. There were the Pops, and then there were the Elite, the secret societies of Eton. If were are called for either, your life would change. And Ben was chosen. His father was Elite. East was chosen too. As was Drew. Their fathers were Elite. Toby and I, our fathers were Elite, but we were their bastard children that they didn't want to see or look at or acknowledge. So whether we would get our summons or not was a question.

Being in the Elite meant seeing my father. Which would be an issue. Why my father denied me, God only knew. He was no longer an active voting member, but he could certainly try to stop me from getting in. He might not stop me though.

He might just make it so uncomfortable that I didn't want to be there. But I knew what the Elite could afford me. The money to look after my mum, the freedom and the power so that no one could look down on me again, and I could actually help people. No offense to my lads, but most of them had never had to struggle a day in their lives, except for Toby.

"Well, let's see what happens."

As the driver pulled over at the train station, I popped the latch of the door, Ben leveled a gaze on me. "If you didn't want to be Elite, you don't have to be, no matter what, mates for life. But if all of us were together? Imagine what we could do together? Who we could be? Not who our fathers wanted us to be, but who we wanted to be. Just think about it."

"You know, when you say it with that kind of confidence, I believe you. We could be our own lords."

His smile was quick on that one. "We could be the London Lords. A new generation who doesn't give a fuck. We don't have to follow their fucking rules. You just think about it, and text me when you're ready to go. Our future awaits."

I glanced over to the train. "Our future awaits." And mine certainly didn't involve Emma Varma.

chapter three

Emma

BRIDGE EDGERTON, WAS THE MOST STUCK UP, UPTIGHT PAIN IN THE arse I'd ever met in my life. He was also one of my brother's best mates. But God, he was just so annoying. He was one of those blokes that always seemed to be doing the right thing. Always seemed to have the right answers and know what you *should* be doing.

I loathed him.

No, you don't. You think he's sexy.

Okay, in my defense, he did have very nice shoulders. But that was hardly anything to get all worked up about. Lots of blokes had nice shoulders.

Sure, but he had nice shoulders, a jaw carved out of stone, and insane abdominal muscles.

There was no point arguing with myself, he was well fit. I saw when he went with us on a holiday to Spain last year. His lips so pouty I fantasized about them. But that was beside the point. The point was I couldn't stand him. And it seemed that the feeling was mutual. So what the hell was he doing at Spin?

My mates and I had come for the Estella Grant special holiday concert. I'd been looking forward to this for *months*. I'd told Toby about it and something told me my brother was the reason I saw Bridge Edgerton here at the Hive. Toby had bailed on me for some school project so no doubt he'd sent Bridge here to watch me.

The Hive was one of London's largest music spots. Record execs would bring their up-and-coming talents here to showcase them. It was a great spot for new talents. It was also a great spot for current talents. It's a smaller venue so your fans can hear you better. I begged Mum to let me come. I'd begged and begged and when she finally said yes, I'd been thrilled and ecstatic. But I hadn't planned on fucking Bridge Edgerton.

My mate, Arabella, leaned over. "Isn't that one of your brother's mates?"

I refused to look at him. What was the point. All that fitness burned the eyes. "Nope, I don't know what you're talking about."

Arabella laughed. "Um, the bloke from last summer. The one we spent half the time staring at and the other half wishing he would just take his shirt off already? That one?"

When in doubt, lie. "No, I didn't see him. It must have been your imagination."

Arabella lifted a brow. "Come off it. Are you guys fighting?"

"For your information, I am not fighting with him. I wouldn't give Bridge Edgerton the time of the day." Lies. "He's a colossal pain in the arse."

Okay, that was true.

"I swear I saw him. Besides, he's perfect. What's wrong with you? Are you still going to pretend you don't like him?"

"I'm not pretending. He's a wanker." And I knew this to be a fact. Last summer, a few of the girls and I had perhaps gotten into Mum's scotch. The stuff she saved just for visitors, which was pointless really because she rarely ever had anyone come over.

We got into it with Bridge when he caught us having fun in the pool in Spain. He'd just been so disapproving. Threatened to grass on us if we didn't stop immediately.

Although there was something just a little bit hot about his disapproving glare. The one that said he wanted to give me a spanking or something.

"No love, I swear it's him. Maybe he's just here to enjoy the concert."

"Do you think he would be at any concert, let alone one of what the media is calling, the next Amy Whinehouse? He's not that cool. He's just not."

Arabella laughed. "He could be. He just needs someone to loosen him up a bit."

"There is no amount of loosening up that makes some ego mildly tolerable. You know this."

She laughed. "If you say so. I don't know why you can't just admit that you like him."

"Because I *don't* like him. See, earlier about him being a complete and total wanker."

"Yes, yes, I know. He came down on us pretty hard for the drinking last summer, but we were drinking underage. And if your mum had found out, she would have been ticked. So he was, in a weird way he was looking out for us."

As it turned out we didn't have to wait long for confirmation. The crowd was like the Red Sea parting for him. His tall, lean frame pushing through. He had that long, large stride and his face was set in a grim mask. When he reached us, my friends, traitors that they were, especially Arabella, smiled and preened.

"Hey, you're that bloke from Spain last year?"

Arabella fluttered her lashes at him and I just rolled my eyes. "What are you doing here, Edgerton? I didn't think you were a fan of Estella."

"Well, there would be a lot you didn't know about me, Varma."

"If you say so. How much did my brother pay you to come and spoil my fun?"

"Toby didn't have to pay me. I'd ruin your day for free."

I scowled at him. "You know, you're such a pain in the arse. What is it you want exactly?"

He tilted his head back and muttered something to himself, and then sighed before leveling his gaze on me again. "Toby wanted to make sure you kept out of trouble. It seems like ***Estella*** can wind up a crowd."

"Oh my God, I don't need a governess. Is that what you are today, you're my nanny?"

He leaned in close, making sure that only I could hear his words. "It depends, do you need a spanking?"

Okay look, I'm as feminist as the next girl. I wasn't down for being told what to do, what I could and couldn't do with my body, who I could be with, who I could see, none of that interested me. But something about the way Bridge Edgerton said spanking made my lady parts tingle.

"No thanks. I'm not into it. Honestly, you can't be here just to babysit me."

He grinned then. "No. I'm also babysitting this group of infants you call your mates."

Arabella frowned. "Oh, I don't need an older brother. You don't have to babysit me."

"If you're with Emma, you're my responsibility tonight. I'll secure the drinks, all non-alcoholic, of course."

Everyone groaned. "Jesus Christ, Bridge, you're ruining the mood," I muttered.

"You're all underage. You think I'm going to let this group of pervs buy underage girls drinks in hopes of getting somewhere with them?"

I grabbed his elbow and tugged him aside. "Oh my God, please stop. Whatever Toby is paying you, I will double it."

He chuckled. "Double it, huh?"

"Yes. Anything just to make you go away."

"Oh, I'm not going away, Emma. I'm here to make good on my word. So you and I, we're going to enjoy this concert, together."

"And if I'm here meeting someone?"

"Well, I guess, he'll have to get used to me too. But just who the fuck are you meeting?"

My brow snapped down. "None of your business."

"Tonight, it is my business."

"You wish it was your business," I spat back. I knew what we looked like. A squabbling couple.

The muscle on his jaw ticked. "Look, I don't want to be here just as bad as you don't want me here. But I gave Toby my word. So, how about you and your mates enjoy the concert, don't get up to anything wild. I'll make sure you lot get home. That's it. I'll just be right here, acting as your silent bodyguard. Does that work?"

I scowled at him. "You know I hate you."

"You know what, you are not the first person to tell me that."

"I don't believe that I would be. Seriously, just please don't say anything. Don't ruin anything for me."

The corner of his lips tipped up and smirked. "I wouldn't dream of ruining your special date. Nope, might as well settle in. It's going to be a rough ride tonight."

"I hate you."

"The feeling is mutual. Believe me, Emma, if I could be anywhere else tonight, I would be. But your brother asked. So, let's try not to kill each other, shall we?"

I knew that was going to be easier said than done.

chapter four

Bridge

EMMA WAS TRYING TO KILL ME.

It was the only explanation. Every time I turned around, she was dancing far too close to some bloke. I kept telling myself it was none of my bloody business. All I cared about, was fulfilling a promise. I'd come here to watch out for her. She was mostly dancing and having fun with her mates. But the sharks were circling, I could see them.

One in particular, had joined the group of girls in the middle of the concert. They'd all hugged him like they knew him so I hadn't complained too much, just sat at the bar, sipping my pint. It wasn't until Emma started dancing with him, all the while over his shoulders, eye-fucking me.

The fuck was she playing at? I didn't have time for games. And the kind of games I want to play with her, were probably not on the brother approved list.

I gritted my teeth, and just sipped my drink, staring right back at her.

I said nothing, when he put his hands on her arms. I just let the irritation boil. I said nothing, when he started dry humping her on the floor. In full view of everyone. I just kept sipping my damn pint. But when he dragged her into the back towards the bathrooms, there was no way I could sit and do nothing. I slammed my glass down and stood.

One of her friends came over to me. "I wouldn't go back there if I were you."

"Excuse me?"

"Back there with Emma and Anders."

"Oh Christ, his name is bloody Anders?"

"Yes. He's a mate from school. But she likes him. So don't go interrupt."

I lifted a brow. All the more reason I should interrupt. Her brother would want me to interrupt.

Her friend, Arabella was it? Just rolled her eyes. "You're not her brother."

"Damn straight I'm not."

And then her sharp gaze narrowed on mine. "Oh, so it's like that?"

I crossed my arms. "Like what?"

I scanned the crowd hoping to see them. When I couldn't find them, I started to move.

But Arabella was hot on my heels. "You like her."

"Nope. She's my mate's little sister. I can't like her."

"When has that ever stopped anyone?"

"It stops the good ones. I'm looking out for her that's all."

I beat my way through the crowd. If Arabella thought she could follow, she was welcome to try.

Surprisingly she stayed hot on my tail like glue. "Then why are you just creepily stalking her, why don't you just ask her out?"

"Because you don't ask out your best mate's sister. It's a recipe for disaster."

"Oh this is rich. I get it now. Why Emma was so intent on bringing Anders tonight. Normally, she loathes him."

I frowned. I turned around and frowned. "What are you on about?"

The music thumped. I leaned close to hear her better. "Anders. She doesn't like him. At all. She said he's a creepy handsy arsehole. But he was the ticket hookup. So he was coming with us. Normally she ignores him. But it's you, isn't it? She wants to make you crazy."

"She knows better. She's not that dumb."

Arabella's grin was sweet. Sweeter than her dark makeup and barely there outfit suggested. "Then you don't know women very well. If you're not into her. I promise you Emma can take care of herself. She'll get Anders off her ass. But if you are into her, I think they went into the unisex bathroom back there."

The fury pumped through my blood. And I wasn't even sure why. She should honestly know better. Blokes were a handful at the best of times. What was she thinking?

I told myself it wasn't my business. Who the fuck Emma decided she wanted to get off with. Not my business at all.

Except Toby made it your business.

Why had he made it my business? This was just torture.

I couldn't have her. Because Toby was a mate. And she knew that. So she was deliberately torturing me.

Now I was going to teach her a very important lesson about how not to tease caged animals.

I fought my way through the crowd of people waiting for the loo.

When I came up to the unisex one, I shoved aside a bloke with two girls waiting with him.

"I'm going in. Try not to make a nuisance of yourself, when I do."

He grumbled but he backed off and the other girls sized me up. I knew what they saw when they looked at me. I had the clothes, the look. A bit of posh. Except I *wasn't*. I'd worked hard to lose that Eastern accent. Worked hard so that none of my former self showed.

And Emma was about to bring all of that to the floor.

I banged on the door, no answer.

The bloke behind me shrugged. "Tough call mate. Who's in there?"

"Someone who shouldn't be."

He chuffed. "Sorry mate. Your girlfriend?"

"No. Dammit. She's not my girlfriend."

"Right. So you're just trying to break into a locked bathroom for no good reason?"

When I heard a thud in the room, I immediately stopped giving a shit. I reached in my back pocket for the lock pick set I always carried with me. Especially when I was home. It was a dumb habit. I didn't need it anymore. I didn't do that sort of thing anymore.

Yeah you do. Only when it's important.

Sure. If you have to tell yourself that.

It was quick work to open the door. And then I found him. Anders, fucking all over Emma. He had her lifted up onto the bathroom sink. And he was busy trying to shove her skirt up. And she was fighting. Pushing him away. Our gazes met over his shoulder. And her eyes were wide with panic. That was fear in her eyes.

I was going to fucking kill him.

I wish I could say I had thought through my next steps very carefully, thought through my deeds. Weighed them against what it could cost me. But I didn't. Me, the always carefully crafted one, who thought through everything. I didn't think. I didn't blink, I didn't breathe. I just moved.

I closed the door behind me, and then I grabbed him by the neck. He choked and fought me, "Oy mate. What the fuck?"

But I was unwilling to listen to any of that bullshit.

"The girl's not interested."

"What the fuck do you mean?"

He tried to square off against me, but I was bigger, and meaner. He just didn't know it yet.

"This girl, she's not yours to touch."

"The fuck. She's-" My hand moved balled into a fist and sailing right for his mouth before he could even get the words out. I hit him once. Good ol' biology rewarded me with blood spurting everywhere.

Emma gasped from the sink.

I glanced back at her. "Are you okay?"

I didn't get an immediate response so I glanced back. Still with a hand on poor Anders.

"I can't hear you. I need to keep an eye on him so I need you to use your words. Are you okay?"

Her words were stilted. But she muttered, "Yes. Y—Yes, I'm fine."

"Good. Now go back outside with your friends. Close the door behind you."

"Bridge it's okay. I'm okay."

"You are not okay. And I'm going to impart on Anders here, how that's a fucking problem for me. Now be a good girl. Off you get."

I could tell she hesitated because the door didn't open. The music remained muffled and silent. Finally, finally I heard it open. And I could breathe free knowing that she wasn't going to see me do everything I was capable of doing. When once again the banging noise of Lil' Wayne was drummed out. I turned to the bloke that had had his hands up Emma's skirt. "Now, you and I are going to have a little talk, about just what the word no means. And it's going to be a long talk so you probably want to buckle in for it."

chapter five

Bridge

I WAS ABOUT TO BREAK OUR DEAL.

My father and I, we'd come to a truce.

I would leave behind the life that I led. No more running around with the lads, nearly getting myself killed more than once. I would walk away from all of that, and he would put me into Eaton, as befitting of a son he didn't want. But I would get the opportunity and access to the kinds of people I would never have known.

I would be educated, and while I wouldn't get my due, I would get an opportunity to stick it to him. An opportunity to show that I wasn't a waste of time. An opportunity to be better. To be different.

Fuck me. I wanted to break our deal right now. I wanted to take every single skill that I had learnt fighting on the streets, and use them right now.

Once the doors closed, I was willing to put my future in danger, because of her. Fucking Emma Varma.

But this asshole, he was going to hurt her. He had been trying to hurt her.

"Mate, didn't anyone ever tell you not to touch what wasn't yours?"

His eyes went round. "Mate, it's not what it looked like. She asked me in here. She was putting it all out there. And then we got started. She likes it a bit of rough, you see."

"You are a vile piece of gobshite. Now, I need you not to scream because this is going to hurt. And I'd rather not get interrupted once I begin, you see.

I'd like you to think thoroughly. Directly. Without dispatch. So, you're going to take it, and you're going to deal with it do you understand?"

He shook his head back and forth. As he backed up smashing into the wall, he put his hands out as if that was going to ward me off.

Pure rage flowed through my system, it was unlike anything I'd ever felt before in my life. Every single dodgy back alley encounter I'd ever had, had been for this.

Before I'd fought to survive. But this, this would be for fun. He'd put his hands on Emma, so that meant he was going to die. And I was going to be the one to deliver the justice.

Quietly, I unsnapped my shirt sleeves, the button down being something that I'd seen one of the lads wearing. Some designer type. I found a knockoff in Camden Market. It was close enough to the real thing that unless you looked, you wouldn't notice.

I rolled up the sleeves, and then with ease, I made the familiar fist. The one that I'd been taught in the martial arts classes that were meant to soothe the rage inside me and not make me more violent. And then I fisted my left hand in his t-shirt. "That's not pretty for me. It's a pain in the arse if I have to go through your lips to get to your teeth. But if you just present them it's easier to knock them the fuck out."

"No. No no no. God please God no."

I caged the rage inside. Because I knew, I knew that if I didn't, the job wouldn't be efficient. I'm going to be sloppy. And I didn't like sloppy or messy. And so I released my fist.

And then he howled. His head snapping back, blood gushing out of his nose. Something cracked in the wall behind him.

With a strong hand, I waited. It was better when they begged first.

"Fuck. No no no. God no. I'll never do it again. I'll leave her alone. I didn't know she was yours."

Snap. Another pop. I was finding that the more I hit him, the more dispassionate I could become. I never had a father around to teach me not to put your hands on women, it's something I just knew. It was wrong.

Pop.

"Fuck." He started to weep then, sobbing and sputtering.

It was the sobbing and sputtering that really got me. And then that carefully leashed control on my rage, slipped just a little. I released his shirt, with my left hand, delivered a left hook swinging my arm wide and connecting, with his cheekbone his head smacked to the side with a crack. More crying.

And more hitting. More fists. More blood. And it was as if I was watching myself calmly deliver the blows that would undo him. Like he had planned to undo Emma.

And then suddenly, there was a voice. Calling my name, and it sounded like the sweetest lullaby. "Bridge. Bridge I'm okay. Bridge."

It was only after another three or four blows that I realized that it wasn't a lullaby but a voice.

Emma's voice.

I turned around, and there she was in the doorway staring at me, mouth open and staring at the arsehole who tried to hurt her.

"I told you to get out Emma."

"Let's go. Someone called the Bill. You're going to be arrested."

With those words, she was the cold slap I needed. "Fuck."

"Let's go."

She grabbed my hand and tugged me outside, leaving the old boy wherever he was to slide down the wall.

"Jesus fucking Christ."

The crowd was packed in. In the hallway it was wild. I kept my head down and tucked so no one could get a clear look at me. All they'd be able to say is some tall prick but lucky for me I knew the bouncers. Tommy O'Rourke, he once lived in my neighborhood. Good and tight once. When I brushed through the door, he gave me a nod. The corner of his lips sort of turned up into a smile. "I see you're still up to the same old tricks."

"Not sure what you're talking about."

He gave me a smirk before saying, "Go that way. Bill's coming from the other direction."

I gave him a nod of thanks, and let Emma tug me away from him. "Jesus." Down the alley she pulled and pulled. "What in the world were you doing?"

I tugged my hand free from hers. "What did you think I was doing?"

"You could have really hurt him."

"Yeah, that was the plan."

"You could have gone to the nik."

"I wasn't going to jail."

"Bridge, you would have killed him."

"Would I? Why would you care?"

"You have a stick up your arse, but you don't want to hurt anybody. You're Mr. Cool, Calm and Collected. You never have any emotions."

I stopped "What?" Couldn't she see? The depths of what I was trying to hold back, for her? Because of her?

We're through the alley and on the other side of street, there are bars around us and restaurants. Way past the public garden. "Look, let's get you a taxi and get you home."

"Me? We have to get *you* home. You probably need to wash your hands."

I glanced down at the blood on them. And I reached into my pocket and pulled out a handkerchief.

Her brows knitted. "A handkerchief?"

The bite of cold, whipped through my shirt. "Time to go Ems."

"No." She held her ground.

Around the garden, there is a coffee stand and behind that, to the left, a water fountain. She stopped, and I let her take my hand and rinse it under the ice-cold water. But I didn't even feel it. All I could feel were her soft hands on mine.

"Why did you do that Bridge?"

She lifted her gaze to meet mine. And she had me gripped. Locked into position. Unable to move or think or do anything. "Don't you know?"

She shook her head. "No. I don't know."

"I would have been destroyed if he'd hurt you. I needed to make sure he was never going to hurt you again."

"Why do you even care?"

"You know why I care."

Emma Varma was in my blood. She was under my skin, and there was no stopping it. But I couldn't tell her that. Because of her brother. I wasn't good enough. "Doesn't matter. Let's get you in a cab."

But then Emma, true to form, lifted her chin and stared me down. "I'm not moving from here until you talk to me. I need to hear the words, Bridge Edgerton. Why would you do that for me?"

Instead of answering, I did the thing that I've been trying to avoid doing. In the absence of being able to use my words to tell her how I felt, I kissed her.

chapter six

Emma

I DIDN'T KNOW WHY, BUT I EXPECTED BRIDGE TO TASTE LIKE BEER OR liquor or, at the very least, sin.

But he tasted fresh and clean, like mint and something so decadent, that I couldn't stop.

He was tall. A lot taller than me. And so I had to stand, even in my heels, on my tiptoes. I expected a brutal tug in my hair, but his hands were a gentle slide. And only when he gripped were his hands at all rough with me.

He waited. He waited for me to give over. Waited for me to give him my permission. And his lips slid away from mine. His gaze burrowed deep into mine.

I nodded.

Yes. God please, yes.

What happened next was more than what I expected. Brutal and harsh slamming back of his lips to mine with a deep groan. His lips owned me. Not just devoured, but completely *consumed* me until I had no breath that he didn't allow.

His hands were gentle in my hair, but commanding. I knew exactly how he wanted me to move my head, I knew exactly the response he demanded from me. He led and I followed behind. It was either that, or be left behind. Jump off the ride, never get to experience this.

I had thought about Bridge Edgerton kissing me since I met him two summers ago. There was something about that lush, cruel mouth that evoked images of stolen kisses and whispered poetry. He was so stiff, aloof. But there was something inherently sensual about the way he moved, if you could get him to smile, the man was a knockout. You had no choice but to stare at his sheer beauty.

He looked like every tortured hero you'd ever been told about. But in this moment, I was being tortured.

My body was on fire. Straining, needing what only he could give it. But instead of giving it to me, his tongue slid over mine, coaxing, teasing, owning. Leaving a wake that no one dared to follow.

One hand slid over my shoulders, molding the curve of my waist, and then over my arse and pulled me close. And I could feel him. The steely, rigid, length of his erection pressing against my abdomen. And I shivered.

Holy hell.

All my mates talked about sex non-stop. It's what we did. We were fascinated, curious, scared, anticipatory. Because none of us had had any.

But the way Bridge was kissing me, was a prelude. Maybe not tonight. Maybe not tomorrow, but one day, Bridge Edgerton was going to be inside me. And I was going to be happy about it and just a little bit terrified. Because Christ, what was pressing against me was never, ever, *ever* going to fit.

But God, did I want him to try because something low in my belly was pulling taut and tight and tingling and it warmed my skin. I need it. I didn't even know why. But I knew I needed it from him.

He growled again against my lips. And his hips moved in this small circular motion that made me want to climb him.

I couldn't stop it. I needed it. I followed suit and he growled, his palms squeezing my arse. Bringing me tighter up against him. And then, just as I was getting into the rhythm, just as something was building inside me, something I couldn't name, but wanted part of so desperately that I would have sold my soul to have it.

He pulled back. Lips swollen, eyes wide, breath tearing out of his chest and ragged pants he glowered at me as if this was my fault. And then his cool mask slipped over his expression and he stepped back.

"That shouldn't have happened."

I was too dazed to think, too tired, too dizzy to focus.

But then it occurred to me what he'd said. "I don't understand. Why would you say that?"

"Let's go. You need to get in the cab."

I blinked up at him. "The hell I do. You'll explain to me what the hell you mean? And first of all-"

I didn't get to finish what I was saying. Because before I knew it, his hands were on me again. And my heart leapt for joy.

But then, he picked me up and flipped me over his shoulder and carried me out of the alley out of the little garden. Next thing I knew his sharp shrill, whistle sounded, and then we were moving again, and a taxi pulled up.

He and the driver exchanged words. And he handed him some money. And then opened the back seat of the car, placed me inside, and shut it with him on the other side.

I tried to roll down the window, but it didn't roll. So I knocked on the window and he shook his head. Through the window from the driver's side of the taxi, he said, "You know where to take her."

"Bridge, what are you doing?"

"I'll see around, Emma."

And then as I drove off in the taxi, I stared at the silhouette of Bridge Edgerton as he walked away from me.

Forever.

inevitable

JENNA HARTLEY

Sumner Gray is my best friend's daughter.
My new summer intern.
But she's no longer the shy little girl in pigtails I remember.

She's got dangerous curves and kissable lips.
A sassy mouth and a killer brain.
If only I could be her mentor in the bedroom, not the boardroom.

I'm used to taking what I want—in business and life.
I can't have her. I shouldn't want her, but I do.
And the way she looks at me tells me she wants me too.

chapter one

Sumner

"THIS CAN'T HAPPEN AGAIN." HIS DEEP VOICE RUMBLED THROUGH his chest and into my ear.

I lifted my head, my dark tresses falling over my face like the wings of a raven. "Be serious, Jonathan."

"I am serious, Sumner." He shook his head, rolling away from me and swinging his legs over the side of the bed. "This shouldn't have happened at all." He cradled his head in his hands.

"But it did." I crawled across the bed on my knees. The plush hotel room smelled of sex and desire, the rumpled sheets undeniable proof of what we'd done. "It happened, and we both know we want it to continue happening."

I trailed my fingernail along his shoulder, studying the way his muscles bunched beneath the skin. His body was...*incredible*. And even though I'd now licked and kissed every inch of him, I wanted more. One night wasn't enough.

Hell, it had taken us months to get to this point. Months of accidental brushes in the elevator and heated gazes across the conference room. Months of pent-up tension begging to break free. But that wasn't even the worst of it, because the truth was, I'd been waiting years for this man to notice me.

Jonathan Wolfe, I sighed, admiring the hard planes of his back. My father's best friend—and my boss for the summer.

To everyone else, he was Wolfe. A successful businessman. A perfectionist. Demanding and shrewd. But to me, he'd always just been Jonathan. Beneath the cool façade was a man of warmth and kindness, a man who had always looked out for me. When I was an awkward teen, he'd always seemed so out of reach. He still did, if I were being honest.

Which was part of the reason I still couldn't believe he was lying in my bed. After a night I'd fantasized about countless times. The reality had been even better than I'd imagined. His beard scratching the delicate skin of my thighs. His hands canvassing my body. His lips…

He stood, and I grabbed his hand, my lower lip jutting out. "Where are you going?"

We still had a few hours until our first meeting, and I didn't want to waste a moment. I wanted to make love and eat room service. Shower together. Just enjoy this freedom away from Los Angeles. Away from the office. Away from my father.

He slid out of my grasp, evading my gaze as he grabbed his suit pants from the floor. "I'm returning to my room to get ready." He pulled them up, buttoning the top before yanking his shirt from the dresser, his movements aggressive, angry. "I suggest you do the same. I'll see you in the lobby at nine."

He's serious. I frowned. I was still coming down from the euphoria of my latest orgasm, and he was ruining it. He was ruining everything.

"What about the rest of the trip?" I'd wanted this—*him*—for so long. I couldn't let the opportunity pass us by. We were going to be in New York for another week. Did he really intend to ignore this thing between us and pretend it had never happened?

"Sumner. I—" He pinched the bridge of his nose, closing his eyes briefly. "You're my best friend's daughter. My fucking intern. Not to mention, you're twenty years younger than me."

Twenty-three years younger. But I wasn't going to remind him of that. Besides, what difference did it really make?

I lifted a shoulder, enjoying the way his eyes flickered to my breasts. "So?"

"So…you have to understand why this can't happen again."

Age didn't matter—at least not to me. I wouldn't be an intern at his company much longer. The summer was nearly over, and then I'd start grad school. As to his final objection, I couldn't change who my father was, but it wasn't like he needed to know.

I climbed off the bed, gratified by the way Jonathan scanned me hungrily. He might claim we were done, but his body said otherwise. I closed the distance between us, grabbing his tie from the armchair and looping it around his neck.

He clenched his jaw so hard, I thought he might crack a molar. *"Sumner."*

"Jonathan." I arched my brow, pulling him closer. "If all we have is this week, then we should make the most of it."

He squeezed his eyes shut, inhaling a deep, shaky breath. "We—"

"Can," I said, already anticipating his protest. "We can, and we should. Now—" I leaned up on my toes, pressing my lips to his jaw. "I'm going to shower." I spun and sauntered toward the bathroom, adding a little extra sway to my naked hips. It was an open invitation, and I hoped he'd take me up on it.

I started the water and wondered if I'd pushed him too far, asked for too much. We'd been buzzed when we fell into bed together last night—on a high after closing another big deal, which was celebrated with drinks. Despite the alcohol coursing through our veins, we'd been sober enough to know what we were doing. But now in the harsh morning light, things were different—at least for him. And I hated the idea that he regretted it, regretted *me*.

I reached out to steady myself. I could never regret our night together, even if he currently wanted to pretend it had never happened. I dropped my head to my chest, disappointment washing over me. I just couldn't see this being the end of us. Not when we were only beginning.

But then a pair of warm arms slipped around me, his scent invading my nose. I sighed, closing my eyes as I leaned into his touch. Much as he tried to deny it, he was just as desperate for me as I was for him.

"I knew you couldn't resist me," I teased, smirking at him over my shoulder.

He growled, pulling me closer. His hard-on sought me out through his slacks, the buttons of his shirt digging into my spine. I welcomed it, welcomed the bite of pain. Because I wanted to etch this week into my memory, tattoo it on my brain the way this man was imprinted on my heart.

"When I'm done, you'll be begging me to fuck you." He whispered the dark promise into my ear, and I shivered.

As steam billowed out of the shower, he ran his hand over my breasts, my hips, my thighs. I leaned my head back against his shoulder, my thoughts as clouded as the mirror. I wanted him. I'd wanted him for so long. But his touch was rough, as if he were angry with himself for wanting me.

"Get in," he rasped.

He released me, and I stumbled forward, into the huge walk-in shower. It was tiled in marble with multiple shower heads—decadent and opulent just like my night with this man had been. But like the shower, Jonathan could be cold, hard.

I pushed those thoughts away, stepping beneath the spray of water so it blanketed me with warmth. My body was on high alert, the droplets running down my skin nearly erotic. I watched as he undressed, soaking in every inch of him as if it were the last time. Because I knew it very well could be.

He was… God, he was so handsome. In my mind, he'd always been the most handsome man I knew. Whether I'd realized it or not, I compared every guy to him. How could I not? Jonathan was intelligent, confident, successful. For a man who owned one of the biggest full-service commercial real estate firms in Los Angeles, he really was very down-to-earth.

Prior to this summer and my internship at the Wolfe Group, I hadn't seen him in five years. I'd graduated high school and moved across the country to attend MIT. I'd studied hard, partied hard—had my college fun. But he'd always been in the back of my mind, and I'd followed his career online and through the snippets my dad told me.

Jonathan swept his hair away from his face, silver smattering the temples and throughout his beard. Did he even realize how crazy he made me? He was still fully dressed, and I was already on the verge of begging him to fuck me.

I ran my hands down my chest, over my stomach, and he watched, Adam's apple bobbing. He stripped out of his button-down shirt, his blue eyes hooded with desire. They mirrored my own. His pants were next, his cock bobbing toward his stomach. My mouth watered at the sight.

No sooner had he stepped into the shower than he smashed his mouth to mine, his kiss insistent, demanding. I met him stroke for stroke, his beard scratching my skin. His body firm against mine as he crushed me to him. I couldn't breathe unless he did. Couldn't move unless he wanted me to. And I wouldn't have wanted it any other way.

He dipped his head to suck on my nipple, teasing my clit with his fingers. I reached out for him, taking him in my hand, stroking him. Water streamed down my face, and I tilted my head back and opened my mouth, letting it fall over my lips, my skin, his skin. It made it seem as if he were everywhere, and it certainly felt that way as he pushed me higher and higher. With every nip of his teeth, every swipe of his fingers, I was that much closer to coming.

When he slid one finger inside me, then another, I gripped his shaft tighter, pumping him faster. Panting. Groaning. Punishing. When he met my eyes, his were dark with lust and anger. I craved it, wanted it all. And when he gripped the back of my neck, groaning my name before slamming his mouth against mine, I came. He followed a minute later, painting my stomach with his desire.

After a day of meetings that seemed to stretch on endlessly, I climbed in the back of the town car. I glanced outside when someone called Jonathan's name. *Holy*...mother. My mouth watered at the sight of him standing on the sidewalk, back upright. His silhouette outlined against the glass front of the Empire State Building. Was there anything sexier than a man in a well-tailored suit?

He said something and waved, then removed his suit jacket, tossing it over his shoulder before joining me. We'd barely pulled away from the curb, and his attention was already glued to his phone screen as if his life depended on it. It had been like this most of the day—he did his best to stay busy, to put distance between us. I'd hoped things would be different once we were alone again, but it looked like I was wrong.

I turned toward the window, glancing at the passing scenery. Not a palm tree in sight. As far away from LA and my dad as we could get without leaving the country. And it still wasn't enough. At least not for him. For me… Well. I pursed my lips, watching a street performer as we waited for a light to change. I hated the idea of hurting my dad. I'd never want to drive a wedge between him and Jonathan. They'd been friends since high school. Over the years, Jonathan had been an ever-present fixture in our family, more akin to my dad's brother than a friend.

"Are you hungry?" he asked, startling me from my thoughts.

I lifted a shoulder. "I saw a street vendor near the hotel."

"Nonsense," he said, lowering the divider so he could give directions to the driver before raising it again. "Besides, we have reservations at La Mer."

I studied his expression to determine his intent, but it was useless. I wanted him to do something, say something, *anything* to acknowledge what had happened between us. But he was silent the rest of the ride, and so was I.

When we arrived at La Mer, Jonathan exited first, waiting for me to emerge. He placed his hand on my lower back, his touch sending sparks up my spine. When we walked into the restaurant, the host greeted us with a smile and then led us to a table in a secluded corner.

Jonathan held out my chair. Once we were both seated, he leaned in and said, "Did you enjoy yourself today?"

"I'm not sure enjoy is quite the word I'd use to describe it, though I did enjoy this morning."

"Sumner…"

Not wanting to give him another opportunity to shut me down, I forced myself to adopt a more professional tone. "Thank you again for bringing me. I'm learning a lot."

He chuckled. When he rested his thigh against mine beneath

the table, I wondered if it was intentional. "Yeah. The first few days are usually pretty tedious. But the rest of the week should be more enjoyable."

I nodded, surprised he was even talking to me again. I couldn't keep up. We were talking; we weren't. We were fucking; we were nothing.

He ordered a bottle of wine, and I stole glances at him over the top of my menu. "What?" He laughed after the waiter had gone.

I shook my head, returning my attention to the words printed on the page. "Nothing."

"You have to tell me now," he said, pulling the end of my menu down so he could see my face.

"I guess I'm wondering...is this what it's going to be like between us from now on? Awkward and stiff. Our conversations limited to surface matters?"

He closed his eyes briefly, his watch glinting from the table as he gripped the stem of his wineglass. "It's not how I want it to be. Believe me."

I blinked a few times as I attempted to process his confession.

"Then why are you doing this to us?" When he opened his mouth, I waved a hand through the air. "I know, I know... I'm too young, I'm an intern, I'm your best friend's daughter." I rolled my eyes, not even sure why I'd asked.

He glanced around as if anxious someone would overhear then blew out a breath. "That's definitely a huge part of it, but..." He dragged a hand through his hair. "Did you know I came to the hospital after you were born? Did you realize I was there for every important milestone in your life? I watched you grow up."

He chuckled, and the action seemed so out of place with his brooding demeanor only moments before. "I can remember days spent at the beach, you flinging off your swimsuit and wiggling your cute little butt around. Then you'd march down to the water's edge buck naked."

My cheeks heated, and I was positive they were an unflattering shade of red. "I don't remember that," I said in a soft voice.

"It was years ago. Hell, I'm sure you barely remember me."

"Barely remember you?" I nearly choked on my water. "How could I forget someone like you? Besides, you were always around, always part of the family."

He nodded, his expression serious. "So, you have to understand why this is a terrible idea. Your dad has always been like a brother to me. He's family, and I can't lose him. Even if you are fucking incredible."

I dipped my head, my hair curtaining my face from his view. I wanted to bask in his compliment, but my mind kept returning to his words about my father, about family. I didn't know everything about Jonathan's past, but I knew enough. He really didn't have anyone else.

Conversation returned to more "appropriate" matters—our meetings, the week ahead, registration, and business school. It was fine, nice even, but it wasn't what I really wanted. If anything, it only reminded me of just how good we could be together. We had a shared past, shared interests, and a similar outlook on life.

We were both silent on the ride back to the hotel. When we stepped inside the elevator, Jonathan's arm brushed against me as he reached across to press the button for our floor. He smelled crisp, clean, and I wanted to inhale him. No, I wanted to taste him. That was something we hadn't gotten to do yet. Would he taste masculine and salty or… When he cleared his throat, I realized he was staring at me expectantly.

"We're here."

"Oh." I shook my head. "Right." I'd been so lost in my thoughts, I hadn't even noticed the elevator stop or the doors open.

He waited for me to exit but didn't place his hand on my lower back. I'd already resigned myself to the fact that I was going to bed alone and it was for the best. But that didn't make it any easier.

"You don't need to walk me to my door," I said when he didn't turn the opposite way to go to his. "I'm not a little girl." It was childish, but I was hurt and frustrated and not just a little horny. I understood his reasons, but that didn't mean I had to like them.

"No." His voice was gravelly. "You're not. But I'd like to all the same."

We walked down the hall in silence, the tension vibrating between us. When we reached the door, I held the keycard up to the reader and stepped inside. "Good night."

I didn't wait for him to say anything. Didn't want to have him reject me again. Instead, I closed the door and leaned my forehead against it. I ached for him, but Jonathan had told me it was a one-time thing. I'd always appreciated the fact that he was true to his word. And so, with a heavy sigh, I turned and headed for the bathroom to get ready for bed.

Just this once, couldn't he...

There was a knock at the door, and my heart stumbled over itself. I fluffed my hair and pulled my dress a little lower. A swarm of bees buzzed within me, and I tried to calm myself as I headed toward the door. I was afraid to get my hopes up, but I couldn't help it.

I peered through the peephole, my breath catching when I saw him standing there. I swung open the door. His arms braced the doorway as if he were holding himself back. His breathing was ragged, and I could feel the energy bouncing off him.

He slowly lifted his head, eyes dark and tortured. "All we have is this week."

His words were an echo of mine from this morning, and I wondered what had changed his mind. Whatever it was, I wasn't going to question it.

"Then we should make the most of it."

He gripped the back of my neck, crashing his lips to mine as he backed me into the room and shut the door behind us. Our bodies collided. And I knew that no matter how hard we tried to fight this—we were inevitable.

chapter two

Jonathan

"HERE WE ARE," I SAID AS I PULLED UP TO THE CURB OF A HOUSE in Los Feliz. The yard was more weeds than grass, and one of the windows was boarded up. I glanced to Sumner, trying to gauge her expression.

I'd behaved since returning from New York last week, and surprisingly, so had she. I still didn't trust myself to be alone with her, and I'd successfully avoided it for the most part. That didn't mean I wasn't thinking about her. *Fuck*... I slid my hands down my thighs, wishing my hands were on her body instead. It felt as if I could think of nothing but her.

Sleeping with her had been a mistake for obvious reasons—I was her boss, her dad's best friend, the list went on and on. But the true reason was something I could never tell her. Now that I'd had her, I couldn't get her out of my head. I thought maybe I'd scratch the itch and be done, but it was like a rash. The more you scratched, the worse the itch, until it was all you could think about.

"Are you buying a new house?" she asked.

I shook my head, unbuckling my seat belt as Alexis pulled up behind us. "I've been flipping houses the past few years. It's a passion project of mine. Come on." I grinned. "Let me introduce you to Alexis."

I should've dropped Sumner back at the office after we'd checked out the commercial properties. I'd told myself I'd invited her out of convenience, but I knew that wasn't true. Because for some reason, I wanted to show her this. I wanted her to know this side of me. To *see* me.

I climbed out of the truck and greeted Alexis with a hug. "Hey."

"Hey."

"Alexis—" I glanced over my shoulder at Sumner, her smile like a punch to the gut. She'd always been pretty as a little girl—raven hair, jade eyes that appeared gray in certain lights, kindhearted. But the woman before me was fucking stunning. She was also my best friend's daughter and my intern. And I'd slept with her. God, could I be more of a cliché?

I cleared my throat and turned back to Alexis. "This is Sumner. She's been working as an associate at the Wolfe Group this summer, and I'm showing her the ropes."

Alexis extended her hand to shake. "Nice to meet you. Are you interested in residential development?"

"I'm here to learn." She glanced at me with a devilish grin.

"Wolfe's the best. Even if he can be a pain in the ass sometimes." Alexis nudged me with her elbow, grinning as she said it.

I wrapped my arm around Alexis's shoulder. "You know I'm your favorite client."

"Come on." She shook her head with a laugh, and I released her. "Let me show you the house."

The inside of the house wasn't as awful as I'd feared. But it wasn't much better either. Alexis showed us around until her phone rang.

"I'll just be outside." She slid open the back door and stepped out to the backyard, which was basically a concrete pit. Algae rested on the surface of the pool, trash and debris littering the yard.

"What do you think?" I asked Sumner.

I was relieved that we'd lapsed so easily back into our friendship. There had been no awkwardness or barely concealed hostility. It was almost as if that week in New York had never happened—not that I could ever forget it. But I was grateful that Sumner had been mature and professional despite what had transpired between us.

"Honestly?" She scrunched up her nose, and it made me want to kiss her. "It's kind of a dump."

"I know." Excitement churned through my bones, brimming with potential. "It's a diamond in the rough."

"Or it's just…rough."

"Maybe I like it rough." *I shouldn't have said that.*

"Mm." She hummed with satisfaction, and I gnashed my teeth at the reminder of our time together. I couldn't stop thinking about it, about her. But it couldn't happen again. It shouldn't have happened in the first place. And if Ian ever found out...

I cleared my throat. "This house has so much potential."

Ian was my oldest friend, and I'd slept with his daughter. I'd betrayed him.

"If you say so..."

I went on to lay out my plan, leading her through each and every room. I loved how she listened with her whole body, as if she were a sponge soaking up my every word. She was passionate, smart, and attentive. She was...perfect.

"How do you make this an economical investment? Because everything you described sounds expensive," she finally said when we returned to the living room where we'd started.

"I do a lot of the work myself."

She gawked at me. "You? The man who wears $5,000 suits and owns one of the most successful commercial real estate firms in Los Angeles?"

"Seven, but who's counting?"

She tilted her head to the side. "Seven?"

"The suit. And commercial real estate has become...tedious. Ian says this is a phase, a midlife crisis or whatever, but I need to do something with my hands. I need to make something. Leave a tangible legacy."

"By building other people's homes?"

I straightened and stared ahead. I shouldn't have brought her here. For all her maturity, she didn't get it. Didn't get me. "I wouldn't expect you to understand."

She placed her hand on my forearm. "I do understand. I was just surprised since you never mentioned it before."

"No one knows, apart from Ian," I said, unable to bring myself to call him "your dad" now that I'd slept with her. "Alexis, and now you."

She peered up at me. "Why..."

The back door slid open, and Alexis returned. Sumner removed her hand, and I mourned the loss of her touch.

"Everything okay?" I asked Alexis.

"Oh yeah." She ran a hand through her hair. "It's our anniversary, and the sitter canceled at the last minute. But Lauren and Hunter offered to take care of the girls."

"Congratulations," I said, and Sumner echoed the sentiment. "Wait." I frowned. "I thought you got married in the fall?"

"We, um—wow, you have a good memory," she said, and I smirked. "This is a, um, different anniversary." She dipped her head, cheeks flushing.

Interesting. Alexis was always composed, in control, a badass. So, to see her ruffled… I laughed to myself but didn't inquire further.

"Anyway, what do you think of the house?" she asked.

I rubbed a hand over my jaw. "The price needs to come down, but I'm game if you are."

"I wouldn't have shown it to you if I weren't." She grinned. "And I'll see what I can negotiate."

She locked up and we said goodbye, and then I helped Sumner into the truck before climbing in myself. The radio played softly in the background, some country song about hot days and warm nights. Her scent surrounded me, and I moved my free hand to the steering wheel to stop myself from reaching out to hold her hand.

She shifted, her skirt riding higher up her thighs. I gripped the steering wheel, struggling to push away thoughts of them wrapped around my head. Her taste on my tongue. My name on her lips.

"You and Alexis seem close," she finally said. "Are you business partners? Friends?"

"A bit of both. She owns a very successful residential brokerage, and she wanted to get into development. Sometimes, we collaborate. I'm her silent investor, and I do some of the work."

She nodded, though I could tell she still had questions. "Why did you decide to share this with me?"

"Because…" I blew out a breath, twisting the steering wheel beneath my hands. Sumner was heading to business school soon, and I wanted to make sure it was because she wanted to, not because she thought it was what was expected. "You might think you know what you want out of life, but it will change over time. It will evolve. And I think you should be open to the possibilities. You should create the life of your choosing. Not the one everyone else expects for you."

"I wish you could follow your own advice when it comes to us." The words were said so softly, I'd almost missed them.

I glanced over at Sumner briefly before returning my attention to the road. Out of the corner of my eye, I saw her shake her head. "Sorry. I shouldn't have said that. I knew what I was agreeing to. And I know you're right."

"What am I right about?" I asked, pulling into the parking garage for the Wolfe Group and putting the truck in park. This time of night, the garage was mostly empty.

"You, me, my dad. All of it. It may not seem like it, but I'd never want to come between the two of you. And…" She let out a breath. "I've done a lot of thinking this past week, and I'm sorry if I pushed you into something you didn't want."

I chuckled. "Something I didn't want?" I placed my hand beneath her chin, guiding her gaze to mine. She was so goddamn beautiful it stole my breath. Black hair that hung in waves, those jade eyes that captivated me. "First of all, I wanted you." *Want you.*

I released her chin, placing my hands on the console. "Don't ever think I didn't. And push me into something?" I chuckled again. "Sumner, no one pushes *me* into anything."

"I know and thank you. That means…a lot." She placed her hand on mine, and I didn't know how it was possible to feel both tenser and more relaxed at the same time. Perhaps because my body and head were at war. If it were up to my body, we'd already be undressed in the back seat.

"Fuck, you're gorgeous," I blurted.

She sucked in a jagged breath and removed her hand. "You're not making this easy, and I-I'm really trying to respect your wishes here."

I was trying to remember what those were. Because at the moment, all I wished for, all I *wanted*, was her in my arms.

She leaned across the console to place the softest of kisses on my cheek. "Good night, Jonathan."

I gripped her shoulders, holding her in place. "I want you."

I'd done some thinking as well this week. We'd already slept together; what was one more time? Besides, hadn't she proved that she could be mature about the situation—discreet and level-headed?

Her eyes searched mine, and I nodded. She pressed a hesitant kiss on my cheekbone. Another on my temple. With each kiss, she gained more confidence, and I'd never felt so worshiped or adored.

"Sumner," I groaned when she kissed my forehead, giving me a straight shot down her blouse. "We should—"

She pressed her finger to my lips, her own pouty and begging for my kiss. "Shh."

She slid her finger down my lips, and they parted as if in invitation. I swallowed, the cab filling with tension ready to explode. She reached down and palmed me through my slacks, and I squeezed my eyes shut. *Fuck. Yes. More.*

I glanced around, but we were alone. My belt was released, my zipper drawn, and my cock freed. God, it felt amazing to have her hands on me again. The past week had been torture, plain and simple.

"Sumner—" I reached out with every intention of stopping her. Of telling her we should go back to my place, a hotel, anywhere but the office parking garage. *Christ.* But my willpower crumbled the moment she wrapped her lips around my cock, swallowing me down.

Her head bobbed in my lap as she worked me into a frenzy. "Fuck, baby. Fuck," I hissed, gripping the door with one hand for support while I threaded the other through her hair. The curtain of black silk fell over my fingers, and I knew I was done for.

I pushed my feet against the floorboard, muscles tensing. Her mouth was warm and wet…and then she hummed, and I couldn't take it anymore. I needed to be inside her.

"Back seat. Now," I growled.

I proceeded to take her in the back of my truck like a horny teenager unable to control himself. And despite my age and supposed wisdom, I knew it wouldn't be the last time I took her that way. She made me feel young, powerful, wanted in a way no other women in the past had. It was why I couldn't stay away. Hard as I'd tried, I couldn't fight this anymore.

Just for the summer, I told myself. I could have her until the internship ended. We could keep this a secret, and then she'd go to grad school and we'd pretend this had never happened.

My plan sounded simple enough, but I soon realized it was easier said than done. The more time we spent together, the more I got to know Sumner as this version of her—the adult version—the harder I fell. And the longer it went on, the easier it became to convince myself she was mine.

I continued living in that delusion, sneaking kisses in my office between meetings, cuddling with her on the couch, eating dinner together until the last day of her internship arrived. I was physically pained at the thought of breaking things off with her. But I was just as racked with guilt every time she mentioned Ian or I ignored his calls, which I'd done a lot lately.

"You wanted to see me?" She grinned from the doorway to my office.

"Yes." I stood, smoothing down my tie. "Come on in. And close the door, please."

Her smile widened, and I hated myself for what I was about to do. It had to be done. And though I didn't like the idea of breaking up with her at the office, it was the only way. At her place or mine, she'd find a way to persuade me otherwise. She'd already been hinting that we could keep this going beyond the summer. Much as I wanted to, I knew we couldn't continue long term. It would be a disaster. What the hell would I tell Ian?

"Sumner," I said, debating my words, even though I'd rehearsed this conversation a million times in my head. "This summer has been...amazing."

She threaded her fingers through mine, peering up at me with the most brilliant smile. She pecked me on the lips, and I tried to savor the taste of her, memorize it.

"But today's your last day, and we agreed that our arrangement terminates along with your employment."

"Arrangement?" She jerked her head back. "'Terminates along with your employment,'" she said, attempting to mimic my voice. "Wow, Jonathan." She took a few steps back. "Just say it—you're breaking up with me."

I had to stand firm. I couldn't let this continue. So, I closed myself off to her, adopting the mask I often assumed in business—cold, demanding, shrewd. It was for her own good, even if I knew she'd hate me for it. "How can we break up when we were never together?"

She looked at me as if I'd physically slapped her. It certainly felt as if I had. Fuck, this was painful. It was so much worse than I'd expected, and I was almost tempted to tell her it was a mistake. To beg her to stay and promise to tell Ian about us. *Almost.* But I reminded myself that I was doing this for her own good.

"Never together?"

I studied her expression, watching as she crumpled but then quickly recovered. She concealed her pain with anger, and I hated myself for it. Hated myself for ever making her think she meant nothing to me. That our time together hadn't been the best six weeks of my life.

"How can you say that?" She pressed her hands to my chest. "You don't mean that."

I had to make her believe we were over. Unless I made it absolutely clear that we were done, she would never move on. And she would move on. She'd find someone else, someone more appropriate. My heart squeezed at the image of her with another man, but I quickly pushed it away. This was the only way. Because this would devastate Ian, ruining our friendship and ripping apart their family.

"Thank you for all your hard work and dedication this summer," I said, adopting a formal tone. "You did a great job, and I've written you a glowing recommendation."

She shook her head and scoffed, her eyes glittering with unshed tears. "I thought being with an older man would equate to maturity. I guess I was wrong."

She swiped her tears, squaring her shoulders before turning for the door. I wanted to grab her wrist and beg her to stay. I wanted to apologize. I wanted to… There were so many things I wanted to do. But instead, I pushed my wants aside and focused on her. It was time to let her go.

And then she walked out of my office like the goddamn queen she was. She certainly ruled my heart, even if I wouldn't admit it. What would be the point? We could never be together, and I'd already let things go on long enough.

If I'd thought life before Sumner was tedious, it was absolute hell after her. At my house, at the office, I couldn't escape the memories of her. And it wasn't just the sex—it was the conversation, the intimacy, the laughter, and the life she infused into everything. And now, it seemed as if all I did was go to work and workout. Over the past few weeks, my life had become monotonous and tiresome.

Someone knocked on the door to my office, and I glanced up to find Ian standing there, basketball tucked under his arm. He'd been trying to get me to meet up with him for weeks, and I kept putting it off. I was being a chickenshit, but I couldn't face him.

"Long time, no see," he said. "If I didn't know better, I'd think you were avoiding me."

I laughed, standing to greet him. "I've been—"

"Yeah. Yeah." He waved away my words with a grin. "Busy. Right? Then it's a good thing I made an appointment. See you on the roof in twenty."

I glanced at my computer, at the emails waiting for me there. I'd avoided him as long as I could. "Sure."

I finished up some emails and then met him at the executive gym on the roof. We played for a while, and I was happy to let him lead the conversation. He talked about everything except the one thing I really wanted to know—how Sumner was.

I couldn't get her out of my head. But it wasn't the quiet moments we'd shared or the feel of her writhing beneath me; it was the haunted look in her eyes when I'd finally ended it. It was the resignation and hatred shining back at me when she realized I was serious this time.

"What's up with you lately?" Ian tossed me the basketball.

I dribbled, keeping my eyes on the ball, the court, anywhere but him. "A buyer approached me about selling the Wolfe Group, I took on another property with Alexis—"

"*Another* project? I barely see you as it is."

"What are you, my wife?" I teased, though when I shot the ball, I missed.

I'd needed to fill my days so I'd be exhausted at night. *Too* exhausted to think about Sumner or wish she were in my bed. Too busy to consider all the ways I'd fucked up. Fucked her over, was more like it.

God, I wanted to ask about her. I wanted to know if she was as miserable as I was. Or worse still, if she'd moved on. Ian didn't mention her, and I didn't ask.

He shoved the ball at me a little harder than necessary. "Wait… rewind a sec. Someone approached you about selling? Are you considering it?"

I lifted a shoulder, watching as he retrieved the ball from my latest shot. "Maybe."

He stopped dribbling, tucking the ball against his side. "You're serious?" He shook his head. "You? The man who's married to your job."

"Maybe I don't want to be anymore."

He shot the ball and sank it in the net. "If you're burned out, step back. Don't step down."

"It's more than burnout," I said, jogging across the court to collect the ball.

"You built that company from the ground up. You're one of the most demanding sons of bitches in the field, but also the most successful. And now… What? You're just going to let it all go?"

I blew out a breath. "That's just it. I *have* been successful. It's not just about wanting a change. I need a new challenge." Flipping houses with Alexis had helped, but after Sumner, nothing seemed to hold my interest.

"I thought that was the point of your little side project." He carried the ball over to the bench and set it down before grabbing some water. "You're not—" He tilted his head to the side. "You're not dying, are you?"

"What?" I jerked my head back.

"Well..." He grabbed a towel from his bag and wiped the back of his neck. "I don't know. People usually want to make huge changes like this when they've had a near-death experience or..."

"What? Are diagnosed with cancer?"

"Yeah."

I blew out a breath. "No. I'm not dying." Though it felt like it most days, felt as if I were watching life pass me by.

"Okay." He scrubbed a hand over his head. "I may tease you about having a midlife crisis, but you know if you ever need to talk, I'm here for you."

I nodded, swallowing past the lump in my throat. "I know."

But there was no way I could talk to him about this—*ever*. He could never know I'd slept with Sumner. And the fact that he was being so supportive only made me feel worse. I was an awful friend. Not only had I slept with his daughter, but I was lying to his face about it.

"Maybe I should sell and move," I said.

"Move where?"

Far away from Sumner. But I knew it didn't matter. She was in my blood, stamped in my soul. Even from her first day in the office, I'd known—known she was a part of me.

I could remember it vividly.

The door to my office had swung open, and I'd smiled, expecting to see the same little girl I'd known since she was born. A shy girl with a sweet smile and pigtails. Later, a teen blossoming before my eyes. But in had walked a woman with confidence and curves. A woman who made my mouth water and my eyes bulge.

At first, I was positive it wasn't the same girl. I hadn't seen her since she was nearly seventeen. It had been five years, but…wow. My mouth had gone dry as I'd scanned her figure. Her dark hair fell in waves that caressed the tops of her full breasts. Her suit nipped in at her waist before flaring out over a pair of luscious hips. Who would've guessed she'd grow up to be such a…bombshell?

I'd told myself if she were anyone else, I wouldn't have hesitated to make a move. And then we'd hugged. And the feel of her in my arms…

"You know…" Ian rubbed a hand over his chin. "I haven't seen you this out of sorts since—"

I held up my hand. "Don't say it." *Don't.*

"You and Rachel broke up. Have you been seeing someone?" When I didn't say anything, he said, "You have, haven't you, you sly old dog?" He pointed at my face with a smug grin that made me want to punch him.

Even so, my heart rate skyrocketed, my pulse racing faster than it had the entire time we'd been running around the court. Fuck. Fuck. Fuck.

Ian leaned in, butting his shoulder to mine, a knowing grin on his face. "*So*, who is she?"

I shook my head, sweat dripping down my back.

"Maybe I'll have to ask Sumner if she has any ideas. Hell—" He laughed. "She's seen more of you this summer than I have."

I choked on my water, setting it aside before wiping my chin with my shirt. "Drop it, Ian."

"Ooh. Somebody's touchy." He held up his hands in mock surrender.

I rolled my eyes and lowered my voice, knowing he wouldn't stop badgering me unless I gave him something. "No one can know, okay? We work together," I said, scrambling for a plausible reason to get him to drop it before I blurted the truth. "And she's younger."

"Gotta love a taste of the forbidden fruit," he mused, and I wondered if he was thinking of his wife, Lea. They'd both been married when they met.

"Well, it's over now. So, will you please just drop it?"

"Fine," he sighed. "But I hope you guys will find a way to make it work. Anytime we talked the past few weeks, you seemed so happy."

I had a feeling if he knew the woman in question was his daughter, he wouldn't be so supportive.

chapter three

Sumner

WEEKS PASSED, AND I HEARD NOTHING FROM JONATHAN. MY classes were beginning soon, so I'd packed up and moved to Palo Alto, eager for a fresh start. Even so, my stepmom, Lea, had made me agree to return to LA for my dad's surprise forty-fifth birthday party. I couldn't say no to her. I knew it was important to her, and she'd always been there for me.

Of course, she'd also taken it upon herself to set me up with a date. And while I was grateful not to have to attend the event alone, I wasn't in the mood for a date, especially not when my heart was still shredded from what Jonathan had done.

It was going to be a long weekend, and this was just the beginning. Tonight was the surprise party with 100 guests. Tomorrow morning, a small, intimate breakfast. Golfing or spa treatments for anyone who wanted to join. A night at the rooftop club. Lea really did love my dad.

I smiled and nodded politely at whatever my date, Damien, had said. But I wasn't listening. All I could think about was the fact that I'd be seeing Jonathan again at the party, and I'd have to pretend as if nothing had happened. As if he hadn't ripped my heart out and stomped all over it. I placed my hand to my stomach, trying to quell the nerves there. The pleasant hum of bees was more of a riotous war cry.

I gulped down some more champagne while we waited with the other guests for my dad and Lea to arrive. I hadn't seen Jonathan yet, and I braced myself for it. Steeled myself for the idea that he—like me—might be here with a date.

Damien excused himself to the restroom, and I didn't seek out conversation but was drawn into it anyway. Some of my dad's friends, my grandmother, my aunt. Everyone seemed to want to talk, and I played the part, even if my heart wasn't in it. I kept glancing from face to face, wondering what they'd think if they knew about Jonathan and me. Not that we were together. But if we were, would my family and friends ever be able to accept our relationship? More importantly, why did I care?

"Quiet, please," a tall blonde said from the front of the room. "Lea just texted that they're pulling up to the hotel."

She dimmed the lights to the ballroom, and everyone quieted down. I glanced around for Damien, knowing Lea would expect me to at least be a good host, even if I wasn't being a good date.

When the doors to the ballroom swung open, light from the hallway filtered in. My dad's and Lea's silhouettes blended together, and I could hear my dad say, "Ooh, Lea. You know I love it when you get frisky."

While others in the crowd laughed, I cringed. And then the lights came on, and everyone shouted, "Happy birthday!"

My dad paused, slowly removing his lips from his wife's and turning toward the room. He grinned when he spotted everyone and straightened. Lea's cheeks were dark pink, and she smoothed a hand down her dress. I laughed despite myself.

Damien appeared at my side and continued to charm everyone throughout dinner, including my grandmother. After we ate, the party moved to the hotel lawn. I still hadn't seen Jonathan, and I was beginning to think he wasn't coming. So, I focused on my date, resolving to put the summer behind me. To move on.

Damien seemed nice, and he was "appropriate." And I tried—honestly. But he wasn't Jonathan.

"Whoa," Damien said. "Your dad looks pissed. Did I do something?"

I followed his gaze and discovered it wasn't my dad but Jonathan who was glaring at us from across the hotel lawn. The sight of him nearly stole the breath from my lungs, but I was determined not to show him how affected I was. So, I played the part—waving with a smile before turning away.

"That's not my dad. It's his best friend." *And my former boss. Former...everything.*

"Oh." Damien furrowed his brow. "Okay. Is he like really protective or something?"

"Something like that," I said, more to myself. "Come on." I linked my arm through his and flashed him a smile. "Let's grab a drink."

"Good idea."

We made the rounds, his hand on my lower back the entire time. He was nice, a talented musician, and I was...bored. God, I was *so* bored. And when I couldn't handle the tedious conversation anymore, couldn't force one more smile, I excused myself to the restroom.

My dress swished about my legs, my strides hurried as I rushed to escape. Finally, mercifully alone, my shoulders sagged. I pressed my palms to the sink and took a deep breath. A few breaths later, I lifted my head to evaluate my appearance in the mirror. The material of my dress hugged my curves, emphasizing my generous breasts before flaring over my hips. I knew I couldn't stay in here all night, but I wasn't ready to leave yet. So, I dug in my purse for my lip gloss.

The door to the restroom opened, and I called out. "Just a minute."

But they didn't hear or didn't listen.

A moment later, Jonathan stepped inside the bathroom, closing the door and locking it behind him. His suit fit him to a T, and it reminded me of our time in New York. Which only made me angry.

"Um, excuse me." I glared at him, lip gloss poised midair. "What are you doing?"

He leaned against the door, crossing his legs at the ankle. Crossing his arms. I shrugged and returned my attention to the mirror, needing to avoid his powerful gaze. I took my time, leaning forward slightly and pressing my lips together. I could feel his eyes on me, scanning my legs. *Good*—I hoped he was thinking about the fact that they could be wrapped around his head, his waist. I hoped he was regretting his decision.

"What are *you* doing?" he asked in a tone that conveyed boredom. Or was that distaste? Either way, his placid demeanor was a façade. He was annoyed with me, and I knew him well enough to know that he was fighting for control. And losing.

"Applying my lip gloss," I said, intentionally misinterpreting his question.

He let out a deep sigh, pushing off the door and stepping closer. I could see him in the reflection, feel his presence. "Sumner," he chided. "I thought you were better than these immature games."

"I'm not playing." My blood boiled. "You're the one who said we were done. You said we were never together. We were nothing." *I was nothing.* I stared at him, refusing to back down.

"I lied."

I pressed my lips together, making sure the color was applied evenly. "Well, I'm not going to wait around for you to decide *if* you even want to be with me."

He grasped my shoulder, walking me backward until my back hit the wall. The cold tile was a jolt to my system. "I. Want. You," he ground out. "But I can't have you."

He'd accused me of playing games, but he was the one yanking me around. He was the one who was hot then cold. He was the one who wanted to fuck me, then act like it was a mistake. Like it couldn't happen again.

I was done. Done caring what anyone else thought. It was exhausting.

"You *can* have me, but you won't take me. There's a difference."

He shook his head, tightening his grip on my shoulder. I welcomed the bite of pain, silently begging him to stop fighting this, fighting us. And start fighting *for* us. In business, he took what he wanted without regard for the consequences. Why couldn't he do that with me?

"What happened to being daring and bold?" I turned his words back on him, thinking of all the lessons he'd tried to teach me in the boardroom. "Or does that only apply to business?"

"Fuck." He pounded his fist against the wall beside my head.

"I—" His body vibrated with tension, and it felt as if he might explode at any moment. The fuse was lit, and I was waiting for him to detonate.

"Fuck." His voice was softer this time, almost pained. He rested his forehead against mine, loosening his grip, though the intensity remained. "If you were anyone else..."

I closed my eyes and let out a shuddering breath. Why did he keep doing this to me? And why did I allow it?

"I can't..." I shook my head. "No more." The words were said more to myself, but he heard them all the same.

He trailed a finger along my jaw, and I broke. A tear slipped out, gliding down my cheek.

I opened my eyes, blinking up at him. "I can't keep serving myself up on a platter to you. I just—" My chest ached, and I needed space. "I can't." I shook my head and ducked beneath his arm.

My legs were shaky, but I was determined to put some distance between us. If only he could let go of the fact that I was twenty years younger and his best friend's daughter, we could be amazing. He knew it just as well as I did, but instead, he continued to fight it.

I stood at the sink, wiping my tears and wishing I had the willpower to tell him to leave. But it had taken everything in me to tell him I was done.

Clearly, he wasn't listening. Because he came to stand behind me, watching me in the mirror. I both loved and hated his attention. I craved it like a drug, but I didn't want to crave it. Didn't want to crave him. Not if he was going to continue to push me away.

"Don't cry, Sumner. *Please.*" He brushed my hair over my shoulder, pressing kisses to my collarbone.

My body quivered from his touch, and my heart...my heart was weak. If I was going to survive, it was up to my head. Because my body and my heart would give in to this man every time.

"Please, Jonathan..." My voice cracked. I heaved a breath, forcing the words out of me. "This is breaking me." Admitting it aloud was akin to ripping my heart out. But I couldn't be his dirty little secret—the summer intern he'd fucked; his best friend's daughter.

He spun me to face him, his arms caging me against the sink. His hips pressed against mine. "Believe it or not, it's breaking me too. But I can't throw away a thirty-year friendship. Your dad—"

I gripped the edge of the sink, anger coursing through my veins. "Should have no say in this."

His nostrils flared. "You're his daughter, his only child. I'm his best friend. If he had any idea…"

"Give him time," I said. "Eventually, he'll accept the fact that we're together."

I knew it wouldn't be easy, but I had faith that it would work out. If only Jonathan could too.

He shook his head, resignation marring his features. "Even if I were willing to sacrifice my relationship with him, I'm not willing to sacrifice yours."

"He's my father. He loves me unconditionally. He…" I swallowed down a lump. "You're the man I love. Surely, he'll understand that."

He clenched his jaw but didn't otherwise respond to my declaration. He had to have known. How could he not know that I loved him? Desperately so. The past few weeks apart had only crystallized my feelings—I loved him.

When I realized he wasn't going to budge, I sniffed and lifted my chin. I was done. I'd laid all my cards on the table, and it was time to admit defeat. Time to move on.

"Well, if you'll excuse me, my date is probably wondering where I am."

"Did you bring him to make me jealous?" His voice was low, the words said with an edge of malice.

"Not everything's about you, Jonathan." I'd agreed to come with Damien as a favor to Lea, but Jonathan didn't need to know that. But also, a small part of me wanted to see what it would feel like to give another man a chance.

"Tell him to leave. Tell him you're not interested." Though the words were said quietly, the force behind them had them ricocheting around the bathroom, bouncing off the tile walls and reverberating into me.

I scoffed. "You'd like that, wouldn't you? If you can't have me, no one else can?" I glared at him, challenging. I leaned forward so I was in his face. The air sparked with anger and passion, desire and duty—a storm brewing between us. "Well, you can't have it both ways." I dug my finger into his hard chest, wondering if there was actually a heart in there or not. "I'm done. Let me go."

He stepped closer so that our bodies were pressed together, my breasts crushed to his hard chest. Our pelvises kissing. His nose running along mine. His gaze was so intense, I nearly looked away.

My heart danced within my chest, hope and fear and desire and every other emotion warring within me. *Just do it. Just kiss me. Claim me,* I screamed in my head.

I didn't know what he was waiting for, but I was holding my breath. I'd been holding my breath until he finally pressed his lips to mine, giving me the oxygen I so desperately needed. The breath, the life, only he could give. It was as if I'd been drowning, and he'd saved me.

I gasped when he released my lips to kiss down my neck. I moaned when he pulled my dress aside, releasing my breasts. But then I remembered how it had felt the last time. Not the amazing sex, but the pain that had followed. How gutted I'd been when he'd acted as if I meant nothing to him.

"Stop," I said, even as my body shook when he slid his hand up my thigh. "I'm not doing this. Not again."

He removed his hand, and I stepped back, adjusting my dress so that I was covered and then crossing my arms over my chest. "I will not be your dirty little secret. I will not be a mistake. I will *not* be nothing."

chapter four

Jonathan

NOTHING. THE WORD REVERBERATED THROUGHOUT THE ROOM, pounding into my skull. I'd never regretted saying something more in my life.

I couldn't win. I'd tried to stay away from her out of respect for my friendship with Ian, and it had nearly broken me. But loving her would wreck Ian and destroy a friendship spanning decades. Worse still, though, it was hurting Sumner. *I* was hurting the woman I loved.

I squeezed my eyes shut. I was fucking this up even more than I already had. "You're not nothing, and I'm sorry I *ever* made you believe that. And you're right. You absolutely deserve more, better."

"Well, at least we agree on something," she said with a deep sigh. "But, otherwise, it seems as if we're at an impasse." She moved for the door.

I couldn't let her leave. I *couldn't.*

"I sold the Wolfe Group," I blurted.

She paused, turning to me. "You did what?" I nodded, and then she asked, "Why?"

"My heart was no longer in it." I held her gaze. "A raven-haired beauty ran away with it."

She smiled, but it quickly turned into a frown. "I'm glad you realized you needed a change, and I hope you did it because it was what *you* wanted. Not to prove something to me."

"It is what I want, just like *you* are what I want." I stepped closer, taking her hands in mine. "You gave me the courage to make a change I'd long desired."

If only I could find that same courage in my personal life. But the stakes were different, higher. My relationship with Ian meant more than the money in my bank account. He'd known me before the success, before I was Wolfe, when I was just Jonathan. But Sumner…Sumner was ingrained in me. She was…she understood me, she challenged me, she completed me in a way no woman ever had. I couldn't let her go.

"I'm glad," she said, but her smile didn't quite reach her eyes.

"I want to find a way for us to be together." I cupped her cheeks. "I *will* find a way," I said with more conviction. "Just—" I blew out a breath, brushing my thumbs along her jaw. "Give me time, *please*. Because I can't live without you."

Her lids fluttered closed, tears falling down her cheeks. I kissed them away, hoping they were tears of happiness.

I didn't want to leave any doubt in her mind. "I love you, Sumner."

Her shoulders relaxed, eyes opening. "Finally."

I chuckled, pressing my lips to hers. This girl was something else. And I loved her. Loved the strength of her spirit and the beauty of her heart. Cherished that I was a part of her past, reveled in the fact that I was part of her present, and hoped I would be her future.

"I know you asked for time, but I don't like keeping this secret from my dad," she finally said, and I nodded. "If you're serious about us, I want to tell him—sooner rather than later. Because we both know the longer this goes on, the worse it will be when he finds out."

"You're right." I tucked a strand of hair behind her ear. I wanted to keep kissing her and forget all about Ian, but she deserved more than vague promises. "Tomorrow." I swallowed down the words and the anxiety that idea produced. "I'll tell him tomorrow—after breakfast."

"No." She shook her head. "We'll tell him together."

Together? She couldn't be serious. "I'm not sure that's—"

She pressed a finger to my lips, her expression unyielding. "We'll tell him together or not at all."

I knew she wouldn't relent, and I respected her even more for it. She truly was my equal. So, I let out a deep sigh and muttered "Fine" behind her finger.

I placed my hands on her hips, pulling her against me. "Now

that that's settled…" I leaned down, pressing a kiss to the delicate skin of her neck. I paused, taking a moment to just inhale her, enjoy her. Love her.

We stood there, arms wrapped around each other, safe in our embrace. Tomorrow, I was going to destroy one of the most important friendships in my life. But this moment—this woman—left no doubt in my mind. I would walk through fire for her.

"Let's go upstairs," I said, wanting nothing more than to be with her. And not in the back of my truck or in the hotel bathroom, but in bed. Where I could worship her body and savor every drop of pleasure.

"What about Damien?" she asked, giggling as I continued to kiss my way down her neck.

"I don't care what you tell him, but get rid of him. Hell, I'll get rid of him myself." I moved for the door, and she circled my waist with her arms, pulling me back to her.

"I'll take care of it. But we at least have to stay for the speeches."

I groaned, knowing she was right. Hell, I was supposed to give one myself.

"After the speeches, meet me upstairs. Okay?" She peered up at me with the sweetest smile. How could I ever possibly say no?

"What room are you in?" I asked as she handed me a keycard. Lea had booked a block of rooms for the weekend, insisting that I stay at the hotel so I wouldn't miss out on anything.

"Number 440."

I pecked her lips. "You go out first."

She nodded, her fingertips slipping against my palm as she made her way across the room. When she reached the door, she glanced over her shoulder and grinned at me. "See you soon."

I pressed my hand against my hard-on. I couldn't believe I was letting her go. But I told myself it was just for a little longer. After a sufficient amount of time had passed, I left the bathroom and made my way toward the ballroom.

"Jonathan Wolfe, right?" a guy in a suit asked.

I hesitated, then said, "Yeah."

"Oh, thank god." His shoulders relaxed, and he pressed a button on his headset. "I found him."

I furrowed my brow. "I'm sorry, but do I know you?"

He shook his head and held out his hand to shake. "I'm Landon, and I'm with Juliana Wright Events." Then he added, "The event planner for Ian's birthday weekend. We're about to do the slideshow and speeches."

I was going to have to toast Ian and pretend I hadn't just kissed his daughter. Hadn't told her I loved her and would do anything to be with her. I'd never felt so torn—between my loyalty to Ian and my love for Sumner.

"It's okay if you didn't prepare," Landon said, misinterpreting my anxiety as he guided me toward the ballroom. "You can wing it." He leaned in and lowered his voice. "Most people do."

"Right." I smoothed my hand down my shirt, following him to the front of the room. I grabbed a glass of champagne from a passing waiter, taking a large gulp.

"No birthday party would be complete without some toasts," the blonde spoke from the stage, microphone in hand.

I tuned out her words, my attention focused on Sumner, who was standing near the stage, drink in hand. Damien was at her side, and I nearly growled at him. She gave me a subtle shake of the head, just as I heard my name called.

Ian and Lea stood at the side of the stage, warm smiles on their faces. They were happy, buzzed, and they had no fucking clue. *No one does*, I thought when the room burst into applause. I climbed the stairs to the raised platform and accepted the microphone.

"Ian." I cleared my throat. *Fuck.*

"You can be an annoying ass at times," I said, and he chuckled, flipping me off on the side of his glass. I took that as a good sign. "But you're also one of the most loyal, persistent, smartest people I know."

I inhaled a deep breath. I'd intended to keep this short and sweet, but if Sumner and I were going to tell him about us tomorrow, this might be the last time he looked at me without hating my guts. So, for once, I didn't hold back. By the time I was done, the crowd had laughed and cried, and I had even wiped away a tear. So many incredible years of friendship.

"That was a really nice speech, Jonathan," Lea said, pulling me into a hug.

"Thanks."

Ian slapped my back. "Must be the girl," he teased, but I could tell he was just as affected as me. Though I stiffened at his words.

"What girl?" Lea asked, her ears perking up. She was always trying to set everyone up. She said it was because she was so happy with Ian that she wanted everyone to get to experience that type of love. I'd never understood until now, until Sumner.

"He was seeing some girl this summer, and he's been such a mopey bastard lately. Does this mean you fixed things with her?"

I nodded, watching Sumner approach out of the corner of my eye.

"That's great, Jonathan." Lea grinned. "When do we get to meet her?"

"Thanks," I said, my stomach churning. "Tomorrow," I blurted. "I'm bringing her to breakfast."

Lea clapped her hands together, and Ian wrapped his arm around her shoulder. "Oh, I'm so happy for you."

I chuckled, though it felt as if I were choking. *Fuck.* This was so fucking messed up. Thankfully, before they could pry further, Juliana finished introducing Sumner. Sumner stood on the stage full of grace and poise. She spoke with such eloquence and love, and it was clear that Ian was proud of her.

He leaned over to me at one point. "You did a great job with her this summer. She really blossomed during her internship."

How the hell was I supposed to respond to that? I couldn't. So, I didn't say anything, keeping my attention on the stage.

I stayed at the party a while longer before slipping out. After a quick stop by my room to grab my bag, I headed for Room 440 and Sumner. By the time I finally made it, I was fucking drained. And she was just as quiet, undressing before the mirror with a contemplative expression that spoke of sadness. For me, at least—and I assumed for Sumner as well—the reality of what we were doing was sinking in. The possibility that, come tomorrow, my best friend would hate me and her father likely wouldn't speak to her. We climbed into bed, and I pulled her to me, tucking her into my side.

"My dad seemed so happy tonight." Her voice was wistful and tinged with regret.

"Are you having second thoughts?" I asked when she sniffled.

She spun to face me. "Are you?"

"About us?" I brushed her hair over her shoulder. "Never. But I think we both know things will change tomorrow."

She nodded, burying her head in my chest. "I just... I hope he can accept us."

I hope he can forgive us.

I didn't want to promise anything I couldn't guarantee. Instead of answering, I slanted my mouth over hers, losing myself in her touch. And when we made love that time, it was slower, more deliberate. It felt even more amazing than I remembered, even better now that I'd stopped fighting this, us.

Us. I'd never really been part of an "us," apart from a failed engagement. Rachel and I hadn't belonged together; we never should've let it get that far. But Sumner... Wrong as we were in many ways, we were right in so many others. In the ones that really mattered. Hell, I was about to risk the single most important relationship in my life to be with her.

I lay awake for a long time, staring at the ceiling and thinking about life. I must have drifted off at some point, but when her alarm chimed, I didn't feel rested. Far from it—I'd barely slept, and I didn't think Sumner had fared much better. But we got up and pretended as if everything was fine. We showered and got ready, neither one of us speaking much.

I stood before the bathroom mirror, and she turned me to face her, smoothing down my collar. "Ready to take a risk?"

I nodded. "Are you?"

She pressed her lips to mine. "Let's do this."

With time, Ian would forgive her, love her. But he'd be looking for someone to blame, and that blame would fall squarely on my shoulders, rightfully so. I just wondered if our friendship would ever be the same.

Sumner and I were the first to arrive at the restaurant. Sumner kept turning her bracelets on her wrists, fidgeting with the napkin, anything. I placed my hand over hers but quickly removed it when I spotted Ian and Lea making their way over from the hostess stand.

"Good morning." Ian rubbed his hands together before taking the seat across from me.

"Hello." Lea smiled, her voice cheery as she took a seat. "We need another chair, right? I thought we were expecting someone."

"Yeah." Ian rested his arm on the back of Lea's chair. "I thought you were bringing your mystery woman."

I gulped, rubbing my palms over my thighs. "I did." I glanced to Sumner, and she gave me a hesitant smile. It was now or never. "It's Sumner."

Ian leaned forward, gripping the arms of his chair as Lea gaped at us. Sumner linked her fingers with mine beneath the table.

Ian narrowed his eyes at us and then threw his head back and started laughing. When he finally caught his breath, he said, "You really had me going there for a second." He swiped at his eyes, but Lea was smiling nervously. "Good one, guys." He laughed some more, but no one joined him.

"Dad," Sumner said, and I could hear the hurt and hesitation in her tone. "It's not a joke. Jonathan and I are together."

Ian immediately sobered, blinking a few times. "What do you mean...*together*?"

"Honey," Lea chided, placing her hand on his forearm. "They're a couple, right?" She turned to us.

I nodded.

"No." Ian let out a garbled sound, his complexion paling. "I forbid it."

"Dad." Sumner let out an exasperated sigh. "I'm a grown woman, fully capable of making my own decisions."

"He's twice your age. He's *literally* old enough to be your father. And you—" He turned to me, his skin practically steaming with anger, ready to explode. "How could you? She's my daughter! You're fucking my daughter."

"Ian," Lea hissed, probably noticing that others around us had stopped to stare. I gripped Sumner's hand tighter, hating that she had to hear such crude words about herself from her father.

"How long?" Ian's face was red. I wasn't sure I'd ever seen him this angry. Not even when he'd fought with his ex over the classic Mustang he'd restored. She didn't give a shit about it, but she knew Ian did. He'd loved that car.

"Does it really matter?" I asked.

He banged his fist against the table. "You could have any woman you want. Why her? *Why*? She's... No," Ian sputtered, shaking his head. "She's barely experienced life. Too young to even know what she wants."

"Do you know what she wants? Because you're talking about her as if she isn't even here. As if she's a child incapable of making her own decisions," I seethed. "I'm not—I fucking love her."

Ian stood, throwing his napkin on the table. Lea glanced between all of us, helpless.

"Dad," Sumner pleaded, tears in her eyes. This was such a shitshow. "Please. Don't go. We didn't mean for this to happen. We didn't mean to fall in love."

He held up his hand and glanced away. "I can't—I can't look at you right now." He shook his head then turned to me. "I thought you were my best friend, but you've been lying. Sneaking around behind my back. You're not the man I thought you were."

I stood. "Ian. Wait."

"No." He shook his head. "We're done. I don't ever want to speak to you again."

He stormed out of the restaurant. Sumner was in tears, and I held her, my body pulsating with rage. I deserved his reaction; she didn't. And I vowed to find a way to make this right.

chapter five

Sumner

Four months later

"Hey, Lea," I said, tucking the phone between my shoulder and my ear as I stirred the soup on the stove.

She'd called me every week since the blowup, always checking in on me. Christmas was in less than a week, and my dad still hadn't spoken to Jonathan or me. I'd expected it would take him time, but I hadn't realized how painful waiting would be.

"Hey, girl. How are you? How were finals?"

"Good." I smiled. "I worked my butt off, and I'm more than ready for a break."

"I bet. I'm sure you aced them, like always."

"Thanks. So… I'm hoping you're calling to tell me that you and Dad are coming for Christmas."

We'd invited my dad and Lea to celebrate Christmas with us in Palo Alto, and she'd been cagey for weeks.

She let out a sigh, and my shoulders slumped as I prepared myself for the bad news. "You aren't coming," I said, finally accepting that was the likely outcome.

"I'm sorry, Sum. I just don't know if it's a good time."

"I guess I really hoped if Dad saw us together, saw how happy we were—then maybe…"

"I know, and I'm trying. I've been working on him for weeks, but you know how stubborn he can be."

I switched the phone to my other ear and wiped down the counter. Maybe love really didn't conquer all. I'd been naïve to think my dad would accept my relationship with Jonathan.

"Well, I appreciate it," I said, tossing the sponge in the sink. "And I'm sorry if you feel caught in the middle."

"Thanks. Look—" She was quiet a moment, and then her voice was softer. "Don't give up yet. I have a few more tricks up my sleeve."

I wasn't sure I wanted to know what her tricks involved, so I left it at, "Thanks, Lea. You're the best."

"I have to run, but I'll see you on the twenty-second, even if it's just a girls' trip."

I nodded before remembering she couldn't see me. "I'd like that."

We ended the call, and while I was grateful to have Lea in our corner, that didn't change the fact that my dad still hadn't called, hadn't texted or emailed, hadn't spoken to Jonathan or me since his birthday. Despite numerous attempts on my part—and Jonathan's—to reach out, my dad wouldn't respond. I was beginning to wonder if he ever would.

When I heard the hum of the air compressor from upstairs, I decided to go investigate. I pushed open the door to the future office and found Jonathan adjusting his safety glasses. I leaned against the doorframe and watched him for a minute before he realized I was standing there.

He removed his safety glasses and stepped over some boards to kiss my cheek. "Hey. I'm almost done in here."

"It's looking really good," I said, admiring the built-in shelves he was working on.

He rested his hands on his hips, surveying his hard work. "It feels good."

I grinned, filled with pride for this man. He'd seemed much happier, much lighter since selling the Wolfe Group. And while I knew the situation with my dad pained him, renovating our house helped. It kept him busy, and it made us both happy.

"I just talked to Lea," I said. "She doesn't think they're going to make it for Christmas."

He ran a hand through his hair, which was damp with sweat. "I figured as much."

"I just hoped—" I started to tear up, and he pulled me into a hug.

"I know, baby."

"Ew. Gross," I teased, pushing him away. I didn't want to cry. Didn't want to dwell on this.

"Oh, come on." He stalked toward me, reaching out for me. "I don't smell that bad."

I laughed, backing my way toward the door. "Um. Yeah, you do. Go shower. Dinner's almost ready."

He grabbed me, pulling me against him with my back to his front. "I'd rather eat you."

My core quivered with anticipation. "Mm. I like the sound of that. How about we eat dinner, then you can have me for dessert?"

"Fine," he growled, cupping me through my pants. "But I want an appetizer."

He slid his hand beneath the waistband of my pants, slipping his finger over my clit, teasing me before sliding it inside me. The added pressure from the material of my pants felt so good, and I moaned his name. A moment later, he withdrew his finger and sucked it between his lips while flashing me a wicked grin.

I was one lucky woman. I was building a house, a life, with the man of my dreams. I was pursuing my MBA and excited about the future. But my dad wouldn't talk to me. He refused to talk to Jonathan. And while I tried not to let my dad's silence bother me, it did. I hated that we weren't talking. I knew he was hurt, but I couldn't understand why he couldn't just give us a chance.

A few days later, I was putting the finishing touches on one of Jonathan's presents when the doorbell rang. I furrowed my brow and headed to answer the door, figuring it was just another delivery. I peered through the peephole and blinked a few times, positive I was hallucinating.

I looked again. Shook my head. Then I opened the door. "Dad?"

There was no way he was just "in the area." Palo Alto was a five-hour-plus drive from LA in good conditions.

"Hey." He kept his eyes focused on the doormat, which was red with the word "Merry" printed in a cursive font.

I stood and gawked at him a moment before finally asking, "Do you want to come in?"

"Is he..." He glanced around, as if looking for someone. "Are you home alone?"

I nodded. "Jonathan had to run some errands." He winced when I said Jonathan's name. "Come in. I have coffee, tea, cookies, chips…" I rattled off the items, not sure what to do or say.

"Thanks." He stepped inside but didn't move to take off his jacket. "I won't stay long. But I was in the area for business, and I…" He cleared his throat, toed at the floor. "Nice floors."

"Dad," I sighed, laughing. Leave it to him to comment on the floors when we hadn't spoken in months. But it broke some of the tension, and I was so overcome with emotion that I leaped at him, giving him a tight squeeze around the middle. "I missed you."

He tensed briefly then sighed almost as if with relief and returned my embrace. "I missed you too, Sum."

When I pulled away, I had tears in my eyes and hope in my heart. "Come on," I said, linking my arm with his. "I'll give you a tour."

"I—" He hesitated. "I don't know."

I frowned. "Why not?"

He swallowed, glancing toward the ceiling. "I'm trying here, *really*. But I can't…" He shook his head and blew out a breath. "I'm not ready to see him," he ground out. "Or the bedroom you share."

I nodded. "Of course. Sorry. Um, well, what are you ready for?"

"I'm ready to talk to my daughter again."

I smiled, so incredibly happy and pleased by his words. It was a start. It was a new beginning, and that was all I needed.

"And I want to apologize for how I spoke to you the morning after my birthday," he continued. "I was shocked and hurt and… I'm sorry."

I nodded. "I'm sorry too. I'm sorry that you feel betrayed. I'm sorry that my decisions caused you pain."

He shoved his hands in his pockets and rocked on his heels. "I should've been more…understanding. You never judged me for my relationship with Lea, and I never thanked you for being supportive. Even when you had every right to be angry or disappointed with me for ending my marriage with your mom."

I nodded, appreciating his words. "Thank you."

We were quiet a moment, then he said, "You look good, Sum. Happy."

I smiled. "I am."

He turned for the door. "I should probably get going."

"I know you said you need to take it slow, but we'd love for you to stay for dinner. I know Jonathan misses you too."

He hesitated a moment, some emotion passing through his eyes before he said, "Maybe another time."

My shoulders slumped, but I reminded myself that this was a good thing. It was a start. My dad had opened the door to communicating, and I only hoped it would get better from here. We hugged, and then he said, "I'm proud of you, Sumner. I'm proud of you for having the guts to go after what you want. To seize happiness and love even in the most unexpected places."

My eyes stung as he released me. "Thank you."

"Merry Christmas, Sumner."

"Thanks, Dad. Merry Christmas to you too."

I closed the door behind him and watched as he backed out of the driveway in a rental car. I stared after him, still reeling from the exchange. I was so distracted I didn't hear the door from the garage open or Jonathan approach. When he placed a hand on my shoulder, I startled.

"Hey." He frowned. "Everything okay?"

I shook my head and turned away from the street. "Yeah." I smiled. "Everything is going to be okay."

He tilted his head. "You seem really…I don't know. Calm."

I laughed. "My dad stopped by."

He jerked his head back. "He did?"

I nodded, fighting a smile. I gave him a quick rundown of our conversation, and with every word, I could see the tension leak out of him. I felt it too. It was as if a huge weight had been lifted.

"That's great news." He smiled, picking me up and spinning me around the living room. He set me down slowly, cupping my cheeks. "I love you, Sumner."

"I love you." I leaned up and pressed my lips to his, knowing with every beat of my heart that we belonged together. No matter the obstacles. No matter the pain. We were inevitable.

note to readers

Thank you so much for reading *Inevitable.* I hope you enjoyed Sumner and Jonathan's steamy and forbidden story. I am so incredibly honored to be part of this anthology, and I'm so grateful to you for helping support such an amazing charity. It's been a dream come true for me!

Not ready to leave the *Love in LA* world just yet?

Check out Alexis and Preston's story, *Unexpected*. It's a fresh take on the nanny / single parent story that will have you swooning.

Perspective is an age gap, art professor / student romance featuring Kate and Xander. It's about being brave and taking risks—in art and in life.

Irresistible is a friends-with-benefits romance featuring Lauren and Hunter. Can they follow the rules, or will they break each other's hearts?

Unpredictable is an age gap romance featuring a wedding planner and the father of the bride! It's a story of love after loss, second chances, and hope.

Unwritten is an opposites-attract romance between a former navy SEAL and a bookworm. It's a crossover between my Love in LA Series and Corinne Michaels' best-selling Salvation Series.

Don't miss out on any of my upcoming books, giveaways, and important news! Sign up for my biweekly newsletter.

Never miss sales & new releases!
Follow me on
Bookbub or Amazon

On Facebook, join my reader group to connect with other bibliophiles, talk book boyfriends and chocolate, and just have fun.
Jenna Hartley's Hopeful Romantics.

Like on Facebook
Follow on Instagram or Goodreads

first dance

AMELIA WILDE

chapter one

Dayton

I'M LIVING A DEAD MAN'S DREAM.

Morbid as hell, isn't it? But it's true.

I check my tie one more time in the full-length mirror. It's one of two, side by side in the groom's suite in a New York City reception hall that Summer—or Sunny, as everybody calls her—fell in love with the first time she saw it. She loved the original wood molding and the natural light. Her face lit up when she caught her reflection in one of the windows. Beautiful Sunny, with our baby January snuggled tight to her chest in a carrier so soft that *I* would sleep in it.

A long time ago, when my best friend Wes's house was the promised land, I still thought of myself as the kind of guy who would one day have a normal life. I didn't anticipate getting my foot blown off on a mountain road in Afghanistan. I didn't anticipate everything that came after. Certainly not this reception hall. Certainly not being married to Summer.

The moment the bomb went off was the moment I died.

No—not exactly true. The first moment I died was the last time I kissed Sunny before we deployed. That was the first small death, followed by a series of larger ones until I met her again and was reborn.

It sounds ridiculous.

It's as true as the rest.

I didn't know I was meeting with her that day. All I knew was that my missing foot hurt like a bitch and that I deserved the pain. A man like me always deserves the pain. It's retribution for what he's done.

That's what I thought then. Summer showed me different. Even when her life was on the line she still loved me.

And I love her back.

I love her so much it makes my heart beat too fast. It was this way when we were younger, too. Once when I was fourteen she went down Suicide Hill on a saucer, hit the snow bank wrong, and went flying through the air. My heart hasn't come down out of my throat since. I was the first to move, to run to her. It took her brother Wes too long. He watched me after, like I'd done something wrong in running to her side. How could I not? She was his little sister and gorgeous and funny and strong.

Then, after a while, she wasn't a kid anymore.

If I let myself linger in my thoughts any more, I'll daydream the rest of the day away. That's not an option. I'm not going to miss a second of our wedding day.

Can't say the same for Wes, who is my best friend after everything that happened and who is supposed to be my best man.

It occurs to me now, straightening my jacket, that I'm not supposed to be alone in this room. He was here in the morning, pressing a beer into my hand, but he's been gone for some time. How long? I don't know. We got dressed in suits bought special for the occasion. Then we discovered we had too much extra time and took the jackets back off. I finished the beer and brushed my teeth. I paced around. I re-read my vows.

That must've been why he stepped out. There's nothing more boring than watching a guy read from a paper. I joked about a practiced run and Wes joked about throwing up. I still think there's a part of him that doesn't want me to marry his sister.

Too bad.

The other groomsman, Curtis, really did step away for a phone call. He'll be back any minute. But Wes? No idea.

A light knock sounds at the door. Sunny's mom, Linda, pokes her head in the door. "Hey, handsome."

For a flash, I'm self-conscious about the prosthetic. Summer made me get a new one. The old one caused me nothing but pain. This one is so high-tech that I can hardly feel it, but I still know it's there. Linda knows it's there, too. I swallow down that old shame and smile at her. "Hey. Am I late?"

"Nope. I was coming to see if you guys were ready, but—" She scans the room with its clutch of low furniture and single long table for getting ready. One blink, and her face has pulled itself tight. "Where's Wes?"

"I don't know. He's been gone for a while. I'm sure he'll be right back."

"We've got pictures in an hour." Linda comes into the room like a general on a mission. "And you don't know where he went…" She turns on her heel and moves quickly back outside. A sharp knock echoes through the hall, and then silence. "I don't have his room number." Panic is starting to set in. She's the mother of the bride, sparing precious time to come check on the groom's suite, and I can see the calculations running in her head. There's no time to go up to his room. Not if she wants to help Summer with the last-minute preparations, whatever those are.

I cross the room to her and put a hand on her shoulder. "I'll find him. You go be with Summer."

Her eyes meet mine, and I swear to Christ, she's about to dab away tears. It's way too early in the day for all that to get started. "You're a good man, Dayton."

I open my mouth to argue. That's an old habit, too. I'm not a hero, and I've never been one—I'm just a guy who did my best, and sometimes did my worst. In the end, I got lucky. In the end, I found Summer again and she saved me. There's not much else to say beyond that. So I don't say any of it. Instead, I escort Linda to the door and give her the biggest reassuring grin I can muster.

It's my wedding day, and if there's a problem, I'm going to solve it. Come hell or high water or god forbid another bomb, I'll make this day perfect for Summer.

"I'll go find the best man. Don't worry about a thing."

chapter two

Dayton

I'M NOT SURE WHAT HAPPENS NEXT. I ENTER SOME KIND OF WEDDING-day fugue state on the way up to Wes's room.

Ever since Linda came to find us, my heart has been ticking in time with the clock. I can feel the time draining away until I marry her and god, this has to be perfect. Summer is perfect, and the wedding has to be perfect for her. More than anything I want her to be mine. Officially. In front of everyone. In all the ways a person can belong to another person.

Mine.

There's no answer at Wes's room. Somehow I communicate this news to Summer's best friend Whitney. Somehow her mimosa-bright grin translates into a series of events that end in Wes stepping to my side at the very last possible moment before our fifteen minutes of fame with the photographer. My mind is already on the ceremony, *in* the ceremony. I forget posing for the pictures almost immediately.

Then it's time to take our places at the front of the reception hall.

For the first time since I proposed, the size of the wedding hits home. There are so many people here. People that love us in rows of chairs colored in cream fabric with sage green accents. I only know they're sage green because Summer told me so. I didn't care until this moment about the chairs and how they'd look, but now the sight squeezes at my heart.

This is Summer's idea of a dream.

And I'm standing in the center of it.

The string quartet we've hired is playing something soft and beautiful. The melody is clean and anticipatory. Or maybe that's just how I feel. I turn my head to peer at Wes. He's staring down the aisle at the pair of double doors where Summer and her bridesmaids will emerge from. "What happened to you?"

"Don't want to talk about it."

"Put a smile on, asshole. It's my wedding day."

He shakes his head, seeming to snap out of whatever mood he was in. "What do you know about Whitney?"

I keep my face neutral in case the photographer is getting shots of us now. "Same stuff you know about her."

"I don't know anything about her."

"She's your sister's best friend."

The officiant—a lady with curly red hair whose name doesn't come to mind—takes her place behind us and rests a hand on my shoulder. She seems to sense she's interrupted something important because she bows her head and takes a few moments to collect herself. I don't know anything about weddings, other than this one, but this is probably the kind of officiant a person would want. One who's used to being part of the background. One who can pretend she's not hearing any of this.

Wes gives her a smile and sighs, but his eyes still look dark. "I know they lived together. I know they're best friends. That's it. What's her deal?"

"Do you think I go on their wine nights with them?"

"Dunno, Day. Maybe you do."

"I don't."

Wes blinks and the last of the stormcloud disappears from his expression. I want to press him on what happened with Whitney. Something did—I'm sure of that—but a change in the music pulls all my attention to those double doors.

They're opening.

Summer's mother comes first, cradling my daughter in her arms. January is grinning, all gums and cheeks in a cloud of tulle. Her wispy curls are the same color as Summer's. It's all I can do not to take her from Linda's arms and hold her myself, but this is a special honor for Summer's mom. Plus, I'll need both hands for the vows. That's what I tell myself. Summer and I can hold our baby for the rest of the day.

Hazel, Summer's coworker, is the first bridesmaid, making her way down the aisle with a shy grin. She's pink-cheeked and happy, basking in the attention of all the guests, and breathes a soft sigh of relief when she makes it to the front, with us. Summer didn't want over-the-top decorations, so there's a table with a cloth for an altar and a simple canopy. The white edges of it fall down into my field of vision.

Then comes Whitney.

Whitney entering the room is like a thunderbolt to Wes's stormcloud. He's instantly tense—I can feel it without looking. Whitney doesn't look at him, but the way she holds herself makes it clear that she knows she's being watched.

Not just by the guests.

By Wes in particular.

Her focus is razor-sharp, though her lips form a gentle, almost mysterious smile. This is something the wedding planner mentioned at the rehearsal dinner and Whitney has taken to heart. She's an actress. I'm not surprised it's so good. I *am* surprised she's able to maintain it all the way down the aisle with the energy coming off Wes in spears.

He takes a deep breath in and lets it out like it's *his* wedding.

What happened between the two of them?

I have the strangest urge to stop the proceedings and ask them both right now. But it's only nerves. It's nerves, because the music changes and swells and Summer appears.

My breath stops. My heart stops. The entire reception hall, the entire hotel, falls away. There's nothing left but my own heartbeat coming to life and the smile on her face. The tears in her eyes. My heart, my heart.

She looks like a princess on her father's arm. Her blonde hair is a cascade of curls and seed pearls, a lacy veil making her an ethereal creature and the dress—sweet Jesus, I can't even describe the dress. Something out of a magazine. Something out of a dream. A live man's dream. I'm living now, like I've never lived before.

This is different from every other time I've seen her. Watching her give birth to our daughter was like watching a goddess come to life on earth. God, she was so powerful and strong. And now that goddess has clothed herself and graced us with her presence.

My heart is a forest fire. It would burn down a thousand times for her.

Summer's dad brings her to me, his own eyes shining, and that's the first time I notice my own blurred vision. I try to blink away the tears while I shake his hand and take Summer's in mine. "Hi," she whispers.

"Hi," I whisper back. And then I guide her up into her place beside me. Really, it's me who's lucky to be standing next to her. It's me who's been given a second chance at life. It's me who has been given much, much more than I've ever deserved.

The sunlight streaming in through the windows catches on the pearls in Summer's veil.

She squeezes my hand.

"We've come here today in celebration of the union between two people," says the officiant, her voice warm and rich. "Summer and Dayton. Their entry into the bond of marriage today is like the awakening spring. New. Fresh. Eternal."

Eternal.

chapter three

Dayton

We're married and I can't stop kissing Summer's hand.

Her fingers wind tightly through mine, and she at least has the presence of mind to smile and wave at our guests.

I can't take my eyes off her.

The vows were a whirlwind of words and love and I've never meant anything I said so much as I mean it when I tell her I'll honor her, cherish her, and love her all of my days. My own voice disappears into the feeling of loving her.

Of wanting her.

All I can do in front of all these people is raise her hand to my lips and kiss her knuckles, so I do it. Again and again. All the way back down the aisle in a sea of applause.

By the time we pass through the double doors and out into the fresh air of the hall I'm all twisted up inside with need for her. My skin is too tight and my muscles are too tense and if I don't have her now—if I don't have my wife—there's no way I'll be able to sit through the reception. It feels shockingly close to being in battle. The only choice is to fight it off. I have to fight it off.

For her.

"This way." The determination in Summer's voice pulls me out of the internal war and back into the present. She's hustling me downstairs, in the direction of the bridal suite and then past it. Behind us, cheers and clapping spill out from the reception hall. The swarm will follow us soon. The wedding planner will be herding people to the bar for a cocktail hour while the main room is transformed into a place for dining and dancing and not just watching us get married.

"This way for what?"

Summer pulls on my hand and we make a sharp left into a small room, dusky from the curtains over the windows. She slams the door shut behind us, and then she's on me, this princess in a white gown. She's all over me. Her hands come around my neck and she pulls me down into a kiss that's so hot and so sweet that it pulls a groan from my mouth.

"How did you do it?" She nips at my bottom lip. "How did you stand up there so long without breaking?"

"Because I love you." I'm delirious with her. I've been delirious from a lot of stupid shit in my life, but with Summer—with Summer, it's worth it. "I wanted everything to be perfect for you."

"You're the thing that's perfect." She grips the front of my jacket and pulls back to look at me. "God, you're so perfect, Day. Look at you. *Look at you.*" The sound she makes next is like a sob, only sexier. "Please, *please* fuck me before we have to go to the reception. I can't stand it otherwise."

"You can't stand it?" I wrap a hand around the back of her neck and tip her face up toward mine. "You think *you're* the one who's going to die? Jesus, Sunny. You're an innocent angel if you think I'm not having the same problem."

"Let's fix it then." She pouts a little, wriggling her hips in that dress.

My god.

She really is going to kill me.

"You don't have to beg, sweet thing."

I'm so hard for her I can't breathe. The room she's pulled us into is an in-between space with a chaise lounge and an armchair, and it's the chaise lounge I go for.

Summer hits it knees-first and sits down. I keep my hand on her throat and tip her backward, all the way backward. I only let go so I can shove my hands up underneath the cloud of her dress. All the way to her waist. It's so dirty like this that my cock pulses in my pants. Two minutes ago we were the picture of classy wedded bliss, a cake topper come to life, and now I'm looking down at her bare, glistening pussy.

She wasn't wearing anything underneath the dress.

My blood pounds its way through my veins. "Damn it, Sunny."

Her eyes are so innocent, even while she clutches the bottom of her dress to keep herself exposed for me. "What?"

"You didn't tell me you were naked under all this fabric." I test her folds with two fingers and find her already slick and swollen, like she's been waiting for this. *Planning* this. "Naughty."

"You can teach me a lesson about it later."

"How about now?"

A grin flickers across her face, followed by pink heat. "What lesson, do you think?"

"That naughty brides like you get fucked."

She barely gets a hand up to cover her mouth before she moans. I delve into her with two fingers, and damn, *damn,* I might get her pregnant right now. Nothing would be hotter. Nothing would be hotter than to know she's sitting at our wedding reception with my release inside of her. She clenches around my fingers, ready as always, and opens her legs to me.

"Don't do this again," I warn. "Otherwise I'll have to stop the ceremony and fuck you right there."

"I wish you would have," she pouts. "I wanted you."

I lean down and press a blazing kiss to the side of her neck. "I've always wanted you."

I finger-fuck her for a few strokes just to hear her gasp, teasing at her clit with my thumb, and then I can't take it anymore. I cannot take it another second. I undo the zipper on my tuxedo and let my cock free from the boxers Summer picked out herself. I'm pulsing, painfully rigid. Summer gasps as I guide my crown to her opening.

And wedge myself in.

Slow.

Much slower than I want.

Slow enough that she can feel every inch going in. Slow enough that I can feel how tight she is, how sweet. How she's already shivering around my cock. The little flutters of the muscles deep inside her.

There's nothing like it.

There's nothing like sinking myself into her sweet pussy while she's got her wedding dress hiked up around her waist. Even now, even while I'm pushing into her with slow precision, she looks like a magazine editorial. She could sell a million of these dresses. The delicate flush of her face is the prettiest color I've ever seen. The needy part of her lips makes me want to kiss her.

So I do.

I kiss her and I thrust in the last few inches.

Home.

chapter four

Dayton

SUMMER HOLDS HER BREATH AND I FREEZE HERE, FEELING HER TENSE and clench around me.

"Are you—are you—" She can't get the words out. Oh, it's lovely. It's fucking lovely. I've never heard a better sound than her struggle to beg. "Please, Day—"

"Am I going to make you come?" I murmur into the shell of her ear. "Like this? In this room, with people looking for us and my cock buried inside you?"

Her lips form the word *yes* but no sound comes out.

"Of course I am. What wouldn't I do for you? You're my wife."

On *wife* she clenches hard.

I know what she wants.

I cover her mouth with one big hand and she whimpers into my palm. Summer loves this. She loves having my hand over her lips. She loves it when I'm in control. For a long time I was missing from her life, leaving her to find her own way, and damn it, she did it. Of course she did. She's no shrinking violet. But she craves this. Needs it. Needs it as much as I do.

I reach down between us, under all that tulle and lace, and press a thumb to her clit.

Oh, I could fuck her. I could fuck her so hard, and so deep, but what I want in this moment is to feel every part of it. It's already beginning, in those small jerks of her hips. I circle her clit once, then twice, keeping the pressure teasing and light. Summer bucks her hips to get closer and I reward her with a thrust that makes her gasp against my hand.

"Look," I tell her.

Her eyes meet mine.

It's so difficult. I can tell how much she wants to close her eyes and ride it out, but she doesn't. My sweet bride doesn't. She lets me see the pleasure building in her gaze while I wind her up.

Higher and higher and higher.

I hold my body still and let her fuck me. I coax her hips into a rhythm she can't control, and I watch her expression for the heat in her face and the long blinks and the panting, god, the panting, under my hand. "That's it. That's a good girl."

This is Summer's secret craving, the one that she won't tell anyone about. That she never has. *It's so common,* she would say, wrinkling her nose. *I don't know why I like it so much.*

But she does.

The phrase earns me a burst of wetness around my cock, another frantic rock of her hips, and then Summer comes.

She comes with a cry muffled by my own hand and waves upon waves of muscles working around me. Her hands come up and take my wrist, pinning me in place so I have no choice but to silence her.

What a wedding gift.

And it is, because with her quiet like this, I can fuck her like I want to.

I hold her in place with my other hand, the naked flesh of her ass completely in my power, and fuck into her like this is the last time we'll ever have. It's not. I know it's not. I know Summer would fight tooth and nail to stay with me. I know she'll wring every moment out of this life we have together until we both tumble into the dark at the very end. But this—this is holy. This is special. This is something else, something apart from everything we've done before.

Fuck, it's so right, and so dirty, and so illicit and so perfect that pleasure wraps itself around all my muscles and pulls them in. Summer takes my thrusts with a series of small grunts that tell me exactly how hard I'm claiming her—hard enough to drive the air from her lungs, hard enough to make her hold onto me for dear life.

I love it this way.

I love her this way.

I will always love her this way.

"I'm going to come inside you." The words fall out of me and her eyes go wide. "You're going to keep me inside of you all through dinner, and while we're dancing. You're going to know how much I need you, Sunny, you're going to feel me there with every step you take—"

This makes her clench again, makes her come again, a smaller peak but just as powerful as before.

It draws my own orgasm out of me.

It's a release like I've never experienced. It's the release of all the tension of the wedding planning and the first few months of January's life and this day, this long and exhausting and perfect day. I come in huge, hot spurts, feeling my own slickness mix with hers.

I fuck her all the way through it.

My vision goes dark at the edges, then bright. So bright that for a dizzying second I think maybe I've done it—I've died doing what I love the best. But then the room comes back into focus. My heart settles back into place. I brace myself over her with both hands and Summer reaches up to stroke my face.

"Wow." The curl of her voice is the thread that keeps me here on earth instead of wherever I've been, away in the stratosphere.

Summer keeps me here on earth.

"We're married," she says, and she blushes—actually blushes, even though we have a child together, even though we've just fucked while our wedding guests wait upstairs. "You're my husband."

"You're my wife."

Summer throws her arms around my neck and kisses me. It's the sweetest possible kiss, hopeful and hot all at the same time.

She tastes like a plane touching down after a year in the desert.

She tastes like mint and sugar and hope.

She tastes like love.

chapter five

Dayton

WE LINGER ON THE CHAISE LOUNGE FOR EXACTLY AS LONG AS WE can. It's not long—about five minutes, and then I hear Whitney's voice in the hallway outside.

She'll be looking for Summer and me. The reception can't start without us. Well—the reception *can* start without us, and probably has, but it would be appropriate for us to go. We've got a first dance planned.

I help Summer off the chaise lounge and her dress drops back into place, somehow looking exactly as perfect as it did when we walked in. The only hint of our little detour is the mussed hair on the back of her head. I turn her around and run my fingers through it until she laughs and reaches up for the clips and the pearls. It's magic, what she does.

She's magic.

That's not something I'm used to thinking about people. I was always aware, on some level, that all humans are flawed. If Summer has flaws—and I'm not convinced she does—then they only make her more of a goddess.

My new wife turns back toward me, a wide smile on her face and gorgeous color in her cheeks. "You ready to go to the reception?"

I put a hand on her waist and pull her close. Soon we'll be dancing in front of too many people, family and friends and everyone crowded close. For this moment it's the two of us alone.

It feels right to dance with her.

I take her hand in mine and hold her close, swaying to the silence. "I'm ready to be married to you."

"Good thing you already are." She rises on tiptoe to kiss my cheek. "I could stay in here with you forever."

"In this room?" I run my hand along the curve of her hip and turn her to face the door. "Here, when we have such a nice bed at home?"

"Let's skip the reception," Summer laughs, and I almost pick her up in my arms and run.

Almost.

Our families are waiting upstairs, and our friends, and our baby daughter. There's no running off into the sunset for us now. But that's all right. My running days are over. I was only ever trying to get back to her anyway.

Summer opens the door, back straight and smile on, ready to hug anyone who's waiting outside.

No one is.

Not Whitney, not Wes, not anybody. I guide her out into the hall and she takes my arm. It's so natural and intimate that it takes a minute to catch my breath. "Your brother seemed hung up on Whitney," I tell Summer. "Before you came out. It was like he was waiting for her."

"Well, yeah." Summer snorts. "He was waiting for the wedding to start so he could get it over with." She shakes her head, worry and affection in her eyes. Wariness, too. I wonder what that's about. I'd sit down and talk to Summer about it—about anything—but if we get to talking we won't make the reception.

It wasn't just waiting for the ceremony, though. There was that energy between them. "When she came out and walked down the aisle it was like…" I search for the words. "Like something was pulled tight between them. Ready to snap." A shiver runs down my spine. It didn't remind me of the way I feel about Summer—not exactly. But it did remind me of possibility. "Do you think they had a moment?"

"A moment?" Sunny's laugh is so musical when she's delighted, and my comment delights her. "Wes and Whitney? No way. No. They're way too different. You know that. You've met them both."

I *have* met them both. "Opposites attract," I tell her sagely, then lean down to nip the shell of her ear.

Summer yelps and presses herself closer in. That's the girl I've always known. The one who thrills to risk and adventure, even when she shouldn't.

I'm not a risk to her anymore. It's the thing in my life I'm proudest of.

That, and January.

I'm seized by the desire to see her and hold her and dance with my wife and daughter at my own wedding. Summer picks up the pace alongside me. "You really think they had a moment?" she asks as we go up the stairs. The hum of conversation is already loud, music filtering out, and when we're back in the hall it's clear the reception has started without us.

"Maybe. But you know what?"

"What?" She takes my hand and threads her fingers through mine. In a minute, we'll be into the chaos of the reception, and the evening will carry us away.

"The only moments I care about are the ones I have with you."

Now it's her turn to raise my hand to her lips and brush them across my knuckles. "I love you," she says. "Come dance with me."

I do.

Thank you so much for reading *First Dance*! Want more of Summer and Dayton? Their epic military romance *Before She Was Mine* is available everywhere now. Happy reading!

about the author

Amelia Wilde is a *USA TODAY* bestselling author of steamy contemporary romance and loves it a little too much. She lives in Michigan with her husband and daughters. She spends most of her time typing furiously on an iPad and appreciating the natural splendor of her home state from where she likes it best: inside. For more books by Amelia, visit her online at awilderomance.com.

the scene

MARNI MANN

the scene

James

"CUT!" THE DIRECTOR SHOUTED ACROSS THE SET, HIS LOUD, baritone voice vibrating through my ears.

My co-star, Sabrina Perry—one of Hollywood's most respected and sought-after actresses—glanced in his direction, watching as the director observed the playback on the camera.

I did the same, the anxiousness building in my chest as I waited for his response.

Today was the first day of shooting and the room was full of executives and our other cast members and every assistant and grip who'd been hired for this movie. Everyone wanted to see how Sabrina and I were going to transform into our roles. So far, she had been outstanding.

Me … not so much.

This was only the first scene and we were already on our fifth retake.

I'd rehearsed my lines for hours last night, practicing my facial expressions and body placement, and the emotions I needed to conquer to deliver my best performance.

But something was off.

The words weren't clicking when they came out of my mouth. My face wasn't matching the angst I needed to show. And each attempt was only getting worse.

The director's eyes landed on me and I sucked in a breath as he said, "James, go take thirty." He shook his head, his disappointment so obvious. "When you come back, prove to me that you're worth the millions we're paying you." He stood, his arms crossing, brows pushed so far together there was a valley of wrinkles between them. "We certainly don't have the budget to retake every scene this many times, so don't make me regret casting you."

Dick.

Except ... maybe I deserved that.

Ugh.

Sabina and I were huddled near the fake fireplace, a scene where, as her daughter, I was admitting to having an affair with my high school teacher. One that was supposed to involve heavy tears on my face and quivering lips and a consuming amount of guilt in my expression. None of that had happened, not even during my fifth attempt.

Just as I was about to get up from the rug, I heard the director mumble to one of the executives, "Brett Young promised me she would be the best for this role. Is this what the top agent in the industry considers the best? If so, that man is fucking delusional." He chuckled, the sound dripping in sarcasm. "The best, my ass."

"I'm sorry," I whispered to Sabrina.

She put her hand on my shoulder, the small wrinkles around her eyes deepening the longer she gazed at me. "Go get some fresh air and we'll try again. I know you can do this, James."

I nodded and hurried toward the back door, ignoring the eyes of everyone I passed, too afraid to see their disappointment as well. Once I was outside, I filled my lungs with the cool night air and rushed down the row of trailers until I arrived at mine. I flung open the door and locked it behind me, shutting all the curtains in case anyone could see in.

I didn't need them to judge my tears.

I also didn't need anyone lecturing me about the Diet Coke I was about to drink, and I knew they'd tell me it would only bloat my cheeks for the upcoming scene. The assistants had stocked my fridge with just soda and water since I was only eighteen years old, but what I needed was a bottle of champagne.

I needed something to take the edge off from all the uneasiness that was eating away at me.

I found a soda in the mini fridge and pulled open the top of the can, guzzling the freezing liquid until the bubbles hit my stomach. Then, I picked up my cell off the counter, taking a few more sips as

I called my best friend, knowing the quietness of my trailer wasn't going to help calm me.

"Aren't you supposed to be filming right now?" Eve asked as she answered.

"If you can even call it that at this point."

"What does that mean?"

I sat at the small table, holding my face up with my palm. "The director kicked me off the set for thirty minutes because my acting sucked so bad."

"Tell me you're kidding."

"I wish I was and I'm so embarrassed." I sighed, fighting the tears. "The set was packed, everyone and their mother saw how dreadful I was. And do you know what the director said to me? That when I return, he wants me to prove I'm worth the millions he's paying me." The first drips fell from my eyes. "Kill me now, Eve. Just take me out of my misery, so I don't have to see their faces again."

"God, that man is an asshole. I'd like to kick him in the fucking nuts."

"I love you for that, but he's right. I was so awful—"

"James," she interrupted. "If you were about to agree with him, then I'm going to march my ass over there and kick you in the lady nuts." She paused. "I know this movie is challenging and the cast is an epic line-up of actors and you're feeling all the things, but you're just as talented—probably even more so—than all of them. I don't want to hear you say otherwise, got it, girl?"

Eve's words were warming my chest, but they weren't enough. The anxiety, worry, fear of having to show the director and cast what I was capable of was still very present. "What if I ruin this movie and no one ever hires me again? What if I can't get my head in the right space? What if I go back out there and I can't cry or give them the angst they need? What then? I … quit?"

"Have you lost your mind? None of those things are going to happen. You're James fucking Ryne, Hollywood's hottest, most talented actress. Directors from all over the world are vying for you. Stop doubting yourself and start believing in yourself—now."

I stared at my nails that had been painted black and purposefully chipped for this scene, the ripped jeans and cut-off sweater that wardrobe had dressed me in. I traced the holes over my knees, feeling the smooth skin beneath. "You know the press is already all over this film, everyone is saying it has Oscar potential. After my last blockbuster, I feel like there's a spotlight hanging over me and I'm expected to have an even better performance." I dropped my head onto the table, my cheeks slick from the wetness that had dripped. "I guess I'm just feeling the pressure, that's all."

"That's allowed, but don't forget, you were hired for a reason. So, stop freaking out and start remembering why you're such a badass."

"Eve …"

"Listen, we rehearsed your lines last night, you know them by heart. Just relax and go have fun." She giggled. "I mean, you have thirty minutes and I'm assuming you're in your trailer, all by yourself. Why don't you go rub one out, and then go show them your most Oscar worthy performance? We both know that's the *only* way to relax."

"Seriously? You're nuts."

"But you know I'm right."

I finished the rest of the soda, swirling it around in my mouth while I stared at the empty can.

She was right, if there was one way to get me to relax, it was that. "Maybe—" I began but was cut off by a knock at my door. "Shit, someone's here. I've got to run. I'll call you on my way home, hopefully I'll still be employed." I stood, wiping the tears that lingered on my face as I made my way to the entrance.

"Oh my God, girl, we both know you're going to go out there and kill it. Now, go. Love you, bye."

I hung up and just as I was reaching for the handle, the door began to open.

I swore I locked it and I knew I was the only person who had a key aside from maintenance and they definitely wouldn't come in without my permission.

It wasn't ajar more than a few inches when I heard, "James, turn around," in the most alpha, dominating voice.

Turn around?

The lights outside my trailer had unexpectedly turned off, hiding the man's face. Still, there was something about his voice that wasn't triggering me to want to scream or hide or run.

Just the opposite was happening, and I found myself wanting to take a step closer to get more of his delicious sounds.

"Who are you—"

"Turn around," he growled.

My feet moved in the direction he wanted, my back now facing him.

"Put your hands behind you."

The more I listened, the more familiar he became, I just wasn't able to place him. But underneath his gritty, masculine tone—one that I hadn't heard on set today—was a hotness that was causing everything inside me to melt.

I continued to follow his instructions, moving into the position he had requested, my hands joined, resting on the top of my butt.

Incredibly submissive.

"Good girl."

I smiled at the compliment, goosebumps rising over my skin as I heard the door shut and lock, his footsteps getting louder until he stopped directly behind me.

"Are you going to tell me your name—"

"Quiet."

"Quiet?"

His chest pressed against my back, his hard-on grinding into me. His arm then circled my neck, his palm cupping my tit with a strength that made me moan. "That's the only sound I want coming out of you. A moan just like that one. Do you hear me?"

"Yes—"

"What did I just say?"

He pinched my nipple, and I made the noise again, but this time louder.

"That's my good fucking girl." He bit the edge of my ear, holding it in his mouth while he said, "You'll get rewarded when you follow my orders."

Each time he touched me, breathing over my neck, it felt almost as good as an orgasm.

"*Ahhh,*" I exhaled as his tip ground into the back of me, wetness now pooling between my legs.

"Someone is hungry for my cock."

"*Mmm,*" I responded, not wanting to break the rules.

"How badly do you want me to fuck you, James?" His hand dropped down the front of me, rubbing my pussy from the outside of my jeans, his other fingers pinching and pulling my nipple.

My head leaned back, hitting the muscles of his chest, each exhale giving him my answer.

"Do you want me to fuck this"—he cupped my pussy—"or this"—he slid to my ass, his thumb rubbing that forbidden place.

"*Fuuuck.*"

His lips went to the shell of my ear where he whispered, "Looks like I'll just have to surprise you while you're …" His voice trailed off and there was a slight shift in his body, suddenly everything turning black as he tied a dark piece of cloth over my eyes. "Blindfolded." A second piece of string went around my hands, binding them to their position.

"What are you—"

"*Shhh,*" he said in my ear. "Only moans, remember?" Seconds after he finished speaking, he lifted me into the air as though I were completely weightless, and tossed me over his shoulder.

"Oh!" I squealed, knowing it wasn't the sound he wanted, but the sensation of being in the air was so much different than the ground. I felt us move across the trailer, a breeze whipping past my face as he tossed me onto the couch, landing on my butt.

His hands found me the moment I hit the cushion, unbuttoning my jeans, loosening my heels, both instantly off my body until I was left in only a thong and my sweater.

"You're fucking gorgeous," he roared, that tone so achingly

familiar again, I just couldn't remember where and when I'd heard it.

But I couldn't focus on that, not when I felt the intensity of his gaze wrapping around me. And even though he'd taken my vision away, I could still feel his stare boring through me, tugging at my release.

I rubbed my legs together just so I could have a little friction.

"Does that feel good?" he asked, his hands now keeping my legs apart. When I didn't answer, he added, "I'm giving you permission to speak."

"Yes."

"Does this feel better?" He blew on my pussy, the thin fabric between us warming from his air, each burst like a pumping bass, blasting against me.

"Oh God," I groaned. "Yes, that feels better."

Something began to penetrate into me, and it took me a moment to realize it was his nose, running up and down my clit. "You smell so fucking good."

He was inhaling me.

The thought was almost enough to make me come.

I heard the sound of a zipper and clothes falling to the floor, my hearing much more sensitive now that he'd taken away my sight.

"Do you want my tongue, James?" He continued the rise and fall with his nose. "Or do you want my cock?" I felt something much larger press against me and I knew it was his crown, the thick head circling my clit.

"*Ahhh*," I sighed, the breath trembling out of my lungs.

"Sounds like someone wants me to keep surprising her …"

My head fell against the couch cushion as he slid my thong to the side and his warm, wet mouth dove in.

"*Yesss*," I hissed, his tongue lapping around the top of my clit, sucking, eventually using his teeth to graze me. My legs tightened, so I could feel more of him, the softness of his hair rubbing my thighs, the smoothness of his cheeks. None of them signs of who this man was.

I was rocking my hips at the same speed as he licked, my breathing turning louder, the build taking a hold of me.

"Don't come."

It was a warning, but I was so close. The tip of his tongue was flicking that high point where I was ultra-sensitive, and I wasn't sure I could stop my body from reacting.

"James ..." he cautioned and that only added to the feeling in my body and it increased even more when he plunged two fingers inside me, curving them upward, aiming for my G-spot. "You're not listening to me." His mouth pulled away and I cried for it to return. He gave me a single lick and my hips bucked. "You're getting far too close when I've told you not to fucking come."

"But I can't—"

"No words," he barked. "Only moans or I'll stick a ball between your teeth."

"Mmm," I sang in the most high-pitched voice, letting him know I was screaming inside.

"I know my mouth feels good." He licked harder, but only once every few seconds, unhurriedly gliding his fingers in and out of me. "And I know you want to come, but you're going to have a wait a big longer for that." He didn't move his face away, he just kept his movements slow, his tongue raising all the way up and lowering back to his hand, treating me like the most decadent meal, savoring each bite.

Just as I would get used to his movements, he would switch things up, using a different speed, alternating between one finger and two. The moment he would feel me tighten, he would pull back and the whole thing would start over.

"I'm waiting ..."

I wanted so badly to ask for what, but I knew better. He was torturing me for something I had done, I just didn't know what. And then it hit me—he wanted my moans, not the loudness or hissing of my breathing. So, I leaned my head back, spreading my legs as wide as they would spread, putting my feet on the edge of the couch, toes curled around the lip. I then let my sounds do all the talking for me, each sensation coming out boisterously.

He responded just the way I wanted, giving me more pressure, adding another finger, the friction bringing me right back to that place.

I turned louder.

My voice grew more guttural.

My legs shaking as I neared so close to that release.

And as I was seconds from the peak, his mouth was suddenly gone and he was plunging his thick, long, hard cock into me.

"*Ohhh!*" I yelled.

There was no pause, no gentleness as I stretched to fit him, just a relentless pounding that took me by surprise.

One I couldn't get enough of.

"So fucking tight," he groaned, my legs circling around him, my feet locking at the top of his ass.

I wanted to scream his name.

To dig my nails into his shoulders.

To tell him to go harder.

Faster.

To rub my clit with those deliciously strong fingers.

But I couldn't do any of those things.

And as if he was inside my head, listening to my thoughts, he reacted. His speed increased, he used even more power, his hand went to the front of me, brushing over the top of my pussy, and I was bursting with pleasurable sounds.

"Damn, you're so fucking tight."

He didn't need encouragement, this man was driven by my wetness.

There was so much momentum in each of his movements, so much rhythm every time he twisted his hips, his tip reaching that spot deep inside that his fingers had grazed earlier. But I learned he didn't like patterns and the moment I began to build, he flipped me onto my knees, my chest pressed into the couch cushion. Before I could take a breath, he was diving right back into me.

This position was more intense, I could feel him deeper, reach farther. And he fucked me like he was angry, like he was full of emotion, like he was trying to hit the end of me.

I loved every fucking second of it.

"*Ahhh*!" I shouted.

He held my hands that were tied behind my back and used them to thrust into me, his face in my neck, teeth biting the little skin my sweater wasn't hiding. With every pump of his cock, I felt myself get closer to that peak again and this one I wasn't sure I could fight off.

"Not yet," he growled, another firm warning.

He reached beneath my bra and clamped my nipple, pulling the small bud to the point where I screamed again.

The pain awakened me, causing me to get there even faster and before I could grow sore, he was moving to the other side, doing the same thing to that one.

"Fuck," I breathed, making sure it sounded more like a moan.

"I need to know how badly you want to come. I need to hear it in your voice, James." His teeth were on my ear, sucking the lobe into his mouth. "When I hear that need owning you, then I'll let you get off." When he bit down, to the point where I thought he would draw blood, he added, "But I need to see your face when you do it."

I was suddenly in motion again, my ass now on the couch, my legs spread wide. I felt him kneel in front of me and when he entered, his movements were slow, deliberate. His thumb was on my clit, swiping across it like I was the screen of his phone.

Each inch that slid into me was the most fulfilling sensation, feeding my pussy to the point where I was lost. My mouth was open, air panting in and out at the same speed as him. I couldn't hold on, I could only allow the feelings to bring me there. And it all began to happen much faster when his hand dropped, a finger finding that other hole, the one in the back that was the tightest part of me.

"Oh God," I cried. "Yes!"

He took some of my wetness and lubed it across his nail and knuckle and he pushed his finger all the way in.

"*Mmm*!"

"You like your ass touched, don't you, James?"

"*Yessss*!"

"And you like being a good girl for me."

"*Ohhh*, fuck, yes!"

Every time his cock pounded into me, his finger did the same. I couldn't control anything that was happening—not the sounds that were pouring out of me or the way my legs locked around him or the climb that was overtaking me.

"You're so fucking tight, I don't think I can hold off for much longer."

I couldn't give him words or he'd punish me, so I groaned the deepest noise I could find in my throat.

"Your pussy is so fucking naughty, it's trying to suck the cum out of me." I moaned again. "Is that what you want? For me to fill you with my cum?"

"Hmmm."

"Beg for it, James."

Each exhale came with a scream that was dripping in need, my body tightening around him, the wetness in my pussy even making its own sound. I found his neck and bit down with my teeth, my tongue swirling around the neighboring skin to sooth it.

"Baby, you know I like that."

I couldn't process what he had said, my body moving too quickly to that place I couldn't return from.

His hand was hammering my ass, his cock was doing the same to my pussy, and that familiar tingle was in my stomach, taking over my muscles, spreading up to my chest where a heat was turning to fire.

"Fuuuck!"

The top of my head was banging into the cushion, sweat was dripping down my back. I could taste the saltiness of his sweat on his flesh and the sexiness of his cologne and the lust that was pulsing in his neck and I was swallowing every bit of it.

"Now!" he shouted.

It was like a switch inside my body that only had to be flipped, his demand instantly filling that need. The shudders started in my navel and burst up to my mouth, screams filling the air around us. *"Ahhh!"*

"You're fucking milking me," he moaned. "My fucking God you feel good."

I could feel his cum hitting the depths of me, each pulse causing his cock to grow even harder. His thrusts came with a strength he'd reserved just for this moment. And every one made me shout out in ecstasy, like his orgasm was causing ten more of my own.

"James," he roared. "Fuck!"

He continued that ruthless pattern, my pussy and ass quivering until he slowed, but he kept himself buried inside me.

When he finally pulled out of my pussy, his face landed on my stomach where I felt his breaths warm my flesh. "Fuck me," he sighed. "You're my dirty, dirty girl." His finger was still in my ass and he swirled it around, giving it a few final dips before he gradually popped it out.

"*Mmm*," he moaned. "I already miss that hole."

He reached behind me and loosened the tie from my wrists, the string falling to the couch, and then I heard the sound of him putting on his clothes.

Within only a few seconds, his mouth was hovering above mine. "Don't take off the blindfold until you hear the sound of the door."

I expected his mouth to land on mine, rewarding me with a good-bye kiss.

But he didn't do that.

Instead, he leaned down to my pussy where his lips gently pressed against the top of my clit. He kissed that spot several times, giving it a small swipe of his tongue, before he whispered, "My good fucking girl."

I smiled and gave him a final moan.

I heard the sound of footsteps and then the door closed, the lock clicking into place.

I was alone again.

My heart was pounding, my breath barely returning, my body feeling like it had been through the most satisfying war.

Knowing it was finally safe, I reached up and took off the blindfold, taking a quick inventory of the space around me. Everything looked the same, like that man had never even entered my trailer.

I had no idea how long I had been in here, but I knew I was cutting it close.

I found my thong and jeans and heels on the floor and I quickly put them back on. I rushed into the small bathroom, checking my face, making sure the tears hadn't stained my cheeks or the sweat hadn't ruined my eye makeup. There were a few smudges but nothing my fingers couldn't take care of. I ran my fingers through my hair, ensuring the back didn't look like I'd just been fucked.

When I was sure I looked presentable, I hurried through my trailer and opened the door, going down the steps and across the lot, entering through the back. The set was as full as I had left it and, like before, I didn't make eye contact with anyone I passed before I returned to the spot on the floor, directly in front of the fireplace.

The hair and makeup staff immediately came over to me, something they did every time we left the set. With pallets and brushes in their hands, they touched up my face and hair, making sure my long locks looked slightly messy and the black liner was smudged, like the teenager I was supposed to be for this role.

Sabrina joined me on the floor, professionalism covering her expression, a calmness in her demeanor. "Are you ready?"

I nodded, "Yes."

"James!" the director barked from several feet away. "I hope you're finally ready to perform. I'm expecting perfection and I'll accept nothing less at this point."

"I'll deliver," I replied.

The whispering on set quieted, the assistants disappeared from around us. I was staring at Sabrina, waiting for the countdown until I finally heard, "Fireplace scene, take six and … action!"

"Mom," I started, the breath in my chest warming, the knot sliding into my throat where I needed it to live in order to gain the full emotion this scene required. "Oh God." I shook my head as though I didn't know what I needed to say, but the lines were just waiting to be spoken. "I … I don't know how to tell you this." I paused, shifting my legs like a fidgety teenager full of nerves at the news I was about to give her.

But the movement caused something else.

It triggered the cum that had been shot inside me to begin

dripping out of my pussy. I felt the thickness hit the underside of my thong and within a few seconds it would slowly be running down my legs.

Instead of smiling, like I wanted, remembering those yummy moments of passion, I found the tears that I needed.

The angst.

The expression that I had to dig deep for, but I knew was showing on my face.

The Oscar worthy moment was here and not a single thing in this world would stop me from delivering.

As I opened my mouth again, a tear now falling from my eye, I heard, "Baby, it's time to wake up," in that voice that had growled at me from inside my trailer.

Wake up?

"You're going to be late for your first day of shooting," the same voice added.

Late?

My eyes flicked open and the sight of Brett was the first thing I saw.

It had all been a dream.

But it was his hands, his deliciously long cock, his blindfold.

He'd been the star of my fantasy, of course.

"You were sleeping so hard, you slept right through our alarm," he said. He was on his knees, next to the bed, his face in my neck. "What were you dreaming about, baby? It almost sounded like you were moaning."

As he pulled away to look at my face, I smiled, feeling the heat trickle over my skin. "You."

"Is that so?"

I nodded against the pillow. "You showed up to my trailer on set and …" I shook my head, remembering each of his movements. "Whoa, things got extremely steamy."

He kissed my cheek and stood, going over to the doorway where he gripped the frame, gazing at me. "I want to hear all about it tonight when you get home."

"Don't worry, I'm going to make you reenact it."

He chuckled, knowing he was the one who made the dominating demands, not me. "Good luck today, fucking nail it."

"I will."

He continued to stare at me, his eyes narrowing. "And if you're a good fucking girl when you get back, I'll reward you with anal."

Before I could respond, he was gone.

If you would like to read more about Brett and James, check out their novel, Signed, a super steamy, forbidden, Hollywood romance.

about the author

USA Today best-selling author Marni Mann knew she was going to be a writer since middle school. While other girls her age were daydreaming about teenage pop stars, Marni was fantasizing about penning her first novel. She crafts unique stories that weave together her love of darkness, mystery, passion, and human emotions. A New Englander at heart, she now lives in Sarasota, Florida, with her husband and their yellow lab. When she's not nose deep in her laptop, working on her next novel, she's scouring for chocolate, sipping wine, traveling, or devouring fabulous books.

Want to get in touch? Visit Marni at …

Facebook

Instagram

Website

MarniMannBooks@gmail.com

also by

MARNI MANN

Stand-Alone Novels

Before You (Contemporary Romance)

The Assistant (Psychological Thriller)

The Unblocked Collection (Erotic Romance)

Wild Aces (Erotic Romance)

Prisoned (Dark Erotic Thriller)

The moments in boston series—contemporary romance

When Ashes Fall

When We Met

The agency series of stand-alone novels—Erotic Romance

Signed

Endorsed

Contracted

Negotiated

The Prisoned Spin-Off DUET—Dark Erotic Thriller

Monster—Book Two

The Shadows Series—Erotica

Seductive Shadows—Book One

Seductive Secrecy—Book Two

The BAR HARBOR SERIES—NEW ADULT

Pulled Beneath—Book One

Pulled Within—Book Two

The Memoir Series—Dark Fiction

Novels Cowritten with Gia Riley

Lover (Erotic Romance)

Drowning (Contemporary Romance)

Made in the USA
Columbia, SC
19 January 2021